No longer
the Property of the
Seattle Public Library

ONE
BLOOD

ONE
BLOOD

Denene Millner

TOR PUBLISHING GROUP
NEW YORK

For my birth mother, who loved me enough to give me away.

*And my mother, who found me, raised me, and loved me
with every fiber of her being.*

I am the lucky one.

This is a work of fiction. All of the characters, organizations, and events portrayed in this novel are either products of the author's imagination or are used fictitiously.

ONE BLOOD

Copyright © 2023 by Denene Millner

All rights reserved.

A Forge Book
Published by Tom Doherty Associates / Tor Publishing Group
120 Broadway, New York, NY 10271

www.tor-forge.com

Forge® is a registered trademark of Macmillan Publishing Group, LLC.

Designed by Steven Seighman

The Library of Congress Cataloging-in-Publication Data is available upon request.

ISBN 978-1-250-27619-3 (hardcover)
ISBN 978-1-250-27620-9 (ebook)

Our books may be purchased in bulk for promotional, educational, or business use. Please contact your local bookseller or the Macmillan Corporate and Premium Sales Department at 1-800-221-7945, extension 5442, or by email at MacmillanSpecialMarkets@macmillan.com.

First Edition: 2023

Printed in the United States of America

0 9 8 7 6 5 4 3 2 1

The Blood.

The blood that runs through my veins, my brain, my heart.

The blood, the biggest puzzle piece making me. And only me.

I cannot fathom how much blood.

The same blood that was running through my veins when I took my first breath. When I made my first appearance, my first impression on my people. On this world.

I cannot fathom how much blood.

The same blood that is just one ripple, one little wave, one teaspoon, in the sea of blood.

The gallons and gallons of heritage.

The big body of being, with everyone's little ripples and little waves and little teaspoons coursing through it.

Until millions of different families become one.

I cannot fathom how little blood.

But my little teaspoon carries the world.

My blood flows back to Somalia and Ethiopia hundreds and hundreds of years ago.

My blood flows back to my enslaved ancestors.

My blood flows through everything, everyone.

People interconnect and reconnect.

Blood flows and mixes together.

And we know that we are the same.

That is how the beautiful blood works.

The Blood.

The blood of generations that found its way into your veins.

It is golden.

All of that blood.

It trickles down to you.

That little teaspoon

In the body of being.

—"THE BLOOD" BY MARI CHILES

THE BOOK
OF GRACE

1965–1969

1

The blood never much bothered Grace. Maw Maw Rubelle got her used to it early on, when she was little ol', way before she let her only granddaughter, her apprentice, tend the stove at her first baby catching—before, even, Grace's first blood trickled down her thigh. There it was, her monthly making a dark red liquid trail past her calf and ankle, dripping into the thick, fertile Virginia dirt she'd planted her feet in as she reached for the pins on the laundry line. Grace cocked her head and stared at it in wonder for just a moment, then went on in the outhouse and made her sanitary pad, just like Maw Maw Rubelle had taught her to do with the pins and ripped pieces of feed sack. *Just as natural and nasty as slopping hogs,* Grace thought.

Now her best friend, Cheryl, she didn't see it that way. She cried holy hell when her blood came in. Nobody—not her mama, not her big sissy, not nan auntie—bothered to tell her what was inevitable. They held it to their chests like a big secret Cheryl had no right to know. She near killed her fool self when she saw the red puddle on her little piece of school bench and realized it was oozing from her poom-poom—knocked over the desk, tripped down the rickety schoolhouse steps, and just took off running down toward Harley pasture, hollering and screaming like a stuck pig, the laughter of the boys and the screams of Ms. Garvey, their school teacher, chasing behind her.

But Grace, she understood the power of the blood. Maw Maw Rubelle saw to that—made her look straight at it for sport and for practicality's sake.

Maw Maw knew, after all, that her grandbaby would have the calling—saw it in a vision just as plain as day one afternoon as she pulled poke sallet roots from the ground deep in the woods down by the river, where she had gone to forage and be still and make offerings to the spirits of her mother and her mother before that. In the vision, there'd been Grace's hands—small, delicate, strong—gently twisting, pulling a baby's head as it emerged between its mother's legs. The movements, the way Grace's fingers fluttered about the infant's curls, had made Maw Maw's heart beat fast. She could feel her granddaughter's happy in the tingle of her own fingertips, in each of her own palms. Maw Maw had slowly fallen to her knees, sticks and pebbles digging into the thick of her skirt; she'd kissed those palms, and pressed them—warm, pulsing with energy—to her cheeks. Love was there. Grace would continue in the tradition of the Adams women. Maw Maw's dead did not lie. *Show her the blood*, they'd whispered in the breeze, in the beams of light rushing through the leaves. *Show her what she already knows.*

Maw Maw had pulled a hand towel from her bosom, wrapped the root, leaves, and berries from the small weed stalk in it, and, with a heave, leaned all her weight against her walking stick as she struggled to stand. As quick as her thick legs could take her, she'd hobbled through the brush, across dirt and grass, past the great pear tree and the bumbleberry bush, back to the clapboard shotgun house she'd called home since she was a little girl being taught the ways of a midwife by her own grandmother.

Maw Maw pushed through the back door, squint-searching the tiny, two-room house, her eyes traveling from the bed and small bureau to the kitchen table and three wooden stools Mr. Aaron had fashioned from a fallen oak tree in exchange for two months' worth of Maw Maw's Sunday dinner plates, past the fat-bellied wood-burning stove and huge iron kettle standing sentry atop it, over to the corner beneath the window she'd opened to let the breeze carry in the scent of the gardenia bush planted on the side of the house. There was Grace, splayed like one of the little rag dolls her mama had sewn for her last Christmas, stitching baby clothes Maw Maw had commissioned her to make for a client due to have a baby any day now.

"Come here, baby," Maw Maw had said as she placed the pregnant dish towel on the kitchen sideboard. She'd carefully unfolded it and separated the leaves from the roots from the berries as Grace scrambled to her feet. "Bring Maw Maw Ruby her bag."

Grace, then eight years old and therefore eager, had practically flown to the chest where Maw Maw kept her special bag. Somebody was having a baby and Maw Maw had to hop to, Grace knew, because that's what her grandmother did—she waited on babies and when they came, somebody would call on Maw Maw and she would get her bag and her walking shoes and play with the baby until the mama was ready to play with the baby herself. Or something like that.

"Who baby coming today, Maw Maw?" Grace had asked excitedly as she struggled to gently place the weighty black bag on the table next to her grandmother.

"Nobody, chile," Maw Maw had said. The chair she dropped into creaked as she settled herself onto its frame. She'd torn off a small piece of a newspaper she had tucked in the bag and gently placed a few berries in it before stashing it in a small pocket she'd sewn in the seam of the leather tote. She'd planned to run them by Belinda's place on the way to the ice-house the coming Saturday, as the young mother-to-be was due sometime in the next couple weeks, and a woman with a stomach stretching out as far and wide as she was practically tall needed a little pick-me-up to remind her that she was still a lady, worthy of affection. Worthy of touch. Pretty. A smudge of those berries across her lips would have Belinda remembering her fine—Belinda *and* her man, who Maw Maw had heard was down there at The Quarters, drinking and smoking and grinding and forgetting he had a beautiful pregnant wife back home. "Come here, baby," Maw Maw had said, signaling to Grace. "Stand right here."

Grace inched between Maw Maw's knees and melted her face into her grandmother's fingers.

"One of these days, this here bag and everything in it gon' be yourn," Maw Maw had said, looking into Grace's piercing brown eyes. She let her thumb rest in the one dimple Grace had, a subtle dent in her right cheek.

"You mean like in my picture show, Maw Maw?" Grace had asked.

Maw Maw pulled her face back from Grace's and wrinkled her brow. Always, Grace woke up next to her grandmother, snuggled up under her arm, and recounted her dreams—she called them "picture shows" on account she imagined that's what it would be like to watch a film in a theater, something she hadn't yet had the pleasure, money, or right skin color to do—before the two of them put their feet on the floor, fell to their knees, said their morning prayers, and set out water and bread for their dead. Maw Maw always listened intently, as she knew the power of dreams—understood they were not at all dreams but a nod of things to come. Messages. Sometimes warnings. Surely, Maw Maw had thought, she would have remembered Grace telling her about a dream that involved her midwifery bag. "What dream you had, chile, you ain't tell me 'bout?"

"I was 'bout to tell you, Maw Maw," Grace had said sweetly. "I was playing with a baby, but she had blood on her face. I was scared."

"When you had this dream, baby?"

"Just now, Maw Maw, while you was down by the river."

Maw Maw should have been surprised by her granddaughter's vision and the synching of their connection to what was to be, but she knew better than to question what was natural, true. It was time. "Blood ain't nothin' to fear, chile," Maw Maw said simply. "It got your mama and daddy in it, me and my mama, too. Being scared of blood is like being scared of yo'self."

Grace felt something in her stomach, though it was far from her idea of joy. It felt more like what she imagined the hatchet felt like on the neck of a freshly rung cock headed for the pot. She wanted to let Maw Maw know right away that she got her monthly—wanted to know what was to come next. She could count on her grandmother only to tell her the truth. Her mama, Bassey, had long ago traded in what Rubelle taught her about menstruation for what the Bible, the pastor, and the rest of the men had to say about it, so she was tight-lipped on the subject. The most Grace got out of her was that this was a woman's lot—the curse of Eve. But Maw Maw, she knew nothing of temptation, disobedience, and atonement—of apples and talking serpents with tricky tongues. What she was sure of was what the women who spanned the generations before her were sure of, too: menstruation was a gift. The blood carried the ingredients of life: purification. Intuition. Syncopation between the rhythms of body, nature, God. Her talking to her granddaughter about it became more urgent as Grace's hips began to stretch the fabric of her flour-sack dress and her buds got round and full. "Mama told me, she say, 'When you become a woman, the moon will make the waters crash the shores in your honor,'" Maw Maw had told Grace on more than one occasion. "She say Simbi will make a dance in your womb."

Maw Maw was heading for the clothesline with a freshly washed sheet when she saw her granddaughter walking slowly through the outhouse door, practically doubled over; instinctively, she knew why Grace looked pained, but she asked the child anyway. "What ails you, gal?" Grace's answer made Maw Maw toss her head back and laugh from her gut. "Come here," she said, extending her arms and folding Grace into her bosom. "Oh, Simbi gone dance tonight! Go down there in them woods and scrape up some cramp bark—let Maw Maw make you a little something to ease that pain."

Grace did as she was told, only to emerge from the brush to see a white man riding bareback on a horse, rushing the animal practically up to her grandmother's nose. He didn't bother hopping down; just tipped his hat and got to it: "Granny, I need you over to the house. Looks like Ginny getting ready to have that little one."

"Good day, Mr. Brodersen," Maw Maw said calmly. She was not in the least fazed by the man's gruffness; indeed, she was used to—and slightly amused by—how direct and bossy the white folk tended to be with her when they were procuring her services. Like she was beneath them, even though they were standing in her yard, always in a huff, always desperate, looking for her to step into the middle of a miracle. Hell, most of them were in the same predicament as the colored folk they looked down on: not a pot to piss in, and barely a window to throw it out of. They paid with chickens and promises just like everybody else, except they did it with expectation rather than gratitude. Maw Maw didn't concern herself with the particulars of it all, though. The only thing that mattered to her was her divine mission: assisting in the safe arrival of new life into the world. Color was not specified in her soul contract. "'Bout what time her water broke?" Maw Maw asked politely, shielding the sun from her eye as she looked up at Brodersen.

"Water came about thirty minutes ago," he said.

"And her pains? 'Bout how far apart are they?"

"She got to hollerin' straight off, but she only had the one pain before I left."

"Well, this ain't her first baby, so ain't no telling if this one here gonna take its time or come on out and see the world, is it, Mr. Brodersen?"

"I reckon not, Granny," he said, using the nickname the white folk called Black midwives.

"Well, let me go on ahead and get my bag. Shouldn't take me no more than about an hour to get over, lessen ol' Aaron is here and he agree to drive me to yo' place. In the meantime, you know what to do, and that's exactly what you did the last time I came over there to catch those sweet babies a yourn. Put the water on the stove, get your bottles and sheets in place, and make your lovely wife as comfortable as possible."

"Yes, ma'am," Brodersen said, tipping his hat. And with that, he rode off into the direction of the Piney Tree Mill—the largest employer of the town of Rose. To get to it, his horse would have to cross Piney River by way of the Piney River Bridge, and to get to his home, he'd have to circle around the huge wooden and steel building, where freshly cut trees went to be shaved, chopped, ground, and pulped and white men worked hard and Black men worked equally hard but got 60 percent less money pressed into their palms come Friday evening. White men used that extra money they made to live in the tiny town behind the mill, where Black folk found themselves only if they were there to work for the white families who lived segregated lives in their segregated community with segregated ideals— and even then, Black folk didn't find themselves there after sundown. The only somebody who was safe there was one Rubelle Adams—the granny whose hands were the first to touch practically three generations of white Rose's residents. Ruby was neither proud of nor ashamed of this fact. It was what it was.

And now her granddaughter would join her in being the Negro who could visit white Rose in the dark. "Come on in here, baby," Maw Maw said to Grace, signaling to her granddaughter, who'd stood immobile by the wash line, waiting for the white man to get on. "Let me make you some tea and talk to you a bit. It's time."

From the moment Maw Maw had seen the vision of Grace catching babies, she dutifully set about teaching her granddaughter the ways of the women who wait on miracles—the ways of her own self. And now, on this day that the spirits saw fit to make her capable of producing her own miracles, Maw Maw would bring Grace along to her first birth.

She quickly prepared Grace's tea, and then sat the child down to once again go over what was tucked in her midwife's bag—what was supposed to be there according to the Board of Health, from where she'd gotten her license almost twenty years earlier, and what was supposed to be there according to her visions, experience, and the natural order of things among women whose hands were sacred, ordained. *This is so-and-so paper for this and such, this herb here gets the mama calm, that root you need to ease her pain.* Maw Maw had gone over the bag's contents enough times for Grace to know what was what; she never tired of looking at all the equipment in that bag—and especially appreciated that she no longer had to sneak and peek when her grandmother wasn't around. But she could hardly contain herself with the thought of finally getting to see firsthand how bodies and God helped mamas push chi'ren from "a woman's sacred place."

Just as Maw Maw twirled the bottle of iodine drops in Grace's face, Grace's mother—tall, lithe, and as fancy as one could be for a country gal with not much more than what she was wearing and carrying in a small sack on her back—meandered through the front door, lost in the thought of how she was going to wash out her clothes, press her hair, and hightail it back over to Willis Cunningham's place before the sun made its slow dance across the sky. It was Maw Maw's voice that snapped her out of her trance. Her eyes got good and narrow when she caught sight of the jar in her mother's hands.

"Mama, don't you start that mess with my baby," Bassey said, her voice firm. "She don't need to know about this here."

"And what do you know about what this baby needs?" Maw Maw snapped. "Ain't like you been 'round here to take an accounting."

"Now, Rubelle Adams, don't you worry none about whether I been here or not. What I know is you stay trying to get somebody to run all around town, spending they days catching babies in exchange for a couple dollars or a chicken or two if they lucky. I told you I'm not about to spend the rest of my life walking up and down these dirt roads, listening to all these po' folk hootin' and hollerin' while they pushing out babies they can't even afford, and I sure don't want that for Gracie."

Maw Maw carefully placed the iodine back in the bag, followed by the red belly bands, the newspaper, her sack of herbs, the berries, and the stack of tiny pieces of cotton sheets and then she kissed her teeth. "And what would you have her do?" Maw Maw asked as she pushed herself out of the creaky chair. "You want her running around town after some man don't want her none? Let him black her eye as a thank-you for her pleasure?"

Bassey instinctively grabbed her cheek and winced at the tenderness the thoughtless action announced. Willis had been in a mood the night before. Bassey had calmed him the best she knew how, but not before he taught her one of his "lessons" for getting smart in the mouth. "Better she learn how to make peace with a man who can take good care a her than run behind these white folk, scrubbing they dirty draws for a few pennies here and there while you wait on these niggers to have babies that'll grow up to wash dirty draws, too. That's not my wish for my daughter."

"Your wishes for her can't ever be bigger than what the ancestors got in store."

Bassey knew the argument was futile; while she'd shunned the profession passed down from the hands of her mother and her mother before her and so many more women in the Adams line, stretching all the way back to before the ships spilled their family's blood on Virginia's shores, she could lay no claims to how Maw Maw chose to raise Grace. After all, Bassey was not of their world. Not anymore. She'd long ago pushed her visions and the ones Maw Maw saw, too, down deep, where darkness blotted out the ghosts and their prophecies. She wanted no part of them—saw no value in listening to their whispers, paying attention to the messages they left for her in her dreams. They simply did not serve her. She chose, instead, to serve herself. Bassey believed she alone was responsible for her destiny, and her destiny resided in the arms of Willis Cunningham, assistant pastor at the Church of the Nazarene, where Bassey was a faithful and dutiful member of the flock and a first lady-in-waiting, holding tight to the notion that if she just kept a firm grasp, if she just did what he said, if she proved the depths of her love, Willis would do what was right, what was necessary, what was divined by Jesus and God and the Holy Spirit himself: make her his wife. She cared for Willis, sure, but she cared even more about what he could do to assure she'd never have to touch another washboard again—at least not to tend wash for ornery white ladies. The respect he commanded both at Nazarene and down at the High Plantation, where he worked as a foreman charged with overseeing a bunch of shiftless niggers chopping tobacco stalks, brought in enough money and prestige to assure her place on the front pew every early Sunday morning, in front of the deaconesses and their oversized hats and pursed lips, next to Lady Stewart, Reverend Stewart's wife and the first lady of Nazarene, and directly in front of Willis, whose occasionally roving eyes needed a clear focus from the pulpit.

"Now, Mama, I don't have time to get into this with you today," Bassey said, snapping. She twirled in three different directions, unsure of what to tackle first. "I have to get myself ready for Bible study at Mr. Cunningham's place and I'm going to be late if I stand here and entertain this talk on the Good Lord's Thursday." She turned her attention to Grace and softened her tone just a bit: "Daughter, put some water on the stove for me to wash up."

Yet again, there stood Bassey and Rubelle, like two prizefighters—angry, anxious, silently stalking their opponent from their respective corners, blood and sweat and snot betraying the brutality of their rage. The only thing unbroken between mother, daughter, were the bones.

This is just the way it was. How it would always be. Neither's spine was pliable and so there would be no bending. Each was rooted in exactly who she was. Rubelle received from her daughter the same restrained respect she got from the community she served. Bassey appreciated her mother's skill as a midwife and healer, but for a woman who craved both modernity and roots in God's word, accepting her mother's unusual ways was no easy feat. It shook Bassey to her core that her mother would never allow so much as her shadow to darken the doorway of the Church of the Nazarene, the place where Bassey was convinced her new life—spiritual, physical—began. Frankly, she was embarrassed by Rubelle—this woman who trafficked in haints, worshiped the rush of the river waters, and believed a sack full of leaves and dirty roots could heal better than the hand of a doctor with school learning. The community put up with her behavior because options were few: segregated hospitals and white country doctors would just as soon heal a sow than a nigger, and most of the people in the tiny colored section of Rose were too poor to pay for professional care anyway. Rubelle was all they had.

Rubelle knew that she was all her daughter had and it angered her that her daughter refused to see it as such. Bassey was so blinded by her ambition—so busy turning her back on her destiny—she couldn't see that truth, much less the trinity of dangers that stood at the ready to end her: the church mothers of Nazarene, who thought she was nothing more than a trollop angling to lure their beloved pastor into the Adams family's web of evil and sin; the men who smelled Bassey's desperation and dabbed it on their bodies for sport; and that Willis, the darkest of them all, draping his lies in forever and dangling it before Bassey's eyes. None of them meant Bassey well. Rubelle warned her, but to no avail. Bassey was Bassey and that was all she had in her.

The two had remained silent as Grace tended Bassey's water; she treated it as if it were a precious perfume being prepared for royalty. Just like Maw Maw had taught her, Grace took a flower from the gardenia tree and pounded the tender leaves into a handful of Epsom salt. When she was sufficiently satisfied with its scent, she pinched the salt between her slender fingers and sprinkled it at the bottom of the large iron washtub that sat in the corner between the kitchen and sitting room, and when the water was warm enough, she poured that into the tub, too. Three more trips to the tub with warm water, and a few gardenias sprinkled on top, and it was done. "Mama, your bath is ready," Grace said proudly, standing back from the vessel.

Bassey nodded, tossed her sponge into the water, and let her dress drop to the floor. Her back was turned to her mother and daughter, so she hadn't seen the shadow of horror that darkened their eyes. The bruises on her back and thighs were shocking to all but Bassey; she'd been too preoccupied with getting herself ready for Willis to let the pain or evidence of it slow her down, and she sure wasn't about to harp on details of how it all happened to her mother and daughter. No, this was business between her and Willis and that was that.

Grace stared in her mother's direction, but she wasn't watching Bassey wash. Instead, she stared at the picture show—in technicolor, grotesque—flashing before her. In it, Bassey was laid out on a slab of wood stretched between two chairs, her hands resting at the sides of her smoothed-out dress—the one with the yellow flowers, her favorite. Maw Maw was putting coins on her eyelids and painting her lips with berries. Mama was perfectly still, but she was not at peace.

Grace wasn't quite sure what was unfolding in her picture show—or even why she was seeing one while she stood, rested and wide awake. But Maw Maw knew.

She knew because she was watching the picture show, too.

"We have to get on down the road," Maw Maw said, finally breaking the silence. Her voice cracked, but neither her daughter nor granddaughter saw the water welling in her eyes. "Miss Ginny's baby ain't fittin' ta wait."

2

Grace had already gotten a talking-to on the walk over to the Brodersens' place and so she knew to stand in the corner and not so much as breathe unless Maw Maw instructed her to do otherwise. She was there to watch, learn, hop to and help with Ms. Ginny's four other babies, all of whom sat in the kitchen whisper quiet as they listened for their mama's moans. The children were aware that a baby was coming, but the particulars were inaccessible to them because asking questions wasn't an option. Their father, stern, gruff, and not much of the talking type, would just as soon smack them in the mouth and his own mouth, too, rather than answer to children. And so they were reduced to the conjuring of their wild minds, which served up fantastically ridiculous scenarios for what was to happen with the kettles of boiling water on the stove and the scissors being dipped in the hulking bubbles and the brushes and the fabric cotton squares the granny, a vision in all white from the top of her head to the stockings in her white nursing shoes, had piled high on the little serving tray they craned their necks to see every time the lady or Mr. Brodersen opened the creaky door to enter or leave the bedroom. "Maybe they gone cut the baby out her stomach," the oldest, age seven, whispered when their father was out of earshot. "And maybe they gone tie her belly with those sheets," another, five, added, pulling the three-year-old baby sitting in her lap closer to her chest. The four-year-old's bottom lip quivered at the thought and broke into a full-on shake shortly thereafter when a contraction forced a guttural yell from his mama's throat.

"Don't you cry," the oldest warned, her top lip curled as she whispered in her little brother's ear. "Daddy gone come in here and skin yo' hide if you don't do like he say and set still."

The little boy clapped his hand over his mouth. He'd already felt the sting of their daddy's belt earlier in the day and he wanted no more part of it. The seven-year-old seriously considered taking the hit, though, settling in her mind that a whipping was worth the price of finding out why she had to sit in the kitchen like a little baby while the little nigger gal got to be in the room with their mama. Their daddy, preoccupied with fashioning a baby bed out of a large corrugated box, pads, and blankets, was oblivious to the whispers, whimpers, and wonderings.

"Now, now," Maw Maw said as she helped the moaning Ms. Ginny out the bed. Her water had broken a few hours earlier and the contractions were coming at a steady pace, but her body wasn't demanding she push just yet. It was Maw Maw's job to make her charge as comfortable as one could be while pain dragged like a switchblade across her abdomen, and so, just like all the other birthing mothers before Ms. Ginny, Maw Maw walked and talked to and reminded Ginny of the sweet sweet on the other side of all that sour. "This fittin' to be a beautiful time for you and yo' husband and that sweet little baby. Don't you worry none 'bout the pain. With God's favor, we done did this four other times and every last one of them babies got here healthy and strong. Same gone be for this one, don't you worry. We 'bout to witness another miracle."

"Yes, ma'am," was all Ms. Ginny could muster. There was fear in her eyes.

"Gracie, go on ahead and make this bed, now," Maw Maw gently ordered. "Do it just like I taught you. Put down the plastic on the mattress and then the sheet and then the big pad Maw Maw made. That's in that bag over there, nice and clean. Do that straightaway, and then get the basins together, one for Ms. Ginny here, one for me, and one for this new bundle a joy gone be joining us soon."

"Yes, ma'am," Grace said. She got straight to business while Maw Maw continued handing out orders.

"Now Mr. Brodersen, I'm going to walk Ms. Ginny around a little bit while my grandbaby gets the bed linens in order, and after the basins are set up, me and her, we gonna be right out there in the kitchen with the chi'ren while you and Ms. Ginny go on ahead and spend some quiet time together in here."

"I won't be doing that," he said simply as he settled the baby's new crib on a stand next to the marital bed.

Ms. Ginny moaned again as a contraction squeezed her womb—a pain so strong it radiated down to the tips of her toes. She doubled over and grabbed her belly with one hand and squeezed Maw Maw's arm with the other.

"Oh, Mr. Brodersen, don't get shy on me now, hear? You and your beautiful wife were alone before this baby and you should be together, just the two a ya, as this child makes a way into the world."

"I said no!" he yelled. The base boom of his voice made Grace jump, and that jump made Grace drop the pad, and dropping the pad made Maw Maw's tongue just as sharp, reckless, as the white man's.

"Get that pad up!" Maw Maw yelled, despite that Gracie had already snatched the pad into her arms so quickly only a small corner had actually touched the freshly swept carpet on the clapboard floor. "Know how long we had to work to get them sheets on that pad sterilized? Let me see it!" she demanded, still holding on to Ms. Ginny, who was shifting from one foot to the other, trying to loose herself from the aftershock of the last contraction.

Grace held the pad up for her grandmother's inspection. Spotless.

"You got to be mo' careful, baby," Maw Maw said, her voice softer, sweeter. "Everything in here got to be clean and sterile so this baby and the mama don't get no infections, hear?"

"Yes, ma'am," Gracie said, nodding. "I'll be mo' careful, Maw Maw," she said as she placed the pad on the bed—the end that grazed the carpet positioned at the bottom of the bed where Ms. Ginny's feet would be.

Maw Maw turned her attention back to the ornery husband, but she thought better of trying to convince him to do what should have come naturally, what was exactly right. His wife, nervous, insides on fire, anxious about her new baby's passage, needed her husband's soft parts to balance out all that hard. But he was incapable; something was grating him and love was too weak a salve for the wounds he was nursing.

Maw Maw had seen this before—overwhelmed husbands leading with their nerves, cutting down to the white meat anything that got in the way of their figuring on what, exactly, it would take for them to put food into yet another mouth. Maw Maw felt for the mamas, but she had little sympathy for the pas. They never seemed to take any of this into consideration when they were chasing their wives around with their stiff peckers, refusing, even, to let the women's bodies heal before they were demanding sex. Taking it. And then here come another baby on top of the one or two they already couldn't afford, which, on occasion, would become more than just their family problem; it would be Maw Maw's, too. Poor Mary Patterson, that was her lot. Her man couldn't find work and the two of them had plenty of hungry nights the winter before last, around when the baby was due. Might be some corn pone here and there, some beans if Mary could muster up the energy to take in a load or two of laundry for some spare change to hand over to ol' Bunch Cleary down at the mercantile. Mostly, they bent over small bowls of grits with a little fatback grease to make the taste halfway palatable, while huddled up next to an oven that saw in its belly not much more than a couple small pieces of wood Joe Patterson had managed to scrounge up on occasion while foraging. So malnourished was Mary when she was pregnant with that first baby, Maw Maw was compelled to make an extra special offering down by the river, imploring the ancestors to spare the baby the pain that was to come with what Maw Maw was sure would be its inevitable death. Alas, Mary went into labor on the coldest night of the year; the daddy and mama were so weak from hunger, exhaustion, and the beginning stages of hypothermia, that in their quietest moments, the sole signs of life were the puffs of warm breath making weak clouds against the freezing air. Maw Maw, who, upon walking not but three steps into the house, had become alarmed by their condition—the hollowness of it all—and immediately summoned a neighbor to run her back to her place for provisions: a spare quilt, some preserved beets, a bag of beans, coffee. Soap. She'd already sewn a flannel gown for the baby, but she grabbed a few more pieces of fabric, a box, and six small bottles to fashion a warm bed for the baby, knowing its mama's bones would be insufficient comfort against the winter cold. Mary Patterson had a hard labor—one of the hardest Maw Maw had seen in all her years catching babies. Can't be no weak woman in any kind of way when you're pushing a human from your loins. Mary? She'd been strong that day and with Maw Maw's grace, she pulled herself together for her child—for her family. But her husband just sat there, useless. Waiting. Incapable. A piece of a man. Had his poor wife up, sore, struggling to fix his food before, even, she could give their little baby some ninny. "Now Joe, you gone have to let Mary rest," Maw Maw had told him when she stopped by a few weeks later to check on her patient and the baby, only to find the baby in the box, wet and fussing, while Mary stood over the stove, breast milk soiling her raggedy dress, spooning grits and a portion of bread into a bowl.

"She all right," Joe said, grabbing his wife's waist in a way that made Maw Maw avert her eyes—shamed. This, she thought, was no way for a man to carry on in front of company. "Mary and me and our young'un, we gone be just fine, ain't we, sweets?"

"Yes, Joe," she said quietly, simultaneously placing her husband's bowl on his lap and adjusting her dress, which was soaking and clinging to her body. She rushed to her baby and, in one quick motion, put her frustrated, hungry son on her breast. He was slurping and sniffling by the time Mary, exhausted and near tears herself, practically dropped onto the unmade bed.

She was pregnant three weeks later. Had another mouth to feed eight months after that. Joe Patterson still owed Maw Maw the five dollars from the first delivery when he came knocking on her door to tell her that Mary's water broke and she needed her to deliver their second child—a child that would join an ever-growing list of people he could not, would not feed.

Maw Maw thought babies sacred and so there would never be a time when she would use her root work—a gift handed down through the generations—to pull an unwanted baby out a mama's belly to die. She didn't want that on her soul. But the Pattersons, and all too many more couples like them, made Maw Maw clear about why some women made that choice and why it wasn't hard, at all, to find someone to help them carry out the mission, if that's what the parents aimed to do. Judging never saved a baby from the abortionist's hook or stopped a baby's stomach from rumbling.

Through the bedroom window overlooking the backyard, Grace watched Mr. Brodersen, ax in hand, stalk a hunk of a black locust tree he'd been chopping for firewood. He looked angry, which confused Grace, because who could be mad about a wee-bit coming into this world? Babies, to Grace, were like Maw Maw's Sunday lemonade—filled to the brim with goodness, made with love. A couple times, she babysat Nearest Dandy's little baby, Evermore, and Grace just couldn't get enough of how he smelled when she nuzzled her nose against the line of his jaw or how he would gnaw her cheek with his gums when she put her face in front of his mouth. His breath was so sweet—the sweetest thing she'd ever known. Mrs. Dandy warned her not to hold the baby the entire time she was sitting. "He gonna get ruint with you holding him all the time and ain't nobody got time for no spoiled baby," she warned. "Put him down, even if he fussin'. He need to learn how to get on in this world without all that coddling."

"Yes, ma'am," Grace would always say, and then, before Mrs. Dandy could get all the way out the door good, little Evermore would be back in her arms. She was addicted, and that wasn't even her baby. Why Mr. Brodersen was acting so funny style about his own child was beyond Grace.

Ms. Ginny's scream shocked the girl's attention back to what was going on in the room. The woman's knees buckled beneath her, and had Maw Maw not been there, surely, she would have fallen clean to the floor.

"Rubelle," Ms. Ginny said, struggling against the weight of her own breath. "It's time. I need to push."

"Now hold on there, Ms. Ginny. You know you can't push until we know for sure it's time. Come on now, I gotcha."

Grace shifted from one foot to the other as Maw Maw pulled back the sheets and helped Ms. Ginny onto the pad-covered bed. Dutifully and quickly, she fetched from the kitchen the kettle of hot water to pour into the white basin at the foot of the bed, which sat on a small table on which Maw Maw had assembled all the tools from her bag.

"Okay, Ms. Ginny, now you lay on back now and settle against your pillow," Maw Maw instructed. "I'm going to see how far along you are. Whatever you do, don't bear down just yet, okay? Don't want that baby getting stuck and we shole don't want you hurting yourself, now, you hear? You remember the breathing, don't you?"

Ms. Ginny, face contorted from the pain of a contraction dragging across her groin, nodded.

"Okay, then breathe through it, okay? It'll help with the pain. I'm going to get my hands washed up and then we'll go on ahead and get down to business," Maw Maw said.

For what seemed like an eternity to Grace, Maw Maw stood over that basin and, with great care and precision, scrubbed her hands, fingers, fingernails, and forearms with a brush—the bristles scraping against her skin so hard, Grace thought that for sure she would scrub her skin clean off her bones. When she was finished, she held her hands up in the air and then reached for one of the white sterile towels she'd set next to the basin, her eyes surveying the room as she toweled off. Scissors. Iodine drops. Vaseline. Soap. Scraps of sterile fabric. Slop jar. Scale. Box and clothes for the baby. She was satisfied; all was in order.

"Okay, let's get your legs on up and see what's what," Maw Maw said as she reached down and lifted Ms. Ginny's nightdress.

There, splayed before her, was a sight Grace had never before seen in her thirteen years—something she wasn't sure she should be seeing for herself: a grown lady's privates. A white woman's poom-poom. Closest she'd ever gotten to seeing a poom-poom had been not much long ago, when she looked at her own out in the outhouse. Just like a few times before, while Maw Maw was by the river, she snatched the old, cloudy handheld mirror and rushed into the backyard on her mission to discover what her privates looked like now that she was "a woman" with her monthly. The first time she'd checked, she was eight years old and curious on her own accord—wanted to see the folds and the pink and what was making it feel funny when she put her pillow between her legs as she fell asleep or when she rubbed it with her pointy finger. She snuck the mirror again when she noticed all the fine, curly hair sprouting on her groin area. She knew she would get some under her arms, sure, because she'd seen evidence of it on a few of the older girls in her school one afternoon when the boys were getting on Mabel Tawny for stinking. "All that hair got yo' pits smelling like a heap a scraps on a hot fire," Lewis Melton had yelled during recess, with the obvious intent not to inform Mabel about the stench but to call her out in front of the schoolyard full of children who had long, sharp tongues and a short supply of grace. Mabel had cried that day over all the taunting, and Grace, doing her best to be invisible to Lewis's gaze, said a silent prayer that she never grow hair under her arms for Lewis or anyone else to jones. That afternoon was the beginning of her obsession with hair—where it grew, why it grew where it did, what was supposed to happen when one got it, if everyone had it or if Mabel was just the most unfortunate girl in the world to have under her arms hair that smelled like hot garbage. Grace, armed with that cloudy mirror, would find out a few years later that underarms and heads weren't the only place hair took up residence. A couple years after that, she would find out, too, that her poom-poom pretty much looked the same as it always had, even if, like Maw Maw said, she was officially a woman and could have a baby on her own. She expected it to be bigger—round like her hips and behind, thick like her thighs, maybe more dull, seeing as only the skin that got kissed by the sun was darker, shinier, and much more pretty than the parts that stayed up under her gunnysack dresses. Not much about it, she was sad to find, had changed after she started bleeding.

But here was Ms. Ginny's poom-poom—a whole different color from the rest of her pale white skin, and hair that looked much more like that which grew on the top of her head, straighter than curly. And peeking from the flaps and folds was a mass of dark, curly hair and blood and goo, pulsing at the crown of Ms. Ginny's hole.

Grace grew faint. There was a baby in there.

Maw Maw's voice snapped her to. "Now you gone feel my fingers right there on the rim, Ms. Ginny. You remember how I massaged you with the other chir'ren?"

"Yes, ma'am," Ms. Ginny said.

"Okay, good. Keep still and let me go on ahead and rub it. Give you a little relief and make it stop burning, so that baby come out without tearing you to pieces. We don't want that."

"No, ma'am."

Grace watched in equal parts awe and disbelief as her grandmother massaged her patient, rubbed her legs with the back of her hand and encouraged her to "bear down" when a contraction rumbled across her belly. She knew what was to come, of course; there was no way Maw Maw would let her attend a birth and assist with it all without explaining to her how babies made it into this world. Grace knew the particulars. But it was something altogether different to see a human—what Maw Maw called "a miracle between a mama and her God"—emerge from between somebody's legs.

"Okay, Ms. Ginny, this baby almost here," Maw Maw said as she positioned her hands in front of Ms. Ginny's Vaseline-slicked poom-poom, one up top, the other below it, almost as if she were about to catch a ball. Ms. Ginny made a low, guttural grunt and then pushed with every ounce of energy she could muster—a push strong enough to get the head, full of bushy curls, out of her body. Maw Maw gently cupped the baby's head in one hand as she deftly wiped the baby's eyes with sterile cloth and dropped iodine in each one. Just as she set the drops back on the small side table, Ms. Ginny gave a final heave, sending the entire squirming body into Maw Maw's waiting hands.

"Whew, look at this pretty baby!" Maw Maw shouted over the baby's cries. "You got yourself a healthy girl. She just as pretty as she can be. Look here, Gracie!"

Maw Maw was right: she was beautiful—prettier than any of the Brodersens' other children, who were all fast asleep on the kitchen chairs.

"Let me see her," Ms. Ginny demanded with intensity; Maw Maw jumped ever so slightly.

"Now hold on there, now, Ms. Ginny. Let me get her cleaned up for you and get her weighed and dressed. There's an order to this thing."

"Please," Ms. Ginny said, this time more gently.

As if perplexed, Maw Maw gave a long, hard look at Ms. Ginny, who was giving a long hard look at the baby. Maw Maw followed Ms. Ginny's eyes to the infant, and that's when, she told Grace later, she saw it: the little girl, moments old, with only a half a minute's worth of fresh air in her lungs, was wearing the weight of the world on the tips of her ears. They were brown. Not quite the color of those that belong to a black sharecropper, but certainly the tan of a landowner whose family had been working hard to weed out the slavemaster's offence from generations before. It didn't take much more than that for Maw Maw to understand what she was looking at—what the stakes were.

"Please," Ms. Ginny whispered, pleading.

Maw Maw was quiet. She looked nervously at Grace, who was too smart to be oblivious to the heaviness of the room, but too fresh and new to know that both Ms. Ginny, the white wife of a white man with a small farm and six mouths to feed and the pride of every white man who'd come before and would follow behind, and her Black baby were in severe danger.

"Now, now," Maw Maw said, trying her best to stay calm, as if to keep Ginny calm. "You know we need to get the afterbirth out of you and I gotta get yo' baby weighed and check her over." Ms. Ginny opened her mouth to speak, but Maw Maw raised her hand to cut her off. "It's gone be all right now, don't you worry, hear? This baby is healthy. She shole is pretty. And the whole world gon' know she a Brodersen, hear?"

Maw Maw turned her attention to Grace. "Baby, go into Maw Maw's bag and get out my paperwork and set it up out there on the kitchen table. I'll fill it out when we finish up in here."

"I can fill it out, Maw Maw," said Grace, who was anxious to show off her schooling.

"Naw, baby. The law say I got to fill out that paperwork," she said. Turning her attention to Ms. Ginny, she added: "And it say I have to be truthful on the birth certificate, too. The truth, that be important."

"Yes, ma'am," Ms. Ginny said, nodding. "And we know what the truth means around these parts, don't we, Granny?"

Maw Maw nodded as she finished bathing the baby and wrapped her in the belly holder; she attached the cloth to a hook weight and held the little girl up with one hand and leaned in to take note of the numbers on the dial. Seven pounds, three ounces. "Yes, ma'am, we do," she said finally, as she unhooked the baby and swaddled her in a blanket. "Now I need you to bear down one mo' gin', Ms. Ginny, so we can get that afterbirth out and I can check it and make sure you and this little one is okay."

The placenta, bloodied but intact, slid easily from between Ms. Ginny's legs and onto the birthing pad, on which Maw Maw examined it, checking for tears and any other indiscretions that could indicate her patient might have complications. All was well. Maw Maw would make sure of it. So many other times when the little babies' ears betrayed the lies, Rubelle Adams made sure of it.

"Grace, baby," Maw Maw called to her granddaughter, who'd returned to the room, as she wrapped the placenta in several pages of the weekend newspaper. "Take this here and go on out to that pear tree out yonder in the backyard. Ask Mr. Brodersen for his strongest shovel, and then you go on out there and dig up a nice, deep hole, hear? Bury this in it and cover it up real good. You know what to do, baby. We talked about it; you remember?"

"Yes, Maw Maw, I remember," Grace said as she cradled the package.

When she turned around to leave the room, she ran directly into the mass of Mr. Brodersen's broad, hard torso. He smelled of earth and sweat and black locust wood. Anger.

"Won't be no need to bury that up under the pear tree," he said simply, gruffly.

"Oh, Mr. Brodersen, of course we'll put it under the pear tree—just like we did for all the other babies. You remember, right? It's the old way. My mama and my grandmama, too, say you bury the afterbirth under the tree and your babies will never, ever leave you."

Mr. Brodersen looked Maw Maw in the eye and held her gaze until she got uncomfortable enough to shift from one foot to the other. Her rubber shoe squeaked, the sound piercing through the thick in the air.

It took him only one long stride to push past little Grace and take his place directly in front of Maw Maw. He held her gaze, even as he reached down and took the baby out of her arms. His long fingers, strong, steady, pulled the blanket back from the baby's head, and only then did he switch his eyes from Maw Maw's face to that of the newborn. He stared long and hard, his eyes washing over her tight, black curls, her forehead, her nose and lips and neck. The baby craned her neck and licked out her tongue.

Mr. Brodersen stepped back and turned his attention to his wife, then Maw Maw, then to Grace. There was not even a hint of emotion in his voice, but his command shook Grace to her core. "Take that package and burn it in the stove. Now."

3

They came for Maw Maw before she could get her daughter into the ground. It did not matter that her heart was shattered, or that Bassey's battered body was laid out on the cooling board, her bones still settling into their new state of being, or that Maw Maw and her sister healers were in the middle of singing and stomping her child's spirit away home. The men saw more that they could break and so they did.

They moved like wild boars, their dirty boots crashing against the wooden floor already in full sway beneath the dozen feet that dragged and stomped and jumped in a ring shout around Bassey's body. The men's voices cracked like thunder over the women's high-pitched, mournful chants but failed to penetrate the trance that the funereal song produced among the lot of them. And so, the strangers, four in all, made their presence known. One, red-faced, sweaty, angry, pushed through the circle and grabbed arms, pushed backs and thighs, causing one woman to topple over the other. Another, redder, sweatier, knocked over chairs to snatch at the women's faces. "All this savage shit! Stop it, this blasphemy. Before the living God, you will stop this!"

"Which one is it?" the third yelled over his shoulder to the fourth man standing by the door, as he, too, set upon the women. Their chanting morphed into screaming. As if for sport, the third sliced his arm across Maw Maw's altar, sending plates full of food and cups of water and moonshine and vases of flowers crashing to the floor, before stopping in front of the floor-length mirror set against the living room wall. He was a

Southern man of tradition and so he knew full well that the black cloth hanging over the mirror was there to keep the dead's spirit moving, but he obviously cared not for Bassey's soul or the women who were tending to it, and so he snatched the cloth and smirked as he caught sight of his own reflection, a gummy face contorted into a sickeningly gleeful grin. His lips straightened, though, when his eyes caught sight of the rest of the reflection: there was the young girl, petite, Black, stoic, standing sentry over the dining table where the dead body lay. He likely struggled to distinguish the two bodies, so close was the girl to the dead, her hand resting on the Black-eyed-Susan-filled hand of the deceased, which, too, was dressed in a white flower-print frock, covered with a worn, hand-sewn, white quilt, the head resting on a small white pillow and surrounded by a halo of white gardenias. On the dead girl's eyes were two silver dollars, shimmering against her skin. Though the commotion rocked the table and door slab on which the body lay and sent the quilt sliding and some of the gardenias scattering, somehow the two coins, locked in the recesses of Bassey's deep-set, bruised eyes, stayed put. The man had seen dead bodies before, and he'd attended a few country wakes of his own before his own family had collected enough wealth to mourn its dead in the modernity of the whites-only funeral home. But this—the girl's penetrating stare, the disturbed body, the sight of the two in the mirror he purposefully, callously uncovered—this, it was certain, would haunt him for the rest of his miserable life.

Grace just stood there and watched. She watched it all, knowing her mother would never find rest.

It was the last position Bassey expected to find herself in—lying in the dirt with her pretty dress lifted up to her waist, legs splayed, bloomers exposed, head split, eye socket smashed, teeth sprinkled like pebbles among the sticks and roots and rocks that had served as unwitting accomplices in her brutal death. She thought, after all, that she had fixed things. The clandestine night at The Quarters was supposed to make things right between them after a disastrous morning that had ended with Willis pulling his strap from his pants and whipping her body over a transgression she still didn't quite comprehend. Up until the beating, the morning had been every bit as perfect as the sound of the sparrows that had announced the new day—as beautiful as the hot pinks and oranges that had slow-dragged across the sunrise. It was his favorite time to have relations and so it became hers, too, despite that she loathed letting him see the havoc sleep wreaked on both her eyes, which, against a morning pillow, always looked swollen, and her hair, which, sweated out and nappy from night-before sex and hard sleep, always drew up closer to her scalp than she liked. In the sweet moments of that early morning, he'd told her she was the prettiest thing he ever did see, and she believed it to be so because that was the way he usually treated her—pulling out chairs, scrubbing her back in the tub as he fawned, staring into her eyes, his gaze so intense she could only shift and avert her own eyes under the weight. "I would kill a ox dead with my two bare hands for you, girl, you know that, don'tcha?" he'd said, leaning in to whisper the words in her ear, like he was sharing a secret. "I wouldn't do that for nobody else but you."

She'd believed him, too. She was rooted in it as deep as a hundred-year-old oak was in a Virginia forest. And she was pleased, so much so that she stood and danced naked around his small room, giggling and jiggling, calling out "Mrs. Cunningham" from her gut.

That's when he hit her. Just rose up from the side of the bed and, in one swift move, picked up his pants off the floor where, the night before, in their throes of passion, he'd thrown them, snatched the belt from its loops, and cracked the brown leather, buckle and all, against her hide.

"*My mama* is Mrs. Cunningham," he yelled, raging as he swung. Bassey's surprise was quickly usurped by the sheer terror that rose like the welts and bruises on her back, buttocks, and thighs.

"I'm sorry, baby," was all she could think to say, all she could think to do to defend herself from the barrage of blows that sliced the air before raining down on her bare skin.

"How dare you stand here naked, The Jezebel, calling out that sacred name before God!" he yelled as he swung.

"Please, Willis, I didn't mean it!" she yelled as she cowered against the blows, grabbing at her face and head to protect them.

She sought neither explanation nor apology; he gave both just as freely as the beatings—"Satan got a hold a me," "My daddy used to do my mama like this and I can't hep it," "I do this on account I loves ya, Bassey, and you need to learn iffn I intend to make you my wife." She swallowed all of Willis's foolishness whole—grilled it up and ate it like Sunday dinner. It was more filling than the thought of spending the rest of her life alone. The rest of her life without him.

But later that evening, after she'd made up with her man, cleaned her wounds, and shushed her own mama to hightail it back over to Willis's house, Bassey, looking like a star that could give Lena Horne herself something to envy, draped herself on Willis's arm as they walked into The Quarters, only to face off against disrespect so grand, so unapologetically, almost unforgivingly bold, there was no amount of sugar that could help it down her gullet.

The Quarters was supposed to be a safe space for Bassey and Willis, and it was—a place the two of them could go to have themselves a little dance, a little liquor, without the judgment they found Sunday mornings in the pews of Nazarene. The owner called the establishment a "speakeasy," like one of those fancy jazz clubs they'd all heard about up in Harlem, but really, it wasn't much more than a slightly more gussied-up version of the average juke joint, a shack held together with spare, rusty nails and worn wood. What made The Quarters shine wasn't so much how it looked, but how it made its patrons feel; one hard swallow of anything served beyond the heavy barn door—whisky, gin, corn—made everybody equals. Made circumstance and sin disappear.

What the atmosphere couldn't do was make Bassey tamp down her penchant for jealousy. She'd stepped away just a moment—just long enough to grab the chow-chow from the other end of the eating counter and squeeze and bump through the tight crowd to get back to her and Willis's plate of greens and cornbread—and there he was, leading some woman by her dainty hand to the dance floor, the two of them just grinning. It wasn't the laughter that got to her or the proximity of their bodies as they fell lockstep into a slow dance that was half the meter of the fast groove the band was jamming. It was the way he looked at her and how she responded to his gaze. It mirrored the look they'd shared just that morning, when he promised his love was strong enough for him to kill for her.

There was no time and no space between; Bassey was at the counter and then she was standing in front of her man and that woman, having neither sense nor care of how she'd gotten from one place to the other. "You know what's good for you, you best git off my man," Bassey said, seething as she yanked the woman's hair, pulling hard enough to toss her to the floor while keeping a clump of her hair suspended above her body.

"Woman, what the hell . . . ," Willis started yelling as the patrons on the dance floor quickly scattered, leaving the man, his lady, and his mistress to it. There was no chance to finish his query, though; Bassey didn't give him time to. The palm of her hand connecting against his lips won priority over the rush of his words, the sound of it echoing off the walls that, just moments before, had been absorbing the sound of the trumpet, saxophone, guitar, piano, and drum before the commotion enticed all the band members to stop playing and start watching what was unfolding before them.

Bassey was distracted by her rage but only momentarily. Willis's grip on her arm, just as tight, strong, and furious as his eyes, snapped her back to gentle, small. "Please," she begged. "No, no, no, I didn't mean it, baby, I'm sorry. I don't know what came over me."

She shrunk herself as she pleaded, prepping for the blow. Willis didn't want her words. Didn't need them. He grabbed her by the gullet and practically lifted her off her feet; his eyes were red, his nostrils bull-like. "Getcha ass outside," he said, pushing Bassey by the throat through the crowd, which parted like Willis was Moses and the people were the Red Sea.

There would be no saving Bassey. No one thought to try. They just left the man to do what he was to do and so he did it: Willis pulled Bassey out into the woods just beyond the clearing of The Quarters and, under the red moon, bloodied the eyes and lips of the woman he proclaimed to love.

And when he was through proclaiming his manhood, when he was satisfied the lesson had been taught and learned, Willis pulled Bassey up off the ground and stood her in front of him, using his hand to brush off the dirt and sticks that were stuck to her dress and hair. Like she was some rag doll he was retrieving for a wayward child who'd dropped it.

"Why can't you just do right by me, Bassey?" he asked. Brush, brush. Tug. "You know I love you, don't you?" Brush, brush. Tug. "Don't you?" he asked, more forcefully.

"Yes," Bassey said, struggling to get the word through her fattened, bleeding lips. It was all she could muster, so she nodded additional confirmation.

"But you can't just go hitting your man in the mouth, Bassey, you know that, don't you?" Brush, brush. Tug.

She nodded.

"Now is the perfect time to repent, baby," he said. Brush, brush. Tug. Push.

Bassey was back on the ground, but this time, she was on her knees. Willis brushed the back of his hand lightly against her cheek as he deftly used the other to loosen his belt.

"Willis, please . . ."

"You want to be my wife? Huh?" he asked as he unzipped his trousers.

"Please . . ."

"Please? Please what?" he said softly, menacingly, as he adjusted his undergarment and pulled out his member. "What you begging for? Say it."

Bassey's tears choked her words and her lips were too swollen to let them out anyway. She managed a yelp when he grabbed her by her hair and pulled her face toward his crotch.

"Go 'head, beg for it, lil' bitch. You want to be Mrs. Cunningham so bad. Beg for it."

Bassey tried to crumble, to make herself small again, but she struggled against his grip, which only made him angrier. She felt the first blow, saw the second one coming. And then, there was her baby's face, sweet Gracie, giggling and walking toward her, a freshly picked black-eyed Susan in her little fist, a field of the yellow flowers at her baby's back.

Beyond that was the sun.

Grace knew something bad had happened to her mother before ol' Jussie Mack found his way up the steps and to the front door of the Brodersens' house to tell the news—before Maw Maw could comprehend his words. Grace had seen Bassey's body in a picture show while she was emptying Ms. Ginny's slop jar in the outhouse: there she was, laid out in the pitch-black woods in the stark white dress, with the flowers in her hair and the coins over her eyes, shimmering like stars against a clear night sky. Grace couldn't quite comprehend what it all meant or how, even, her mother had gotten there in the first place. But she knew that as peaceful as her mother looked, she was not at rest.

Maw Maw was just finishing filling out the birth certificate for the Brodersens' new arrival when Jussie Mack pulled his wagon into the driveway. Ms. Ginny was sounding out the spelling of the baby's name—"That's Sandy with a 'y,' Granny, and Annabelle with two 'n's and two 'l's"—when Mr. Brodersen met Jussie out on the porch. When she heard the front screen door slam, Ms. Ginny struggled to sit upright and stated her case. "Granny, listen," she said. "She gone pass, ain't she? She light enough to be my husband's baby. Tell me she is."

"She shole is a beautiful young'un," Maw Maw said in an equally hushed tone. "But I can't guarantee nothing but that the sun gone rise in the morning and set in the evenings. That's all, Ms. Ginny."

"But you can mark that certificate to say it's so—that my husband is her pa and she is white," Ms. Ginny said, getting flustered, teary.

"I can," Maw Maw said. "But it won't be the truth, and if'n I lie on this here gubment document, I can go to jail, Ms. Ginny, and you know that."

But each knew the alternative—what would likely happen if Maw Maw marked "Negro" on that baby's birth certificate. It would be the same as signing a death sentence for that child. Maw Maw had heard about it time and again and seen it happen with her own eyes, too: little brown newborns abandoned by the husbands of cheating wives on the side of the road, left to the elements or the animals, whichever got to them first, or dropped off in the colored orphanage, where motherless children did some hard living. One family Maw Maw had heard about put its little colored baby in a gunnysack with a rock and dropped the child to the bottom of the Sussex River, and when the child washed up on shore, white folk shrugged and kept on living, as if it were the baby's fault for being and for dying. All the Negroes could do about it was mourn.

"Granny, I need you to come on out here now," Mr. Brodersen said as he appeared in the doorway. He was less gruff than earlier, when he'd been cross with Gracie.

"Yassir," Maw Maw said quickly, hiding the pen behind her back as if she were hiding the secret in her starch whites. "I'm just finishing up the birth certificate and waiting on my grandbaby to come on back in here and help me get the rest of the baby's things settled, Mr. Brodersen. I'll be there directly."

"No, now, Granny, I need you to come on out here right now," Mr. Brodersen said. "Nigger by the name Jussie is out on the porch and he got something to tell you."

"Jussie?" Maw Maw said. "Lawd, Belinda done gone into labor sho'nuff? She still had a couple weeks on her."

"That's not it, Rubelle," Mr. Brodersen said, this time gently.

Never once had he called her by her first name. She didn't even realize he knew it. Maw Maw looked down at the birth certificate and Ms. Ginny, then back at Mr. Brodersen. Something was wrong. Terribly, tragically wrong. She could feel it between the heartbeats that picked up pace in her chest. Maw Maw dropped the pen and the birth certificate, gathered her skirt, and took off running, out the bedroom, though the kitchen, onto the porch, down the porch steps, straight past Brodersen and Jussie, and right up to the back of Jussie's wagon.

There, she found Grace, the slop jar hanging precariously off the fingers on her right hand. Beyond her granddaughter was Bassey's body, in a bloody heap in the back of Jussie's wagon. "Maw Maw," Grace said, her eyes looking past her grandmother. "Mama sleep."

Brodersen stood at the door, caring nothing about the desecration of Rubelle Adams's home or how the men—deputies in the town of Rose's sheriff's department—handled the old lady, her friends, or the body of the woman they were about to put into the ground. She had committed the ultimate sin against him and so he wanted them to get on with it and he didn't care how they did it, so long as it got done. He pointed his finger, and at the end of it was Maw Maw, the woman whose hands were the first to touch the heads of each of his children, but who also used her position as a midwife to try to saddle a nigger baby in his care. This was the white people's worst nightmare—that generations of that good blood, that pure blood, would be tainted by the one drop, the blood of savages. The unclean. So many days before this particular one, the good white folk of Rose knew how to handle this kind of betrayal. The trees told those tales. Brodersen considered himself more evolved when it came to Rubelle, though, seeing as she'd been his family's granny midwife and her own child had been beaten to death, and so he took mercy and suggested the deputies spare her the business end of the rope. But Brodersen wanted Maw Maw to pay. Needed her to. Because right there on that bastard baby's birth certificate, she'd cosigned the lie, swearing in ink and through her duties as a midwife that the newborn was a white man's baby. His baby.

This was a lie. This was against the law. And though he had already dragged his wife and the nigger baby and all of their things out of his home and banished her from his existence, he was not satisfied. He needed more. He needed the granny who'd perpetuated his wife's lie to suffer for her most egregious sin.

"That's her, right there," Brodersen said, pointing at Maw Maw, who, by now, was second from the bottom of the heap of root women, their white dresses stained with footprints and tears, struggling against the weight of each other and the precariousness of the moment. Nothing good ever came for Negroes who stood at the end of a white man's pointed finger.

"Please, Mr. Brodersen, I don't understand what's going on, but I promise you we can fix this," Maw Maw said as she struggled to her feet. She tried to straighten out her dress but two of the men grabbed her by each arm. "Just tell me what did I do?"

"You know what this is," he said, seething, jabbing his fingers in her direction.

"Sir, I . . ."

"Shut up," one of the men yelled at Maw Maw. Then, to Brodersen: "Who is this nigger sassin' you? Tell you what, we can go on and handle this right now, just like we used to when niggers got outta line."

Maw Maw stiffened, Brodersen held up his hand as to shush his cohorts, and the entire room fell silent, save for Grace, who was draped over her mother's body, sobbing. "Please don't take my Maw Maw. Please," she said, screeching as she clung to Bassey's body.

"Enough talking, let's go," Brodersen said, grabbing Maw Maw and marching her to the door. She had no other choice but to surrender to their will.

"Watch after my Grace," she ordered her friends as the men pulled her out the door.

"Yes," her friends said simultaneously.

"And watch after my Bassey," she yelled as the men pulled her out into the yard.

"We will," they said, calling after her as the screen door slammed closed.

4

Grace's eyes were transfixed on the black ant—specifically, its spindly, threadlike legs. She was fascinated by how hard the tiny insect paddled them against the water—calculated that, had the ant been on dry land, it could have easily made it across the mound of dirt piled atop Bassey's body and probably halfway to the blackberry bush. Coulda had itself a mouthful of that sweet and dragged some of the flesh back to its queen mother, too, if it had sense enough not to climb its fool self into the metal cup of water Grace had left as an offering for her mother. It probably had its fill of the cornbread she'd left for her mama, too, Grace thought, glaring at the ant. Whatever death it was about to meet—drowning, a slow burn from the light of the sun—it had it coming. Served it right for taking what wasn't its to have.

That's all Grace had for that ant in that moment. All she could muster. Saving it was not an option. Maw Maw had taught her better than that— told her to care for all living creatures, be responsible to them, as they each served a critical function in the chain of being. Roosters get the day going, announcing the sun, waking everybody up; bees and spiders kiss the flowers, so food can grow and skeeters can find something else to chew on. Even snakes deserve to be. "Now you quit all that hollering," she'd once yelled at Grace, smashing her hands together for emphasis, jarring her granddaughter from a loud and boisterous jog away from the vegetable garden. Freshly picked sugar snaps were flying every which way from Grace's gathering skirt as she took flight, spooked by a black rat snake slithering around the pea bush and her bare feet.

"Maw Maw, that's a great big ol' snake over there!" Grace had said, wide-eyed, pointing as she backed away.

"What you runnin' fo'?" Maw Maw asked, waving a stray weed she'd punished for trying to marry with her marigolds. "You ought to be thanking that lil' ol' snake for prancing in our garden, all pretty and proud. He helpin'."

"But Maw Maw, that snake long as my arm. Look like he helpin' hisself to the whole pea bush."

"He heppin' that pea bush by making the mice run. The mice run, they take a few seeds wit 'em and somebody get a new pea bush right where they need 'em. Or a eagle eat up the mouse, so he can grow strong and fly high up in them trees and shake a seed, make a new tree for all the birds and squirrels to play in and such. Them squirrels make a fine stew. And that pea bush, well, the snake hep the pea bush, and that pea bush hep us, so we can eat. We eat, I can hep the mamas bring the babies into the world, and they grow up sweet, like you. Hep they mamas plant flowers and make squirrel stew," Maw Maw said, bending over, peering between the marigolds, inspecting for more weeds. "Make the whole world fat and pretty. Make all us smile and thank Mama Earth for giving all us life. One big circle. Way I see it, that snake is life. Thank the snake. Pick them peas."

Now, Grace pressed her cheek and chest and stomach and hip and palms into the dirt that was covering over her circle. Bassey was no more to this world than a mouse driven into the ground by a snake that people saw fit to let slither around the pulpit, big and black and bold in his presence. His fearlessness. They ate up his lies about the jezebel—didn't bother doing the figuring necessary to make his rationale for beating a woman to death with his bare hands make sense. She was lust. A menace. A threat to the goodness of their pristine, productive gardens, and so ashes to ashes, dust to dust was all that was meant for her. All she deserved. Same for the jezebel's crazy mama, mixing up potions and talking to trees, talking to the water, like they could hear her. Like they could talk back. A sin against the living God, the omnipotent, is what it was. Her evil caught up to her, is what they said. Didn't matter that she was the town's most prolific midwife; babies had wriggled from pregnant bellies just fine before her. They reckoned they'd do the same without her. Let that circle be broken.

Lying on her mother's grave, stomach rumbling, having spent the last five weeks foraging for work and food, Grace knew nothing of the scriptures the neighbors used to justify their own lust—that blood-filled rage the white folk employed to deny the child the wash work Maw Maw had, for years, taken in to earn a few extra pennies, or that which compelled her grandmother's acquaintances to pretend that girl didn't need their helping hand. In fact, they'd become mean about it—like they didn't care none whether Grace breathed in God's good air or suffocated under His good dirt. What she was asking for was so little in the scheme of things: a dollar or two in exchange for cleaning the rugs, scrubbing the floorboards, dusting, taking down the cobwebs, so the missus could keep her hands pretty. It's what she'd been doing before Maw Maw had been taken away, before Bassey got taken away. What she'd have to do the rest of her life, Grace supposed, now that everything was destroyed.

"Whatever it is you're looking for today, you will have to find it somewhere else, I'm afraid," said Mr. Horowitz, the head of one of the families Maw Maw had worked for, taking in their laundry and cooking their meals and such. Often, their benevolence had extended to Grace, who'd watched after their little babies whenever Maw Maw had an extra job to do and Mrs. Horowitz had to run to one of her lady functions or otherwise ingratiate herself in a town of womenfolk who neither understood nor cared for the Horowitzes' brand of religious doctrine. Her white skin and her husband's checkbook made her palatable. Always, she would drop a silver coin in Grace's hands for wiping her babies' bottoms and tending to the things mothers were called to do, even and especially when they didn't want to. "Just like I told you yesterday and the day before that, I can't have you working here anymore."

"But Mr. Horowitz, suh, I ain't looking fuh no handout. I just want to hep out like I been doing when my grandmama be here doing her work," Grace said, pleading. "I . . . I'll even do it for just a little something to eat. Anything." Beyond his shoulder, she caught the eye of Arlie Stephenson, a friend of Maw Maw's, stiffly tending the stove and trying, but failing miserably, to not cut her eye in the direction of the front stoop, where she could hear her friend's grandbaby begging for sustenance—a little something to save her very life. Just weeks before the Brodersens had reigned terror down on Grace's family, Ms. Arlie had been standing on Maw Maw's porch, making practically an identical plea, fiddling with the broom, going on and on about how she'd been let go from her job for leaving one too many pieces of silver a little too dull for her mistress's taste. Soon as Maw Maw gave her a spoonful of corn pone and a scoop of lima beans, she swallowed them practically whole and got on down the road like she had some kind of pressing appointment to tend to. Shame gives feet wings. Ms. Arlie was intimate with Grace's struggle.

Mr. Horowitz followed Gracie's eyes to Ms. Arlie, who quickly snapped her attention back to the pot roast she was tending. "Look, gal, you need to get off my porch."

"But Mr. Horowitz, please, just listen . . ."

Before she could get the whole sentence out, Mr. Horowitz grabbed a handful of Grace's dirty collar and yanked her toward his face so that she could hear him good. "You need to get the hell off of my porch before you force me to make a scene," he said, his eyes darting from yard to yard surrounding his own. There wasn't anyone watching, but it was clear that just one pointed finger could upset the delicate ecosystem he and his family had worked so hard to create to keep burning crosses off the front lawn and bricks out of his windows. He needed the granddaughter of the woman whose blood would be let to get off his porch. "Now go!" he yelled, accenting it with a shove that sent Grace tumbling down the steps.

Grace scrambled to her feet and took off running without so much as a glance back. She knew the consequences that could easily follow a boss's aggression. Her friend Bobbie had been in the Barnwell Training School for the Feebleminded for the whole of her fifteenth year behind sassing her missus. All she wanted was a little break from scrubbing the stove after she burned her hand while scalding the bread box and trash cans clean. That a blister had bubbled up on half of Bobbie's right palm made the missus no nevermind; it was a Tuesday and the appliances were to be shined with cloudy ammonia, no matter if the cleaning liquid stung nigger hands. "Oh, stop being so delicate!" she'd yelled at Bobbie as she cried out.

"But it hurts! I'm not going to do this!"

"What did you just say to me?"

"I'm. Not. Do. Ing. This."

The missus had reeled back, brows knitted, shocked. After a beat, she pointed to the door and, through the air of her gapped teeth, snarled, "Get out." Not more than a couple hours later, a paddy wagon rushed onto the grass in front of Bobbie's papa and mama's meager shotgun house and the truck's occupants dragged the teenager out the front door and down the steps and forced her into the back of that vehicle. To this day, the neighbors whisper about her mama's sorrow cry.

This was the way of white folk; they counted on Black body parts—hands for the wash, backs for the breaking of soil, titties for feeding their babies—but they couldn't stand the actual Black bodies or the souls that inhabited them—the souls that, every morning, had to piece their fragile selves together in order to convince the bodies to submit to the labor again and again, without benefit of break or complaint. Grace knew to walk away—to stop putting her faith in the hands of people who would just as soon hear her grandmother wail than fill a nigger's empty belly.

Maw Maw's friends were much more disappointing. In the beginning, after they came together to wrap Bassey's body in gunnysack and put her in the ground, a few women close to Maw Maw made a point of remembering that a thirteen-year-old girl was alone in that house with neither money nor sustenance and stopped by with a little something here and there: a pot of beans, a little fatback and corn pone, fresh buttermilk, wood for the stove. But they could keep that up but for so long before their own rumbling stomachs and reputations suffered the consequences of putting on for the child who belonged to a dead woman and a jailed baby catcher accused of soiling a white man's bloodline. Soon enough, they fell in line with all the others: hoarded their food, denied the family like Peter did Emmanuel. To them, Grace was a ghost. As dead as her mama.

Consumed with sadness and hunger, Grace did not hear Mr. Aaron's footsteps as he walked over from his yard and circled around Bassey's grave. It was the creak of his knees when he bent down beside her that made her sit up in attention.

"Hey, lil' bit," he said, resting his gnarled hand on her back. "Why don't you get up from there? Them red ants gon' get a hold a ya, and then what you gon' do?"

Grace slowly pushed her body up from the grave and wiped tears from her eyes, leaving streaks of Virginia dirt on her ashy cheeks. She hadn't seen Mr. Aaron in weeks. Hadn't the energy or gumption to inquire where he'd been. Her eyes, her belly did the communicating.

"When the last time you ate something?" Mr. Aaron asked, staring at Grace's stomach and wrinkling his brow.

Grace said nothing.

Mr. Aaron surveyed the yard—saw the garden overrun with weeds but bare all the same. The wood supply, a similar condition. "I ain't been back from Richmond but a minute. Got a little break from laying tracks on the railroad, but I gotta get on back in a few days. Whatchu need, lil' bit?"

Again, Grace said nothing.

"I know you ain't been to see yo' granny," he said. "I know you miss her."

Fresh tears and snot rushed down her face to meet her thick lips, mid-tremble. She wasn't about to explain to Mr. Aaron that she actually had seen her grandmother, repeatedly, in her picture shows. Every night, practically before she could get her eyes closed good, the same image haunted her down to her soul: there would be Maw Maw, curled up in a ball on concrete, her face buried in the creases of her arms. Then would come the shuffle of boots across dirt and stone and a series of loud clangs—metal against metal.

And Maw Maw's face would shoot up, delirious, haggard, grotesque—face swollen, one eye shooting down toward her feet, a gash on her forehead betraying the white meat beneath epidermis and fat. Her dress, crusted over with sweat and dirt and an array of body fluids, was soaked in red where her lap lay.

Every time, Grace felt her fear. Could taste it like bile on the back of her tongue.

Grace didn't need to be at the jailhouse to see her grandmother. But she needed to be there to see about her.

"Can you take me?" she asked weakly. "To see her for real?"

"Listen, lil' tender thang like you shouldn't be down there at the jailhouse. That ain't no place fuh pretty lil' guhs. Especially pretty lil' guhs who got kin in them boxes."

Grace couldn't hold it in any longer. Her sobs and gulps rode the breeze, over the grass and dandelions, up into the spaces between the leaves.

"I know, baby. Let it out. But you gots to listen to me. We don't have no whole lotta time."

He told her to fold herself into his space. It was a gentle command, but a useless one nonetheless; there was no other way, really, to fit in the tiny, underground box—dank and dusty, with walls that demanded Grace's small-but-curvy frame struggle against their sentry. "Now, I know it ain't no comfort in there, and when I cover it up with this here barrel, you gone feel a way, like ya can't breathe. But there are holes at the bottom, it's empty, and there's no top, so you gone get some air down there. This the only way to keep you safe," Mr. Aaron assured Grace as he dropped down after her a small water jug and a sack filled with two apples and a half loaf of bread. "A whole lot mo' people sat right here in this box while they was makin' their way up north, and they was fine. You gone be all right too, now, hear?"

Mr. Aaron's voice sounded like he was questioning the truthfulness of his words, but Grace could see something else in Mr. Aaron's eyes— a certain steeliness that settled her. It was the same look he gave Maw Maw when she got word that they'd found Ol' Johnny Payne's body ripped and strewn all the way down Piney Road, each piece having tumbled off his corpse as an angry husband and a mob of his friends rushed their horses through the center of Black Rose, Ol' Johnny's body in tow. It made no difference that Ol' Johnny, who lived in a small shack just four doors to the left of Maw Maw's place, was down there at the church repairing a roof when he was supposed to have been on the business end of a cheating wife's finger as she cried out, "That's the nigger raped me!" The husband needed to believe that the nigger who took off running from his house when he came home early for lunch was there in violation and not by invitation, and it was a story he needed the good white folk of Rose to believe, too, so a black body needed to be dragged through the streets. A message and a warning. The kind that not only tore up bodies, but families. A community. Peace. Maw Maw and everyone else in Black Rose knew that once the mob had Black blood on its tongue, it would not stop until its appetite was satiated. Any neck would do, and fear would ride the wives and the babies and the husbands and the fathers and everybody else with breath and two brown legs until the white folk were full. Maw Maw was scared. "Don't you worry 'bout me none," Mr. Aaron had told Maw Maw the night they'd pieced Ol' Johnny together and laid him down in the meadow behind his beloved church. "We 'bout done with all this killing 'round here. These crackas need to know we mens use our guns for more than shooting squirrels. They come, we got somethin' for 'em."

And when they came riding into the night looking to desecrate Ol' Johnny's church and any Black bodies they could find along the way, Mr. Aaron and a crew of men, full-grown and ready to both defend and die, were already there, some with pistols cocked, others dropping buckshot into their rifles and snapping them closed. Mr. Aaron was out front, dressed head to toe in red, a machete hanging from his fingertips—just beyond his muscular thigh. As it is oft recounted, nary a word was exchanged, but a conversation was had that night all the same. Man to man.

It had been some time since that dialogue that night, but here stood Mr. Aaron and the men of Black Rose, primed to chew with white men again. This time it would be Brodersen and his men. Word had traveled to Mr. Aaron all the way over in Richmond that the medicine woman and midwife who talked to trees and worshiped the waters refused to bow her head, no matter how hard they tried to break her, and so they would do what they knew would shred her heart as easily as Ol' Johnny's body bouncing along the dirt road: they would come for her Grace.

"No matter what you do, no matter what you hear, no matter how scared you be, don't you move from this place until you hear my sister's whistle and then yo' name, and this here barrel move from on top a yo' head, you hear me, Gracie? It need to happen in that order."

"Yassuh," Grace whimpered, tears streaking down her face.

"Her name Anna. She gone come by here when it's safe and she gone take you somewhere where they can't get to you."

"But what about Maw Maw?" Grace said, panicking. "I can't leave her. She need me!"

"*Shh, shh,* hush up now," Mr. Aaron said. He dropped down to his belly, so that he could lean in and look directly into Grace's eyes as he wiped her tears. His palms, covered in callouses and ash, felt coarse against her face, like they were telling the story of every raw rub they'd withstood against the sledgehammer as Mr. Aaron, sucking hundred-degree air into his wide nostrils, put all two hundred of his pounds into slamming railroad spikes into metal and dirt. "Don't you worry none about Rubelle. She taking care of hersef and you gone have to trust that. She a strong woman. An' her ancestors? They stronger. Now let me be strong for you. You got to be quiet down there, you hear?"

Grace whimpered some more but nodded slowly.

"And don't you move so much as a eyelash until my sister whistle, call yo' name, and move this here barrel. Can you do that?"

"Yes, Mr. Aaron," Grace whispered.

And with that, Mr. Aaron got up off his belly and stood to his feet, his eyes fixed on Grace's, Grace's eyes fixed on his, until the last sliver of light disappeared behind the barrel.

Darkness, followed by bugs and then sweat and then an unshakable fear crawled all around Grace as she sat as still as her body would allow her, each of them intensifying as the sun did its slow shimmy down the horizon and the crickets and frogs sang their songs. Grace covered her ears and buried her head in her skirt, snot and tears free-falling into its folds as she stifled her cries, waiting. Wondering. Trying to call up a picture show of Maw Maw—see if she really was holding her own down at the jailhouse. Trying to remember Maw Maw's face down by the river, licking apples and tossing them into the water—Bassey looking on from the bank's edge, shielding her eyes from the sun as she both shook her head and laughed heartily, tucking away her judgment and even her lust to humor her mother and her daughter and engage with love, real and pure and honest. True. The memory was good for Grace's heart, calmed her breathing a bit, helped her stomach stop rumbling, dried up a few of her tears, even.

It was the tires and hooves that snapped her from her meditation, the yelling and the clicking of rifles and the stench of the turpentine burning on the end of the sticks that made her stomach turn. Grace didn't need to see the torch fires licking the night sky or the dirt, kicked up by both the screeching truck tires and stallions, battering the air or the backs of the white hoods floating on top of the wind. When the Brotherhood rode, each of these things was as inevitable as thunder chasing lightning. Piercing. Consistent. Grace smushed her hand over her mouth to catch her scream and pinched her thigh to will her body to be still. But she was helpless against the beating of her heart, so forceful she thought the organ would shatter against her chest bone. She was convinced she was going to die in that hole, and that Mr. Aaron was going to die outside of it, and Maw Maw would die in her own hole, and Bassey made four dead and the world, her world, would be no more.

But if, by some chance, she could have floated above the trees and peeked between the branches and seen down to the brush, Grace would have seen the beginnings of her new life. A new understanding. She would have witnessed the bold, expensive conversation Mr. Aaron and his men—the brave men of Black Rose, who had finally tired of seeing their women and children and brothers and daddies under the boot of their unrelenting oppressors—were having with the boogeymen, who were courageous in the cloak of night, but nothing more than grotesque caricatures when forced to reckon with opponents who were both formidable and unafraid. Grace also would have caught glimpses of Negro men in their own gowns and hoods—theirs black—with their own shotguns primed and their own torch fires licking the sky and one crazy nigger out front with a freshly cut chicken in his hands, holding the still-wriggling body over a cauldron of boiling liquid on top of a roaring fire, rubbing the blood dripping from the bird onto his tar-covered face and neck and naked chest, the whites of his eyes shining against the dark. Grace would have seen that for every one of the caricatures, there were at least three brave men, standing there ready to die.

She would have known no fear.

The deep, rich timbre of the men's screams filled the air, chasing behind the pop and whistle of the shotguns and pistols, the echo of slaps and grunts when fists and feet met stomachs and backs and cheeks. From the hole where Grace was tucked, it sounded like war.

And then there was a whistle, right on top of her head.

"Grace. This Anna."

Grace grabbed her face even harder, digging her fingernails so deeply into her cheeks that she drew a little blood. Tears sprung every which way from her eyes as the barrel scraped against the wooden floorboards, finally revealing a boot, and then a pair of pants, and then a shirt, and then a woman holding her finger to her lips and squinting, trying to make out the tiny figure burrowed down in the hole.

"Come on, baby, give me yo' hand," Anna said, extending her fat, broad arm down and waving her fingers as if to entice Grace to grab. Grace grabbed her sack and submitted to Anna's grasp, walking her feet against the walls to help give Anna the momentum she needed to lift her up and out. Grace fell directly into Anna's ample breasts and snorted until she cried, like a newborn taking her first breath. "Listen to me," Anna said sharply, giving Grace a little shake to get her attention. "We don't have time for this here. We got to get on out of here while they over that way," she said, pointing toward Ol' Johnny's house, where Mr. Aaron and his men had lured a much smaller gang of the Brotherhood. "We gone ride the horse on outta here. Make it easy for us to cut up through these woods and get over to the train station in Reidsville without anybody noticing or caring. But I need you to be quick about it. Just follow me and do what I say and you gone be just fine, okay?"

Anna grabbed Grace's hand and tugged her toward the opening of the shed. She peeped around the corner first, then made a run for the horse, her hand squeezing Grace's wrist as she tugged her some more. With the swiftness and ease of someone who knew horses and loved them, too, Anna hopped onto the chocolate brown steed and extended her hand to pull Grace up behind her. "Hold on to my waist now, lil' bit, and don't let go, hear? You gone be fine."

5

W ell, don't just stand there with your bottom lip hanging. Come on up here and give your auntie some sugar."

Grace heard the command, but her feet were leaden on the concrete just beyond the stoop leading up to the fanciest house she ever had seen—certainly the fanciest belonging to any home-owning Negro she'd ever met in the whole of her thirteen years. To Grace, her aunt Hattie's terra-cotta brownstone, with its magnificent elliptical arches and Byzantine columns stretching high up toward the dark gray clouds, looked like somewhere she wasn't supposed to be—like a place that little country gals weren't allowed to even dream of, much less walk into with any kind of authority. Even by permission. Especially at Hattie's behest. It was certainly not lost on Grace that even as the woman's smiling lips fixed themselves to welcome her to climb the stairs, Hattie's eyes, coarse, steely, had quickly made a wholly different assessment of Grace and her worthiness of such an invitation. Grace took in Hattie's eyes as they measured the rugged plaits knotted and puffing from the teenager's scalp, and then slowly panned across ashy skin and thick, crusted lips and down the tattered dress and too-small shoes that belied Gracie's origin story—told just how far she'd traveled but just how stagnant life was back in rural Virginia, where time stood still and people who chose to stay there had made their peace with it. Hattie, she'd made that same journey a dozen years earlier—not necessarily to get away from any one person, but more to get away from that one place, to rid herself of that same patina, that stench. To be somebody other than who the town of Rose would allow.

Grace stiffened as she watched Hattie's lip curl in disapproval, and when her eyes finally locked with Hattie's and she saw her mama's—an amber green version to Bassey's deep brown—she instinctively reached for Anna's hand, the likes of which, over the past week as they made their way from Virginia to Brooklyn, had soothed as Anna sowed comfort and detail and instruction. *She yo' Maw Maw's baby sister. Same daddy, different mamas. One a them light brights. Look just like yo' mama, though. 'Round the same age, too. Always was saditty. We loved her just the same but wasn't nobody missing on her when she left the South. She ain't got no chi'ren. No man. Last anybody heard, she was doing hair. Still mean. Still saditty. You family and she heppin', so there's that. Keep yo' head low, don't get in the way. Do what niggers do up there in the city: make it. Promise me that.*

Anna squeezed Grace's hand as the three stood still and the city swirled around them—cars ferrying and neighbors sliding down sidewalks tossing their "Hey, nows" and the children, oh the children and their laughter and all their pretty clothes and the big, big hair and the people everywhere.

"Anna," Hattie said, greeting her old friend through pursed lips and a slight head nod.

"Hattie," Anna said, returning the same energy.

Hattie shifted her eyes back to Grace but continued to address her adult charge. "So, what's wrong with her? Cat got her tongue?"

Anna looked at Grace and ran her fingers over her matted hair. "She just tired, I reckon. Been through a whole lot, you know."

"Yes, I heard," Hattie said, this time her tongue a little less sharp. "I'm sorry about Bassey, rest her poor soul. Shame about my sister, too. It just don't make no sense why she would take the weight for that ol' ofay. She should have just let those white folk go on about their business and handle their affairs without getting into the middle of it. Know them white folk down there like they blood pure. Now look what she done. Got herself into a hell of a pickle."

"She ain't done nothin'," Anna said, snapping at Hattie. "Don't tell me you been up north so long, you done forgot the dirty ways of white folk. You gone take the word of a white man caught his wife cheating over your own sister's?"

"Don't matter none whose word any of us believe, now, does it?" Hattie said, scoffing. "She's in a southern prison in the Jim Crow South. That's judge, jury, and conviction all in one where she is, that much I know . . ."

"Hattie!" Anna interrupted, tilting her head toward Grace to remind the woman to mind her tongue. "Now is not the time for all this here." And then, with a little less bass in her voice: "We're doing everything we can for her, but in the meantime, it sho is right nice a you to mind after Gracie here while we get her grandmother's case settled."

"Yes, yes, you're right. Where are my manners, discussing grown-folk business in front of children?" Hattie asked to no one in particular. She extended her hands and beckoned Grace to walk up the steps. "Come here and let your auntie get a good look at you, now. Don't be scared. I knew you when you were knee-high to a duck. I even watched you a few times while Bassey was out there doing what she do. Well, did."

Anna tossed Hattie another evil squint but pushed Grace toward her aunt all the same. "Go on up there, now. Ain't nothing to be 'fraid of. Hattie family. She gone take good care of you," she said, albeit weakly.

Grace stiff-legged her way up the grand staircase. When she was within reach, Hattie pulled her close enough to her face to smell the fried chicken her aunt had eaten for lunch shortly before they arrived. Grace's stomach answered the smell with a slow but loud rumble. "Come closer, gal, I don't bite," she said, snatching Grace's arm and leaning into her face. "Let me take a good look at you." Something about the way she stood there, piercing eyes wide, deep black skin scorched by the Virginia sun, put Hattie in the mind of a picture that, just a few days prior, she'd scraped out of a family photo album and rubbed between her fingers. She'd pulled that picture close to her eyes, stared at her young face and Bassey's young face, and her eyes, creamy and gray in the black-and-white photo, and Bassey's eyes, just like hers but black, and her body, slender and stiff, and Bassey's, curvy and pressing against the fabric of her dress. On the photo, someone had scrawled "1952." In it, Bassey was two months' pregnant with the child of a boy she didn't care anything about beyond that he called himself liking Hattie until her niece, funny and fast, came along and caught his attention. Angry, a little tipsy off her nightly swigs of corn, Hattie angrily threw that picture in the basement closet, so she didn't have to see it, didn't have to remember the time. Now came all that history, all the mess captured in the one photo—the problem that couldn't be seen by the naked eye—darkening her doorstep. Hattie curled her lip as she took Grace's face in.

Grace took a good look, too. Hattie did look just like Bassey, a revelation that coaxed fresh tears to her eyes. "Now, now, no need for fussing," Hattie insisted, smoothing her face. "Come on in here and get yourself cleaned up. I'll fix you a plate while you wash up. By the time you finish, you can meet the girls in my class."

"Class?" Anna asked. "What class you teaching? Out yo' house? I didn't know you was a teacher now. I thought you was fixing hair. They don't have no schools for the children around here in this fancy neighborhood?"

"Well, of course they have schools here, Anna," Hattie said exasperated. "I don't teach reading and arithmetic. I teach the young ladies in our community something much more valuable than that."

"Do tell," Anna said, folding her arms over her chest.

Hattie's eyes traversed the whole of Anna's body and then shifted back to Grace's. "Why, I teach the young girls of our beautiful neighborhood how to be ladies," she said, half smiling as she tilted her nose in the air. "A life skill. I'm helping them prepare themselves for the fine young men here, the sons of nurses and professors and businessmen, who will go on to college and make something of themselves. Something good. For all of us." Hattie gave Grace one more once-over. "Come on inside," she said, taking Grace by the arm. "Pay attention and you might learn some things."

"Okay, Grace, you take care of yourself, hear?" Anna called after her.

"Bye, Missus Tucker," Grace said, wiping a tear and giving a little wave as Hattie pulled her toward the grand door to her brownstone. Hattie didn't bother with such niceties; she gave a little half wave and slammed the door behind her and her new charge.

Grace was no stranger to hard work; she'd rather liked helping Maw Maw keep their place nice, sweeping and ironing, gathering wood and tending the garden, darning clothes and mending quilts worn thin from the double duty of warming bodies and decorating the beds and sofa and chairs and such. She tended to do each of those things with joy—well, most of the time—because her grandmother insisted upon it. "You gots ta be proud a the thangs belong to ya—take care of them," she'd say. "Ain't you work hard for this here bowl of field peas? This here dress what keep you warm? This here bed what make it so yo' aching back feel better in the mornings?"

"Yes'm," Grace would say, bringing the bowl of peas to her nose to smell the earthiness of the dish, mixed with okra and sometimes corn, if they had it, and a little ham hock, too, if somebody pushed a baby out and filled the hands that caught it with a pull or two of the salty meat as a thank-you.

"Good. That's good, baby," Maw Maw would say. "Ain't nothin' wrong with hard work or a healthy respect for the things it brings you."

"Yes'm," Grace would say again, sweetly. Grateful.

Now she tried to apply that same sentiment to her responsibilities at Hattie's house, but her aunt's philosophy on hard work was cut from a different cloth, and so Grace's response was less silk, more burlap, too. Hattie thought it her charge and her duty to exact from Grace the amount of work the older woman thought would cover the cost to care for and keep the teenager— a kind of indentured servitude that was equal parts taxing and cruel. In the world according to Hattie, no job, it seemed, was too small or too big for the thirteen-year-old. "You damn near grown and country as hell, too. You can handle this one," she'd say as she'd hand down another set of instructions for yet another chore—clearing out the basement, organizing the hair supplies she used in her makeshift salon, preparing lunch for neighborhood girls she was teaching how to be "young ladies." It seemed it never occurred to Hattie that Grace had "lady" potential—that she might make a good match for somebody special. Or even that she should go to school or be anything . . . more. A bony, raggedy mule, meant to be worked, is all she was. A hand-me-down cleared from the home of the dead—not really wanted by its new owner but taken nonetheless because such things had to have a place and throwing them away would be wasteful. Sometimes, Hattie would emphasize the point with a finger poke or a little twist of flesh between her pointer finger and thumb if Grace wasn't moving fast enough—half reminder, half warning when her niece got to slipping on her chores and had to be told one too many times about the care and upkeep of her home. Always, Hattie reminded Grace that it was her home, her way. She meant to wash the country off her niece, so help her God, because Hattie's own survival depended on it. Hattie, after all, had been turning her back on herself for quite some time now, practically before anyone in her then newly adopted home bothered, even, to know her name.

She stored away her sewing machine first—a most necessary step in her immersion into Black Brooklyn society. Hattie could pattern and sew an entire season's wardrobe with the care and attention of an upscale clothier, a skill that was necessary in the backwoods of rural Virginia, where fancy store-bought clothes were every bit as inaccessible as the money it took to buy them, but this was far from impressive to the women of the Negro Women's League. To be exact, Hattie forced herself to lay her skills by the wayside on the day Mrs. Spencer noticed the "Hand Crafted by Hattie Adams" label on a jacket Hattie, warm and anxious to get a scoop of ambrosia before it disappeared from the refreshment table at her first League meeting, had, in haste, rested across her chair. "Oh dear, isn't this . . . quaint," Mrs. Spencer had said to no one in particular but loud enough for all to hear as she ran her delicate fingers across the pink and black paisley fabric tag Hattie had sewn into the back of the silk jacquard jacket. The fabric, ordered special from Sears, cost Hattie the proceeds of seven hairstyling appointments—had her subsisting on cornbread and buttermilk for breakfast and butter beans minus the smoked meats for lunch and dinner for damn near a month. That smile, that pride Hattie wore on her face when she slipped on that jacket before the meeting slid right off the corners of her lips with just one utterance on the tip of Mrs. Spencer's tongue: "Hattie sews her own clothes. Somebody alert Bergdorf!" The giggles and murmurs of the women would drape Hattie's shoulders for years—the evidence of which lay in a heap in the basement closet, beneath her sewing and embroidery machines, a fully stocked sewing kit, and enough fabric to outfit the deaconess pews of a moderately sized church. Hattie had politely begged her pardon and bid her good nights and, ignoring the rub of her corns against the patent leather of her pumps, rushed against the chill of the evening breeze the four blocks to her brownstone and up the steps and through the front door and slammed it behind her so hard, the teacups arranged just so on her breakfront rattled. She silently pledged that the only time from that point forward that she would wear hand-sewn clothes would be over her dead body, and even then, she might resurrect herself from the grave to change into more fitting attire. That night, into her closet, everything was thrown—clothes, material, buttons, and zippers, even pictures of her strutting in what she'd previously thought refined. In the trash went the Moms Mabley records, the Muddy Waters and Elmore

James LPs. And then she stood there, breathing heavy, hands on her hips, eyes trained on the small table at the mouth of the kitchen—stalked to it, stood in front of it, let her pupils slowly wash over the wilted flowers she'd pulled from her garden out back, the black-and-white picture of her dead, the small pouch filled with dirt from her mama's grave, her daddy's old bristle brush, the bowls, one filled with day-old greens, the other, water. The altar she'd built more in those days out of habit than allegiance— a reminder of the old way. Who she used to be. Who she was trying not to be anymore. And Hattie took her arm and quickly, in one big swoop, swept each of those trinkets and reminders off that table and clean onto the floor. The broom quickly followed, and then the trash—into it all the broken pieces, along with any connection to home she would have from then on. Except the corn liquor. That she kept.

Hattie would not have Grace stinking up her home with her country things. "Come here, gal!" she'd yelled when she'd discovered Grace's small altar—a rabbit's foot, a tin of water, a brush, a pouch pregnant with all manner of country shit—piled on the wooden chair in her basement bedroom. Grace, still not used to the yelling, jumped at the sound of her aunt's voice and hustled down the stairs so quickly her back right heel slipped off the edge of the second to last stair. Grace landed in a heap at Hattie's feet.

"What I tell you about this here?" Hattie yelled, her anger betraying her natural southern drawl as she stood over Grace.

Grace quickly hustled to her feet as she focused on the items her aunt waved so close to her nose that she had to reel back her neck so as not to be hit with them. She slipped again.

"Get up, ol' clumsy ass!" Hattie yelled. Grace stood, eyes frozen in terror as she realized what her aunt was holding. "Didn't I tell you about practicing this hoodoo shit in my house?"

"Yes, ma'am," Grace said quickly. "That's not what that is," she insisted.

"Oh, now I got 'fool' written across my forehead?" Hattie yelled. "I know exactly what this is!"

"I . . . I . . . just took them out to look at because I was missing my mama and Maw Maw," Grace said, eyes darting between her reminders of home and Hattie. She wanted so badly to see Maw Maw in a picture show, but the visions, they would not come, no matter how hard Grace squeezed her eyes shut and got still and focused. Those items, they were her telephone—the way Grace had intended to call on her mama for help, her grandmother for a sign. This wasn't anything Grace dared let Hattie know; this wasn't anything with which Hattie dared let anyone know she was familiar. "I'm not doing roots, I swear!"

"Don't you swear! That's a sin against the Lord!" Hattie said.

"Yes'm," Grace said. "I'm sorry, Auntie Hattie."

"Don't be sorry, chile. Be better," Hattie said, shoving the items into Grace's chest. She let her eyes wash over the room. It was neat, well kept. No matter. "Clean up this mess," Hattie sneered. "I don't want to see it again."

And so, Grace focused on making herself small—a shadow that constantly moved away from the light source, so as not to be noticed or stepped on. It didn't take her long to recognize that becoming invisible spared her Hattie's angry words and hands; when breakfast simply appeared on the table or the dirt on the floor looked like it swirled itself into the garbage can, or the beds and rooms straightened up themselves, there was calm. This is what Grace needed. Calm. It was in those moments that she could look for her light. She searched when the moon cast its glow over Brooklyn and when the red sun stretched burnt orange and smoky pinks and grays across the sky before even the birds sang their songs; through eyes squeezed tight, between whimpers and whispered promises and the swiping away of snot and tears, she searched for her picture shows—a connection with her grandmother or some kind of sign from her mama of what was what. If being alone, sad, uneducated, unloved was simply her lot.

It was on a Wednesday that the sky gave her an answer. Grace was out on the front stoop, sweeping dirt off the steps when a flash of the light of the sun bounced just so off the eye of the colorful cock perched like the sunrise in the stained-glass window. From her first day darkening Hattie's doorstep, Grace had been mesmerized by that rooster—how the bloodred, deep blues and purples of its feathers stood like a shock between the lead lines that gave it its magnificent shape. The rooster stood erect—confident—like a jewel in the window, announcing itself the king of the castle. Put Grace in the mind of Jeremiah, the cock that would strut all around Maw Maw's yard, announcing the morning sun, running behind all the hens, reminding them who ruled the roost out yonder, but getting sweet on any one of them that moved anywhere within his periphery. Grace was scared of him—the way he always lunged at and chased her around the yard when she had a little something to eat in her hands. Some bumbleberries, a piece of cornbread. A chewing stick. Jeremiah would see it and take off running, feathers flying this way and that, upsetting the order of everything as he cocked and she screamed, the two of them running in zigzag circles across the yard until Grace either gave up her goodies or outran him into the house. But let somebody, anybody come up on Grace wrong: Jeremiah protected her better than any guard dog, any pistol pulled on her behalf. Maw Maw would just giggle and shake her head. "Ol' Jeremiah just sweet on you, is all. Think he yo' man."

"Me and all the other chickens!" Grace would say, laughing from her belly, even as she shook the scare off herself.

There was no fear, only beauty in the rooster jewel above Hattie's door. Like Jeremiah, it kept after her, this colorful cock casting that flash of light all three times she turned her body toward the front door to sweep the cobwebs and spiders out the corners. Finally, Grace stopped sweeping and held her left hand over her brow, shielding herself from the sun's rays as she pondered what could make Stained-Glass Jeremiah wink at her with such intensity. When Grace turned her face toward the sun, right there, in all its glory, was the answer: a sunbow. It was the prettiest thing Grace ever had seen aside from her mama when she smushed red lipstick between her thick lips and Maw Maw's bosom when she laughed and the sound echoed inside her chest and rode on top of it. There it was, the universe's brightest star, at the very top of the gray clouds, bathing in a rainbow halo prancing around its perimeter. So stunning was it that Grace hardly breathed— refused to blink out of fear that it would disappear into the forever by the time she opened her eyes again, leaving with her the same thing as did the two women she loved most in the world: memories. Nothing.

And so, she stared. She stared so hard, the sun's rays turned into sharp shards of bright yellow light, bouncing on top of and in between the red, orange, yellow, green, blue, indigo, and violet circling the sun.

"Pretty, ain't it?" a voice called out, shocking Grace out of her trance.

She jumped, instinctively thinking Auntie Hattie had launched herself from the house with some fresh insult or command, until eyes and brain found and focused on the direction of the words and then the woman who said them. Grace shifted the broom into her left hand and used her right to shield her eyes from the sun's glare. There was a lady, short, buxom, about Maw Maw's age, running a cloth down the stoop railings of the majestic brownstone next door. She didn't look anything like the fancy women Auntie Hattie attached herself to—didn't look anything like the lady of the house next door, who, in the month since Grace had been in Brooklyn, did nothing more than look in the girl's direction and scowl. This woman, with her apron tied around her waist and her hair pinned and tied down with a white cloth, she looked like . . . home.

"You see how them clouds busy rushing past?" she asked. She paused from her own work to jut her chin toward the dull blue sky. "I like how they make all those different patterns and thangs in the gray. Almost make gray look pretty."

Grace slowly shifted her gaze from the woman and back at the sky—switching her focus from the colors to the patches of gray peeking through the holes in the clouds shifting around the sun.

"It's gonna rain again," the lady continued, sniffing the air.

Grace smelled it, too—a trick she'd learned from Maw Maw, who regularly extolled the virtues of knowing when a good storm was coming—to keep laundry drying out on the line from getting soaked, to keep from wasting time drawing water to pour on the vegetables out in the garden and such. Grace nodded at the sky and said, "Yes, ma'am. Seem like it's always raining."

"Aw, but the gray what bring all them colors. That's just as much the promise as the rainbow. Gray mean joy come in the morning," the woman said. "Gotta love the gray like you do the colors. Can't have the one without the other."

Grace nodded—tilted her chin higher. Let the rays of the colors and the gray shadows wash over her.

It was the slam of the gate and the giggling of the girls that snapped her to. And then, "Grace, get your tail on out the way, so my ladies can come on into my home on this fine afternoon," Hattie yelled, shielding her eyes from the sun but clearly missing the miracle unfurling around its light, staring, instead, at the clouds forming in the opposite direction. "Whoowhee, it smells like rain out here. You ladies come on inside before that water falls down on your heads. Don't want to turn those pretty curls into naps, now do we?"

Hattie pushed the broom back into Grace's hands. "Get to it before this rain gets the stoop wet, hear? I will not be happy if my broom comes back into this house soggy."

"Yes'm," Grace said, tucking her chin. Her eyes were grateful for the reprieve from the glaring sun rays.

"Don't 'yes'm' me, girl. That's for country folk," Hattie snapped.

Out the corner of her eye, Hattie caught sight of the woman, standing there, rag in hand, looking. "How do?" the woman said, waving the rag and her greeting in Hattie and Grace's direction. Hattie frowned. Made like the woman's very existence was a direct affront to her sensibilities. She slow-blinked then turned back to Grace. "It's 'yes, ma'am,'" she said slowly, as if her niece were too dimwitted to understand her.

"Yes, ma' . . . ," Grace began, but Hattie didn't give her a chance to finish; her attention was drawn to the front gate, where another visitor was entering. Grace's eyes, still shocked with yellow spots from staring at the sun, could barely focus, but she could hear the change in her aunt's tone—could see how quickly the corners of her mouth shot upward when she got a gander of who was walking onto her property. Grace turned and blinked a few times to get a clear view of her own, and, upon training her focus on the young man's face, sucked in enough air to make herself cough.

Hattie pushed past Grace and greeted the young fella. "Oh my, well if it isn't Dale Spencer. How are you this fine afternoon?" Hattie asked, her tone soft and proper.

"Hi, Ms. Hattie," he said, giving a wave. "Looks like it's about to rain, huh?"

"Indeed, I was just saying the same," Hattie said, moving a little closer to the teenager. "I can smell it in the air."

Dale closed his eyes and inhaled deeply; the drawn-out breath made his muscular chest rise and push against his tight, green-striped shirt, something Grace would have had a better view of had it not been obstructed by Hattie's shoulder, which, like her voice, had become round and easy in the presence of this, her young neighbor. "I tell you what: I love the smell of rain, but you know what I love even more?"

"What's that?" Hattie asked.

Dale turned his head toward the sky and jabbed a finger at the sun. "Look what the rain brings. It's something else, ain't it? A circle rainbow. Actually, it's called a sun halo."

"Is that right?" Hattie said, shading her eyes.

"Yes, in my science class, we're learning all about rain phenomena. You know, what causes it, the role clouds play in it, what kinds of clouds do what. And sun halos. We learned about those last week."

"Well, isn't that something," Hattie said, her head cocked to the side as if that precise positioning would help her understand a bit better.

"I really like it when rainbows show up in the sky after a hard rain," Grace said. "Look to me like pretty ribbons."

Dale switched his focus from the sky and trained it on Grace, as if noticing her for the first time since he'd walked into Hattie's yard. The two stood perfectly still, taking each other in—he her lips, thick and perfectly shaped, like someone had taken a brown pencil and traced onto her face what God meant for lips to look like; she, his eyes, round like that of a doe, with pupils so dark and glossy they made his thick eyebrows and close-cut black Afro, with the most perfect straight part cutting a line up from his left temple to his ear, glow off his skin. Back in Virginia, somebody would have called him "Red" on account his skin was the same color as a teaspoon of fresh grated cinnamon. All the boys nicknamed "Red" got all the attention for being pretty. Dale was most certainly that.

"Oh, hush up, gal," Hattie said. Her voice was a thunderbolt in the middle of their silent studies. "A ribbon," she scoffed.

"I can see that," Dale said, never once taking his eyes off Grace.

Hattie's furled brow announced her displeasure with Grace making herself seen. Heard. Un-small. Noticed.

"So, Dale, what can I do for you?" Hattie said, shifting her weight as if to break the kids' gazes and block Grace's face from Dale's view. "Are you here to see one of the ladies? Bettye, perhaps? Or Roe? They're all inside."

"Oh, no, ma'am," Dale said, his face turning red. "I'm not here to see any girls. My mother wanted me to return this to you. It's your spoon and casserole dish. You sent it over last week? She didn't want to hold on to it too long."

"Oh, goodness," Hattie said, taking the bag from Dale's hands. "Of course. How is your mother holding up? I know it's a terrible thing to lose a mother."

"It is. I miss my grandmother. A lot," Dale said. "And my mom misses her mother, too. But she's hanging in there, taking it day by day. Trying to pick up the pieces."

"I'm sure," Hattie said, adding in a *tsk* and a head shake. "This community won't be the same without Mother Hilliard, but I know I can speak for all of us in the community by saying she was special to all of us, and we're grateful for the work she did here making our block and neighborhood beautiful." Then, to Grace, she said: "You would bode well to get to know the work of the Spencers and Hilliards in this community, Grace. Dale here comes from good stock."

"That's your name—Grace?" Dale asked, as he extended his hand awkwardly around Hattie. "I'm Dale. I live two blocks over."

Grace looked at his hand, with its long fingers and clean, manicured nails, and then at Hattie, before finally reaching out and resting her own hand in his. It was soft. Electric.

"Yes," Hattie said, "this is my little niece. She's visiting from Virginia. Her first time up north."

"It's nice to meet you, Grace," Dale said, still holding on to Grace's hand.

"Nice to meet . . ."

"Oh, here comes the rain!" Hattie practically yelled as big, sloppy drops of water plopped on the three. "You better get on home, Dale, before you get soaked out here and catch cold. Grace, you might as well get on inside. You can start making lunch for my ladies."

"Yes, ma'am," Grace said, addressing Hattie, but still staring at Dale.

"See you around, Grace," Dale called after her. Her name on his lips sounded like honey dripping on a fresh hunk of cornbread.

Grace didn't know what to make of the boy from two blocks over or why his gaze made her heart jump. She wanted to giggle out loud recalling how his hand had felt in hers, how he had looked at her and through her, like he couldn't see her not-so-perfect clothes and her not-so-perfect hair and her not-so-perfect way of talking—like what he was seeing was something worth looking at. But not because he thought Grace pretty. Because he thought Grace mattered.

And while she stirred the pot of beans and spooned them into Hattie's pretty bowls for her pretty ladies, Grace imagined she and Dale were ribbons, circling around the sun.

6

What did Grace know of love—this instinct that directs the heart, sometimes against the very beat of logic, to play in fire? Sure, she loved her mama; that was both nature and obligation—a fair exchange for the blood and bone and sinew and flesh and nutrients and air Bassey's body had reaped in her womb for her daughter. Didn't matter what her mama did or didn't do or how perfect or perfectly inadequate she was for Grace, that child, whether lil' ol' or good and grown, was going to root for her mama's ninny. Bassey had given Grace life and so her daughter paid her back with love. And Maw Maw—oh, Maw Maw. Well, in Grace's eyes, Maw Maw was the very essence of love. Grace loved her down to the marrow—could slice it and spread it across time and reason. It was thick. Filling. Unconditional. Earned.

But this fawning and falling for a boy—this was new. Though she was now fifteen and should have been a little wiser about worldly things, Grace hadn't occasion to see up close what courting actually looked like, much less how love transferred from boy to girl, girl to boy. When she was about age eleven, she did call herself sweet on Isaiah Wright, some big-headed boy who, let her little girlfriends tell it, liked her back. He took great pleasure in pulling her braids every chance he got, and it didn't occur to Grace, tender-headed and not a particular fan of anyone touching her thick, kinky mane, to actually like it until her friend Lucy shot-called the particulars. "You know he like you, right?" she said, giggling, one afternoon while she,

Grace, and three other girls in their class circle spent recess hiding in the shade of a sycamore tree, cleaning dirt out of each other's fingernails and playing in each other's hair.

"Who, Isaiah?" Grace asked, wrinkling her nose and stealing a glance in his direction.

"Well yeah," Lucy said, jutting out her neck and shaking her head. "He stay tryna get yo' attention. Shole look to me like he interested, don't it, y'all?" she asked. Furious head nods made the girls' collective heads look like fruit in an apple-bobbing bucket.

"There he go over there," Angeline said, nodding in the direction of a mob of boys skipping pebbles against the dirt, trying to make them pop up from the ground and smash against each other's ankles. Isaiah just happened to be looking at the girls when Grace followed Angeline's jutting chin to the jumble of boys. "He cute."

"Mmm-hmm," Lucy said, nodding in agreement. "I wouldn't mind him pulling my hair," she added, with the whole bunch laughing and slapping each other's palms.

"You think he cute?" Angeline asked.

Grace took a second to really take in his face. Though she'd never thought about it, she supposed he was. Prior to, only thing she'd ever truly noticed about the boy was that he stayed ashy, like his mama annem didn't think it important to insist he rub a little grease on his elbows and cheeks every now and again. But he had dimples. Grace liked his dimples. She shrugged. "He cute."

"Go over there and tell him, then, since you in love!" Lucy said.

"Love?" Grace said, confused.

"Y'all make a cute couple. Probably make pretty babies. With dimples and such," Angeline chimed in.

"First comes love, then comes marriage . . . ," Lucy began. And then, in unison, the whole group giggle sang, "Then comes baby in the baby carriage!" before falling out again.

The boys, obviously having grown tired of having their ankles and shins pelted by rocks, heard the commotion and turned their attention to the sycamore tree. Their looks were met with a whole lot of giggling and grinning. Isaiah walked over first; the others were fast on his heels.

"Y'all over here doing hair?" he asked. His voice seemed to want to be deeper, but a little squeak rode on the higher parts of his register, betraying his throat's charge toward manhood.

"Mmm-hmm," Lucy quickly answered as she grabbed one of Grace's braids.

"Look like you gone have to hire a mule to put in the work y'all gone need to get some cornrows into Grace's head," Isaiah said without skipping a beat. "A regla ol' comb ain't gone get it."

The boys fell out in laughter, but the girls, Grace knew, they felt the sting. "Well, if you think Grace hair so nappy, why you always got yo' fingers in it?" Lucy demanded.

"I was just tryna pull summa them naps out," he answered right back, to more laughter at Grace's expense.

Embarrassed, Grace struggled up from the soil but stepped on the hem of her skirt while she did so, exposing her panties. She brushed away hot tears rushing down her cheeks, leaving a finger trail of dirt on her skin. The boys laughed even harder as she pushed past them, her gaggle of girl-friends fast on her heels.

The way she twirled her fork in her supper bowl later that evening was the giveaway that something was troubling Grace, but Maw Maw had kept quiet about it until Grace hoisted her elbow onto the table and leaned her head into the palm of her hand. "What all ail you?" Maw Maw asked.

"Huh?" Grace answered.

Maw Maw was quiet. "Well," she said slowly, "you must be studying somethin' because you got yo' elbow on my table and you just answered yo' grandmama with 'huh.'"

Grace quickly took her elbow off the table and tucked her hand in her lap.

"Is you gone tell yo' grandmama what's wrong or you just gone play in them beans the rest of the night?"

Grace placed her fork in her bowl and tucked her chin into her neck. Then, finally: "Did my daddy and granddaddy go away because they thought we weren't pretty?"

A few of the beans in the forkful Maw Maw had just placed in her mouth seemed to take the wrong route down her throat, forcing a cough where there should have been an answer. Grace knew Maw Maw hadn't come to the table ready to talk about Sonny and Amos, but this was a conversation for which she'd likely long prepared. A girlchild—a curious one like Grace—should know the story of her blood, even if it wasn't a fairy tale, that much Maw Maw knew, even if her own daughter didn't agree. "Being pretty don't make no man stay," Maw Maw said simply. "I done known plenty womens look like they should have all the mens falling at they feet, and quite a bit a them do. But that don't make the men stay."

"Well, what make 'em stay?" Grace mumbled.

"That ain't the right question, baby. Better question is why is menfolk okay with making babies and going on about they way? Only some answer I got is that they ain't no man at all."

Maw Maw could tell by how Grace's head sunk even lower that answering her granddaughter's questions with questions wouldn't do. It was time. "Yo' daddy, Sonny, he won't good for much aside from making yo' mama think he was a good man," she said in a hushed tone. "Came to ya mama with a whole lotta promises about how he was gone get him a farm with enough land to make money off it and feed the family and all. Had yo' mama 'round here falling right into the trap," Maw Maw said, shaking her head. She kissed her teeth. "She needed to believe his lies to do what she always did when some man came along with big talk and all them promises. 'Fore you know it she was running around here cooking and washing his dirty drawers, and then that turned into her cooking and washing other people's dirty drawers while he slept half the day and stayed out all night. Lord, when she had you in her belly, I thought she was gone break." Maw Maw leaned forward and shifted in her chair, as if waiting for Grace to say something. She didn't. "I won't 'bout to let that happen, though. See we Adams womens too strong for that there. We love hard like every other woman that want a family to care for—to grow up. But our kind of love? We pour that into what matters. *Who* matters. And ain't nan nigga run around here making babies but refusing to do what it take to keep 'em alive ever mattered around here. That's why yo' daddy had to go. That's why yo' mama's daddy had to go. That's why my daddy had to go. It was better for me. It's better for you."

Grace, who always followed questions with more questions until her brain had its fill, was quiet still. Grandmother knew granddaughter wasn't finished feeding, so she offered more. "We done lived three generations without mens running around this house we built with our own hands, telling us women what to do while we run it. Ain't nobody taking what ain't theirs, ain't nobody playing small so somebody else can feel big, ain't nobody making promises they can't keep, ain't nobody putting their hands where they don't belong. That's three generations of good living on our own good terms. I'd say we done all right. How 'bout you?"

Grace knew nothing of the broken promises of men or whether running away for her daddy and her granddaddy and the daddy before him was the right prescription for mending broken homes—didn't know if the explanation would stick to the bones. Whether it would be enough. In the moment, she didn't want to ponder that. What she wanted to know was if she would ever know the kind of love that made a boy pull her hair and tell her he did it because he thought she was pretty.

Grace sighed, took a deep breath, and exhaled the reasoning behind her question. "Isaiah called me ugly today."

Maw Maw reeled back her neck, then sat back in her chair and folded her arms. "You mean that big head lil' boy live over there on Clifton? Mama sell eggs over there to the general store?"

"Yes, ma'am."

"Isaiah what knee-high to a duck with that funny lil' squeaky voice?"

"Ma'am."

Maw Maw reached over, grabbed Grace's chin, lifted her head, and looked her straight in the eye. "Don't you ever let me catch you with yo' head down over no nappy-headed lil' boy who wastes his words on lies." She brushed an errant braid from Grace's forehead and ran her hand down her granddaughter's cheek. Just her gaze, just her touch made Grace feel like ruby red. "You know the truth. Believe it down to the bottom bone."

And from that moment and all the moments after that, Maw Maw had poured into Grace in a way that assured she would regard her worth in the same way as she did her very breath. And yet, the same mind that allowed both breath and regard to exist without contemplation was now consumed with theory: What would she have to do to her hair to get Dale to notice her? Her clothes? Was there a particular scent that struck his fancy? Did he prefer smart girls? Those who were cultured, like Aunt Hattie and her "ladies"? Would he care if she always remembered to put her napkin in her lap after grace but before picking up her fork, or would he be more concerned about the crisp of the chicken she wanted to cook for him, or the number of pats of butter she put in the dough to make the crust of her cobbler perfectly flaky? Would he care if, aside from her mama and Maw Maw, the only kisses she'd ever given were to her pillow? Would he care to know that when she kissed her pillow, she thought of him? What if she got herself one of those pretty dresses what looked like triangles, maybe a bright yellow one like Princess had worn that time when Dale's eyes lingered a little extra at her legs as she walked up the front stoop to a "ladies" session—would his eyes linger on her legs, too? He call himself liking Melissa? Could he like her?

"Are you just going to dust a hole into my breakfront, or do you plan on getting to the rest of this room sometime today?" Aunt Hattie asked, interrupting Grace's inner inquisition.

"Huh?" Grace said, instantly regretting doing so.

"What I tell you about saying that to me?" Aunt Hattie snapped. "If you can say 'huh,' you can hear. I declare, you been here three whole months now, and only thing that's grown on you is your appetite. How do you expect to go to school and get your lessons if you can't get simple things right here? Those schools down south ain't worth a damn . . ."

Hattie went on . . . and on . . . and on . . . just like this, regularly, using any occasion to launch into a direct questioning of Grace's upbringing, family structure, education, Bassey's choices, Maw Maw's choices. Their humanity. She'd told Grace snatches of her story here and there: she had been in Brooklyn for more than a decade, having ridden the wave of the Great Migration to keep herself from drowning in Virginia's servant class with the three of them. "Nothing under God's sun or within all his oceans could convince me to step so much as my pinky toe back over the Mason-Dixon Line," she'd once said as she alternately stared at the evening news, on which a community of church Negroes, locked arm-in-arm, were being run over by fire hoses, and her toes, on which Grace was painting clear nail polish. Hell, Hattie wouldn't even leave the confines of Kings County; that's how deep she'd planted her roots, and she had nary a kind word for those who actively chose maidservant over teacher, sharecropper over storekeeper, mill worker over insurance man. She'd arrived to Bedford-Stuyvesant with her head full of big dreams that had been planted ten years prior, when a neighborhood boy, fresh off returning back to Black Rose, having had his leg blown off in the war, recounted the day the glamorous actress, whose beautiful, enviable face wallpapered the lockers of practically every Negro soldier to serve, performed for "the boys" serving overseas.

"Awwww, that Miss Horne, she somethin' else," he'd said, whistling. "I heard tell she grew up rich rich in New York City. Had a gang a money before she even set eyes on the stage. Negro royalty!"

"New York City!" Hattie had answered back wistfully. "Her mama annem in one a them fancy houses, huh?"

"Shole is. I saw it with my own two eyes in the magazine," he had said. "Look like a mansion, made out a brick. Clean as a whistle. She don't live there no mo'. She out there in Hollywood, living the good life. But I heard tell she still go back to New York with all her celebrity friends. Imagine that! A gang a niggers with all that pretty and all that money!"

Hattie reeled back. "Lena Horne ain't no nigger," she'd sneered. "All that pretty hair, that skin. That money. That family. Give her the right not to be referred to as anythang but a lady."

"Yeah, well, she shole is a lady, I give ya that," he'd said. "When she was standing in front of us out there in Germany, won't no mistaking that!"

Hattie hadn't heard any of the other words coming out of his mouth. Already, she was plotting on how she would make it to Brooklyn to grab her a little piece of Lena Horne. A little piece of some free. And when she finally made it, once she had her job and then her business and then her money and then her opportunity and then her home and then her reputation and then her circle, never once did Hattie look back, lest she suffer the fate of the wife of Lot—spending the rest of eternity looking backward, cursed and immovable. Those with the stink of Jim Crow in their clothes, on their breath—well, she had little patience or use for them, blood included. To her, they were as useless as a pillar of salt.

"I tell you this, and I'll say it so that you can understand me: git it togetha, lil' guhl," Aunt Hattie said, employing, for emphasis and insult, the southern drawl she'd stomped off like mud on the bottom of her rain boots the second she entered the North's door. "If you're going to stay here, especially with me, you gone have to grow you some wings and get to flying. These people around here, they smart. They goin' places, and I'm goin' wit 'em. And they ain't got no time to fool with no gal content with carrying everybody else's water. Have some respect about yo'self," she added, clapping between every syllable as she finished chastising her niece.

Grace jumped at the sound of Aunt Hattie's palms meeting; she bit her lip to try to keep the water from filling her eyes, knowing her tears would not inoculate her from Aunt Hattie's scorn and disgust. Her aunt was immovable.

"Now hurrup and finish dusting before my ladies get here," Aunt Hattie snapped. "And when you're through, go upstairs and put on my dress with the white line down the middle. I need you to make a delivery to the Spencer house and Lord knows I don't want you knocking on that woman's door looking like you fresh off the last car in the cargo train."

Grace froze in place, but her mind was a whir of frenzied calculations. Her aunt was demanding she go get pretty, so that she could knock on Dale's mama's door. Where Dale would be. Where she might see him, maybe even talk to him. Where the boy who occupied every inch of space in her daydreams could very well see her through eyes that were new.

"Did you hear me, gal?" Aunt Hattie yelled, slamming her palms together again. "Get your head out ya ass and finish your chores, so you can run this box of flyers over to the Spencers!"

The yelling made Grace hop to, but her mind was still doing the math.

"Well, don't you look nice," Mrs. Spencer said, her eyes traveling Grace from shoe to tendril. Grace stood at the door, struggling under the weight of the box of programs for the debutante's ball, willing that the woman, perfectly coiffed and most proper, would be too preoccupied with the perfect coils traversing her temples and the height and width of the perfectly symmetrical Afro puff to notice how the shoes Grace had borrowed from Aunt Hattie's closet—much less scuffed, less run over, less rural Virginia hand-me-down—bounced around her slightly smaller, delicate heel. Every instinct in Grace's body willed her to bow or curtsy or do something else fancy to greet the elegant woman, who dressed like early Sunday morning even on a Tuesday, in her home, where, presumably, no one but her husband and her son were watching and, therefore, judging. Instead, Grace stood there, wide-eyed and transfixed, unsure of what to say or do besides release a crooked grin. "Come on in," Mrs. Spencer said, moving aside and holding open the door to let Grace enter her home. "My goodness, that box must be heavy. Dale!" she shouted. "Come here, please."

In what seemed like both one second and all eternity, there was Dale, materialized in front of her, his eyes locked in a dance with Grace's. But Grace could not see him, at least not in that moment. Instead, she watched him in flashes—him staring at her as if he could see down to her very soul, him touching her face, his lips on her lips, the two laughing at what was funny only to them, him touching her again, a burst of light so bright, so bright, so bright and full of passion and joy that he was the sunrise.

"Here, let me get that for you," Dale said, grabbing the heavy box with ease from Grace's hands, his words and the action snapping Grace out of her picture show.

"I don't know why Hattie didn't just call me," Mrs. Spencer said, shaking her head. "I could have sent Dale over to fetch these programs. They're much too heavy for a young lady to struggle with for two long city blocks. I appreciate you bringing them over, dear."

"You . . . you're welcome, ma'am," Grace said slowly, picking through her words to say just the right ones, heeding Aunt Hattie's warning to swallow her country drawl in front of this woman, whom Grace's aunt worshiped for all the things she was—for all the things Aunt Hattie wanted to be. Admired. Connected. Important. Big.

"Would you like a cool drink?" Mrs. Spencer asked.

"No, thank you," Grace answered slowly. "I should be going now."

"Well, hold on now," Mrs. Spencer said, pausing and looking off into the distance, as if she were calling to her the memory of what she needed to do next. "I have to send over my heavy stockpots to your aunt. She's offered to prepare the stew for the cotillion dinner, but I'm sure she doesn't have one big enough to accommodate the crowd we have coming. Be a dear and take it to her, won't you?"

"Yes, ma'am," Grace said.

"Dale, baby, put those programs in your father's office and go get my stockpot. The one your grandmother used to make the gumbo."

"Okay, Mom," he said before quickly disappearing into the back of the house. Grace stood awkwardly by the door as Mrs. Spencer stared some more, her silence settling over Grace's head like a gray cloud pregnant with a strong, gusty shower. Soon enough, Dale reappeared with the pot and its lid cradled in his hands. "You know what? This is pretty heavy," he said. "How about I carry it over to Ms. Adams's house so Grace doesn't have to struggle with it." He was addressing his mother, but his eyes were having a whole 'nother conversation with Grace's.

"Oh, well, yes, I guess that's a good idea," Mrs. Spencer said, seeming to take note of the energy between her son and the country gal with the nappy head and the oversized shoes, squeezed into a dress that was not hers, pulled from a closet that also was not hers, in a home that was hundreds of miles away from whatever shotgun shack she'd fled, just two blocks away from her only son, a smart, beautiful boy with an equally beautiful brain who was headed to Morehouse College, home of some of the most prestigious Black intellectuals of their generation, with zero time to waste on a dusty country nigger not fit to run his bathwater. "Don't linger, Dale," she said finally. "I'll need you to make a run to the store for me when you get back."

"Okay, Mom, I got you."

"You what?" Mrs. Spencer said, furrowing her brow.

"I meant yes, ma'am—I'll hurry back," Dale said, yielding to the more formal language his mother clearly insisted he use to impress company—or clobber them about the head when she needed to establish or remind all within the sound of the Spencer family's voices that they were from New Orleans, of good stock unblemished by chattel slavery and its hold on the lineages that sprung from the fields and oversaw them, too. This afforded her a specific standing—a luxury—she rather enjoyed. The kind reserved for her kind of people.

Mrs. Spencer walked over to the door and held it open for her son but never once took her eyes off Grace, who felt as if a hole was being bored directly into the space between her eyes. She stammered a "goodbye" and made herself small as she passed by the mistress of the house, and practically tripped out the door behind Dale, who seemed oblivious to the exchange. Grace clopped down the front stoop steps and folded herself into herself, walking several paces behind Dale, feeling as ridiculous as she was sure she looked. She jumped just a bit when she heard Mrs. Spencer's door slam. She willed herself to not look back.

"So, you going to the cotillion?" Dale asked. His words shattered Grace's silence, but not her shame.

"Huh?" she said absentmindedly, before quickly recovering with, "I mean, um, what did you say?"

"The cotillion," he said, slowing down his pace to allow Grace to catch up. "I know you're not in it, otherwise I would have seen you at practice. That would have at least made all those hours in the banquet hall basement a little more worth it," he said, turning to look Grace in her face. She was too busy concentrating on balling up her toes in Aunt Hattie's shoes to keep them from bouncing up against the concrete to connect with his compliments—the one coming from his mouth and the one that might be seen in the gleam of his eye.

Grace was silent.

"Anyway," Dale said, undeterred. "You won't be missing much if you stay home. Cotillions are a form of torture no one should sign up for."

"What's a cotillion?" Grace said finally.

"Ahhhhhh, she speaks!" Dale said, smiling big, looking exactly as he had in the visions of her mind. "Can I get a little side of smile with that?"

Shyness made Grace drop her head just a little more, but her heart—it coaxed the smile Dale was looking for. She forced some words to her throat: "Is it a fancy party?"

Dale sucked his teeth. "It's torture."

Grace looked his way again, this time confused. Dale explained without prompting. "Every year, the women of the Bed-Stuy chapter of the Negro Women's League force their kids to put on a bunch of itchy clothes and too-tight shoes and perform like a bunch of monkeys in front of our families, our friends, the community, and anybody else who bothers buying a ticket. They say it's to raise money for scholarships, but us kids all know it's to show us off."

"So, you git to dress up and let your parents be proud of you in front of people?"

This time, confusion jumped onto Dale's brow. "I mean, it's not really like that . . ."

"Well, I reckon, I don't really understand . . ."

"It's like, it's a drag, right, because there's all this stuff happening in the world. Negroes are catching hell, getting bit by dogs and spit on and hosed for wanting basic things. I mean, they blowing up babies in churches! Killing Negroes in their driveways in front of their children. They killed

Dr. King! Hell, Bobby Kennedy is fresh in the grave for daring to help us!" Dale said, his excitement growing. He spun himself around and walked backward, so he could look into Grace's face as they walked. "And right here in Brooklyn, the same thing is going down . . ."

Grace reared back her neck. "The same thing?"

"Hell yeah. The schools are segregated, the pigs are billy-clubbing brothers over the head every chance they get. We can't go where we want to."

"You can go to a school and get educated, and go back to your house and do your homework . . ."

"What good is the school if the white teachers aren't teaching us the way they do white kids? Or, or, or the two toilets they put in there for a thousand kids don't work? Or the books in the Black schools are falling apart while over there at the schools where the white kids are, they're getting new books every year?"

"So, you want to be over there with the white people?"

"Man, Grace, this isn't about sitting next to white people. This is about Negroes having access to the same things whites do. Being treated the same."

"And you think your parents don't want those things for you?"

"I think our parents are ignorant to what's really going on because they're not in the South anymore. Instead of taking to the streets to help our people, they got us running around here like some Uncle Toms. 'We just happy to be here, suh!'" he added, mocking a southern accent.

Grace stared at him but said nothing. Her silence, she knew, made Dale understand quite quickly just how offensive was his mocking.

"I'm sorry—I didn't mean it that way . . ."

"Well, what did you mean?" Grace asked.

"I meant, there are some of us who want to do more for our people than show up to fancy parties pretending like the world isn't burning around us."

"But if showing up to that fancy party makes it so that somebody can go to school, why is that a bad thing?" Grace asked.

Dale turned back around and walked forward, as if thinking hard about Grace's ask. "Well," he said finally, "what's the point of going to school if our people can't do anything with what we're learning? What's the point of an education that's not equal? And even if we get good educations, what does it do for us if when we come home, all we can still be is somebody's janitor?"

"What's wrong with being a janitor?" Grace's face got hot as her disappointment in the boy she'd conjured a whole life with in her mind slowly erased the good images she'd used to build a wall around the bad—Maw Maw's imprisonment, her mother's death, her longing for home.

"Man, I didn't . . . I . . . ," Dale said, starting and stopping in seeming fits of caution and a desire to be precise. He didn't like that his tongue was thick. He did like, though, that the diminutive southern girl with the too-big shoes but a quick wit was keeping him on his toes. "Look, I didn't mean it like that. Can we start over?" He convinced himself that Grace's silence meant "yes." "All I'm saying is that what's happening to our people isn't just a southern thing. It's a Negro thing, no matter where we are. We should be fighting for our freedom right here in Brooklyn just like they're doing down south."

"What you know about the South?" Grace snapped. "'Sides from what you see on yo' television set?"

"I know Jim Crow is killing our people."

"Das all you know?"

"I know it's happening here, too, and wherever it's happening, we got a responsibility to stand up."

"You think because one of these ofays gives you a mean look on the subway in the morning, Brooklyn got it as bad as Virginia? South Carolina? Louisiana? Mississippi? Ala—"

"Don't you get it, Grace? It's not about mean looks. It's about segregation, even where it's not the law, and the lack of opportunities for Negroes, wherever we are."

"You git to go to a good school. You live in a fancy house and git to go to fancy parties in your fancy clothes. Yo' mama and yo' daddy live in yo' fancy house with you. And in a couple months, you gone be off to a fancy college to get ya learnin', so you can take it and help people. Our people. Any way you please," Grace said, stopping just in front of Aunt Hattie's stoop. She got in Dale's face and pushed her words through her teeth: "You don't know nothin' 'bout the South."

Aunt Hattie was standing at the door by the time Grace, shoes flopping off the backs of her soles, made it to the top of the brownstone stairs. Her inclination was to push past her aunt, but Grace knew better; she stood in front of Aunt Hattie's lithe body, eyes fixed on the set of string pearls circling her throat. On a few occasions, Grace let herself imagine, just for a moment at a time, what it would be like to squeeze them—both the pearls and the throat they decorated—between her bare hands.

"Dale, your mother sent over her stew pot. Wonderful!" Aunt Hattie said, her voice doing happy, her face doing a mixture of concern and "What did Grace do?"

Dale seemed to force a smile. "Yes, ma'am. She said you were making some of your amazing gumbo and since Grace stopped by, she wanted to send the pot over. I didn't want Grace to carry it. It's a little heavy."

"Well, ever the gentleman," Aunt Hattie said, stepping aside and gesturing for Grace to pass by. "You can bring it inside. Put it on the dining room table for me, dear."

"Yes, ma'am," Dale said, trotting up the steps, grateful he'd at least get to look at Grace one more time before he headed home. Somewhere between Lafayette and DeKalb, he fell in love with the southern girl who was every bit as passionate as she was beautiful. She wasn't like the cotillion girls—no. She was something else. Dale intended to see what, exactly, that was.

7

There was tulle and satin and lace, long gloves that stretched to elbows, and lots of string pearls pulled from the jewelry boxes and handkerchiefs of proud grandmothers—girls whispering and giggling in corners while they practiced curtsies and waltzed with the air. They were careful not to disturb tendrils and delicate curls that had been pressed and slicked and coiffed like sculptural paeans to the mothers—women who, just the night before, had situated daughters on thick books and pillows between knees while lovingly wielding white-hot sizzling hot combs over singed ears and nappy kitchens. The girls heeded both encouragement and warning: ladies of a polite society are delicate, demure. *On this night, remember who you are. Remember what you are not.*

The whir of the room was almost too much for Grace. Plucked from a quiet Saturday night she had looked forward to spending alone on the stoop of the brownstone, away from Aunt Hattie's sharp tongue and never-ending demands, Grace had ended up in the basement of the Colored YMCA in Fort Greene, having been summoned by her aunt to "learn a little something about grace and class" while she helped the cotillion girls get themselves ready for presentation. As if Aunt Hattie had sat them down and given them specific instructions on how to work Grace like a mule in springtime, the girls—twenty-five in all from various well-to-do colored families across the northwestern section of Brooklyn—made quick work of bossing her all around the room. "Adjust my dress." "Help me into my shoes." "Run and get me an extra pair of pantyhose—mine have a run in them." "Pin my curl right here, it's not sitting right." "Adjust my corsage—and you better not stick me like you did Cassandra." "Well, shouldn't you get water for everyone? You think Barbara is the only one thirsty?"

Grace wanted desperately to be somewhere—anywhere—else than among the lot, who somehow became more mean, insufferable, than when they were at Aunt Hattie's house, taking their etiquette classes. Grace snatched bits and pieces of Hattie's lessons on "how to be" every now and again, between fixing lunches and moving furniture for their dance rehearsals and straightening up as they took down their home assignments and pledged to be "outstanding in body, mind, and service to others," their motto. But she just couldn't recall any moment where they were told that the prettier they were, the uglier they should be. And still, here they were.

She had become an expert at making herself invisible. It was how they liked her. It was what Grace preferred. Being bigger, grand, loud, well, that would draw attention, and not the kind anyone would purposefully want to call to themselves among this crowd, which tore down and devoured for sport. No shoe, no garment, no hairstyle, no school, no family status, no familial history was safe from torching among this lot, and so folding into oneself, being neither seen nor heard, was the sole salvation for someone of Grace's background and stature. They'd made that abundantly clear. Grace complied without fuss.

Dale hated that part. "Why do you let them talk to you that way?" he'd asked Grace once while she sat on the stoop beneath the rooster, watching the sun do its slow dance across the evening sky. Most evenings, this is where he found her, feet tucked beneath knees, elbows ashy and rough and pricked with tiny rocks that burrowed themselves into her skin as she propped them on the concrete steps behind her. He'd strut up the sidewalk, books, basketball, something in his hands, having walked, she knew, blocks out of his way to run into the girl who, when he was alone with his thoughts, was every bit as vivid as the pinks and oranges dragging behind the sun's wake. On this particular night, she was more stoic than usual— quieter than he'd become accustomed to. When they were alone on the stoop and no one else was there to push and pull and order, Grace was interesting and introspective, thoughtful. Alive. Just like in his daydreams.

Grace waved her hand in the air and sucked her teeth, the gesture meant to make clear where she stood on the matter before she bothered to say the words. "I ain't studyin' them girls, Dale," she said, wrinkling her brow. Grace knew she sounded like an old southern auntie—wiser than her fifteen years.

Certainly more mature, Dale thought, than the gossipy cotillion girls. To him, she had heft. He loved that about her; she made him work for her attention and he didn't mind that. Didn't mind it at all. "So what, they spit out my corn pone. Dey the ones spent the day hungry," she said with a shrug.

"But did Melissa really toss it on the floor?"

"How you hear about it?" Grace said, finally taking her eyes off the sunset to look directly at Dale. She tried hard not to do that too often—look him in the eye. Out of fear he would find evidence that she'd seen forever with him. Out of fear that he hadn't—wouldn't—see it back and would take away the one small pleasure she'd had the entire time she'd been in Brooklyn: seeing him smiling, leaning on the railing, the sunset a halo around his head.

Dale scoffed. "Everybody knows everything here."

"Well, they don't know me," Grace said quickly.

"Forget about them. I'd like to get to know you," Dale said as he sat on the stoop, a step down from Grace. "For real."

Something about how he was looking at her—his face tilted up, eyes smiling, sincere—put Grace at ease and made her heart flutter all the same. She smiled—looked back at the sky. "I miss sunsets back at home. Dey ain't as nice here. The buildings get all in the way and the lights in the street make the colors weak." She went quiet for a moment and continued. "Back home, Maw Maw and me, we used to watch every night. Sometimes we'd sit and play a game—look at the sunset, close our eyes and count to ten, open them again. See something new."

"That sounds really special," Dale said. Grace didn't see it, but Dale played her game—closed his eyes and counted, then opened them again. She was sunrise and sunset, star and moon. A galaxy that took him away from the scorch of the Brooklyn sun.

"I miss her. I miss my mama. Ain't much else anybody can do to me to hurt me like it hurt when they went away. Melissa, Aunt Hattie, all them girls just mean. I'm used to it."

"That's not something you should let yourself get used to," Dale said, practically whispering.

Grace was quiet. And then: "I miss the water. I miss the dirt under my feet and the way grass feel on my toes. Even the snakes—miss dem, too. The little green ones. They helpful. The snakes here in Brooklyn? Kill ya dead if you let 'em. I know that now."

"Don't let those girls push you around, Gracie." He said her name like it was honey on his tongue.

"What you care about it?" she said, finally looking at Dale.

"I care about you knowing that I'm not like them," he said.

Grace held her breath—the suspension of air meant to make time and space stand still. He was looking up into her face with awe and desire, like the Dale in her daydreams. Her heart could barely keep its rhythm. "Why does that matter to you?" she asked.

"Because you matter to me, Grace, exactly the way you are," he said simply, quickly. "And I want to matter to you."

Grace's heart bloomed as the last of the evening summer sun floated in his eyes.

And so, the second she heard one of the cotillion girls say Dale's name, Grace became an elephant—all ears and ready to charge.

"They practiced together and everything. I don't blame her for being upset," one girl said, sitting back on the sofa, crossing her ankles just so.

"Can you imagine doing all that work and your escort just not showing up?" another said, peering from girl to girl, collecting nods of agreement.

"I'm surprised at Dale, honestly," said another. "That's not the stock he comes from. His mother is practically royalty. It's just in poor taste to stand up a lady on her cotillion night."

"Well, where is Melissa anyway?" the first girl asked.

As the girls shrugged and faked concern, Grace snuck out to the library, where the planning committee of anxious mothers was putting the finishing touches on the evening's event. Dale's mother was the committee chairwoman; Grace knew enough to know that whatever rumor was being spread downstairs would be fact in there. She walked into a full-blown storm.

"Where could he be?" Mrs. Spencer said. Her gown, an exquisite black strapless body-skimming affair with a train attached just below her delicate shoulder blade, trailed like a cape as she rushed over to the couch and practically twirled herself onto the slippery chesterfield cushion.

"He'll be here," Ellen, Melissa's mother, said. Her words conveyed confidence, but they slid tepidly over her tongue. No one in the room was quite sure what to make of Dale's disappearance, though some suspected that Lucinda Spencer's son, the golden child of Bedford-Stuyvesant who had, for years, lamented being trotted out for benefit of family reputation rather than his own desire to be there, had finally taken it upon himself to simply not show up—consequences be damned.

Mrs. Spencer wrung her hands as her fellow moms feigned a symphony of concern: they rubbed her shoulders and patted her knees and *tsk-tsk*ed while exchanging knowing glances, all of them obviously wise to the ways of seventeen-year-old boys and the mothers who could only see the good in them.

"How about we get you some water?" one suggested, touching Mrs. Spencer's arm while twisting her body south, east, north, and west, as if a glass would magically appear. "Some water? Someone?" Finally, her eyes settled on a server who, despite being assigned the high-intensity job of catering to the every whim of the planning committee's quarters, was thoroughly glued to the screen of a small black-and-white television set in the watch corner of the library, a gift gleaned from a Negro Women's League fundraiser a few years prior. Evidently, neither she nor the waiter in charge of folding napkins and placing them at the top of each plate just so was aware of a roomful of delicately painted, angry eyes that were now boring holes in their backs.

"You know they stay killin' niggers in the summertime," the male server said, folding his arms over his chest.

"You ain't lying," the female server said, shaking her head, eyes transfixed on the screen. "You would think they'd put they guns away after what all happened with Dr. King. Ain't been but a couple months and them cops back at it. They not gone be happy until this city tore up brick by brick."

Grace craned her neck trying to take in the chaos that was unfolding on the TV, a tingling in her fingertips—a sensation she hadn't felt and had been unable to access since leaving Virginia and Maw Maw behind—that signaled Dale was somehow connected to it. Unable to get a clear view through the two bodies standing in front of the set, she trotted over to see for herself what she'd already felt in her bones: Bed-Stuy was burning. Dale was in trouble.

"You best get out there and find him," the female server said to Grace. Her eyes never left the television set.

Grace snapped her neck from the TV to the body connected to the voice; it was the lady who'd been cleaning the stoop next door to Hattie's on the day the sunbow was high in the sky. She slowly turned to Grace and issued an order that sent a chill through the entirety of Grace's being: "Go to him. Now."

"But I don't know where . . ."

The woman turned toward Grace and took both the girl's hands into her own; together, they watched the same picture show—Dale standing in the whirlwind of an angry, bloody mob, face contorted in a fit of equal parts rage and fear.

Grace snatched back her hands as if she'd touched hot fire. "How did you . . ."

"I didn't do anything that wasn't already inside of you," the woman said in a hushed tone. "Do what you know to do and go find that boy right now."

"Who are you? What's your name?" Grace begged.

"I'm Miss Ada Mae," she said, her country lilt every bit the balm it was the day they'd first met under the rainbow. "We spirit kin. I felt you before I knew you. Now go now—quick!"

Hattie entered their space like a bucking bull. "We are not paying you to take leisure time in front of the television!" she yelled, the shrill of her voice making Grace, Ada, and the male waiter, oblivious to all going on around him until that very moment, jump.

Grace, small again, backed out of the room and disappeared down the hall and out into the night. Dale needed her. Grace needed to be there for him.

He was broken and bowed—too weak, even, to get through the brown-stone's front gate, which, despite its grandeur, still required both muscle and finesse to lift and twist open. And so, Dale slumped there, his underarm anchoring him to the sharp edges of the iron, his hand, covered in dried blood, clutching the thigh that, just fifteen minutes before, had endured the business end of police officer Mike Humbert's bully stick. Dale, having summoned the adrenaline he needed to wrestle himself out of the clutches of the cop's hands just as the angry mob moved in and launched a barrage of Molotov cocktails at Wilson's Goods and Sundries, was lucky to have gotten away in the midst of pure bedlam, but he knew he needed to be inside his home, away from prying eyes, away from speeding cop cars, away from the gaze of frightened crackers looking to point a finger at any nigger they could. Their stores were burning—their goods had legs and were running down Lexington and Quincy, Kosciuszko and Lafayette. Ungrateful niggers, all of them. Somebody, they were already calculating and demanding, would have to pay, and surely the ransom would flash like a neon sign above the head of the Black bastard bent over and bleeding outside the front gate of his parents' yard.

"Dale!" Grace shouted, rushing up to her friend as he struggled to lift the iron. "Oh God! Oh God!" She worked swiftly, ignoring his groans as she eased her body beneath his shoulder and took on the full weight of his thin but muscular, dense frame. "Just hold on tuh me. I got tuh git tha gate open," she said, her fingers curling around the fastening. In one swift move, she lifted and pulled, made a pathway for herself and her charge, and dug in down to her core to make herself the base Dale needed to struggle up each of the sixteen steps leading to the front door.

Once inside, Grace poured Dale onto the couch and then rushed to the kitchen to fetch him a glass of cold water. She rummaged through the kitchen drawers for a towel and wet that, too, and rushed them back to Dale, who, by then, had stretched himself across the couch, still clutching his leg. "I think he broke it," Dale said, grimacing, as Grace wiped his brow.

"Who?" Grace asked. "Who did this, Dale?"

"Fucking pigs! They shoot Negroes down like dogs in the street and expect us to just stand around taking it!"

"What you talkin' 'bout? I don't know nothin' 'bout what you sayin'," Grace whimpered. With every touch of her skin against his, she could feel his anger, his angst, and she felt every bit as powerless against it as he.

"I told you! I told you, Grace! It's bad here. They got everybody thinking the South is where the problem is and here in New York, we all getting along. But we're not. These crackers just as evil. They aim the rocks straight for our heads and then hide their hands and make the whole world sing their kumbaya songs. But we ain't fooled. They're the worst kind. The worst kind!"

"I don't understand, Dale. Tell me what happened!"

"Haven't you seen the news?"

"What news?"

"The news!"

"You gone give me a heart attack shouting in my face! Just tell me what happen!"

"They shot him. They just shot him, right there like it was nothing. Like he was nothing. Over a cola not worth a quarter."

Grace reeled back. "Who shot who?"

"Darnell. That was my friend, my brother. We been going to school together all our lives. He's a kid. Was a kid. We all are. And the cops shot him because ol' Wilson accused him of stealing a soda."

"He's . . . he's . . . dead?"

The way Dale dropped his head sent a chill through Grace's bones. She sat in silence, wringing her hands, running them up and down her forearms—Dale's pain her pain. Yet another dalliance with death dragging her to the darkness. Dale, seeing her hands trembling, took them into his own and rubbed them gently, the two of them sitting in silence until their hearts finished their race.

Finally, Grace: "You was there? When it happened?"

"Naw, I wasn't there. But my friend Roger, he was. Said Darnell was thirsty, is all. So he opened the soda and drank it in front of the cooler, you know, so he could cool off, too. But he had the money in his pocket to pay," Dale said, tears finding their way to the ducts and then the cheeks, then his chin and neck. "He was going to pay. Roger said Darnell was reaching in his pocket to give Wilson the money and Wilson started yelling and screaming and the cop came in there and shot him." Dale banged his head with his knuckles, each of the thumps making Grace jump as if he were hitting her, too. "He didn't care who got caught in the crossfire. He just shot up the place, and when he was finished, Darnell was . . . he was . . . ," he whispered.

"But I don't understand how you got beat up if you weren't there."

"Grace! Open your eyes! You so busy sniffing behind all those highfalutin folks you not paying attention to what's going on around you?" Dale snapped.

"I knew enough to come get you!"

"How . . . how did you know to do that?" he asked.

Grace hesitated, calculating what explanations would be required to quell the fear and judgment she was convinced she'd have to contend with if she told Dale about the picture show she'd seen through Miss Ada Mae's touch. She hadn't even had the time to process it for herself—how she'd been able to suddenly access the ability she hadn't experienced since those early days when they took her Maw Maw away, how she was able to see them with Miss Ada Mae, or even who that lady was, for that matter. Grace went with, "A lady at the cotillion told me you were in danger."

"What lady?" he asked.

"Her name is Miss Mae."

Dale squinted his eyes as he ran through a mental catalogue of faces. "Oh!" he finally said. "The creepy lady who cleans houses? Who does all that weird stuff out in the park?"

"What weird stuff?" Grace asked. She surmised she already knew the answer.

"You know, she does some kind of church in the park, but she does weird stuff in the grass and by the trees. My mother thinks she practices voo-doo," he said. Then: "Funny how she knew what was going on but none of the cotillion people or you were paying attention."

"But I'm the one here with you! I'm the one who came and got you! You think I want to be there around the cotillion girls? Around my auntie Hattie? You think I have a choice?"

"We all have choices, Grace. You can choose to pay attention to what's going on around you or become just like them and pretend like everything is just fine."

"I know everything is not fine!"

"Then how come you didn't know they're out there rioting up and down Nostrand? How did you not know the neighborhood is on fire? Don't you smell the smoke?"

Dale winced in pain and brushed his fingers against his left cheek and temple, both of which had turned a shade of purple-black that looked like the bruises Grace had seen on Bassey's body as Maw Maw and her friends washed it with warm water scented with gardenia flowers, roses, and thyme and peppermint leaves that grew wild down by the river where Grace and her grandmother made offerings in the water and asked their ancestors for special favor. Though her mother had been gone now for well over a good year, the smell of those specific flowers and herbs always coaxed bile into the back of Grace's throat. Much like Dale's bruises were in that moment.

"Gracie, I'm sorry. I'm sorry. It's going to be okay," Dale said, softer now. The same hand he used to rub his bruises he now used to wipe Grace's tears.

She said nothing.

"Gracie, it's going to be okay. I'm okay."

Nothing, still.

"Gracie." Dale lifted her chin and looked into each of her eyes, studying them with an intensity that was every bit as hypnotic as the rhythm of his breathing. He wiped away one tear with his thumb. Then another. And yet another with his second thumb, until he was cradling her whole face in his hands, their chests rising and falling at the same deep, heavy pace. He let his gaze fall to her lips and chin and up to her cheeks and back to her eyes and then back to her lips. And then he pulled her to him.

Grace, unsure of what she was doing but sure she wanted to do it, did not fuss with the pulling. Instead, she leaned in and let Dale, his hands, his lips, lead her. She was grateful for his tenderness, something to which she hadn't any access since the last time she laid in her grandmother's arms. Every piece of her had been disconnected—her ability to love, to be love, to be loved—for so long that she'd almost forgotten what it felt like to be both human and light. And suddenly, she was both again, transformed by Dale's kiss.

Neither of them heard the key in the lock or the door flying open, or Mr. and Mrs. Spencer rushing through the door in a panic that, when they got their bearings and surveyed the room, quickly turned into an inferno of rage. "Theodale Thomas Spencer! What in the hell is going on here?" Mrs. Spencer yelled first. "Get your ass off that couch with that girl!"

Grace jumped first, clearing herself from the couch and crashing into the cocktail table, knocking over the delicate crystal elephants that stood sentry on the table, their tusks pointed at the door.

"And you," Mrs. Spencer said, turning her gaze to the fumbling Grace as she smoothed down her dress and wiped Dale's spit from her lip. "You get your fast ass out . . . of . . . my . . . house!" she yelled.

"Yes'm," was all Grace could muster as she rushed past Mrs. Spencer, stomping on the woman's cape as she made her move toward the front door. Both of them stumbled, grabbing on to each other as they tripped in slow motion.

"Get your goddamn hands off of me!" Mrs. Spencer yelled.

"Mom, no!" Dale yelled.

Mr. Spencer tried to hold his wife back, but her thrashing proved formidable. She grabbed Grace by the sleeve and held on so tight as she pushed the girl down the stairs that Grace would feel the grip hours later, while she sat in Hattie's basement, trying to find the right words to explain why she'd been on the Spencers' couch, kissing a battered and bruised young man who, at the time, was supposed to be dressed in a tuxedo and tails, waltzing with the girl who, four years prior, Mrs. Spencer, weaned on her family's obsession with being in the precise social circles, schools, vacation enclaves, complexions, and the like, had handpicked to be presented by her son at the debutante ball.

Grace, eyes blinded by tears, slipped down three steps before she thought to grab hold of the railing to break her fall. She held her breath as she ran down the rest of the stairs and through the gate and burst onto the street, and only after her foot touched the pavement did she hear the sirens and smell the smoke and stop short, paralyzed with fear. The riot that had been invisible to her as she rushed to Dale's side was moving like brush fire through the streets of Bedford-Stuyvesant, the intensity parallel to that of her last night in Black Rose. Had Mrs. Spencer not been standing at the top of her steps, loudly lobbing obscenities and cursing the very ground on which the teenager stood, Grace would have dropped to her knees, cradled her head, and screamed until her throat and heart and insides seared.

Instead, Grace cupped her mouth, choking her urgent cry back down into her throat.

And she disappeared into the dark.

8

Maw Maw hadn't much believed in beating children. In fact, she'd been patently against it—thought it so base, she wouldn't even smack a newborn's behind to hear its first cry. It was her mama who'd taught her how to suck the placenta and snot out the baby's nose and employ a simple swipe of the finger to clear their little throats. If that didn't get them going, there was nothing like a knuckle rub between the shoulder blades and a "Welcome to the world, sweet little baby" whispered directly in their tiny ears to open wide to them their new life. "They breath sweet as cane," she'd say. "Get in real close and listen from the inside, them babies, they'll tell you secrets. Tell you what the ancestors sent them here to tell us. If'n you listen."

The old ways—regard for children, how to love them—went by the way of the lash, and what was left in the pot was a filthy stew of practices meant to exact submission. Straps, switches, shoes, spoons, paddles, palms, fists—didn't make no nevermind—all of them were employed to consistently remind children that they were to be seen, not heard, around grown folk. Practice for when they got grown and found themselves around white folk. They were bred to be shadows. All of it, Maw Maw despised, and she taught Bassey and Grace to despise it, too.

But hating it—wanting to remember and practice the old way—that hadn't stopped all the other mamas and papas from beating on their babies. Grace, she'd been the one who had witnessed it up close—saw the welts on her fellow students' thighs, the black under their eyes, the light dimmed as they tried to concentrate on their lessons or eat their food come break time. Looked like they were chewing on sawdust. Grace felt their emptiness, smelled their fear. "I's scared for him, Maw Maw," she'd said one evening during supper, while recounting how Noah's papa, strap in his left hand, came down to the school special to grab his son off his bench and into the air by his neck with his right hand. The boy's offense: he'd forgotten to close the door to the chicken coop.

"Well, I suppose he did have to answer to being so careless. Noah 'bout, what, three hundred pounds on a light week when the food running low?" Bassey had said as she scooped a delicate round of pinto beans into her spoon. "Can you imagine Noah running after chickens?"

Bassey laughed, but Maw Maw hadn't been tickled. Not even a little bit. She pushed her bowl away and slapped her hands together, making both Bassey and Grace jerk in their seats. "That's just terrible! Why on earth you beat on a baby you love? How that make anythang better?"

"Well," Bassey said, spooning more beans in her mouth, "maybe grabbing the boy by the neck wasn't the best thang, but sometimes you do have to get they attention."

"Bassey, if I beat you er time I had to get yo' attention, you wouldn't have no kinda skin on yo' hide."

"You do got a point there," Bassey said, nodding. "I do 'preciate you ain't beat me and all, but I gots to stand firm on this one. Noah's papa know he got to keep that boy in line, or somebody else will. Wasn't it just a couple weeks back some cracka slapped Bobbie Jean's baby dead in the mouf for sassin' him at the general store?"

"And that man ain't have no right to do that, either!" Maw Maw had said, growing more agitated.

"You right, he didn't. But crackas do what they want. She lucky that's all she got was a slap. She shoulda known better. Her mama shoulda taught her better. And sometimes the teachin' come in the beatin', is all I'm sayin'."

"You dip mighty low if you doing to yo' baby what a cracka would. Chir'ren is a gift, and the mamas and daddies running 'round laying hands on 'em like they a dog. Running the god right out 'em."

Clearly, Hattie didn't see the god in Grace. She believed deeply that with every lash, she was running the devil clean out of her niece's body, all while restoring her standing among the neighborhood women, who had cast her aside like the sons of Belial. She blamed Grace for her excommunication. Kissing on that boy, angering the Spencers, refusing to keep her little country ass in her place—each of these things reminded those women of what Hattie had worked so hard to get them to forget—the stink of having nothing, coming from nothing, being nothing. Of course, it did not occur to Hattie that she was equally culpable—that her decision to turn her back on the old ways, on her dead, would hinder rather than help her get to the money, standing, respect she craved. Hattie had handicapped her own self from the beginning. And now, that precarious house of cards she'd assembled for herself had been effortlessly toppled. Grace's doing. Hattie wanted her to pay. It seemed all she could think to do—all that mattered to her.

"Running 'round here like some harlot, witcha fast ass!" she yelled, her southern Virginia tongue slipping out as the belt sliced through air and flesh. This was what Grace woke up to—fury that Hattie had let brew overnight after she collected phone call after phone call, recounting all the things that had gone wrong the night before. Let them tell it, Grace had been single-handedly responsible for turning Dale on to all that civil rights mess, putting him directly into the clutches of the police, jeopardizing his chances of going to college and using sex to steal him straight out the arms of a cultured colored girl from a good family with solid values and closed legs. What was worse: Mrs. Spencer had spread word to them all that Hattie and her little bastard niece were dead to them all. They were not to be talked to, let alone allowed to carry on the ridiculous charade that Hattie was cultured enough to teach the young ladies of Bed-Stuy how to be. Hattie was undone. She meant to get her pound of flesh from Grace's hide. "What gives you the right to take what's not yours?" she demanded as she wielded her belt.

"I . . . I was just checking on him, I swear, Aunt Hattie!" Grace yelled as she tried to dodge the lash of the whip. Her attempts were fruitless; no matter where she moved, no matter how she positioned her hands and arms to guard her face and thighs and head and stomach, the belt carved up her skin, raising welts and bruises up and down her frame. It was a pain—sharp, searing—that Grace had never before felt and would never, ever forget.

"Who the hell you raisin' your voice to?" Aunt Hattie yelled, raining down more blows. When her arm got tired, she tossed down the belt and balled her fist. One of her punches landed square on Grace's right eye, a hit so forceful Grace dropped to her knees and pushed out a scream so shrill, it made Aunt Hattie jerk back. Grace cried and cried. Aunt Hattie stared and stared and yelled and yelled and contemplated whether she would leave her niece sitting right there in a heap on the parquet floors or exact some kind of explanation about why, exactly, she thought she had the right to kiss on Dale in his mama's living room, distracting him, and, more important, turning Mrs. Lucinda Spencer against everything she'd worked for from the moment she set toe in Brooklyn: respect, status, livelihood. Place.

Finally: "I mean, I just don't understand what you were thinking," Aunt Hattie said, dropping onto the couch, adrenaline making way for the fatigue that follows whoopings—for both receiver and giver. "You knew that boy was supposed to be down there at the Y. And instead, you had him hemmed up at his house. Had his mama annem worried sick about him and embarrassed, too. How she look being the chair of the whole event and her own son ditches his debutante and his big debut?"

Grace sniffled but said nothing.

"Answer me, dammit!" Aunt Hattie yelled. Her voice was like a lightning strike against a power grid. The boom made Grace's heart flatline.

"I . . . I . . . I didn't stop him from going to the ball. I was there heppin', remember?"

"Well, his mama seems to think you told him to meet him back at his house. And she think you the one talked him into going to that protest."

"What?" Grace asked gently, wincing as she wiped tears from her now swollen, bruised eye.

"The protest. You were there with him. Filling his head with lies about the movement. Who else gonna tell him to get involved with that mess? You brought all that marching and drama and carrying on up here from the South, where niggers standing around begging for their rights, while we up here in Brooklyn living good lives. Making good moves. That boy is on his way to Morehouse and after that, medical school. Last place he needs to be is in somebody's street getting run over by dogs and hoses and arrested by them crackers. And here you come, inspiring him to tear down everything his parents built for him. How dare you?"

"No!" Grace said, shaking her head violently. "No, I won't there, Auntie,

I swear. I ain't know about the protest. I just knew he was hurt, and I went to hep him."

"How you know he was hurt?" Aunt Hattie said through gritted teeth.

Grace hesitated, unsure how her aunt would respond to her truth.

"How!" Aunt Hattie yelled.

"I . . . I . . . saw it in a picture show . . . ," Grace said.

"A picture show? You went to the movies? What the hell . . ."

"No, a picture show. I saw him being hurt in my dreams," Grace said. She figured it would be best to keep Miss Ada Mae out of it. "When the girls at the cotillion said he was missing, I knew from my dreams where to find him."

Aunt Hattie reeled back and started talking in fits, but she couldn't complete a whole word. The look in her eyes made terror do a slow drag in Grace's. Their chests—one heaving in fear, the other in anger and disgust—were the only things moving. After what felt like an eternity, Hattie narrowed her eyes and pushed words through pursed lips and clinched teeth. "You listen to me and you listen good: don't you ever in your sorry life let me hear you talking about that black magic again. I already told you I will not have you bringing that evil into my house, and I especially will not have you running your mouth about it anywhere north of the Mason-Dixon Line. Some of that evil is buried with your mama and the rest of it can rot in the jail cell with your grandmama as far as I care."

Grace's breath quickened at the mere mentioning of Maw Maw; Aunt Hattie had been short on information about her well-being and her temper grew even shorter when Grace had asked—begged—for details on where her grandmother was, how she was faring. If she was even alive. Hattie guarded the information like the very answer was locked in a vault, deep in the recesses of some inaccessible, invisible fort that Grace had no right to access, no matter that Maw Maw was her whole heart. For just a fraction of a second, Hattie's acknowledgment that Maw Maw was indeed alive and indeed still in a jail cell after all this time had Grace fix her lips to ask about her grandmother. Her wounds—the ones on the outside—reminded her just as quickly that no matter how desperate she was for more information, this moment was not the time.

"Let me tell you this," Aunt Hattie continued, "you will not come here, to where I've built a life and community, and have these people burying me right there next to those witches. There's no place for that hoodoo mess here. Am I understood?"

Aunt Hattie lifted herself off the sofa and stood over Grace. She flinched and lifted her arms, full of welts and open wounds, to protect her eye, which had a heartbeat of its very own. "Do. You. Understand?" Aunt Hattie asked menacingly.

"Yes," Grace whimpered.

"Now get your ass up from there," Aunt Hattie said. She reached into her dress and down into her bra and pulled out a sweaty dollar bill. "Go down there to the corner store and get me a pack of Camels."

Grace slowly took the money from her aunt's hands. "But they still out there protesting."

"Nobody told you to go to Wilson's. Go two blocks over to The Blue Moon and get my cigarettes and hurry back. Don't nobody want you. You'll be fine. And hurry up!"

"Yes, ma'am," was all Grace could say with confidence she wouldn't get punched again. She struggled to her feet, her aunt still holding an imposing pose over her as she stood. Grace hobbled to the front door, every step making her wounds vibrate as if they were still in the midst of their creation.

It was early and so it was still quiet on the streets—eerily so—and Grace was grateful for this. Though Aunt Hattie wasn't at all worried about whether it was safe for her to move through the neighborhood that, just the night before, had been an active war zone, Grace had been worried that the rising of the sun wouldn't make any kind of difference to the Negroes, who tottered on the ledges of rooftops as they rained bricks, Molotov cocktails, pieces of cement—whatever their hands could touch and lift and heave—on the heads of police officers and anyone else standing on the street who happened to be either moving through their day or out demanding justice. Brick, baton, Grace had been sure she'd have to reckon with one, maybe both, the second she got to the bottom of her aunt's front stoop—or at least as she walked the two blocks over to a convenience store that, despite the damage it sustained, was still functioning. But the chaos had ceased, worn thin by a gang of arrests the night prior, an appeal for calm from the community leaders who leaned more on the protest stylings of Martin rather than Malcolm, and the much more practical, mundane reason: Negroes had jobs to get to, and so protesting would have to wait until shifts were over. Grace was grateful for the reprieve. She dodged the broken bits of Bed-Stuy and forced a bouquet of "hellos" to her lips for the colored men and women who nodded their heads and pushed the brooms and said, "Morning, little sister," as they filled garbage cans and swept up shards and took accounting for all that had been lost in the night's fire. On a more practical day, Grace may have been moved to try to understand why people would tear up their own neighborhoods—why they would light a match to the stores owned by their own, or that they worked at or lived next to and above. But really what she needed to do was get Aunt Hattie's cigarettes and get herself back to the house before someone lifted their eyes and saw the shame and anger her aunt had carved on her body.

"Who did that to your face?"

Grace's eyes were focused on her shoes and so she couldn't see the inquirer, but she knew his voice. She groaned and kept moving toward the store's door.

"That happened when you left my house last night? Who did that? Where did it happen? Was it the cops?"

"I can't talk to you right now," Grace said, pulling open the store's door, which had been reduced to a glassless frame in the prior night's events. "I can't talk to you ever."

"What do you mean? Grace!" Dale grabbed Grace's shoulder in a way that made it impossible for her not to scream out in pain. The curdling made Dale pull back his hand like he'd just touched white-hot coals; his reaction stopped her in her tracks. And so, the two just stood there in the glassless doorway, Grace rubbing her shoulder, Dale trying to fix his face, as if not to have it reflect the horror that stood before him. The sound of trash being dumped into the butt of a garbage truck broke the silence. "Gracie," Dale called out quietly, the way he'd done the night before when his lips touched hers.

Grace finally met him eye-to-eye; the two of them stood there, battered and bruised, looking like two prizefighters center ring, waiting to hear who would take home the belt. Grace closed her eyes and leaned into his hand as he caressed her face and quietly asked her, again, who had laid hands on her.

"My auntie don't want me seein' you no mo'," she said simply, letting her quick pronouncement stand in for the details Dale sought, but she was too afraid to give.

"Ms. Hattie did this to you?" Dale asked, reeling back in confusion.

"Auntie Hattie. Yo' mama. Yo' little girlfriends down there at the Y. All them done this to me, Dale," she said, seething.

"My girlfrie . . . mama . . . what?" Dale said.

"All I know is I tried to help you and my eye got blacked for my trouble. Everybody told yo' mama I was the one talked you into looting the store and kissing on me and now my auntie on the war path 'cause everythang she built just gone now. Gone."

"What?" Dale asked, flummoxed. "I went out there for Darnell. On my own. What do they know about any of this? So busy trying to be the good Negroes and hiding and letting us kids put our lives on the line . . ."

Grace stood there staring at Dale, who had turned the volume on his voice down low. What she knew was that she needed protection, tenderness, and here this boy stood before her, turning her beating and the sentence his mother had meted out on Grace's family based on evidence built upon assumptions, stereotypes, and lies into a referendum on his protesting. On his friend. On his family's lack of empathy for the movement. Dale's selfishness was dirty fingernails in Grace's fresh wounds. "Look, I can't be here with you," she said forcefully, interrupting his tirade and pushing past him into the store.

"Grace," he said, scampering behind her. "Baby, wait. I'm sorry. I'm so sorry. This is my fault. All of it."

Grace lumbered to the cigarette machine, uncrumpling Hattie's dollar bill as she walked.

"I shouldn't have pulled you into it," he added.

Grace put the dollar into the machine and pulled the knob for the Camels, but instead of retrieving the cigarettes, she leaned her palms against the machine and slowly took in air through her nose, then blew it out through her mouth, just like Maw Maw had taught Mrs. Brodersen to do when she was panicked and the labor pain threatened to swallow her whole and she needed to find some calm.

"Grace," Dale said softly, pushing his words ever so gently between her breaths. "I'm sorry. Look at me, Grace. I'm sorry."

She let him touch her chin and gently turn it toward his—watched him as he took in her pulsing eye and the scratches and welts and grew big across his shoulders. He meant it. Her heart told her so.

"You two, get the fuck outta my store!" someone shouted, making Grace and Dale jump. Instinctively, Dale pushed Grace behind him and turned toward the angry voice. "I see the two of you, all beat up and limp. Them cops got you good. That's what you get for making trouble around here where there ain't none," the man said, rushing toward them from the back of the soda pop aisle, where he'd been sweeping up debris from the looting the night before. "Ask me, they should have thrown your nigger asses in jail. Now get the fuck out before I call the law." Grace grabbed the cigarettes from the dispenser as Dale pulled her arm and led the way out of the store. The two of them limp-ran down Nostrand, dipping around the first corner they could, and then another, until they were sure they were far enough away from the shop owner to slow their pace.

"I gotta get back home," Grace said, slightly out of breath from the sprint and the fear.

"I know, but listen, Grace, I need to see you. Tonight." She shook her head, but before she could get in a word, he shushed her, putting his finger on her lips. "Listen to me: my parents are sending me away soon to go stay with a family friend in Atlanta until I start college. They're afraid the pigs are going to figure out who I am and come get me for protesting yesterday."

First came the nose stinging, a warning of the impending tears. Then, the tears. Aside from Miss Ada Mae, Dale was the only somebody who saw Grace—who, despite his oft single-track focus on things that hardly registered on Grace's list of concerns, bothered to say and show he cared about her. She was suffocating without her mother, without Maw Maw, without place, without love. Dale was air.

"I'll be at my buddy James's house. My parents are scared for me to leave home but I talked them into letting me go over to his place to say goodbye before I leave. They don't know his parents went down south for a couple weeks to visit family. I'm going to go over there and cool out for a while. I want you to come with me."

"I don't know," Grace said, wringing her hands. "Auntie Hattie is plenty mad wit me. She barely let me out the house to get her cigarettes. I gotta go, Dale. She waitin'."

"Just come to four-three-two Williams Street. Nine o'clock. Promise me you'll try."

"But . . ."

"Promise me."

Grace pressed her face into his cupped hands as he drank her in. She could smell on his breath the maple syrup he'd drowned his pancakes in and swallowed down before he slipped out the basement door to survey what, if anything, was happening in the smoldering streets. Grace wanted to taste that sweet on his lips, and so she did just that, savoring the taste as she lingered on the fatty part and waited for his tongue. "I promise," she said when he pulled back. "I'll try."

Grace stood in the doorway of the kitchen, staring at Aunt Hattie's chest as it lumbered up and then down and up and then down. Her aunt was spread out precariously on the couch—one leg and foot dangling over the side, one arm sticking straight out from beneath her head, which she'd propped onto a decorative velvet pillow. Her snore—loud, crackly, steady—made Hattie's body rub and squeak against the plastic sofa covering, a symphony of noise that accompanied the rumble of air and snot that forced itself through Hattie's throat and chest and nostrils. Grace watched with a wrinkled brow and her hand on her own nose, sure that the passageways carrying air to Hattie's burned like coal. Black, like her heart.

Hattie was exhausted, having spent the day making phone call after phone call, trying to redeem herself, her reputation, and her business. It had taken only one good slap across her cheek for Grace to figure out it would be best to huddle down in the basement, as far away from her aunt as she could get, while Aunt Hattie argued, begged, promised, and denied culpability in the mess Dale's mother had laid at her doorstep. No matter how Hattie shined it up and presented it, the truth of it all wasn't good enough for those who pointed fingers, and as Hattie slowly began to realize that alliances had been made and redemption in the court of public opinion would likely prove elusive, she started searching for salvation at the bottom of a bottle of corn. Three quarters of the way through, that bottle transformed from escape to sedative, giving Grace the opening she needed to steal away and find reprieve in Dale's arms. Grace was scared—scared her aunt would wake up and find her missing, scared she would get swept up in the riots outside, which had ratcheted back up almost as quickly as the sun had found its rest. But neither outweighed her desire to get her air, her Dale. And so, after checking to see that her aunt was in deep slumber, Grace snuck a light sweater from Aunt Hattie's closet and creeped down the stairs to avoid the creaks, quietly pulled open the back door leading out into the small backyard garden, and stepped into the open air.

Rather immediately, Grace saw the shadowy figure pressed against the brick; her scream might not have been heard by her aunt, but surely the Millers, who were out talking to their back neighbors over the fence about how the overwhelming noise and smoke rising into the Brooklyn air sounded like war, would have heard it if he hadn't used his palm to muffle her scream. Fear made bile burn Grace's throat and nostrils, but when the shadowy figure said, "Shhh, Gracie, I got you, be calm," she instantly devolved into a heap of breath and adrenaline.

"Listen to me, Gracie, it's okay. You're okay," Dale whispered quickly. "I came to get you because I didn't want you walking to James's house by yourself. It's dangerous out here."

"I 'on't think we should go," she said as soon as he took his hand off her mouth. "What if we get caught out here by the police? What if my auntie wake up? If they don't kill us, she will."

Dale shushed her and grabbed her fingers with his hands. "Grace, do you trust me?"

More than anything in this current iteration of her world, she did. Grace nodded yes.

"Where's your auntie?"

"She's on the couch, sleeping. Drunk."

"Good. Good. Hold on to me. I know how to get us there without us being seen, and I'll have you back in plenty time before your aunt knows you're gone," he said.

The couple said not one word as Dale weaved them through alleys and backyards and side streets covered by night, the result of the city's neglect. Despite repeated requests that the streetlamps be tended to in the mostly Black neighborhood, New York City's Department of Transportation was much too busy answering to the needs of those who lived in the truly affluent Brooklyn Heights neighborhood just four miles over, and on any other evening, Dale would have had a half-hour-long soliloquy about said neglect primed for a choir—the likes of whom were just blocks away, throwing rocks and being bitten by dogs and police batons—but on this night, he seemed singularly focused on getting himself and Grace to safety.

Finally, they climbed through a small hole between a row of boxwoods separating the backyards of two modest brownstones. Dale looked over both his shoulders as he rushed toward a small flowerpot on the back porch. He quickly fished out a key and used it to push his way through the door of the house, dark save for a kitchen light left on by the house's occupants to make the rest of the neighborhood think they were home, rather than seven hundred miles away in Orangeburg, South Carolina. Grace didn't take a single breath until Dale peeped around corners to double-check that they were, indeed, alone, and said, "We're good."

"Come here," he said, folding Grace into his arms. "We made it. I told you I got you."

They stood there, breathing each other in, swaying to a rhythm that couldn't be heard but certainly was felt. "Wait! I got something for you!" Dale said suddenly, pulling from their embrace. He reached into his jacket pocket and pulled out a multicolored candy necklace. Grace felt her lips spread across the whole of her face.

"I love to see you smile," he said, turning her chin up to his. He ran the back of his fingers across her blackened eye; she recoiled, but he touched it anyway. Gently. And then kissed her. Gently.

She took the necklace out of his hand and dropped it over her hair and around her neck. "Thank you," she said simply.

"Hey, we should go down into the basement. No telling who can see in the windows and I don't want James's nosy neighbors to think there's a break-in. We don't need anybody knocking." Grace tried, but she couldn't hide her concern. "Don't worry," Dale said, as if reading her body language. "It's nice down there, and safe. Nobody will know we're there."

That was one item on Grace's list of chief concerns, but she didn't say that out loud. Instead, she took his hand and followed him down the steps.

The room downstairs was modest but prettier than anything Grace had seen back home, even the houses she'd dusted and polished up and in which she'd chased around children who were in her charge. Wood paneling draped each of the walls and the face of a bar that stood sentry in the far corner of the room. A series of diamond-shaped mirrors struck a stately pattern on the back wall, giving all who faced that direction a clear-eyed view of the brown bar stools, a plush, lime green sofa, a cocktail table stacked with board games and ashtrays, and two teenagers who did not belong there and were nervous about that fact. Grace fiddled with her candy necklace as she stared first at the room, and then herself, and then Dale, who'd been watching her take it all in. "Nice, huh?" he said. "Me and James come down here and hang out with our friends. His parents are cool about it, so long as we don't tear up the place. One time, Ellison got into a fist fight with Tommy and they smashed into the wall right about there," he said, pointing to their right, "before they fell into one of the stools. Broke one of the legs clean off. I don't know how we did it, but we hurried up and got some glue and put it back together. It was all good until James's big brother sat on it. Smashed it to pieces. Their parents still think he broke it." Dale shook his head and chuckled at the memory. Grace looked down at her shoes. "Anyway," Dale said, like he was looking to lighten the heavy room. "You want to play a game?"

He rushed over to the cocktail table and called off the offerings: "Let's see, they got Monopoly, The Game of Life, Checkers." He laughed big. "Ohhhh! They got Twister!"

"What game is that?" Grace asked, walking over to check out the box.

"It's this game where you spin the arrow and whatever color it lands on, that's where you have to put your hands and feet." Grace felt the look of confusion that took control of her face. "It sounds weird but it's crazy fun. You'll see."

In no time, Dale and Grace were a jumble of giggles and intertwined limbs, feet and hands slipping across plastic, grazing each other's bodies, his shirt, her skirt, flopping about, exposing skin and awkwardness and, somewhere along the way, desire that whirled in circles as quickly as the plastic arrow on the cardboard spinner—all air and lightness and target. And when they landed in a heap, her foot having slid across the plastic mat, her body on top of his, his lips against hers, her tongue licking his, his hand rubbing on her thigh, her hand caressing his bulky chest, his fingers stroking the pink of her panties, her breath heavy on his neck, his private parts heavy on her private parts, her scream muffled in his neck, his sweat dripping down, down, down onto her forehead and her cheek and her neck, her insides bearing down on the sharpness, his moans sounding the alarm in her ear, her blood gushing where they lay, she saw stars and space and time—a burst of energy that rained down a divine . . . perfect . . . light.

She knew.

Grace knew that together, what she and Dale had created was love.

9

Now some might call it plain old dumb luck that Grace got pregnant the first time she had sex, when she was neither trying nor all that sure how an innocent game with Dale had put her square on the road to being somebody's mama. Hattie, well, she would call it plain dumb. First thing came out her mouth when Grace had first darkened her door were the threats and the warnings: "Being here is an opportunity," she'd said, sounding more angry than welcoming. "You better treat it as such. Keep your head down and your legs closed. Stupid country gals come up here all the time, wide-eyed and fast—nine months later, they're right back in the dirt where they started. Only somebody who'll be bringing babies into this house will be me, understand?"

But for Grace, the marriage of seed and egg, its journey to womb and growth in the belly—a baby, life—that was a miracle. That much she'd come to understand by watching Maw Maw's work, sure, but also from having Maw Maw reluctantly explain to her the what of it all—of sex and new life. Grace had been about the age of seven or eight; she'd stumbled in on a friendly visit Ben Charles had been paying Bassey out in the woodshed—the kind of visit not meant for children's eyes. The kind of visit that absolutely demanded explanation.

With the promise of a warm slice of Maw Maw's shoofly pie, Grace had been anxious to complete her pre-dinner chores, so she could get to her dessert all the quicker, and so she went to the woodshed to gather up a few pieces of chop for the stove, only to walk in on her mother bent over the pile, dress hiked up to her waist, hollering like Mr. Charles was beating her tail, but with his waist instead of his strap. His pants, well, they were around his ankles, the belt still in the loops, so he definitely wasn't hitting her with his strap, Grace surmised as she tried to make what she was seeing fit with what she thought was actually going on. It was Bassey, in a throw of passion, twisting her neck as she grabbed hold of Ben's ass, who saw Grace first.

"Get yo' lil' fast ass on!" she'd yelled.

As if startled, Ben's eyes quickly traveled to where Bassey's were trained; he had wrinkled his brow, but his body continued on, like that part of him was unaware that it was wrong to do adult things in front of a little girl. Bassey—well, it seemed never to have occurred to any part of her body that stopping was a consideration. Grace had seen what she'd seen, but little girls who grow up in the sticks of the South saw a lot of things they didn't need to before their time, and they learned to get over them, too. Quickly.

Grace had taken off running, scared more for her mother's safety than she was of her mama's ire. She'd sought refuge in Maw Maw's arms.

"What ail you, gal?" she'd asked, pushing Grace from her body and inspecting her head to toe, looking for injury, bruise, blood.

"That man out there beating on Mama," Grace said. Terror stretched from eyebrow to pupil, down to her nose and thick pink lips.

"What man?" Maw Maw had said. She'd grabbed her shotgun and was at the door before she could finish asking the question. But she stopped equally fast at that door as she made out two figures by the woodshed— one smoothing down her skirt, the other pushing his belt through the buckle, both giggling and wiping sweat and chests heaving up, down, up, down. When Bassey finally looked up and saw her mother standing in the doorway, shotgun cradled in her rough hands, she grabbed Ben by the arm and led him in the other direction, back out into the street. Back where he came from.

Maw Maw took a deep breath and slowly turned to her granddaughter. Truth, no matter how harmful, embarrassing, was her virtue. She just hadn't seen herself telling this particular truth to an eight-year-old. But she did it.

"He wasn't hurting your mama, baby," she'd said simply, putting her shotgun back in its place. "They was just doing what grown folk do."

"I don't understand, Maw Maw," said Grace.

"Well, when a man and a woman want to show how much they like each other, they kiss and hug."

"Like how you kiss and hug me and Mama?" Grace asked.

"It's a little different than that, baby," Maw Maw said, pulling Grace close. "Set down and let Maw Maw talk to you a spell."

Eyes wide as saucers. Wrinkled brows. Hand-wringing. Poom-pooms and pee-pees. Holes and pushing. Seeds and eggs and little babies turning into big babies in stomachs that drop into Maw Maw's hands, grow up big and strong and look for somebody to love and love them back and use poom-pooms and pee-pees to grow more babies like bees and things make flowers. It was a five-minute explanation, but it traversed the terrain of an hours-long lecture.

Finally, after everything had been said and the air got thick with quiet, Grace asked the obvious. "Do Mama love that man?"

Maw Maw could do many things but explaining sex and pleasure out of the context of marriage to an eight-year-old, well, that wasn't one of them. "You go on out there and get that wood now, hear?" she had said to Grace, pushing herself up from her chair. "Supper be ready soon and you not gone want to bathe in cold water, is you?"

"No, ma'am," Grace said.

"Well, then you best get the wood for the water."

Bassey, upon hearing that Maw Maw had explained the birds and all the bees to her child, bucked. "You ain't have the right to tell that baby that!" she said. "She don't need to be knowing all that!"

"She ain't need to see it either, but here we are," Maw Maw said simply, unbothered by her daughter's tone.

"I got needs, Mama," is all Bassey could say.

Neither would ever understand the impact the entire affair had on Grace seven years later—how Maw Maw's words about babies being the evidence of love between a man and a woman would dance a jig in her brain in the days following her encounter with Dale. She'd wake from wet dreams in both the still of night and in the morning time, when the birds started singing their songs and ladybugs tickled the mops of purple hydrangea scrubbing against the window; Grace would hump pillows and the armrest of Hattie's couch, her panties wet with anticipation and memory and want. Maw Maw hadn't mentioned that part—the wanting. But it was as real as the nausea that quickly settled in the space between her left rib and the right, as tangible as the subtle buzz that settled behind her belly button, just above the part of her stomach that felt like Thanksgiving after she had pushed herself back from the plate she'd greedily relieved of its beans and rice and cornbread and extra ham hocks. The fullness, the evidence of the evidence, it was immediate. Grace knew her body. She knew her heart. She knew she wanted both Dale and his baby—that she would love them with the same fervor with which she had loved Maw Maw and Bassey, the feeling of soil on her soles, the way rainbows danced around the sun.

Grace aimed to tell him—she just didn't know how. Dale, he was gone—this she knew for sure after passing by his house a couple times, hoping to see him, hoping he'd see her, only to arrive on the last of those occasions just in time to watch Dale's parents hustle him and his suitcases into a light blue Buick with Georgia plates. They were too preoccupied with their teary goodbyes to notice her; Grace's eyes were too watery to catch that someone—Miss Ada Mae—had walked up to her side. Grace smelled her first; gardenias, just like back home. She reached for Grace's arm and the girl jumped at her touch.

"Shh . . . don't say nothing," Miss Ada Mae said. "Come with me," she added, gently pulling Grace by the arm into a small alley between an empty bar and a furniture store with a boarded-up storefront that had been run all through in the riots.

"I have to get home," Grace said, pulling her arm. "I'mma get in mo' trouble if I stay out here."

"Don't worry yo' pretty head, now, I'm not going to keep you long," Miss Ada Mae said. "That boy ran me down and made me promise to give you this," she added, as she shoved an envelope between Grace's two hands. She placed both her own hands on top of Grace's and pulled her close—let her eyes wash over each of the welts and bruises pockmarking Grace's face and down the girl's neck and chest and belly and back up to her eyes. Now she knew, too, and where there had been worry on her lips, there was joy. "Oh, Simbi is dancing!" she said as she rested her hands on Grace's belly. "Oh, you sweet, sweet girl, this is a blessing!"

Miss Ada Mae pulled Grace into her bosom and folded her into an embrace the likes of which Grace hadn't experienced even once since she'd crossed the state line into New York. She had craved this very specific affection, this storge, for so very long, but it proved elusive in Hattie's cold home, and eventually it began its slow fade, disappearing, even, from her dreams, until there was nothing but empty where love was once so natural, so pure, it didn't need to be a thought. It just was.

At first, Grace resisted what she couldn't remember. But muscle memory is strong and quick. Where there was struggle, now there was surrender. Grace let her body and her tears surrender into Miss Ada Mae.

"Now you listen to me and you hear me good, hear?" Miss Ada Mae said. "This ain't fittin' to be no cakewalk. But you not alone. Remember what you already know. You got everything you need right there inside you. Call your people to you, baby. They don't know anything other than how to do right by you." She pulled Grace from her breasts and, with her hands on either of Grace's shoulders, she stared into the girl's eyes, her soul. "Trust that with everything you have in you, understand?" she said.

"Yes'm," was all Grace could muster.

"Go on now," she said. She gave Grace's face one last gentle caress that Grace would long for when, later that night, tucked in the basement, having procured a break from Hattie's anger, she read Dale's simple, succinct note, which said, "I'm leaving for Morehouse, Grace. I'm sorry we didn't have more time." The words were an arrow to her heart.

And then Grace was alone again. But this time, it was different. A baby—her baby—was coming, and Grace just knew that her little baby and all the love that child would bring to its mama would save her.

It was easy enough for Grace to hide her growing belly from Hattie and anyone else looking. That was the beauty of growing into that country gal thick, all booty and thigh and jiggle everywhere. The belly, it fit a sixteen-year-old from the sticks of Virginia. Hattie noticed but dismissed it with her usual insults and general abrasiveness: "Your greedy is catching up to you. Might want to push away from the plate every once in a while," she said one night when Grace lifted her arms in such a way that shifted her shirt just so, exposing her belly. Hattie caught sight of the bump out of the corner of her eye, and then stared at the helpings Grace had heaped on her plate. "You around here eating like you got a full-time job."

The nausea, the pulsing, aching breasts spilling out of her already worn bra, the butterfly flutters morphing into little heels, palms, booty skimming her uterus, leaving imprints against her stomach, hanging on her ribs—hiding all of that was a different proposition. Grace tried hard to remember what Maw Maw kept on hand for expectant mothers whose babies turned their stomachs, and she would sneak a little of it for herself when she could without Hattie noticing. A few mint leaves in her pocket to chew on when she felt the throw-up winding itself up to her esophagus. A real good scratch or two on lemon peels, so the smell would stay up under her fingernails. A whiff of that here and there helped. But Grace knew time would come when she wouldn't be able to hide—knew that she would be all stomach and wobble and whatever that pain was that made Mrs. Brodersen cry out for her God and hang on to the sides of the bed so tight her knuckles turned to cotton—that would be her lot. That scared her. Not the pain, but the discovery. The response. The judgment that was sure to come—the whispers and lowered eyes that would turn to stares boring a hot hole into her belly. The misunderstanding of the miracle and how a baby made in love was everything good.

In the meantime, Grace knew what she had to do. With barely two months to go before she gave birth to her and Dale's child, and with barely anything to her name or complete autonomy over her own body, Grace's mothering instinct activated. She hunkered down, sought refuge, recounted again and again what Miss Ada Mae had said to her—prayed in the way that she knew how. It did not take her long to gather what she needed; there was the faded black-and-white picture of Hattie and Bassey that Grace had dug up from a box tucked away in Hattie's basement, Maw Maw's pipe, filled with tobacco Grace had carefully saved from the cigarette butts her aunt snuffed out in ashtrays throughout her brownstone, the floral print handkerchief Mr. Aaron had wrapped that pipe in when he slipped it into the food bag he'd sent with Grace for her journey up north. A glass of water. A small piece of cornbread. Prayers. Prayers. Prayers and secrets, whispered in the corner of the junk closet where spiders and all Hattie's memories went to die, but also where Grace bartered for her child's life. From her ancestors, she sought counsel and favor, just like Maw Maw had taught her to do when she was just a wee bit: "You set out your food, first, see?" Maw Maw had said sweetly as she placed a tin plate with beans and a few scoops of rice atop a smooth patch of dirt blanketing the simple pine box in which her mother's body lay. "And then you take something special—something meant to call them to you and remind you of the one you missing. You set that down, and then you put your water next to that. See how Maw Maw doing that?"

"Yes'm," Grace had said. She fiddled with her skirt as she watched Maw Maw arrange the assortment like a bouquet on the grave.

"Now, you thank them for watching over you and ordering your steps. They mean good by you. You just got to let them know you know and mean it, understand?"

"Yes, Maw Maw," Grace had answered, eyes fixed on the pipe dangling from her grandmother's lips.

"This here a conversation," Maw Maw had said, smoke floating from her lips and nose, floating on her words. "Talk to your dead. Do it out loud. Your peoples will answer you back and lead you to the light."

Grace would learn over time and with practice that it mattered neither the day nor time for these talks; there was no waiting for Sundays and church pews or tents at the summer revivals. Pipes were lit at sunrise on a Tuesday, at midnight when hearts needed tending; potlikka was placed in cups with a scoop of biscuit when birthdays came along. Didn't make any never-mind; it was always the right time to talk to the dead. But Maw Maw had warned, sometimes the company one kept dictated when these moments were lived out loud; God-fearing Christians just couldn't see the hypoc-risy of falling to their knees and praying to a dead white man who existed solely in the pages of a dusty old book while simultaneously marking the heads of those who speak to the spirits for which their hearts longed. That made tending to the dead a solitary matter—asking them for help a quiet, personal proposition. And so to spare herself the wrath of Hattie and any-one else who valued Jesus over their own blood, Grace did what she was taught to do: she told her secrets in corners.

Grace carefully laid out her offerings, then struck the match and in-haled deeply, puffing on the pipe like she remembered Maw Maw had done when she visited graves and talked to the dirt and the water and the trees. The heat of the tobacco smoke burned Grace's chest, coaxing a cough she quickly tried to tamp so as not to wake Hattie. Her aunt, passed out drunk on the floor directly above Grace's head, had already set the law on such matters. "Don't think you're going to bring that mess into my house, hear?" she'd said the first time she found a pile of Black-eyed Susans and some leftover spoonbread on a paper plate perched on a small coffee table in the basement. Hattie was familiar. She also was keenly aware that the old southern ways had no place in her new northern disciplines. She'd slammed the plate and its contents into the bottom of the metal trash can just outside the back door and then pushed her way back into the house and up the stairs, leaving a teary Grace in her wake.

But now, a pregnant Grace's need to commune was bigger than her fear of her aunt. Her charge was to draw to her Bassey and Grandma Lizbeth and all the ancestors who kept her spiritual being in their care. She intended to thank them for her miracle and also for favor. For herself. For her child—this marvel that traversed treacherous terrain it was not meant to survive, hurdling every physical obstacle and a mountain of emotional distress to become a being. To become Grace's someone. She had but one simple appeal: that in all things, her baby would have the joy Grace once had. That she longed for. The family, the home she needed like air.

The moment she made the petition, a picture show, grainy, dark, staticked its way into her line of sight. Grace struggled to make out what was what, at first, and then there was Bassey, smiling just as pretty, in her favorite dress, the white one with the flowers, holding her belly with one hand, pointing at Grace's with the other. Bassey was beaming, proud. Grace could feel that—could feel the tingle in the pads of her fingers, the tips of her swollen breasts and toes. Her little baby felt it, too—got to shifting around in Grace's stomach like it was backstroking across space and time to smile up in its grandmama's face. Bassey tossed back her head and laughed big— from her chest.

"Mama," Grace said sweetly, "where Maw Maw?"

Bassey's laugh was a flower, perking up and stretching toward the morning sun; her shoulders shook from its intensity. She spoke no words, but the glint in her eye was light—a tome of precise messages Grace had waited years to hear: *She is strong. The ancestors are at her back. Don't you worry. Don't you worry. Don't you worry. Focus on your joy.*

It was in her quest to follow her mother's directive that Grace, in the middle of her thirty-second week of pregnancy, was finally found out. The baby clothes she'd been sewing from scraps of fabric that had been stacked in Hattie's basement closet, that's what betrayed her. Hattie, who was slowly working her way back into the community that, the prior summer, had turned her out, was looking to sew herself a new outfit—something she'd decided to make based off a pattern she'd found in Woolworth's. It looked elegant, refined. Perfect, considering she no longer could afford to buy outfits off the rack. A humble return to the pastime Hattie had eschewed. She'd long ago thrown her sewing machine and materials in the back of her basement storage closet—a necessary step in her immersion into Black Brooklyn society. But times were hard, and her shunning hit not only her pride, but her pockets. There would be no more trips to department stores—no more money spilled on fine clothing and shoes purchased to impress. She had to get back to what she knew. On this particular day, she woke up from one of her drunken spells ready to sew herself something fine. Something body skimming and tight. Demure, she'd decided, wouldn't keep her warm at night.

It was the neat of the closet that caught hold of her attention first. She was in a rage when she shoved what she loved into that hole—tossed it all in in a heap along with a photo album or two of pictures that served as evidence of her former life, the one she'd left behind, tried desperately to deny even existed. Hattie had shoved all of it in that dark closet and slammed it shut, pretending it, too, never was. But there was that fabric, all of it neatly folded and organized by color, piled on top of the machines and topped with garments she hadn't herself sewn. Little tiny things that she had no use for. And next to that, an assortment of items, distinctively laid out—that looked and smelled and called out . . . home.

Hattie ran her fingers across the tin of water and also the pipe and lifted the latter to her nose—inhaled deep and was transported to Black Rose and the woods and the dirt graves and the cool of the water on her ankles when she was little and she and Bassey held hands as Rubelle talked to the winds and asked them for favor. The memory soothed—daresay coaxed the corners of her lips to lift ever so slightly. But the feeling, it was fleeting; Hattie's mouth quickly reverted back to its persistent scowl when she spotted the baby clothes; she picked them up between pointer finger and thumb, as if they were rancid—nasty to the touch. She did the same with that black-and-white photo of herself and Bassey—the one she'd warned that thickheaded girl to put away—that was now right there in her face again. Reminding her of what she'd lost in Virginia. What she'd tried to forget in Brooklyn. And then Hattie was fire.

Enraged, Hattie took the pile of baby clothes and the pipe and the photo into her hands and ran back up the steps two at a time, so anxious was she to get to Grace. And when she found her in the kitchen, draped in an oversize floral dress and a heavy sweater, hands dipping a dishcloth into hot soapy water, she heaped the items at Grace's back with all the force she could muster, then, before Grace could even begin to process that something was happening, much less what it was, Hattie spun the girl around, snatched open her sweater, and squeezed her belly. Grace's stomach, small but bulbous beneath the fabric and Hattie's fingers, pushed back, meeting force with force.

Hattie jumped back, looked Grace dead in the face, and, after a beat, smacked her charge so hard with the back of her hand that spit sailed through the air, landing on the breakfast dishes the young mother-to-be had just washed clean.

Had she been in her right mind, had she employed the logic and cunning that had bought her the favor on which she had staked her new life up north, Hattie would have thought better of what she did next. But rage, jealousy, they are an intoxicating mix that can make one neglect subtlety for more direct, contemptable pursuits. With no coat to speak of in twenty-one-degree weather, house slippers slapping against the sidewalk still wet from an early morning rain, Hattie stomped and slipped and stomped down the street, her pregnant young niece sliding behind her, knowing better than to struggle, scared of what was to be in the next moments. When they turned the corner at Nostrand and made their way toward the Spencer house, Grace finally tried, albeit unsuccessfully, to struggle from Hattie's grip. "No, no, no, no," was all Grace could think to say as she pulled and writhed beneath Hattie's fingers. But it was to no avail. This was happening.

"Lucinda Spencer!" Hattie yelled from the bottom of the steps, Grace looking on, mortified and still trying to extricate herself. "Lucinda Spencer, I know you hear me! Get out here!"

There was a tiny movement from the curtains—subtle but noticeable. That made Hattie yell louder and Grace wriggle a little harder as the woman struggled up the stairs, her little niece still firmly in her grip. "Lucinda Spencer, if you don't open up this door, the whole neighborhood gone find out the dirt your goody-two-shoes son did before he slipped out of town. You better come on here!"

Not soon after, the front door opened slowly to reveal Mrs. Spencer, barefaced and in curlers, an elegant silk nightgown draped down to her ankles, a cigarette dangling from her delicate, manicured fingertips. Eyes locked with Hattie's, she took a long drag of her cigarette and blew the smoke from her mouth and nose directly into her loud, unwelcomed visitor's face. Undeterred, Hattie pulled Grace in front of her and snatched open her sweater. Mrs. Spencer stared at Hattie for a lifetime before finally letting her eyes fall to where her nemesis was drawing her attention. Mrs. Spencer stared as she took another drag of her cigarette and stared some more as she let the smoke roll over her tongue and, again, through her nostrils. She let her eyes slowly trace from Grace's belly, up to her swollen breasts, up to her fat face, nose spread wide, a universe of pimples dotting her skin, up to Grace's own eyes, puffy with fear and grief. She scoffed, flicked her cigarette, took one delicate step backward, and slammed the door in Hattie and Grace's faces.

10

⁕

No one sings lullabies for sixteen-year-old colored gals with babies in their bellies. There are no melodies with promises hung on stars, no moonlight kisses and a word about the dawn—how the sun will rise in the morning and shine, shine, shine on the mamas and the children who stack the muscle and make the world strong. They are neither home nor future, they are no one's merry, pious dream. Their bellies betray their imperfection. They are wild. They are to be tamed. At all cost, they will be tamed.

Hattie assumed the position with great haste—was running around telling anybody with ears and a second's worth of time to spare her woeful tale of how, out of allegiance to family, she'd exposed her heart, only to have the organ ripped from her body and stomped by a no-count niece she didn't even really know. "That gal came in here like a boll weevil. Just ruined my whole crop. Now I have to be responsible for her little bastard baby?" she'd hollered from the stoop at an acquaintance who'd paused at Hattie's iron gate to get and give gossip and such. Hattie's words floated on the cold March air, finding their way through crack and crevice and straight to the ears of those who took delight in clucking about the jezebel who was out there whoring and carrying on—carrying sin.

None were aware they were stepping stones toward Hattie's own redemption. She was carrying the weight of having to answer for her niece's sexual proclivities, but with just the right mix of air and water she could both feed and tamp the scandal's fire to her will, a skill that did a yeoman's job of rescuing her reputation from the ashes. Grace's pregnant belly, full with the evidence of her scurrilous, wholly indecent ways, absolved Hattie from the public shaming she'd faced just months earlier. There was no controlling a fast-ass country hussy, everybody knew that. Lucinda Spencer, anxious to reframe her son as victim rather than willing participant and expectant father, made sure of it. "Oh, goodness—that could be anybody's baby," she'd said again and again, her words skipping like a scratched record to magnify their importance, even as she waved her hand in blithe dismissal. "There's no telling who she laid down with or how many."

Reframing Grace's narrative was easy enough. Neither Lucinda's nor Hattie's theatrics were even necessary, really; God himself could have done Grace like he did Mary and produced the second coming, and still, Grace would have been a pariah. Neighbors, acquaintances, strangers, none of them had an ounce of gentleness to spare for her. Even the nurses at the clinic, sworn to care for and extend kindness to their charges, tucked both away when Grace and her belly stood before them. "This is a whole world of trouble she done got y'all in, isn't it?" one said to Hattie as she tossed a patient's robe past Grace's outstretched hands and onto the examination table.

"Yes, indeed," said Hattie, who'd taken Grace to the clinic to have her and the baby checked out—not because she cared about their health so much as it afforded her another instance to play martyr. "You can't imagine what I've gone through behind all this."

"Oh, I know it," the nurse said. "All these young girls coming in here, missing their morals, dragging their poor families down into the gutter with them. Barely know how to wipe their own behinds, and here they come with all these babies for everybody else to look after."

Grace stood there, absorbing the verbal blows, her spirit sinking into the hard faux leather examining table. She could feel her heartbeat pounding in her chest as her tongue thickened; she knew better than to say a single word beyond "Yes'm" and "No, ma'am" and whatever basic information the nurse asked of her to fill in the medical chart, but her body was demanding more of her. Her baby shifted its weight and stretched, dragging its foot across its mother's groin, as if it could hear every slight. As if its mother's pain were its pain—her stress was its stress. Both writhed in discomfort.

"Well, don't just sit there looking dumb, get undressed and put the robe on," Hattie said. She gave a curt smile to the nurse and shook her head.

Sensing Grace's hesitation, she piled on. "Don't get shy with it now. Clearly, you weren't shy about taking your clothes off all those months ago for that boy."

The baby hooked a foot on Grace's rib and stretched its butt against her stomach, forming a bulging circle against her bulbous belly. Grace's gentle rub coaxed the bulge into retreat, but the pain of it all was acute. Grace took a few cleansing breaths, forgetting, however briefly, how the adults' dug chunks out of her spirit.

The door flung open as she struggled to fit herself into the robe. She quickly pulled the fabric as best she could over her naked body as the doctor took the nurse's chart, looked it over, looked at her, looked at it, looked at her. "And this is the first time she's seeing a doctor for her pregnancy?" he asked.

"Yes," Hattie said. "She hid it from me for months, otherwise I would have brought her sooner."

"Frankly, where she needs to be is Booth Memorial," he said as he pushed Grace back on the table. Like she was an inanimate object. Like her body was not hers. "They take care of the girls there, help them have their babies. Heal their minds. She can put the past behind her, and the babies get the chance for a future. A good life. The nurse can give you some information about it on the way out." Then, to Grace: "Put your feet in the stirrups," he said, patting the cold metal footrests. Then to Hattie: "Now if you'll excuse me."

Grace, having eyed the collection of hooks and knives and forceps splayed on a tiny table next to the doctor, tried to control the tremors coursing through her body as she lay under his probes and fingers and dead eyes, but her attempts proved fruitless. The doctor explained nothing, said not a word. Under his hand, her body was an incubator—a machine—something to be explored but not discussed. Not with her. On the paper, for formality's sake, sure. But he had already decided her narrative before he darkened the doorway, before he knew anything of her, and Grace could feel that. It was every bit as palpable as the snap the gloves made as he wriggled his fingers into the latex, every bit as tangible, shocking as the feel of those fingers on her inside. Grace wriggled. The baby wriggled. The doctor saw her tears. Nothing was said. That was the extent of their exchange.

Grace held tight to the robe and stared at the popcorn pattern in the ceiling as the doctor removed the gloves, washed his hands, gathered the paperwork, and walked out. She was unsure whether there would be more probing, so she lay there, deep breathing and rubbing her belly to calm the baby. Herself. Within moments, the door burst open, with a frantic Hattie rushing in, purse in one hand, fistful of papers in the other. "Get up from there, girl. The hell you still laying there for?" she snapped. "We have some things to discuss."

Hattie said not one word on the subway ride home—just took a seat on the crowded train and sat there with her purse and those papers while Grace stood holding tight to the pole, her belly flopping about with every creak of wheel on track. She knew not what to make of her aunt's pursed lips or what there was to talk about, and so her mind raced with queries and pronouncements: *Is my baby okay? Am I okay? What Hattie need to talk to me fo'? She ain't hardly said a word to me since she found out. Everyone staring. There are eyes everywhere. My stomach hurt.* Grace rubbed her belly. The woman sitting next to Hattie stared at Grace's stomach and then directly, boldly, into her eyes and shook her head. Grace slowly panned the train and found more of the same: men bathing her body with lasciviousness, women holding their children's hands tight, kissing their teeth. *Come on, little baby. It's gon' be okay. We gon' be okay.*

Grace barely made it across the threshold before Hattie pounced. "It's time you put some thought into what you're going to do with this little baby," she said, tossing her purse and the brochures on the cocktail table and unbuttoning her coat. "This is a burden you are not ready to bear."

"But I can take care of it, Auntie. I made a whole buncha clothes and diapers and I used to look after a bunch of babies back home and Maw Maw, she . . ."

"Rubelle is not here. I am."

Grace pressed her back against the front door and made herself small. It had been so long since she'd heard her grandmother's name on anyone's tongue. It was only at night, when silence settled over the dark and the baby wriggled in her womb, that Grace even allowed herself to think of

Maw Maw, so acute, so painful was her absence. When she squeezed her eyes tight and summoned the sweetness, Grace could feel Maw Maw's fingers in her hair, smell the earth in the sweat on her grandmother's neck, could see the way she leaned into her right hip when she stood looking out from the porch. For months, Grace had begged her grandmother to come to her in her dreams, to give her counsel. The rest of the time, there was only the quiet and the memories. Hearing her name, formal and angry on Hattie's tongue, laid reality at Grace's feet: it was just her and her baby. But she inquired all the same. "Is . . . is Maw Maw still . . . is she still alive?"

"We're in the middle of discussing something important, life-changing. What you bringing her up for?"

Grace dropped her head. "I . . . I was just wonderin' about how she . . ."

"She's fine, okay. The best any Negro can do in a prison with a five-year sentence over their head," Hattie snapped. "But we're not going to discuss that right now. Now I told you when you first stepped foot in my door: do not bring any babies into this house. And what you do, Grace? What did you do? I opened my home to you and all you've given me in return is shame," Hattie continued, unmoved by Grace's fear, sadness. She watched Grace wrap her arms around her belly and shook her head. "Tell you what: tomorrow, we're going to go down there to this place," she said, snatching off the table one of the brochures she'd been holding tight in her hand on the walk home, "and we're going to see about you staying there until that child comes. They're going to help you get yourself together, get a nice home for the baby . . ."

A sharp pain ripped through Grace's womb, like a serrated knife through watermelon rind. Grace grabbed her belly and buckled. "Aunt Hattie, please don't send me away. I want this baby. I'll do right by it, I swear," Grace said through gritted teeth, as the pain bore down.

"See? Look at you. You don't know how to have no baby, and you damn sure don't know how to raise one, either. And you won't be figuring it out on my watch. I didn't sign up for this shit here."

"But I can do it," Grace insisted. "I . . . I can get a job, something and . . ."

"A job where? Where are you going to work with a baby strapped on your back and limited education?" Hattie asked. She smirked. "There aren't any fields in Brooklyn."

"I . . . I was hoping you . . ."

"I suggest you stop that right now," Hattie sneered. "There is no hope for an unwed teenage mother out here. Get that through that thick head of yours." She was moved neither by Grace's cries nor the pain she was trying to breathe through. "Tomorrow. We're going to this place tomorrow," she said, tapping the brochure. "You go downstairs and get your things together, so that we can go over there first thing in the morning. The nurse said they have a few open beds and I intend to have you in one before lunchtime."

With that, Hattie slapped the brochure back down on the cocktail table and went into her room with not another word to spare.

Grace, bent over still from residual pain and the baby's kicking, stared at the brochure like it was one of those snakes in her grandmother's garden. She had to force herself to touch it, to look at the words, to understand what the "hospital" and Hattie intended to do. But the anguish, that came freely.

The blood did not bother Grace. Maw Maw Rubelle had gotten her used to it, early on, when she let her tend the stove at her first baby catching, way back when she saw her first blood trickle down her thigh. There it was, first the gush of water splashing on the bathroom tile, creeping along the crevices and into the holes around the sink and toilet that Hattie had long neglected to fill, and then the blood, crimson on both the snow-white toilet tissue and the pale side of Grace's fingertips. She watched that blood trickle down her thigh, dripping from her insides, thick and fertile and full with life that stretched and rumbled and announced its coming. Grace stopped and cocked her head and stared at the blood in wonder for just a moment, before the pain forced her to her knees. *Breathe*, Maw Maw whispered in her ear, and so Grace did, through her nose and out her mouth, through her nose and out her mouth, and then from her belly she forced pants, short and quick, past her lips. And then, there was another pain and then another, so sharp, so searing, there was no breath to give, only long, guttural sounds through knitted teeth and furrowed brow. Grace's knuckles could barely withstand the force she employed to hold on to both the commode and the bowl of the sink, the only things, it seemed, that were keeping her from falling face-first into the pool of water and blood puddled around her toes. The pain, it wouldn't let up. *Breathe,* Maw Maw said again, and so Grace did, again. When she could catch enough of her wind, she closed her eyes and saw her Maw Maw plain as day, scrubbing her hands and looking around . . . used the strongest voice she could muster to call out to Hattie, but it was of no use—much too small to travel from the bathroom, through to the front of the basement, up the steps, through the closed door, around the corner, past the kitchen, and behind a second closed door, where Hattie sat at her makeup desk, smoothing Noxzema on her skin and humming to Billie Holiday's "Good Morning Heartache." Grace, her baby, they were on their own.

Grace let go of the sink and turned her whole body toward the tub; she focused on the towel neatly folded across the tub's lip and reached for it as she rode another contraction, this one so intense, so breathtaking, she slammed both her hands into the pool of water and blood and cried out for all she loved, all she ever had: "Maw Maw. Mama. Please," she cried. "Please."

Push.

The pressure radiating from her private parts was almost too much to bear; Grace ceded her control over it and did what is natural and beautiful and a miracle to all living things: she grabbed tight and bore down.

Push, Maw Maw said.

Grace's poom-poom felt like fire and gush and skin ripping, rippling, stretching every which way. When she reached between her legs, her fingers slid across the bloody mound struggling toward the light, struggling to get free. Another push and that mound turned into eyes closed and nose and mouth and cheeks and curly hair swimming in fluid. Grace hoisted her body up into a squat and, while cradling the contents of her womb between both hands, she bore down once more and pushed with all her might and grabbed tight to the little body as it slipped its way from its cocoon of warmth and safety into a cold world that, the second it found out she had breath, would try to steal it away.

Grace, sobbing and heaving, sat on the floor and grabbed the towel off the tub; she wrapped it around the baby and kissed her head as the tiny being cried into her mother's breasts. Grace wiped the blood and gunk off the baby's face and sucked her nostrils to make it so her daughter could take in air between her gulps and her screams. "I love you so much, little baby," she said, holding her like it wasn't an option to let her go.

"Turn off those lights down there!" Hattie screamed from the other side of the door at the top of the basement steps, completely unaware that she'd just hosted Grace's miracle. Fixated on the stream of light coming from beneath the door and pegging it to what she quickly surmised was Grace's disregard for the cost of her light bill, Hattie screamed again and more, too, before she snatched the doorknob and made her way down the stairs. "Don't you hear me, gal?" she demanded. "Or are you just as deaf as you are tragic?"

Hattie turned the corner into the bathroom at the precise moment Grace, on all fours, was catching the placenta sliding out of her body. On the floor next to her was the baby, bloody, wrapped in Hattie's good white towel. "My God, Lawd Jesus, you done had the baby?" she asked, despite the answer laying in a bloody pool on the bathroom floor. "Why didn't you call me? How did you do this by yourself?"

Grace couldn't talk. Didn't want to. She laid the placenta, fully intact, on the floor and picked up her baby, watching with awe as the child rooted her head toward her breast, latched on, and suckled.

"My God, stay right there. Don't you move! I'm going to go get some towels and help you over to the bed. Stay there, okay?"

Grace nodded.

In the moments after that, Hattie, too, was new, handling Grace with gentleness and care as she cut the umbilical chord and helped Grace clean up and climb into fresh pajamas, and as she bounced the baby in her arms, cooing and inspecting her from her curly mop of hair to her fat cheeks and soft little fingers and toes. "You go on ahead and get yourself into the bed," Hattie said softly. It was a voice Grace had never heard Hattie direct toward her, never once in the entire two years she'd been in Brooklyn, except in her dreams. Hattie's tenderness took her aback. She could hardly make out the words. "Come on now, let me help you. The baby ate, she's full. Bathe and then go lay down and get you some rest. I'll watch her for you while you sleep."

"But what if she needs . . ."

"I'll be right here, don't you worry," Hattie said, bouncing the baby in her arms. "She's safe. I'm going to clean her up and wrap her up good. When she's hungry, I'll bring her back. From the looks of that bathroom, you've been through it. Let me help you."

Grace ran the back of her hand across the top of her baby's head and her cheek and kissed her forehead. She said not another word, but she kept her eyes on her child as she settled herself, as Hattie walked up the stairs, until all she could see was Hattie's back and then the door closing behind her. Grace stared at that wooden frame, too, until her eyes went limp and she could fight sleep no more.

The sun was yawning out the dawn when Grace's eyes flew open and she bolted upright in her bed. She thought she'd heard a single, loud handclap over her head, but when she could finally focus, she was the only one in the room. Like a fog slowly creeping in front of a headlight, the events of just a few hours before came back to her, the pain and the blood and the grunting and pushing. Maw Maw's voice. Her daughter. Grace tried to rise quickly from the bed but her body wanted no such parts of that folly. Instead, she creaked with the speed of someone who, not even a half day prior, pushed a human being out of her loins.

While she tried to lift herself from the bed, she made note of how neat everything was—bare. A tighter focus revealed the absence of everything: her comb, bonnet, lotion, sweater, shoes. There was only one dress and a pair of boots—the same outfit in which she arrived to Hattie's house—laid out neatly on the chair across from the bed. Confused, Grace went to the bathroom, wiped herself clean of afterbirth, pulled on the clothes that had been set out for her, washed her face, and, upon realizing her toothbrush and toothpaste were missing, tottered out the bathroom and stood staring at that wooden doorframe at the top of the steps.

It took Grace quite some time to hobble across the room. To hobble up those stairs. To pull the door open. To walk out into the open living room. To settle her eyes on the bag Mr. Aaron had sent with her up from Virginia, sitting there by the front door. Hattie sitting there on the sofa, in the corner, cool as she pleased, gently blowing the liquid in her teacup. Grace looked her in her eye and saw death. Frantic, she hobbled to the kitchen, then the small dining room and bathroom, then down the hallway, toward Hattie's room. "Where is she? Where is my baby? What did you do with her?" she screamed.

Hattie sipped her tea.

"My baby! Please! Where is she?"

Hattie gently sat her teacup on the saucer resting on the coffee table and rested her chin in her hand. "You know, one of these days, you'll see. And you'll thank me for saving your life."

The look of horror that creeped across Grace's face moved at the same speed as the loss of air in her lungs—the breaking of her heart.

"Now, now, no need to worry, she's in good hands, I saw to that myself," Hattie said quietly, matter-of-factly. She puckered her lips, blew the liquid, took a tentative sip. "I even put together a little petition for her, like they used to do back home. You must remember, don't you? I'm sure Rubelle showed you how. Always stuffing little things in pouches and such."

Grace stood there, frozen, in that same space of silence as when a child is popped hard and they're in a state of shock so immense they can't catch the breath stuffed in chest and throat and all the vital organs hold still, hold still, hold until toes tingle and chest burns and their owner thinks, surely, this is how death announces itself before the darkness comes.

"I used the pouch that ol' Aaron sent up here with you. And the rabbit's foot. Your grandmother's handkerchief. I told you to throw them out, but you don't listen," Hattie continued. Cool breath, gentle sip. "It's no nevermind. They came in handy. Your baby got a lil' piece of you with her. She will have a sweet, protected, prosperous life. That's what I wished for her in the petition, on your behalf, of course, but I wish her the same. I prayed over her, too, but the old way; that can't hurt things, I suppose."

Finally, the air released itself, Grace's frantic words, cries accompanying the gush. "Where is my baby?" she said over and over and over again as Hattie rose from the couch . . . and picked up Grace's bag and coat . . . and gripped Grace's shoulder . . . and opened the front door . . . and pointed at a beat-up blue Chevy sitting just beyond the gate. "No, no, no, no, no, where is my baby? You have to give me my baby!" Grace screamed as Hattie pushed her out the door.

Hattie slammed the bag and coat into Grace's chest and said words devoid of both emotion and volume that would forever ring in her niece's ears: "I don't have to do shit but stay Black and die. She will have a good life. I suggest you do the same."

And with that, Hattie stepped around Grace, pushed her from in front of her vestibule, and, with the fanfare of someone picking up a newspaper and going back in the house for morning coffee, closed the door behind her.

THE BOOK OF DELORES

1967–1999

11

It was hot as hell in the Right Church of God and Fellowship and LoLo, sweaty, clammy, was itching something terrible right around where her stockings clung to the meaty parts of her thighs, and no amount of fidgeting or swishing the worn-out cardboard funeral home fan in front of her face and neck could bring her relief. This, she thought, served her right. God didn't like her particular kind of ugly—meant for her to be uncomfortable. She'd lied to her Tommy, after all—the only somebody who'd done right by her, who loved her, who said he would do anything in this world for her—the one she'd got down on her knees and prayed and prayed to Emmanuel for when the sun climbed into the sky and when the moon did the same and so many times in between. The prayers, they were humble but specific, from the lips of a human who was woman and Black and therefore poor, powerless, and out of options: *Lawd, I know you are a good God, a generous God, who kept me in the land of the living when I thought I was surely gone die and wanted to. I come to you, humble as I know how, asking you to send me a man. A good, hardworking one who will be my shield against all hurt, harm, and danger and be willing to let me lay down some of these here burdens. In sweet Jesus's name.* So faithful was LoLo to this ritual, this begging for Jesus to bring her a good man, that she had to tend to her ol' knobby knees with gobs of Vaseline to keep them from getting hard and black on the worn linoleum floor of her tiny room in the basement of a good but strict Christian woman who took LoLo in when she escaped to New York. The prayers—what she was asking for—

they were meant to keep her heart from getting hard and black, too. Then, He delivered. There was Thomas Lawrence, standing before her with his ring and his steady paycheck and his love. His protection. He promised her that with him, she would never be hungry again, would never worry about where she would lay her head. Tommy promised LoLo forever, and she believed him. And after that, what she do? *What did she do?* Not six months after they said, "'Til death do us part," LoLo looked Tommy, her love, her husband, dead in his face and told him lies, and then got up the next morning and plopped her butt right there in the church pew, sitting up in the Lord's house like she ain't have a bunch of the devil sowed up in her bones. A crime and a shame.

LoLo smushed the back of her hand across her forehead, sopping up beads of sweat, and stared at the white Jesus painted on the wall-sized scroll behind Pastor's pulpit, His hands outstretched, blue eyes piercing directly into her own. She rocked and fanned, rocked and fanned, wiped her brow, stared at Jesus. *Don't cry, little baby,* she said to herself. *Don't cry. Forgive me, Lordy.*

LoLo had her reasons for lying. Good ones. She needed to hold on to Tommy. She'd had, after all, her share of relationship calamities—a line of men who would quickly declare their devotion and, just as easily, devolve into distorted collages—cutouts of men with small hearts, big fists, handsome faces, ugly ways, fancy suits with stinginess sewn up in the pockets. Zero desire to be men. To hold true to the exchange set and baked by thousands of years of gender roles shackled to the ankles of humans according to their genitalia: he earns, she keeps. No matter how she'd contorted herself to fit neatly into their ideal—the cooking, the cleaning, the organizing, the arranging, the mothering, the being the end-all-to-be-all—none of them had the glue to fashion themselves into the perfect piece of art for LoLo's frame. All they had to offer were the lessons; men were happy to take but could not be trusted to give, could not be counted on to hold up their end of the bargain. Closest she got to getting herself out of that squalid, one-room tenement she'd been suffocating in since escaping her cousin's house and stealing away up north was saying yes to Sharpe Williams's proposal. But even he, the best among the lot of men she ran through looking for her savior, couldn't work himself up to excuse her from the sole piece of this exchange she could not make.

"What you mean you can't have no babies?" he'd asked her, pushing her off his lap when she casually revealed the news to him.

"I just . . . can't."

"How you know? And why you just telling me this now?" he'd demanded. "We're supposed to be married in less than two weeks and you didn't think this would be something I need to know up front?"

It was a conversation—rather, explanation—that hung like a weight over each one of her relationships. Felt like her lovers smashed it down on her head, the gravity of her inability to plant their seed, to grow their flowers, all too much for them to bear. Too much for their manhood, which demanded her body—her womb—guarantee their legacies.

"Baby, I just thought this wouldn't be a big deal, you know? You traveled all during the war and got to see all the pretty parts most of us won't ever see in a lifetime," LoLo had said, picking up the pace of her words, moving directly into the space from which he'd pushed her, her breath sweet on his face. She lowered her eyes and slowly batted her lashes. She was hoping this would get him to a slow buy-in, rather than the quick walk away she'd gotten for all the others all those times before. She didn't want to lose Sharpe. Couldn't. "Don't you see? This is a blessing! We could travel to all those places and more, together. We won't have to worry about no babies and family and being tied down. Not having kids, it gives us wings."

"So, you been standing in my face, lying all this time, knowing you can't make no babies?"

"I . . . I didn't lie, honey, I just . . . I just kept that part quiet is all. I was always gonna tell you, Sharpe. I promise you, honey."

"But you know what kids mean to a man. To me. You know I want a family."

"I'm your family," LoLo had said. She stood up tall, squared her shoulders. "Ain't I enough?"

"The hell you talkin' 'bout, woman?" She'd seen Sharpe's softness—his center full of kindness and high regard for those he loved. LoLo also had witnessed his rage—saw him punch walls and run through tables and chairs to snatch up those who dared show even a smidge of disrespect. His eyes, already black, piercing, would have this midnight about them—a darkness. It was crouching in his iris as she stated her case. Made the little hairs on her forearms stand at attention. She thought he would hit her.

He did not. Instead, he disappeared. Not even a year later, she would see him rushing toward the door of the corner market, his hand on the small of the back of another woman, pretty and round and bright, waddling across the threshold, the sun gleaming off her wedding band just so.

LoLo promised herself she would not make the same mistake with Tommy. He was a player but also a hustler—dependable, quick. Fun. Demanding. The latter could, on occasion, be a lot to handle, but she didn't mind giving him exactly what he wanted—a hot meal, clean drawers, the promise of sex, even—because she'd taught him relatively early on to make sure she always had what she wanted: a man who would provide for and protect her in a world that would just as soon nail a Negro woman to a cross rather than afford her the basic ability to feed, house, clothe, and otherwise sustain herself. This wasn't so much about each other's happiness as it was the order of things. Earn. Keep. This is what LoLo had made clear to Tommy the first time he disappointed her—when she burst through his door, not a care in the world about who was there with him, and laid him flat for standing her up.

"I don't know who the hell you think you are, but let me tell you something, you ain't as special as you think you are," she'd said, standing in the threshold, the half-metal, half-screen door smacking against her behind. She had no intention of stepping into his little house and so there was no need to let the door close. She was mad as hell and had decided before she even stomped up to the front stoop that she was going to say what she needed to say and get the hell on.

"Whoa, whoa, whoa!" Tommy had said. His heart was in his throat, ushered there by fear for the sudden appearance of an intruder in his door and the thrill of seeing her standing there in his house, the tall, pretty, healthy, tender thing he'd rapped to just a few days before as he made his way to The Corner to put fifty cents on 976, the number he always played when he dreamed about death. He'd whistled. She had smiled. He stopped. She stopped. He said some things to make her giggle. She giggled and looked at him with those eyes. He asked her out. She accepted. He'd promised he'd pick her up at 7:00 P.M. on Friday night so they could make the 7:30 P.M. train into the city, go see a show. She sat there until 9:00 P.M. in the hip-hugging black dress she sewed special for the occasion, her pantyhose making her long legs itch, the size nine-and-a-half heels she'd squeezed her size-ten feet into crushing her bunions, getting hotter by the minute over being stood up by the little man who thought he was so hip, so big, he could make a date with two women and choose the other over her.

"Don't 'whoa' me! Lana told me you got plans to go on a double date with her and her man and some other broad, but let me tell you something," LoLo had said, wagging her neck and finger. "Just as sure as my name is Delores Whitney, you won't be running around this neighborhood making me out to be no fool! You ain't special," she'd sneered, slow-panning him from his stockinged feet to his boxer shorts to his barreled, bare chest to his deep brown chiseled face.

"Naw, naw, let me 'splain," Tommy had insisted.

"I don't need you to explain shit to me. I need a man who do what he say he gon' do. You can keep all that other shit."

"It's already done."

"Boy, what's done?" she'd asked, folding her arms to match her brows. She wanted to be mad. But he was so pretty. Prettier than she remembered when he whistled and she gave him the time of day. Her brain demanded she focus on his offence. Her heart laughed.

"Me and her are done. Now it's you and me."

"How it gone be you and me if you can't even get your girls and days straight? I'm not some side bitch you can keep hanging around until you finish with the next broad. You got the wrong one."

"Naw, you the right one," Tommy had said, his eyes shining. He liked her fire. It burned every intention he had for all the other women who flitted around him like bees did a honeycomb. From then on, all that shined in his sky was LoLo.

LoLo picked at her nails, lips twisted, while Tommy did a whole lot of fast talking to get her into his car. The city, that was out; it was too late to get a seat at the jazz club he'd originally planned to take her. And he knew to steer clear of the house party he was on his way to, as he didn't need to run into Billy and his loud-mouthed girlfriend, Lana, just primed to get in his business. "How about we go for a drive, just me and you," he had asked. LoLo liked the way he said "just me and you"—like a plea. She obliged. And on that warm evening, on that most perfect drive deeper into Long Island, they settled on a side road where mosquitoes and fireflies burned their wings against the streetlights and the crickets sang their songs. They feasted on Honey Buns, Coca-Cola, and Kool cigarettes, telling their sad stories, exchanging their sorrows, commiserating over their lot.

"My mama, she had this real pretty hair, on account she was part Indian, you know? I'd come running up to her with the brush and she would sit on the floor, low like, so I could reach up and run the bristles from the root all the way down her back," LoLo had said as she traced her finger around the lip of the Coke bottle. This was the stock memory she kept on hand for those who needed a little seasoning on her purposefully dry origin story—the particulars of why she left South Carolina and how she found her way to New York. *Mama died, kin took me in. Always wanted to come to New York. Right Church made room for me in the basement—let me work off my keep. Saved up for a room of my own. I'm a seamstress. I makes do.* The rest she didn't want to tell. Just couldn't. Secrets, shame—both kept the knot in her throat tied tight, just like they did most everyone else whose eyes and bodies had witnessed the unspeakable—whose knots kept them from telling, reliving, risking.

But Tommy, he wanted more. LoLo could see it in his eyes—the way he turned his whole body toward her and watched her lips as she talked, like she was a film he was analyzing, dissecting, because he was curious about the actress's choices, her motivations. She liked that he was really listening to her. Not grabbing on her soft parts or forcing what she wasn't ready for, but, instead, genuinely curious. Where there had been steel in LoLo, now there were butterflies. LoLo spread her wings—flew back to her past for Tommy, to a few places she'd never before taken any other man. "Mama died when I was six, right after my little brother, Freddy, was born. My daddy, he wasn't no kind of father to me. To none of us, really. When Mama died, he just left us at that house. Left us to die. My three big brothers, they did what they could, but they was kids, you know? They found places to stay, but me and Freddy, we stayed in that house after Mama's funeral for a long time, seem like. My daddy, he left a little food, some formula for the baby. But that couple days we were there alone? Seemed like all of eternity when Freddy got to crying. I guess my brothers got a hold of my mama's best friend. She was like kin to us. She found out me and Freddy was at the house all alone and she came and got us. Later on, my little brother got sent to family somewhere in Blacksburg, South Carolina, and I ended up with some cousins over in Columbia." LoLo quickly bit her lip to stop it from trembling, but she couldn't hide, not from Tommy. He reached for her hand. She let him.

"After my mama died, my daddy did the same thing yours did," Tommy had said. "He sent the little ones away, but he kept us older ones around. Beat on us. Made us do all the work—fixing on the roof, chopping wood, driving his truck, making deliveries and such. Made me drop out of school and all. He wasn't no kinda father to me."

"Your daddy wasn't shit. Mine wasn't either. But here we are, huh?" LoLo had said. She retightened the knot. "We still standing." LoLo clinked her lukewarm Coke bottle against his and took a swig.

"Still standing," he had said, taking a guzzle from his own bottle. Then, quietly, he added: "I want to be better than that to my kin. My brothers, they got kids—the older ones do, at least. And one of my little sisters got kids, too. I want that. I want a family of my own. A wife, couple of babies. I intend on being the kind of father and husband my daddy never could be."

"You really like kids, huh?" LoLo had asked slowly. Tommy seemed to miss the uncomfortable shift LoLo made as she adjusted herself in her seat.

"Love 'em," Tommy had answered quickly.

"That's your dream? To be somebody's daddy?"

"I got a lot of dreams," he'd said. "But won't nan one of 'em matter if I can't share them with the people I love."

"What make you think you can do better? 'Cause it seem like my mama and your mama thought they had good men, too. And all they got for their troubles was a bunch of kids and a ticket to an early grave."

"I am not my father," Tommy had said gruffly. The way he looked at LoLo, like he could see clean through to her soul, made her squirm a little. He meant that; she felt it. "I'mma do right by my family. Take care of my kids. Do like the white folk do, make it so my wife and children never know struggle. That's the life I'm promising to you. I keep my promises."

"Oh? That's why I found you standing in your drawers, ironing your suit for the next girl?"

"There is no other girl. Only you."

And that is the way it was from then on. LoLo appreciated Tommy wasn't like the others; he didn't beat her like Cindy's old man did, didn't give her reason to run up on girls like Lana did when her man got to publicly tipping on her, bringing all that Negro theater to street corners and front yards all around Amityville. He took out her garbage and bought her milk and cigarettes—made her cover her eyes when he walked her into his new place and open them after he slipped that cold piece of metal into her hand. A key. His key. LoLo focused on slow breathing to keep her heart from jumping clean up into her throat, out her mouth. It was she he'd promised the world, she whom he'd taken all the way into Midtown to pick out a wedding ring. She trusted that Tommy was a man who meant to do right by her; she intended to hold on to him with all her might.

"I want you to go to work tomorrow and walk right up to your boss and tell him to kiss your ass," he'd said. "Tell him yo' man got it from here. Tell him just like that." And she did. And at the Justice of the Peace, decked in a body-skimming dress it took her weeks to sew—one of those dresses like Dorothy Dandridge used to wear, like a satin hug for her mahogany skin— LoLo said "I do" and smiled so big the clerk down the hall could see her back teeth. They were going to have a good life. He promised. She believed.

In return, LoLo allowed Tommy to dream out loud and yanked his chain when he got off track. He liked that—her support. Her loyalty—devotion. He told her often she was the very beat of his heart. "You can't do nothing without a good ticker," he'd say. That's what he called her, sometimes: Tick. LoLo thought it a small price to pay for what Tommy had to offer.

She had no intention of losing this good man to anybody—not to Lana's fast-ass friend, or to any other woman, for that matter, not to the streets or to the cracka-ass cops who locked up colored men for sport. Especially not to her empty womb. Keeping him on his toes but letting him have his way—feeding his manhood—would be her strategy, from the moment that white man down at city hall said, "I now pronounce you man and wife," to her last breath.

But this required her to lie—required her to submit her body to him again and again, month after month, pretending that this time it would take, that eventually there would be a little baby, his baby, forming and growing and becoming in her womb. Required her to pretend to be surprised by the outcome, which, unbeknownst to him, would always be the same. Would always be counter to what he desperately wanted. Would leave both her womb and him empty. It was her blood, her monthly, that she presented as evidence that the problem was his, not hers.

"How you know that for sure, though, LoLo? How you know we just not trying hard enough to make this baby?" he asked, his voice shaky. They were sitting in their living room, side by side on the couple's three-legged pea-green velvet couch, a castaway they beat the garbagemen to on a curb two blocks over. A small, oval coffee table with wiggly legs stood sentry next to their knees. Beyond that, a small black-and-white television stacked on three small milk crates, antennas stretched wide and at least two lengths larger than the set itself, blared in front of them. On it was a commercial featuring a little white girl swimming in a bathtub bounding with suds, running a rag across her chubby arms as a narrator went on about how this particular soap floated in water and produced a creamy lather safe enough even for a baby's skin.

LoLo fidgeted with her hands in her lap, eyes trained on the lines buried in the folds of her palms. She'd practiced this part, but she couldn't look Tommy, this man who desperately wanted children, in the eyes when she said it, lest she crack and lose her love forever. "I get my monthly," she said quietly. "Means my body works just fine," is what she said, and then not another word after that.

Tommy, devoid of a working knowledge of biology and its intricacies, dropped his forehead into his hands and rubbed, first his eyebrows, then his temples. Finally: "I'm sorry, Tick," he mumbled. "This my fault. This my curse to bear and I done dragged you into the middle of it. What kind of man can't count on God to bless his wife with a baby? What kinda . . ."

Tommy didn't bother finishing his sentence. He hopped out of the chair so abruptly, the coffee table crashed to the hardwood floor. LoLo felt like she could jump out of her skin. Tommy rushed to the front door and then through it. LoLo let him.

So busy was LoLo staring at that white Jesus behind Pastor and his pulpit that she almost missed her blessing; she snapped to when a woman perched on the pew behind her shook her tambourine in praise, the miniature cymbals crashing just behind LoLo's right ear. LoLo shifted her body on her own pew and swished the fan more furiously, peeping every which way to see if any of her fellow congregants had picked up on her stress.

"Oh, suffer the little children!" Pastor Wright shouted, his voice sounding like an echo in a tunnel to LoLo's ears. He pulled back from the microphone, relishing in the tambourine shakes and "Yassuhs!" and "Preach, preachers!" that rushed his worn, rickety pulpit. LoLo perked up, zoned in. "God was so clear about his love for children and our duty to them as Christians," Pastor continued. "Proverbs fourteenth chapter, verse thirty-one: He who oppresses the poor shows contempt . . . hear me now, church!" he shouted. "I said he who oppresses the poor shows contempt . . . for their Maker . . . but . . . but . . . whoever is kiiiiiind to the needy . . . honors GOD!"

LoLo's back prickled; she bolted upright, upsetting the delicate balance of her Bible, purse and prayer cloth spread just so across her lap and knees. She snatched the lot of them into her sweaty palms as she leaned, turning her left ear, her good ear, toward the pulpit, just to make sure she was hearing right. Surely, she thought, this was no coincidence: just as she was silently begging sweet Jesus to forgive her for lying to her husband about her inability to get pregnant, here was Pastor Wright, using God's holy gospel to encourage his flock to adopt babies. LoLo's stomach did a quick somersault. "Gloray!" she yelled as she balanced her bottom on the edge of the pew.

LoLo, taking the sermon as a message from God himself, slipped out of that service and, with her church heels in her hand, ran a hole into her stockings rushing back to 333 Penny Drive with her idea, so divine. "Baby," she said, sitting gingerly on the couch, breathing heavy, staring at her husband staring at the Mets on the TV as they pissed away a four-to-zero lead over the Astros.

The television, his beer; the two had been Tommy's sole solace for days on end since he'd helped himself to a reality he wasn't ready to face, much less discuss—even with his wife. He continued to sip one and stare at the other.

"Baby, listen to me," LoLo implored, this time, her hand on his knee. "Look at me, please."

Finally, Tommy broke his gaze, dead, blank, and slowly turned to look his wife in the eye, something he'd avoided doing from the moment he finally accepted that they would never have a baby of their own and that it was probably his fault. Tommy shook his head and squinted at LoLo. "What?" he asked, emotionless.

"Let me tell you about the Negro Children's Society," she said as she wrapped his free hand, the one not holding his third warm beer, in her own.

Eyes wide with excitement, spittle rushing over her chafed lips, dry and brittle from swallowing hot air as she ran to her man, LoLo let all the right words tumble through the gap in her teeth, the rush of statements so fast she was practically whistling in the quiet parts. Tommy heard all the key words like "less fortunate" and "blessing" and "God's will" and "family is family, blood don't matter," but he wasn't prepared to register the idea, even if it did sound like right. What self-respecting, virile man couldn't make a baby? How much of a man could he be if he were incapable of giving his wife a child? What man could bear the curse of his own legacy withering and dying at his own doorstep? Tommy wasn't no praying man, but this, God knew, was important to him. All those times Tommy had promised Him he would be a better man than his own daddy and LoLo's, too, all those times he told the clouds his intention to fill their house with children and raise them up with the direction and love he and his wife never witnessed for themselves—all of it was for naught. This God had nothing more to offer than LoLo's empty womb, his own broken heart. The pitch from the snake oil salesman in the pulpit? Didn't want to hear it.

His sullenness was a match for neither LoLo's enthusiasm nor her gift of persuasion. She could get most anything out of her man and this, especially, would be no exception. They needed this baby. It would be had.

A week's worth of Sundays would pass before Tommy came around to the idea of adopting. LoLo's words had been logical, but it was at their friend Sarah's house where his heart had finally given way. Pastor Wright was there: new suit, sweaty brow, breast pocket full of money from the welfare check he'd scored from Child and Family Services. A son. "Yeah, this here is my boy, Samuel," Pastor Wright had said. He'd pulled a handkerchief from that money pocket and wiped his upper lip as he watched the four-month-old child be shuffled from arm to arm. "It's something else to have a new little blessing in the house just as my older ones have their feet practically out the front door."

"You have your own kids?" Tommy had asked as he watched Sarah bounce the baby's cheeks between her fingers and coo.

The pastor wrinkled his brow. "Well, my wife and I have two sons together and we took in her sister's daughter when she passed. Samuel here is our fourth child."

"So, the older two, they're blood," Tommy had said.

LoLo, leaning into the baby as she pulled back his blanket for a clear view of his cherub face, cut her eyes at Tommy, but her husband was too busy demanding a straight answer from the pastor to notice his wife's discomfort.

"I birthed those two older ones, yes, but Samuel is no less my child," First Lady Wright had said. "All babies are a blessing from God. It doesn't quite matter how they made it to your arms."

LoLo, instinctively understanding that Tommy was sharpening his swords, reached for the baby before her husband could say something slick—nestled him in the crook of her left arm, and gently swayed and bounced as she patted the baby's little bottom, like she'd learned to do a lifetime ago, when shushing babies, making them feel at ease and comforted, saved her own hide. "Whosasweetbaby? Whoseasweetbabyboy?" she had cooed as she nuzzled her nose against the baby's cheek. She closed her eyes and inhaled deep. Yes, she thought, a baby like this, a son Tommy could learn to call his own, would make everything right between her and her man. Would get them to forever. She would make him see.

There was something, Tommy would say later, about the delicateness of LoLo's fingers—the way her digits, calloused from the cotton fields she'd worked as a child, gently pulled the baby to her chest. Tommy watched as she bounced the baby in her arms and was, indeed, new.

12

W hat's down there?" Tommy asked, jutting his finger at a narrow stairwell he and LoLo zoomed past as he trudged excitedly behind the social worker. LoLo, her clammy hand rubbing against Tommy's dry, calloused palms, trailed a measure behind the pair, taking much smaller steps than her long legs could have allowed, which, to anyone bothering to observe, gave the appearance of her being dragged through the hallways of the Negro Children's Society, rather than walking willingly. She rubbed her right temple with her free hand. The clomping of the social worker's kitten heels against the tiled floors echoed off the empty, gray walls—bounced around the inside of her brain, too, coaxing a dull headache that sharpened with each step. She held back her tears best she could. She could barely handle the one baby. Barely even wanted him. What was she fittin' to do with two? With a girl who, surely, would worry her into the ground?

And now LoLo was standing in an orphanage, swallowing her screams. The first baby they got, the boy, did not require all of this. Under the direction of Pastor Wright, the Right Church of God and Fellowship had become a favored partner of The Society, which leaned on the benevolence of Black churches to rescue little souls in need of good Christian homes. Initially, Pastor Wright had underestimated how easy of a sell it would be to convince his parishioners to take in children pockmarked by the whips of abusive parents, abandoned by drug-addicted mamas, surrendered by families ashamed that their daughters had spread their legs. But when he shined a light on The Society's questionable tactics—how the institution provided the children beds, food, clothing, and, in exchange for that benevolence, lent the kids out as indentured servants to earn their keep, learn a trade, be useful—convincing his flock to foster and adopt those poor souls made for easy propositions. Couldn't nobody rest their heads at night knowing there was a gang of Negro innocents being forced into modern-day slavery right there in their own backyards. The bonus: each one of them chil'ren came with a small monthly stipend that could come in handy for this flock of poor Negroes for whom steady employment remained somewhat elusive. Best believe this latter point was not lost on Pastor Wright, either. The collector and the decider of the tithes would have his 10 percent. With everyone clearly motivated, procuring a baby from The Society was easy enough: Tommy and LoLo joined a half dozen other families down at the church on a Tuesday night, took turns looking through a book filled with the names and vitals of available children, and picked one. About a month later, in no less than three hours, in less time than it took for Tommy to fix the line engine down at the cake factory, they were walking out of The Society with their new baby boy, their son, a child named John whom, in time for his birth certificate to be drawn up, they would later name Tommy, Jr., or TJ, for short. Tommy was happy. This pleased LoLo. Being a mother, this did not. Getting a second child, a girl, just two years later, well, that was a fool's proposition that sent LoLo back to her knees. *Lawd, give me the strength,* LoLo had prayed the night Tommy came to her, jammed into her hands a catalogue of little bodies that needed to be moved out of the system. "I think it's time for TJ to be a big brother," he'd said. Tommy spread his legs and lips wide as he sat back on the sofa, grinning. "We can still have the family we always wanted, right? We can have a whole house full of kids if we want."

LoLo bounced little TJ on her hip. She'd fed him, bathed him, put him in warm pajamas and rocked him, gave him milk, and still, he would not settle. Wouldn't stop all that fussing and grabbing on her when all she wanted to do was wash up the dinner dishes and sit down somewhere. She bounced some more, out of nervousness. Out of fear of what would come if she told Tommy the truth: she did not have it in her to keep up with her end of their deal to be a homemaker and mother, especially so if a girl child was involved. LoLo was convinced there weren't enough shadows, enough dark corners and hidden places adequate enough for her to hide a girl from the troubles of this world—that she hadn't enough muscle, prowess to box with a man.

I know what I asked for, Lawdy, LoLo prayed silently. She stared at Tommy and forced a smile to her lips. Bounced the baby. *I'm calling on your strong name, Jesus.*

Seemed like God was more in tune with Tommy. He had decided he wanted another—a girl—and so a girl would be had and waiting six months for the next church adoption rally simply would not do, so he hustled LoLo onto a 7:00 A.M. train into Manhattan to make sure they were standing at the front door of this cold, sterile relic of pre–World War II institutions, where he was convinced he'd find another baby—a daughter. This is how LoLo found herself tipping around The Society, whispering to herself, "Don't cry, little baby," and avoiding dark corners, heart racing as she passed closed doors and children with empty looks where there should have been light. She walked stiff-legged. Tommy did not notice. He did not notice a lot of things.

"Oh, down there are more babies," the social worker told Tommy as he doubled back to the doorway and peeked down the dark set of stairs. "You and Mrs. Lawrence are in luck! We had quite a few children come in over the past month or so. We did the math; looks like these all were popped into the oven after Bobby Kennedy was shot. It's like clockwork. Something traumatic happens and nine months later, here we are," she said, shoulders shrugging, lips twisted into a smirk.

LoLo wanted no parts of the basement. "I'm going to go out and take a look at the children out on the playground again," she said, turning on her heel and run-walking down the hallway without giving Tommy a chance to object.

Tommy paid this no nevermind. "You mind if I take a look?" he asked the social worker, bounding down the steps before she had a chance to respond. The social worker's face folded as she watched him disappear.

"You know, it's usually the wives who are the excited ones," she said, calling out to LoLo, who had made it halfway down the hallway.

LoLo halted, hesitated, slowly turned to face the social worker. "Yes, well, he comes from a big family. He always wanted his own big family to love," LoLo said simply.

"Well now, that's a lovely sentiment. It's a shame you can't have babies of your own," said the social worker, with complete disregard for her callousness.

"Who said it was me who can't have babies?" LoLo snapped. Just as quickly, she rubbed the angles from her words to make them less sharp: "Can you tell me where the restroom is?"

The social worker narrowed her eyes. "Yours is down the hallway, around the corner, to the right, past the utility closet."

"Thank you," LoLo said curtly as she rushed toward the COLOREDS ONLY sign. She stood in the tiny box of a room, its size hardly big enough to fit a commode and sink, and paced, which was really just her turning in tiny circles. *Don't cry, little baby. Please don't cry.* LoLo ran the words through her brain—repeated them slow, letting them wash over the social worker's jabs. But they just couldn't clear the grime off truth, memory, scars.

1953

LoLo learned how to tend to babies at the tender age of six in a place just like The Society, before she knew how to tie her shoes—before she had a good pair, even, of her own. The women who worked at that children's home would have this no other way. They called themselves "The Mothers," and they were particular—liked neither noise nor the children, those soulless little niggers born to the ones who fucked like wild boars and left their litters for someone else's care. The extent of The Mothers' giving was Bible led: Deuteronomy was clear about their responsibilities to the fatherless, and so they made sure the bastards had food, a place to rest. But that particular verse of the Good Word that they favored said nothing of love, of nurture, and so they had no tenderness to give—only requirements as long and as hard as their rods, which they did not spare. LoLo learned this practically at the door, having skipped right up to it, the sucker with which Auntie Bessie had lured her out of the house sticky on her grinning lips, perfectly unaware that yet another adult she trusted would betray her with abandonment. LoLo was standing there quiet, fingers salty with sweat, picking off her molars the thick candy she chose to bite rather than lick because this was the expedient thing to do with such a rare, magnificent treat, when she slowly began to listen to and then understand the exchange between Auntie Bessie and the women—that this wasn't a friendly visit but a destination for her and her newborn brother, a departure for the only adult who saw fit to come see about her and Freddy when hardly no one else had—not their daddy, not their older brothers—in the week after they put her mama in the ground.

Her heretofore hazy reality coming into full focus, LoLo wriggled out of Auntie Bessie's firm grip, backed away, chest heaving with every clumsy step; she fell over a rock as big as her foot for her troubles, watched her chewed-up lollipop bounce across the same pea gravel that buried itself in her knees and palms, pocked with raw and blood from the spill. Where there had been sweet on her tongue, now LoLo tasted bile and the salt from her tears. "Please, Auntie Bessie," she pleaded, shaking her head furiously from side to side. She crumbled from the weight of the shock pulsating through her stomach, down to her feet. "Please don't leave me here."

"I know, chile, it's a sad day. But yo' Aunt Bessie done all I can do," she said to LoLo as she handed the newborn, LoLo's baby brother, to the one woman, crinkly and gray, and then helped the little girl to her feet.

LoLo tightened her grip on the folds of her auntie's skirt as her mind did the figuring, flashing moments over the last few days where she may not have been at her best. She smushed her body against that of her care-taker and grimaced through the prickly pain shooting from her skinned knee and palm as she stared hard through glassy eyes into her aunt's and shined her teeth—tried to make herself look pretty, sweet. Like how she did in church when Mama was on the ground, not beneath it, and Auntie Bessie would pinch her cheeks and ask her for some sugar and say, "Whew, you's a pretty little thang. Smile so bright." LoLo's mind raced. *What I do wrong? She mad at me! Freddy cry too much. No, no, I shoulda kept out the bacon grease. She mad 'cause I ain't ask before I put it on my biscuit, like how Mama used to do.*

Little LoLo had, indeed, heard snatches of the not-so-kind words Auntie Bessie's husband had yelled just the night before, as Freddy screamed and LoLo sat in the corner, simultaneously consoling her baby brother and picking salty biscuit bits off her teeth. Auntie Bessie's two kids—a boy of about nine and a girl about LoLo's age—sat stiff on the other side of the room. Didn't make a peep. "What we 'sposed to do, Bessie? You expect me to give more of a damn about some kids that ain't mine than I do the two of us? Our own chillen?"

"What you want me to do, Georgie? I can't just put 'em out on the street. They my best good girlfriend's babies . . . ," Auntie Bessie said.

George was hearing none of it. "That's right, they Lila Mae and Ford Whitney's chillen, they ain't none a ours. Let they daddy feed 'em. Where he at, huh? Leaving his own blood to die. Ain't no kinda man to do that to his own family."

"He . . . he working, baby. This just temporary, I told you."

"Shole is. That's exactly the right word: temporary," George said, pushing it through his teeth like a toothpick. "It's been two weeks a me bringing what lil' bit a money I make in here to feed chillen they own daddy done left behind for someone else to take care of. Not my responsibility. Time's up. I want them kids down there at the orphanage before I come back in this house from work tomorrow. That's all there is to it."

LoLo heard the word "orphanage." Didn't quite click what that was until she was standing in front of the dingy white building, she and Freddy about to be deposited into the hands of strangers, like somebody's hand-me-downs—like things to be cleared out, discarded. Then, frantically: "Please, Auntie Bessie," LoLo begged. "I won't sneak bacon grease on my biscuits no mo'. I'm sorry. I won't do it again, I promise. Please . . ."

The second woman, younger, her puffy hair rolled into two tight buns that made her temples stretch, tightened her fingers around the little girl's shoulders, fighting her squirm. Bessie sighed and wiped the tears and snot that raced toward her lip. Then, to The Mothers, Bessie said: "I kep' 'em long as I could, but they mama gone. Died a couple days after she had this one here," she said, nodding at the baby, Freddy. "The older ones, they can fend fo' they selves, but these two babies, they daddy . . . ," she said, taking her time with the words, "he workin'. Ain't no time for a man to tend a job and babies, I understand that, but we just can't do it for him. Lila Mae was my best good friend. She got family over in Blacksburg and maybe Columbia, I believe. I'mma find 'em, tell 'em where they kin is. I know they'll be here directly. I'd take 'em myself if I knew exactly where they was and I had a way to get there. But in the meantime, if you could just take 'em. Take 'em and be good to 'em until they family come get 'em."

Bessie, unable to push any more words past the choking of her tears, bent down and kissed the struggling LoLo on both her cheeks and then stood and brushed the back of her hand on Freddy's temple. With that, she rushed across the porch, down its steps, and out onto the street, the swish of her skirt wrestling with the thick of the cold March air. Sixteen years later, while she laid on her deathbed, the cancer finally having had its fill of her insides, Bessie would still hear LoLo's shrieks and pleas, and she would search her heart for the words she would say to her best friend in Heaven to atone for leaving her babies at the Beacon Baptist Home for Orphans.

LoLo was only six years old and though she'd been raised in a country household where children were expected to be seen and not heard, she hadn't yet mastered the art of checking her emotions, so The Mothers, they helped her to it. The older one had enough decorum to at least wait for Bessie to reach the dirt road before she addressed LoLo's fit at the door, but the younger caregiver didn't bother to even pretend like she cared if Bessie witnessed her actions or the little girl's response. In one smooth motion, she whipped LoLo around and used the back of her meaty right hand to strike the child across her ear and cheek, an action so sudden, so quick, so vicious, LoLo's very breath got stuck in her little chest and throat. Desperate for air, desperate to get the cry out of her gullet, desperate to stop the ringing in her ear, desperate to run to the dirt mound underneath which her mother lay and claw deep down into the soil to shake Mama awake and lie in her lap and let it be like it used to before Freddy came, Lolo dissolved into a quivering heap on the wood floor. The younger Mother would have none of this, though; she snatched up LoLo by her arm and held it in the air while she sneered between gritted teeth, "Shut up! You . . . shut . . . up!" Terrified, LoLo choked down her shrieks best she could.

"Now that we have your attention, let's come to an understanding," the gray-haired one said quietly, almost sweetly. "I am Mother. She is also Mother. This is how you will address us. You will stop that crying because I do not tolerate noise. You will put away your things because I do not tolerate filth. You will do as you are told because this is what God requires of his children: obedience."

LoLo stood there, shivering, even as the noon sun cooked the Vaseline Auntie Bessie had slathered on her skin to shine her up. She snuck a peek at the small white clapboard building that stood ominously just past the woman's shoulders, swallowed her whimpers as she watched the older woman look down at the baby and rock him lightly as he began to fuss. *Freddy stay fussin'*, LoLo thought, a flash of anger scorching her fear. *Mama gone on account of him, and now we here 'cause Auntie Bessie and Mr. George ain't want to hear him crying either.*

"Now, now," Older Mother cooed as she loosened the blanket from around Freddy's head and neck. Smirking, but without lifting her eyes from the baby's face, she continued: "Isn't it something how cute they are when they're this little? Look like a little baby monkey. Who'samonkeyboy? Who'salittlemonkeyboy?" Still without taking her eyes off Freddy: "You will take this little monkey and make sure he keeps himself quiet. You're his kin, you take care of him."

And with that, Older Mother shoved the baby into the whimpering LoLo's arms and headed down a short hallway. LoLo, skinny, diminutive, cowed by the force of the baby being pushed against her chest, nimbly stepped back on her right foot to keep from falling, but had a harder time trying to hold on to her little brother, wriggly and heavy in her tiny arms. She knew better than to linger, though; she quickly followed the woman, the sting of the slap still burning her sopping wet cheeks.

Mother led her to a small room filled with three rows of cots, a third of them occupied with children of various ages and stature. When they walked in, each one of the children—the ones playing, the ones with their heads down, the ones talking, and the ones quiet—scrambled to their feet and stood next to the cot closest to them, heads bowed, hands clasped, feet together. LoLo almost ran into Mother's legs, so busy was she taking inventory of the room that she'd barely noticed the woman had stopped.

"Children, this is Delores Whitney and her brother, Fredrick Whitney," Older Mother said in the same even tone in which she'd spoken by the front door. "I expect you to teach her the rules and the consequences, or suffer the little children." Then, to LoLo: "You and your little monkey will sleep over there," she said, pointing to an empty cot in the far corner of the room.

LoLo, struggling under the weight of her baby brother, walked as fast as she could over to the cot, eyes darting all around at the other kids for clues on how she was to stand, too. Freddy wriggled in her arms and started to work up a little cry, but then settled as LoLo bounced her arms, like she remembered Mama doing between the first days after she gave birth and the one on which she took her last breath, when Freddy got to fussing and nuzzling his head in Mama's chest, rooting for some ninny. LoLo took a quick look at her own chest—wondered if she was supposed to give Freddy her ninny. Older Mother, she quickly surmised, would be too stingy to give him some of hers. *How Freddy gonna eat?* she asked herself, her six-year-old mind prone to distraction, even then, even under those circumstances.

Older Mother had said not another word. She turned on her heel and disappeared back down the hallway, her exit releasing all the breath the children had been holding in their throats. Freddy, seeming to feel the energy shift, worked himself into a wriggly cry—one that, this time, he clearly intended to see through. Almost as quickly as he whimpered, a girl, of about twelve in age, appeared by LoLo's side. "Let me have the baby," she said, as she tried to pull Freddy from his sister's arms. LoLo resisted—tugged him away from her clutch and turned her back to keep the baby away from the stranger.

"Listen to me," the girl insisted, scream whispering as her eyes darted to and fro. "You cain't have that baby in here cryin', or else we all gone get it. You know how to keep a baby from cryin'? Clean his butt? Feed him?"

LoLo shook her head no. Bounced her arms to keep Freddy quiet.

"Well, you best ta learn, 'cause don't none a us want Mother in here," she said. "Now give me the baby."

LoLo had been a quick study, but it did not come without struggle. Freddy was impossibly impossible, and all LoLo had a hankering to do was to crawl up under the tiny cot, cuddle herself up in the darkness. Hide. The girl snapped her to.

"My name Florence. When I got here, I had to take care a my brother the same way," the girl had said as she laid Freddy on the cot. LoLo, hands finally free, used the hem of her shirt to swipe at her tears and snot, nearly dried on her face and therefore rendering all the skin they touched tight and itchy. "When the last time he ate? He might be hungry. I hope that's not it because don't nobody want to ask Mother for no milk right now on account she on a tear. Hope he just wet, need his bottom changed." The girl kept on like that, words colliding into one another so fast, LoLo couldn't keep up with what she was saying, much less doing. So she just stood there and watched, scratching at her face as the girl pulled up Freddy's gown and undid his diaper. "Yep, just like I figured. Look here," Florence said, stepping aside to give LoLo an unfettered view. "He wet."

LoLo leaned in and, for the first time, took a good hard look at her little brother's private bits—watched how his pee-pee and the mound of flesh beneath, wrinkly and black, jiggled as Freddy slammed his legs and arms up and down and up and down, his throat rumbling with a cry he intended to let fly, no matter how dry his bum. LoLo didn't feel right staring at his ding-a-ling. Her brothers, her father had always made her turn her head when they climbed into the tin basin to wash, and she never peeked, not even once. She didn't want to see Freddy's, neither.

"Now you got to hurrup and get his little butt clean, hear? Or else he pee right in ya face then the both y'all gotta wash and you don't want to 'splain that to Mother, either," Florence said, working quickly, Freddy's privacy the least of her concerns. "Go over there to the basin and water down one of them rags so we can wipe him down. Bring back one of them diapers, too."

LoLo followed Florence's pointed finger to a small counter backed up in the opposite corner of the room and rushed to it. She felt the eyes of the children all over her body—her hair, pulled into four big puffs on each corner of her scalp, her dress, scuffed with dirt, her legs, dusty and bare—and she felt shame. Small. But that wasn't anywhere near as big as her fear of Mother coming back into the room behind Freddy's fussing. She poured water on the rag with haste and hustled it, along with a dingy but clean white cloth diaper, back to her cot.

"You got to tell him not to cry," Florence said as she wiped. "Go 'head, tell him so he understand."

LoLo trained her eyes on her brother and leaned in. "Shhh . . . baby. Don't cry. Don't cry, little baby," she said as she pressed down on the cot, bouncing it against her palm so that it could bounce against his back.

"That's it, that's how you do it," Florence said as she pulled the one diaper off his butt and slipped another beneath it. "Hush him up, dry him up. We all stay outta trouble."

Within the week, LoLo was changing Freddy with confidence—feeding him, burping him, too. If he fussed, she could get him to hush up quick. Getting him to drift off into wherever babies went when they fell fast asleep, she had that down, too. This ability was neither nature nor nurture. She understood its necessity. But never did she do it with joy—glee. The Mothers' paddles and straps assured this. "Children . . . must . . . be . . . obedient," Older Mother would say with her even voice, each of her words a staccato to match the whizz of the long, black leather belt soaring through the air, landing on LoLo's thigh, arm, cheek, knee. LoLo's curdling cry grew deep down in her gut, rushed up like hot lava through chest and neck, across tongue and teeth, echoing against the walls of the overcrowded but austere living quarters that would be her and Freddy's home for two years until family ushered her off to a fate even more fraught with sadness, danger. That was the first time she got hit—the second, the fifth. By the sixth, LoLo was standing by the cot, the itchy gray uniform barely hanging onto her thinning frame, Freddy on the bed, squirming and fussing over she didn't even know what. She'd fed him and changed him and burped him and rocked him and still, he wouldn't shush up—*like he want me to get beat,* she thought as she watched Older Mother navigate her thick, buxom frame around cots, children scattering and flattening themselves against walls, heads bowed, saying silent prayers that she was coming to see about somebody else, not them. Older Mother rested her heavy feet in front of LoLo and bore a hole into her forehead with her angry eyes. When the words began, the strap swung. LoLo inched a little closer to her cot where Freddy lay, stiffening herself against the blows, face as still as she could muster, heart hoping that the leather would slip in Older Mother's hand just a little, maybe land on the baby who killed her mama, and drove away her daddy and Auntie Bessie, too, and kept making The Mothers mad and her, too.

Truth was, if there were some kind of innate love LoLo was to have for her little brother, some kind of intrinsic ability to care for this child who shared her blood, it had not one chance of blooming. Just as easily as the six-year-old could grow love, Freddy had come along and killed their mother, rotting out love's roots. LoLo's garden had no flowers, only rocks—for Miss Bessie, her daddy. Her two older brothers, who found refuge somewhere where little girls were not welcomed. Wilting under the sting of the strap every time Mother heard Freddy's wails, under the weight of her lot, this motherless child, heart full of rocks, became her baby brother's mama, a role and title she neither relished nor wanted until she would find out much later that she couldn't have that title—mother— the way God intended it. This she laid squarely at Freddy's feet—would hold him accountable for the death of their mother and the successive ca- lamity of events that would shape her very being, all the way through to their old days, even when he would try to reconnect and make amends, even when she should have found the courage to unearth the true source of all that anger and pain and dig it out of her thick, hardened parts 'til she got to the meat of some joy. "Shhhh . . . don't cry, little baby. Please don't cry," she would say, the words no longer for her baby brother, but herself.

There were no napkins or towels with which to wipe one's hands, as this was a "coloreds only" affair, which meant one had to make do with what the establishment bothered to avail, so LoLo wrapped toilet tissue around her hand five times, ripped it off the spool, and trickled a little cold water on the wad. She dabbed at her face with the wad, careful not to leave little tissue bits on her cheeks and eyes. She pulled her compact out of her purse and flashed the mirror all around her face to confirm, then stared into her own eyes. *Don't cry, little baby. Please don't cry.*

Only the tip of her well-worn heels had breached the threshold of the bathroom door before Tommy popped up in her face.

"I found her," Tommy said, the bottom of his face spread wide with teeth and gums. "I found our daughter. She's down there in the basement. Come meet her."

LoLo shined her teeth, but there was no light in her eyes. "Okay, baby. Let's go on down there."

13

Tommy's Ford Mustang, prized because it was both pretty and had been built from scraps by his own hand, was already rumbling down Penny Drive when the baby stirred. It had been a long night, what with TJ wetting his bed and needing fresh pajamas and linens, and LoLo wasn't ready to rise much less tend to the baby's cries, but husbands like their coffee hot first thing before work and their liverwurst folded just so between two slices of white bread, and the children, well, they knew nothing of savoring sleep, of keeping their eyes closed, especially when the light of day beamed through the sliver of open curtain before it was time for them to wake, so LoLo had to get on with it, whether she was ready to or not. She said not one word as she sat TJ, a mass of yellow-brown skin and bone with thick lips and great big ol' eyes, on top of the stack of yellow-page phone books tottering on the kitchen table chair and pushed his body up to the edge of the table, but she popped his hand all the same when he reached for his spoon without saying his grace. "You know better," she said, folding his hands together. "Say your blessings like I taught you."

"Godis greaaaaaat, godis goooood, let us thank him for our food. Aaaa-men," TJ sang with his little baby voice, the sound coaxing a smile to LoLo's face. It took some time for that—for LoLo to look at her son and see joy rather than burden. Her titties were bone dry—she had not a drop of ninny for him, but still—*but still*—he clung to her from the beginning and that, LoLo could not stand. All that fussing and grabbing at her thighs. Burying his head in her lap, her breasts. She couldn't pee without that boy following her to the toilet—couldn't grab the milk out the milk box on the side porch without him whining, "Up! Up!," and raising his arms in the air so he could ride on her hip as she set out the bottles and brought in the fresh ones. Put her in the mind of Freddy, and she knew that was an unfair comparison, but still, her little brother's dependence, his fussiness, cost her a pound of flesh, maybe even two in the almost two years they spent in The Mothers' care, and that made LoLo stingy—made her hold back what little bit of affection she was able to muster while she fought to bury in the recesses of her memories all she was forced to pay on account of him. And so, in the beginning, there was the push and the pull—TJ pushing for attention, LoLo pulling away. "You can't just be carried every damn where!" she'd yell and leave him standing right there in the middle of the floor, his little hands like lobster claws, grabbing as he begged. Push, pull . . . push, pull. This is what it was. TJ, all energy and tumble and warm—LoLo, thick ice.

It remained this way until the day came when LoLo thought she'd broken him, and an intractable fear made way for heart melt where there once was only bitter cold. He was supposed to be sleep, but not more than ten minutes after she made TJ lay down, there he was. "Mama," he'd whined. LoLo groaned, hearing only his voice, not his words as she scraped peanut butter off the side of the Formica. She lifted her eyes toward the ceiling, cocked her ear toward the voice. Stood statue still. There was silence again. *Good, he went back to sleep*, she told herself. She scrubbed the gooey mess and then set to scraping her memory for tricks for getting stains out of fine fabric, because of course, where there was peanut butter, there was jelly. Was it baking soda? Vinegar? *Didn't I see somebody dab club soda on a carpet where some red wine spilled?* she asked herself as she rubbed. *Swear I don't know how the hell that boy got grape jelly on the wallpaper and the sofa.* LoLo clicked her tongue; a scowl chased behind it. *Damn running through this house like the Tasmanian Devil.*

"Mama!"

The little voice was bigger, and now there was the patter of little feet across the wooden floor. LoLo deep-sighed and mouthed a cuss as she ran the dishrag under a stream of warm sink water and rung it out, lamenting the fact that her plan to sit and simply be had evaporated in the matter of a finger snap. "Boy, you 'sposed to be sleep!" she said as TJ turned the corner into the kitchen.

"Mama," he said, this time in the form of a whine.

"Boy, if you don't go get back in that be . . ."

LoLo's eyes came to rest and slowly focused on TJ; her scream curdled in the air. TJ, wont to totter on his tiptoes—a practice that would earn him the nickname "Tip" by the time he was a sixth-grader and his friends were ribbing him for the way he bounced on the pads of his feet as he rushed around the hot concrete at the community pool—was bouncing around in front of her, a puddle of red dripping from his mouth, down his neck, onto the blue of his shirt and the white of Superman's imposing, chiseled face. Even the "S" on his chest.

"TJ!" she yelled as she rushed over to the boy and pulled him to her. Frantic, she lifted his neck. *Maybe he got a hold of a knife and cut himself!* She looked all around the halo of his head. *Maybe he fell out of the bed and slammed his head on something sharp.* She looked at his lips and teeth. *Did this boy pull out his teeth?* Finally, when TJ's tears had turned to wails and his mouth trembled wide, she saw it; it was as if his tongue had come disconnected from the small bowl of pink gum beneath it. LoLo reeled back. "Sweet Jesus, Lawd!" she screamed, which of course made TJ cry harder and then there was the two of them, scared and frantic, he trying to hold on to her, her trying to push him away.

"Mama!" he wailed through the blood. There was so much blood.

LoLo grabbed the toddler and rushed out the door, her slippers slapping against each of the concrete steps and across the gravel-lined walkway and down the driveway. Little rocks popped up into her slippers as she booked it up the neighbor's gravel driveway, screaming. "Skip! Skip!" she called out to her neighbor. She held TJ with one arm—banged the aluminum screen door with the other, loud enough to wake the neighbor, who'd just settled in after pulling an overnight shift. "Skip!" she hollered.

"I . . . I . . . I don't know what happened; he was napping and then got to screaming and crying and when I saw him, he was like this!" LoLo cried as her neighbor's door creaked open and he appeared in the screen.

"Whoa, whoa, what ail him?" Skip asked, rushing to unlock the door, a look of horror pulsing across his face. He pulled LoLo and TJ inside.

"I don't know, I don't know, I don't know, I don't know," LoLo said like it was one long word.

"Okay, okay, try to be calm," Skip said. "Just let me get my keys, okay? Meet me on the side of the house. I'll run y'all down to the clinic."

A few hours later, LoLo was back home, slow rocking TJ in his bed, mashing his head to her chest as she croaked her way through a whispered version of "Hush Little Baby," the two of them, finally, at rest. Tommy, oblivious, sauntered into the house, later than usual, not a care.

"Hello!" he sang as he gently closed the door, looked around. He was primed for his greetings at the door, but there were none. "LoLo? TJ?" Still, nothing. Tommy hesitated and listened. "Where's my wife? Family?"

"In here," LoLo called out.

She kept rocking, kept singing, kept nuzzling her son as he nestled himself in the groove between her neck and breast. Her fingers were prickly cold from the ice pack she was holding against his tongue, but she paid it no nevermind. Just kept singing.

Tommy appeared in the doorway and cocked his head to the side, leaned in to survey what was splayed before him. "What happened? He fell again? Busted his lip?" Tommy asked. TJ squirmed a little, nuzzled so close to LoLo's skin it was almost hard to tell where one and the other began and ended.

"His tongue was tied, Tommy," LoLo said finally. "He ripped it somehow. Never seen so much blood in my life." LoLo rocked. "I tried calling you down at the factory but I couldn't get them to put me through." She nodded her head toward the heap of bloody clothes on the floor. "Got ice on it. Got two stiches to keep him from bleeding."

"What?" Tommy practically sang. "Oh man! Where you take him, down to the hospital?"

"Naw, Skip drove me in his taxi to the clinic. He gone be fine. Just sore and scared is all."

Tommy reached down to pick up TJ, but the boy wriggled from his grasp. Whined. Nuzzled deeper into LoLo's neck and bosom.

"You know, he called me 'Mama' today," LoLo said as she rocked. She looked down at TJ and kissed his forehead. "First time he ever called me that."

"Oh, you with Mama now, huh?" Tommy said, tossing a little smirk.

He reached down and dug his fingers into the boy's underarm, trying to elicit a giggle. TJ shook him off. "Oh! You don't want me, huh?" Tommy added. He stood up straight and crossed his thick, muscular arms as he fake frowned. "That's it for me and you, lil' man?"

TJ whined again. Nuzzled again. Wrapped his little hands around Lo-Lo's body best he could. LoLo pulled him closer, kissed his forehead, sang her song. Her son, her baby, didn't want nobody else but her. And finally, LoLo, she wanted this baby back.

"Good. That's good, baby," LoLo said as she placed her hands over TJ's. She kissed his little fingers. "Now eat up your oatmeal. Make you big and strong!" LoLo said. Then, her voice was coarse. "And don't you touch that milk until you finish. Shouldn't let you have anything to drink no way, witcho peeing in the bed last night."

TJ scooped the oatmeal into his mouth, half of it making it in, half smearing across his cheek. LoLo let him have at it, though, as she had to turn her attention to baby Rae, who was fussing in her high chair, waiting for her scrambled eggs and bottle. "All right, all right, all right, it's coming," LoLo said as she used a fork to push the eggs around on the plate while she blew on them to cool them off. Babygirl was no fan of oatmeal; she would sit in her high chair and purse her lips in protest the few times LoLo tried to feed it to her, even when it was sweetened up with a little cinnamon and an extra splash of milk. The girl wanted one thing only, and that was eggs, scrambled soft and fed to her not with a fork, but by LoLo's fingers. She was a stubborn little thing, that one.

"Okay, okay, here they come. I have to cool them off, little one. You don't want me to burn your mouth, do you?" LoLo said, blowing the small yellow mound between her words. The baby smacked her lips and drooled in response and made a *buh buh buh* sound. Finally, LoLo pinched a small bit of egg between her thumb and pointer and middle fingers, gave it a final blast of cool breath, and pressed the whole affair into the baby's mouth. She, in turn, leaned into LoLo's fingers, mouth wide and then not, tongue and lips wrapped around food and skin, pulling and sucking until fingers were clean and her little mouth was full. She waved her arms in approval, or satisfaction, excitement—probably all three—and this brought LoLo immense joy, this simple, loving act that connected her not only to this little girl who she now called her own, but also to her mother, who she remembered fed her the same way. That was one of the only memories she had of her mother. Every now and again when she leaned her whole self into mothering the children and she felt strong enough to endure the ache of recollection—the latter of which did not come often—LoLo would sit and shut her eyes real tight and try to remember what her mama looked like, but even when she focused real hard and burst into tears searching for the memories, she couldn't see her mama's eyes, her cheekbones, her smile, her hair. Just her fingers, long and nimble and calloused, digging into the eggs and reaching for LoLo's mouth. This was tenderness that she never did experience again after her mother died. This was the most meaningful tenderness she knew how to extend to this new baby, so much more dependent than even TJ was when LoLo and Tommy brought him home at age two.

"That's good, ain't it, baby?" LoLo said, smiling as the now eighteen-month-old sucked and swallowed the eggs. "You like that? You like that, Rae?"

That name, like the baby, was just starting to grow on LoLo. For much of the whole year before that, LoLo was tentative about all of it—taking in not just one but two kids, dealing with the issues that crept up with the boy—his clinginess, his bedwetting and aggressiveness, this child of a drug-addicted mother who wanted her needles more than her baby. Waiting on what might pop up with the baby girl. The unknown. Rae's origin story—the real one, that LoLo and Tommy would never know—was a bit more dramatic than that of their typical charge; a nurse on her way into work at a home for unwed mothers had made the discovery on the building's stoop. There in the bitter cold was a pile of blankets and a pissy, cold, but otherwise healthy baby with a small white pouch full of an odd assortment of contents—a rabbit's foot, a small poof of Afro hair, a pipe, a piece of handkerchief dipped in what looked like blood, and a folded brown paper bag square with "this baby" written three times in a row, and "a sweet, protected, prosperous life" written in a circle around those rows—attached to her gown. She was inside a Nordstrom's bag, left out like Tuesday's trash. With no clue of who that baby was or where she'd come from, the home for unwed mothers made a few half-hearted attempts to alert the neighborhood that someone had given birth to a child and left her to be someone else's responsibility, but they counted on no one coming forward—counted, too, on the cut of the foster care and adoption fees they could trade the orphanage in exchange for a healthy, pretty newborn for whom they had no use. Wasn't no telling where she came from or from whom—what she carried in her blood, in her sinew beyond that. Whoever her mama was, she was country as hell. A rootworker, is what they called them back in South Carolina. Who people in the town of Bluffton turned to when they needed medical attention but couldn't make it over to or afford the one Negro doctor tending to Black folk at least five towns out to the north, south, east, and west. LoLo remembered being scared of them, on account The Mothers told their charges they were pure evil—"a sin against the Living God," they'd say, even as they procured their services when the children of the Beacon Baptist Home for Orphans fell ill. There they'd be, pulling out little sacks filled with tree barks and leaves and herbs and powders for poultices, coins and little pieces of paper with scrawlings that wished for the childrens' best, no matter that the intendeds they were designed to help believed quite the contrary. It wasn't until LoLo experienced the tenderness of one summoned to break Freddy's fever that she thought otherwise. "Come here, baby," the lady, named Lena, beckoned, taking each of LoLo's hands into her own. She leaned in and swizzled her neck and shoulders, trying to capture LoLo's eyes with her own. Finally, LoLo obliged her—stopped moving her head to and fro and lifted her downcast eyes long enough to acknowledge she was listening but also quick enough to keep the lady's curses from sneaking into her eyeballs, like The Mothers had warned. "You okay, sugar?" the woman asked. "How is your heart?" LoLo said nothing, though her darting eyes betrayed her fear—of what The Mothers, the other children would think of any perceived connection between the two. "It's okay, baby. It ain't gone be easy, but you gone make it. Just remember that. You gone make it and be a light to someone else." LoLo didn't know anything about that, and she didn't think much about the rootworker's words until she held Rae's little sack in her hands for the first time and kept it for safekeeping after that. Maybe the person who assembled it put a root on it, meant to bring harm to whoever dared toss it rather than save it for the baby, she thought, or maybe the baby's mama meant for her to have it one day. Either way, The Society put it in an envelope and gave it to LoLo and she, in turn, put it away for safekeeping. Every now and again, she'd pull out that pouch and then sit and stare at the girl and wonder about her. Wonder how in the world she would protect that little girl in a world that meant little girls nothing but hurt and harm. LoLo was nervous about that part. LoLo was nervous about raising Rae.

Tommy, all he'd seen when he laid eyes on her was sunshine. Joy. "Let's call her Rae," he'd insisted one evening, weeks after they brought her home from the orphanage.

"Sound like a boy's name to me," LoLo had said. She'd thought maybe she'd want to call her Lila Mae, after her mama, or Bettye, after her grand-mama, but she needed to know who this little person was figuring to be. If she was worthy of those names. Tommy beat LoLo to the punch, though.

"Rae sounds like the sun," Tommy said, picking up the baby out of her crib and bouncing her in his arms. The baby yawned and stretched a bit, but she didn't fuss. Just stared into Tommy's eyes as he cooed and hummed along to the radio. Stevie Wonder was singing "A Place in the Sun," like he'd made that song just for that very moment. "She a little ray of sunshine."

Letting Tommy name the baby, that was easy enough. She could live with Rae.

"*Buh buh buh buh,*" the baby said as she drooled and leaned into LoLo's fingers for the last of the eggs. She smacked her lips and gave a slobbery smile.

LoLo collected the plate and wiped the baby's face and disappeared. Already, her mind was on the list of things she needed to complete before she could lay her head back down on the pillow that night. Before Tommy would be tugging at her nightgown and burying his lips in her neck and his fingers in her private places. "No" wasn't yet an option—certainly not for him. Not for her, either, just yet. He was gentle, tender, and if she kept her eyes open and watched his hands, his lips, his eyes, his shoulders, round like cannons, and held on to him tight, she could almost enjoy him.

That required real effort, though. Rest. And these days, with two ba-bies and a house to tend to, rest, well, that was not easy to come by. Pulling a double shift in the cold, dank cement basement of the sewing factory during holiday season was infinitely easier than wiping shitty behinds and changing pissy sheets in the middle of the night and combing hair and keeping the house straightened up and calming crying babies and bathing them and getting them dressed, too, and making breakfast, lunch, and dinner and grocery shopping for the week and fucking on demand and teaching babies how to fold their hands and say grace and be grateful for this new life Tommy promised and delivered.

LoLo pulled her housecoat tighter around her chest and dropped the plate into the sink, already full of dishes, and then turned to the refrigerator to pull out the jar of potlikka she'd saved from a big pot of greens she'd cooked the night before. She poured some of the liquid into a small pot and lit the gas on the stove, at first turning the flame low to better control the liquid's heat, but quickly turning it up higher when the baby slammed her hands on the plastic high chair table. *"Buh, buh, buh,"* she yelled as she heavy breathed and wrinkled her whole face, preparing for a cry.

"All right, all right," LoLo said as she grabbed a small glass bottle and assembled its nipple. "It's coming. Your bah-bah is coming."

And then came a crash. Milk was dripping everywhere—across the small folding table pushed against the wall of the tiny kitchen, down the chair seats and legs, across the floor, most of it puddling on the laminate and some of it easing its way toward the wood floor in the living room. "TJ!" LoLo yelled as her eyes traced their way back to the source of the spill. She slammed her hand against the boy's head, freshly shorn from the shape-up Tommy had given him the evening before. She grabbed him by the arm and lifted him out of his chair and swatted his behind as she flung him out of the kitchen. "Get out of here, making all this damn mess," she yelled after the boy as he scrambled into the living room. His wail startled Rae; her little body stiffened, her eyeballs bugging like she'd just witnessed holy horror. And then she wailed, too.

LoLo snatched the glass off the table and TJ's spoon and empty oatmeal bowl, too, and crashed them into the sink. With her hands on the sink's rim, she bent forward and leaned her body back, stretching her spine and deep breathing through her nose, choking down a cry of her own. The potlikka began to boil.

It wasn't even 8:00 A.M.

14

Summer, 1970

LoLo didn't have a problem with Pat Cleveland. She liked her, actually, but thought the regard for her beauty was much too obvious. Tall. Thin. Pretty hair. Didn't none of those things make her any different from every other light bright who whipped crooks in people's necks simply because she didn't look like the garden-variety colored woman.

Now Luna, that was LoLo's girl. She had those great big ol' eyes, looking like an owl scared of the dark, and all her limbs stretched like branches of a spindly oak tree in the wintertime. She had a bit more color to her skin, but she didn't have any titties to speak of, or hips and ass, like the girls who found their way to the centerfold of *Jet*. Every week, colored men licked their fingers and left their spit on the corners of the magazine's glossy pages, hurriedly wading past the cigarette ads and the quick stories about the goings-on of Negroes, in search of those half-naked pictures of Marilyn, who likes to swim and read, and Eloise, with her 38–24–36 body parked behind a secretary's desk at some Negro college down south. Black men, they wanted those girls—real women with soft, thick parts to hold on to. Luna wasn't the one for them and that's what LoLo liked about her. That's what made her feel all right about her own tall, lithe, awkward body that defied stereotypes of what a Negro woman's body should look like. What the men wanted. LoLo was otherworldly, a pretty Martian, just like her idol. She secretly loved that all her friends even took to calling her "Little Luna," on account she was "a skinny ol' thang," just like the supermodel, who had managed to become the toast of the white fashion industry despite being a Negro. "Y'all even got them same great big ol' eyes," Cindy said one afternoon during their lunch break at the tailor shop. LoLo sat chewing on a Spam sandwich, thumbing through an issue of British *Vogue* she kept hidden in the middle of the stacks of magazines their boss kept handy for "inspiration," which was really just a less sinister, singular word to describe how he passed off European fashion as his own "original" gowns and such to his well-to-do, none-the-wiser white clientele. They all thought buying overpriced, tailor-made clothes from a personal designer made them infinitely more fashionable, like the ladies in the society pages of *The New York Times* and *The New Yorker*, and so he actively stole designs to keep up. He'd thrown away Luna's issue, though—the one on which she made her cover debut. Didn't see anything worth stealing off Luna's body. But Para Lee had salvaged the magazine from the trash for LoLo, and Mr. Deerfield, he was none the wiser for it.

"You really think I look like her?" LoLo asked. She cocked her head and squinted her eyes, searching Luna's face for her own, and allowing herself just a moment to imagine herself outside of that basement, outside of Amityville, outside of New York and the United States and prowling down a runway on her hands and knees, like Luna, or making that finger symbol over her eye for Avedon's camera. Maybe kissing Mick Jagger on his thick lips and making him profess his love again and again.

"Hmmph, she pretty, but that can't be no way to live," Para Lee said.

"What you mean?" LoLo asked, finally looking up from the magazine's pages.

"People love to see that girl act the fool, running all through these streets like she don't have a lick a sense," Para Lee said, picking imaginary lint off her perfectly starched, demure dress. "But they don't love her. There's a difference."

"Well, for somebody who isn't loved, she sure looks like she's having herself a groovy time," Cindy said, peering over LoLo's shoulder at the now well-worn pages featuring the model. "I know this much: the men she's dealing with ain't no squares."

"Ugh, who would want that Andy Warhol weirdo making googly eyes at you? He treats her like she's his pet."

"The kind of bread he has, maybe his leash wouldn't be so bad, am I right, Little Luna?" Cindy said, giggling.

LoLo grimaced, her stomach roiling at the thought of a leash—a physical restraint—being used to control Luna's body. Her body. It was one of her cousin Bear's favorite things to do, when his wife left for errands and the house was still; LoLo knew he would find her, no matter where she tried to hide, no matter how she folded herself into corners, and he would control her, with his hands, a belt. After a while, all it took was his command. "Come here," he would say to LoLo, his eyes dark, his voice matching them. Slowly, she would find her way to him and stand in front of this man, her long body, five foot eight in her stockinged feet, slumped into submission before his short but muscular, stocky frame. Always, he would toy with her—make her stand there, waiting, anxious, guarded. Never would she be ready for what came next. No matter that it happened over . . . and over . . . and over . . . and over again. Never was she prepared.

"I ain't interested in being anybody's pet," LoLo said, abruptly slamming the magazine shut and sitting back down to her sewing machine.

But tonight, her intention was to be the gazelle in the middle of the circus Tommy was creating at their new place—an epic housewarming party he was throwing to show off the spoils of his war. He wanted everyone he knew to see his babies, the new house he'd procured for them to totter around in, that sweet ride he had sitting out front. LoLo happily assumed the position as the dutiful wife who could fry up the fish and make the best macaroni and cheese this side of Long Island, all while looking like Luna, with her man's arm draped around her waist. She'd sewn up something magazine-worthy—a knee-baring version of the shimmering golden Paco Rabanne dress that practically dripped off Luna's body in her David Bailey shoot in *Vogue*. LoLo had found the material and a simple pattern at Woolworth's, and, employing the magic she'd practiced for two years during her gig at Deerfield's Tailoring and Design, spread the tear sheet she'd carefully ripped out of the magazine on her sewing table and got to work. Of course, it fit like a glove. Of course, while Tommy was at work and the babies were taking their naps, LoLo slipped into her creation and slinked around the house, sitting daintily on the green velvet couch, back straight, shoulders square, long legs stretched out in front of her, size-ten feet pointed in a way that made her body look a foot longer.

She fake laughed and waved her cigarette and struck poses for the camera until she had her fill—until she was sufficiently satisfied that she'd excised her desire to run away from her new home and her pretty babies and her hardworking husband and, like Luna, who insisted she was from Mars, be somebody otherworldly instead of the regular housewife living the regular life of a regular colored woman who didn't dare consider what was possible beyond the stars and bigger than the moon.

"I didn't say I don't like the dress. It's out of sight," Tommy said, circling around LoLo as she stood before him in her glittering golden frock that, when she first slipped it on, made her feel like Venus. Now, she was Pluto. Small. Insignificant. "I just don't know no woman who dresses up like a movie star to fry fish for a Spades party."

And yet, this was what Tommy had proclaimed he dug about LoLo when he was trying to win her heart. It was nothing for LoLo to sit at her sewing machine and conjure up extravagant affairs that made Tommy puff out his chest when they walked into a room—he, short and dark, with a welterweight's build and muscular shoulders bulging through his suit jacket, and she, modelesque and a quarter foot taller in her heels, looking like a rock star's girl. She would wear sheath dresses with gloves and matching kitten heels to buy bread and cigarettes at the A&P just as easily as she would to check out a set at Minton's. Always a show. She'd spent, after all, quite enough time being average. Being told who and what she couldn't be. Up north, in the streets of New York, she was her own invention. That is who Tommy chose. And she liked being the prize. His prize. In a world that refused her protection, she was a jewel he coveted—safe in his arms.

Surely, for her, he'd made concessions; her physicality, her breasts more nipple than fatty flesh, her hips more angular lines than curve, none of it was his ideal. But she was sexy, alluring—the kind of woman who made necks swivel, even when she wasn't trying hard but especially when she put in effort. Tommy liked the attention. Liked having her on his arm. With her, back then, he was taller. Stronger. If anyone looked at her sideways, Tommy was quick to square up. "She don't need you buying her drinks," he'd once growled to a potential suitor who'd arranged to have a cocktail sent to LoLo while she stood by the bar, swaying and snapping her fingers to The Supremes' "Where Did Our Love Go," waiting for Tommy to come back from the john. Tommy'd snatched the drink, a bourbon, neat, from her hand and slammed it, along with his hand, into the man's chest as he walked up with his hand outstretched, looking to greet the girl who'd caught his eye. LoLo wasn't impressed by how Tommy knocked the man over—by how willing he was to fight to prove his worth to her. Instead, what caught her attention was the way he put his hand on her hip and pushed her behind him, like he was a protective wall against anything that thought to rush her. He'd caused the chaos but made her feel safe in its aftermath. He fast became her superhero, her protector.

But now, for his friends, in the home—the life—he'd built, he was bigger when his fish was fried hard and the beer was poured cold. LoLo hadn't quite gotten used to recutting her patterns, nipping and tucking and tailoring herself into more sensible pieces. But this was what she was supposed to do, right? This is who she was supposed to be, right? Somebody's wife? Somebody's mother? Somebody's peace? The woman who was worth protection?

And so, she cut.

Hours later, she'd forgotten all about that dress and its grandeur and leaned into her right hip as she dropped another few pieces of cornmeal-coated perch into the bubbling grease. "Y'all go on 'head and get you a cold beer out the cooler," she said, smiling wide as Cindy walked in with her old man, Roosevelt, and Tommy's brother, Theddo, kissed her on the cheek. "I don't know where Tommy at. He might be out there on the—"

"I'm right here, woman," Tommy said, playfully smacking LoLo on her behind, which now was covered by a green, yellow, and brown plaid mini-skirt. He gave his wife some sugar and reached around her to grab a hot, fresh piece of fish off the mass of paper towels soaking up the grease. LoLo smacked his hand.

"Ah ah! You're going to burn your tongue," she said. "And then what I'mo do with a man can't use his tongue?"

The whole room burst into oooooohs and all-right-nows as Tommy chuckled and leaned in for a kiss, mouth open, tongue ready. LoLo stared at it as she licked out her own and took his into her mouth. "Mmmph," Tommy said. "I got me a sexy-ass wife, I tell you that," he added as he pulled away, grabbing a piece of fish and shoving it into his mouth before LoLo could stop him. "She can cook, too!"

"Go' on, get outta my kitchen, man!" LoLo yelled, feigning anger and dodging another ass slap. "Won't be no fish left messing with you." Her laugh was full-bellied. Honest.

The night stretched on just like this—easy and pure. LoLo tended the fish, a pot of turnip greens with ham hocks, and a pan of her beloved macaroni and cheese, while Cindy kept the beer stocked in the cooler and did her best to keep Roosevelt out of the brandy bottle. Sarah was doing a coordinated dance with LoLo in the kitchen, hand-cranking batches of fresh vanilla and strawberry custard from her ice cream machine while the three talked shit and swayed to Marvin Gaye and the Temptations.

"Wooooooo, that Marvin got a voice that cuts like a hot knife through sweet cream, I'll tell you that," Cindy said, swirling her hips to the beat of "How Sweet It Is (To Be Loved By You)" pumping from the record player. "That man smooth."

"Hmm, Eddie Kendricks, now that's my man," Sarah said as she leaned into the crank and turned and turned, her biceps dancing to the rhythm. "All he'd have to do is growl in my direction and I'd be out these hot pants directly."

Tommy slammed down the high joker so hard, it made the whole table rumble and buckle under the weight of his hand. "Run 'em, muthafuckas!" he yelled, and the whole house shook with laughter—the women in the kitchen, the men at the table with their legs spread wide and their cigarettes dangling from their lips, eyes pink from smoke and drink, the couples doing their slow grinds beneath the red light bathing the walls, their bodies dripping sex.

Beyond the music and loud talking, LoLo could hear the faint sound of a baby's pitch—a whine that would, within moments, turn into a full-on cry. The children had been put down hours ago and were in a deep sleep by the time the first guests had arrived, but LoLo hadn't made calculations for how to keep them in their slumber through the good time that was being had. She craned her head around the kitchen's corner and trained her eyes on the doors behind which the children were supposed to be a sleep, listening.

"Them kids all right," Tommy said, shuffling the cards, while he watched LoLo watch the doors. "Let 'em be."

"I thought I heard one of them," LoLo said, still staring.

"TJ just turning over is all. He'll be fine. Go on back in there, now, before that fish burn. Finish up so I can slow-drag with my fine-ass wife."

LoLo giggled and gave Tommy those eyes she knew made him want to clear out the fish and the beer and the card table and all the people attached to each of them, so that he could fold her limbs around his waist, her body beneath his.

The doorknob to TJ's room wiggled. Rae's whine turned into a wail. Tommy and LoLo tucked their desire back in and groaned. "I gotta turn over this fish," LoLo said quickly, flashing her cornmeal-covered fingers for emphasis.

"Come on, baby," he said, flashing his cards. "I got a winning hand. Cindy will watch the fish."

"Aw nawl, you don't put Cindy on the fish," Roosevelt slurred as he moved his cards around in his hand. "She'll fuck up your fish, now. Unless you like it bland and burnt." Already, Roosevelt had stared at the bottom of three glasses of brandy and a couple beers, just the right combination to unlock his belligerence, which, unleashed, always found its way to Cindy somehow, in the form of an insult or two, some yelling, sometimes a slap. Roosevelt would get going and everyone knew to ready their feet for the egg-shells. "All she good for is tending to the ice in the cooler. Hell, come to think of it, she can't even get that right. My beer was warm when she brought it over." And then, to Cindy: "Aye, bring me a cold beer this time. Damn."

"Say, you don't have to talk to her like that," Sarah said quietly. She stepped in front of Cindy, this woman who had been her friend long enough for her to keep her secrets and tend her wounds when they were fresh and deep.

"Who you talking to, bi—"

"Whoa, whoa, whoa!" Tommy said, dousing the fire before it got more oxygen. Looking at Roosevelt but addressing LoLo, he let his words tumble quickly: "I got the baby. You go on and make another batch of that fish, hear? I ain't trying to mess with perfection. I got him."

LoLo, uneasy, anxious, took Cindy's hand and led her back into the kitchen—away from Roosevelt's line of sight. She knew the drill. Sarah did, too. As did Tommy, though he really made a point of not concerning himself with another man's affairs, particularly how he handled his money and his lady. He'd encouraged LoLo on many an occasion when she recounted how Cindy came to work with her eye blacked or a bluish-brown bruise perverting her redbone to "just leave it alone." "That's her business," he would say. "She don't like it, she leave."

"You think a woman likes being beat by her man?" LoLo said to him one particular night when they'd argued much too long about another couple's affairs. "You must be crazy!"

"I'm not saying she like it," Tommy had insisted, using both his hands to signal LoLo to calm down. "I'm just saying when a woman gets fed up, she'll stop trying to make it work."

Together, in the quiet of the kitchen, with fish grease popping and Sarah's churning scratching a rhythm against the ice cream maker's metal bucket, LoLo wondered when Cindy would stop trying and start doing for herself. But they all knew this was no easy proposition. The women, they knew.

A chorus of "Awwwww" and "Hey, little man!" in the living room shook them from their thoughts. "Mmmmm mmmph," Sarah said, taking a break from churning to peek around the corner. "Y'all sure did pick some pretty babies."

Cindy tipped over to get her own look. "She picked a good man, too. Look at Tommy in there wit 'em. Know he love them kids." Then, to LoLo: "You a lucky girl. Got you a man who loves you and takes care of you and those kids ain't even his."

"They are his," LoLo quickly interrupted.

Sarah gave Cindy "the look." "Yes, they are," Sarah said without taking her eyes off the offender. "A big happy family is what we all deserve."

LoLo shook the cornmeal off her fingers and walked over to look for herself. Tommy had taken a seat on a small chair at the end of the room, cradling both TJ and Rae in the crooks of his arms. Rae hid her face in Tommy's chest, her little Afro, crooked and peasy, practically the only thing her audience could make out beyond her white onesie and bulking cloth diaper. TJ sat stoic, rubbing his eyes and yawning, unphased by the peering, the music, the smell of cigarettes and reefer and musty bodies sweaty from a full night of dancing and laughter. He wasn't fazed, either, by the flash of the Polaroid camera. Months later, TJ would find his mother sitting in that same chair, smiling at that instant picture, completely un-aware that the gaze he saw was that of LoLo, looking at her family, this unit she'd hand-created, and falling, fully, finally, in love for the very first time with what she'd long believed she'd never have. Protection. Love. A family of her own that loved her back.

Later that night, after the babies were back deep into their slumber and the last of the guests had delivered their half-hour-long All right, nahs and Sarah had helped LoLo pick up the plates and cups and wipe up traces of beer and cigarette ashes that had splashed onto the floors as the guests shook with laughter and slow-dragged their bodies to Marvin Gaye, LoLo washed her face and peeled out of her miniskirt and went to their bed with her night scarf balled up in her hand. She was still too woozy from reefer and brandy to pin-curl her hair and didn't want to, anyway. Tossing onto her nightstand the worn, raggedy scarf, musty from hair grease and night sweat, was a signal. She, still high on brandy and the reefer, wanted Tommy. And he would gladly submit.

Now, LoLo never actually said out loud to her husband that she wanted sex; she knew that was the way he liked it, this man who, like any other, fully expected his wife to come to the marital bed pure—ready to let him lead just as easily in the dark as he was expected to in the morning light. The hippies were screaming "free love" and "revolution," but the wives knew. The men, they were in charge. Leaving her scarf on the nightstand would be as close to bodily autonomy LoLo had come in her entire twenty-three years on the earth.

The moon's glow cast blue light on Tommy's bare chest and one of his muscular legs resting like a hunk on top of the white sheets. LoLo focused on the whites of his eyes as he shifted his body toward her, angling for a better view as she slowly unbuttoned her nightgown and let it drop to the floor. Reefer, brandy, they controlled the strings to her marionette, laying her body down, spreading her wide from limb to limb, her torso wav-ing and surrendering and flipping and bouncing on the squeaky mattress. *Moan,* they said, and so she did. *Open your mouth wide,* they said, and so she did. *Tilt your neck, run your fingernails down the black of his back, moan again,* they said. And so, she did. Reefer and brandy always knew just what to do. Reefer and brandy were loud and raucous—Tommy's favorites. Reefer and brandy relaxed the muscles, choked and drowned the memories. Made what was dead breathe again. Made it so Tommy could drive fast with the windows down, the engine hot and rumbling. Made it so LoLo could ride free.

Both were dissolved in a sweaty heap, bodies twisted in sheets and pillows and a sleep deep enough for neither to notice TJ standing there on the side of the bed, eyes wide, staring into the dark, trying to make sense of the skin and body parts. With his right hand, he held his pissy pajama bottoms, with his left, he self-soothed, his thumb slobbery and stinking of hot breath. TJ looked at his father's penis and then down at his own—at his mother's nipples and then down at his own. Usually, someone would have hopped to at the sound of his door opening, but in this moment, his parents were dead. A push of his mother's shoulder made her spring to life, her scream and sudden jerk resuscitating Tommy, too.

"My God, boy, what ail you!" LoLo yelled, squinting to adjust her eyes to see her son standing there, staring. The white of the pajama pants came into focus first, and then his body, naked from the waist down.

Tommy looked, too, shook his head, and laid back down.

"TJ, boy, you wet the bed again?"

He slowly nodded his head.

LoLo rubbed her eyes and laid back down on the pillow. Her forehead and temples had their own pulse. She closed her eyes again. Maybe it was a dream. Yes, a dream. She would go back to sleep and wake up normal, like everyone else, rested and feeling like everything was right with the world.

Tommy nudged her. "LoLo, get that boy in the other room. He smell like piss."

His voice was a hammer against her forehead. "I can't . . . move," she said, struggling to push the words past her teeth.

The two parents, drunk and half-high, fell back to sleep again, the sounds of the night—the crickets and cicadas and still of the air—lulling them. TJ pulled his thumb out of his mouth and pushed his mother's arm, his slobber leaving a track on her skin. "TJ! What!"

"LoLo, go change that boy. I'm trying to sleep, damn!"

LoLo sat up fast and, in her head, said all the things she wanted to say out loud—*Me too, damn. Is something wrong with your hands? They too good to wipe little pissy asses? I fried the fish, I cleaned the kitchen, I swept the floors, I fucked you. You can't do this one thing?* And then she swung her feet over the side of the bed, taking the sheet with her, and covered her breasts as she reached for her robe and concentrated on holding the bile creeping up to her throat at bay. TJ stood there watching as LoLo struggled herself into the fabric, their eyes locked, no words exchanged. LoLo tied a knot with the fabric belt, their eyes locked still. She stood. And then, without warning, she swiftly smacked the boy across his face with the back of her hand.

His wail was like a siren in the room—made Tommy sit straight up. "LoLo, what the fuck! What you hittin' on him for?"

LoLo snatched the boy up by his arm and, through gritted teeth, said, "He needs to learn not to wake up his daddy," as she pulled him behind her through the bedroom door, out into the hallway, and into his room, thick with the smell of piss and fear.

15

The sun was supposed to blister in July, but on this particular day, it perched itself high up in a cloudless sky, aiming to crisp the green leaves on the bush beans and the purple on the hydrangea petals and anything else that shined a light in LoLo's world, and so LoLo was determined not to let anything get in the way of the tending. The pole beans, the kale, the green onions, and squash would make for fine Sunday dinners beginning in a month or so, but they needed protection—water, care—and she intended to give them just that.

She could hardly get the baby down for her nap fast enough; Rae was still fussing a bit when LoLo tied up her hair in one of Tommy's bandannas and slipped out into the backyard, sans shoes, with a hoe, rake, and hose in hand, TJ hot on her heels. The baby, she would find her peace soon enough. In the garden, so would LoLo. Standing in the patch of lawn next to her plot, LoLo lifted her face to the light of the brightest star as she massaged her toes and foot pads in the thick of the grass blades, down to the dirt. TJ looked down at his mother's feet and then his own, and did the same, wriggling his little toes so hard he would have fallen over, had not his mother caught him by the arm. "Feels good, don't it?" she said, her smile, her laugh sincere. As if it were acknowledging their presence— their grounding—Mother Earth sent a gentle breeze their way, kissed their cheeks with a quick blast of cool. LoLo closed her eyes and breathed in deep. Today, she decided, would be a good day.

"Mama!" TJ called out to her. Quick as that wink, he'd made his way over to the top of the back porch steps. "Look!" he called out. As LoLo raised her hands but before she could get out the word "No!," TJ bent his knees and swung his arms out in front of his body and took flight—came crashing down on his knees just beyond the concrete, hard into the grass. Got up giggling. Which made LoLo giggle, too. Used to be she'd swallow her heart, see the little boy's life flash before her very eyes. She'd forgotten in the beginning how rough little boys could be—how hard they ran and tumbled, roughhoused and searched, with the accuracy of a missile, for all the dirtiest, messiest things to get into. Mud puddles. Trash cans. Worm and ant homes deep down in the dirt. In TJ's world, they were lakes in which to paddle his boat—fishing holes full of perch and whiting that could be caught with imaginary poles. LoLo learned quickly to let her streak of tomboy—that which was groomed in the back fields and woods beyond the orphanage, where she and her fellow foundlings ran wild and free, far away from the Mothers' gazes—soar. When she let herself, she enjoyed TJ. Rae was another matter.

"Whoa, that was a good jump!" LoLo called out to TJ, her smile wide, genuine. "You Superman today? Where you flying to? Can I come?"

"Come on, Mama! Let's fly to the moon!"

TJ took off running, his arms waving behind him as he circled the yard as fast as his legs could carry him. LoLo bent her long legs and took tiny steps behind him, her arms flapping, too, her smile wide, too, the two of them pretend flying through space, the good guys on their big adventure. They went on and on like this, flying beyond the moon, to Saturn and Venus and Mars.

"Okay, okay," said LoLo, out of breath and anxious to get to what she'd originally intended to do. "That's enough, lil' man. Go over there and get your ball and play while Mama gets to this garden. Before your sister wakes up."

TJ dutifully retrieved his blue-marbled plastic ball and got to kicking it all around the yard as LoLo surveyed the neat rows of vegetables she'd grown from seeds to seedlings to plants to sustenance for her belly and her heart. Every single day, she looked forward to these transcendent moments—the buzz of the honeybees as she pulled up the weeds, how the fertilizer, rich with chicken manure or horse shit, whatever she could get her hands on, flavored the fresh air, reminding her of what little bit of good she managed to take for herself growing up in South Carolina. The cotton fields were brutal under the Carolinian sun, and her cousins, the ones who rescued her from the orphanage and chained her to a different kind of hell, used her up out there. All of them worked hard—that was the nature of sharecropping. Wasn't nothing glamorous about it for any of them, but the most tedious tasks on the land, Bear, her father's first cousin, and Clarette, his wife, had saved for LoLo. Plenty nights she crawled into her bed, everything hurting: blistered feet, skin burned raw, knees crooked from kneeling in the soil, picking rocks out the long rows, or mounding up the dirt over the seeds with her bare hands. The worst of it was in the chicken coop, mucking out the thick crust of feathers and cobwebs and shit as hard as cement, with no air to speak of and only wisps of light streaming through the wooden planks. Keeping down her morning ration of oatmeal—on generous days, maybe a biscuit with a slice of salt pork— was every bit a challenge as it was to survive another day on the land. But survive was what she did. Eventually, she came to relish it—the serenity, the connection to the earth. The escape from Bear's hands, full with the bounty of the land instead of LoLo's parts. Farming danced in her bones. Tending the garden moved her.

LoLo leaned into the stream of cool water flowing from the garden hose and took a sip, then placed her thumb over the hose's opening to turn the water into a spray. The water shimmied in the sun's rays, coaxing a ribbon of colors in its shower. LoLo smiled and began a humble, warbling hum of one of her favorite songs. To her left, TJ kicked his ball and ran after it like it was his job. Behind her, the driveway gate slammed. LoLo glanced in the direction; Cindy was snapping her fingers, a little bounce in her stroll as she sang along to LoLo's hum: "'Another Saturday night and I ain't got nobody . . .' Yeah, that's that Sam Cooke right there," Cindy said as she took her place next to LoLo and watched her water. "That man know he was fine. And I'll bet you he had plenty to choose from on his Saturdays, mmm hmm!"

LoLo laughed but kept her eyes on the task at hand. "You a mess!"

"But am I lying?"

"I reckon you right. Probably had a whole lineup to choose from," LoLo said, laughing easily. Until she turned and saw Cindy's face. Her friend's cat-eye sunglasses hid some of the bruising, but not enough. LoLo kept watering, but her smile slowly faded off her lips. "What's going on, Cindy? What bring you this way this fine afternoon?"

"I don't know," she said quietly. She shifted from one foot to the other. "I was driving by; knew I'd see you out here in these pole beans." She turned her attention to the two huge hydrangea bushes lining the fence. "Whew wee, Tommy sure got them hydrangea looking right. He done turned them deep purple for you, huh?" she said, using her hand to shield her eyes from the sun.

LoLo was quiet. Didn't feel like talking about anybody's flowering bushes. "Look like Tommy ain't the only one turning things purple."

Cindy reached for her left cheek, but the words, those she couldn't seem to force out of her gullet. After a long silence, LoLo helped her to them. "Roosevelt somewhere preparing his sorrys?"

"I don't know where he at," Cindy snapped. "Don't care."

LoLo continued to water her garden, the cool of the spray numbing her thumb. Finally, when she felt like her vegetables and flowers had gotten their fill and Cindy had relaxed her shoulders a bit and the sound of the birds blanketed their sorrowful thoughts, LoLo released her thumb, sending the water tumbling at her naked feet.

"Give me a sip of that water," Cindy said.

LoLo held up the hose and watched as Cindy leaned in and kissed the stream. She took a few quick sips, then stood up straight and reached into her purse for her pack of Kool cigarettes and a matchbook. Offered LoLo a smoke. LoLo accepted. The two stood in silence, the water running at their feet as they inhaled the nicotine and tilted back their heads to blow rings toward the cloudless sky.

"I'm pregnant," Cindy said finally.

LoLo looked at her friend's belly and took another pull of her cigarette, but she didn't say a word. She walked over to the side of the house and twisted the water knob to shut off the stream, then took a few more tokes as she trudged back over to her friend, trying to find the right words to say on her way back to the garden.

"I'm late on my monthly by about six weeks. And my stomach feels . . . weird. Like there's something in there multiplying and dividing—getting hard and growing at the same time." She took another puff and dropped her cigarette hand by her side, revealing the start of the tears streaking down her cheeks. "I can't do this."

LoLo bent down to snuff out the top of her cigarette in a small puddle that had formed at the tip of the dirt by the pole beans. "Not with him, you can't. We see eye to eye on that. We got to find you a place to lay low while you think on your next move with the baby—"

"I'm not keeping it," Cindy said, cutting off LoLo.

LoLo wrinkled her brow. "What you mean you not keeping it?"

Cindy was quiet.

"Cynthia Clayton," LoLo snapped. Her words made her friend jump. "I'm sorry, I'm sorry—I'm sorry," LoLo said quickly, understanding that her yelling was scaring her already fragile friend. She tried to hug Cindy, but her friend's body was stiff against the embrace.

"I've made up my mind. I can't bring a baby into this world with that man. The way he do me, ain't no telling if he'd do that to our child."

"But I don't understand," LoLo said. "You have a choice. You can choose that baby over that man."

Cindy scoffed. "And do what? Raise a baby on my own?" she asked. "Have you forgotten how hard it is out here for us? How hard it is to feed our damn selves, let alone these children? How the whole world think you ain't nothing but a cheap nigger hussy if you running around here with a bunch of snot-nosed kids with no daddy to speak of? Not everybody got a Tommy, willing to go out there and work like he do to keep y'all alive."

"What you care about what other people think about your baby?"

"I care about staying alive," Cindy said. "I can't do that with a baby."

"But you can do that with Roosevelt?" LoLo asked. She grabbed Cindy by her chin and looked her in her eyes. "That man gone kill you."

Cindy snatched her face away. "I can handle him. I can't handle being alone. I just can't," Cindy said. She wiped a stream of tears making its way down her cheek. "And I didn't come here to be judged, LoLo. I came for your help." She lifted her eyes and looked into those of her friend. She placed her hand on her belly and beckoned LoLo to look at it.

LoLo slowly shook her head. "No. No, no, no, no—you can't do this," she whispered. "Don't do this, Cindy—please."

"I don't have a choice, don't you see?"

"If you do it this way, they will take away any choice you got left, don't you see?" LoLo begged. She grabbed Cindy's belly with the one hand and grabbed her own with the other. "I know this. I just know it. You don't want this, you don't want this, you don't want it," she said, shaking her head no, tears and snot glistening on her skin.

Fall, 1963

Most people—Negroes, anyway—can remember the details of September 15, 1963, like a painter does his brush strokes: the sun was hanging in a clear, blue sky and the fish were practically jumping onto Zachariah Wilson's line in Mill's Creek out there in the Virginia mountains, and Deaconess Bunche, the one with that heavy early Sunday morning voice, keep the butterscotch candies at the bottom of her pocketbook, was calling the angels down right from heaven in the front pew in a church over in Texas, when word got to spreading from east to west to north to south about those four poor little lambs murdered by a wretched cracker's hand during the most sacred moment of the week: the beginning of Sunday school, when children dressed in their church best get sent by their parents to learn The Word. Lynchings, well, they were all gruesome—Black bodies twisted and broken and even cut into pieces, faces contorted and frozen into that final moment when necks snapped and the last breath left the body and the victims, the poor victims, most likely innocent, definitely terrified, certainly unprepared for the finality, watched all their lives' moments flash before them and looked into the light shone by ancestors calling them home. It is a fright to see. But the thought of four little babies, girls, hair pressed just so, pretty cotton dresses brushing their knees, Mary Janes shined up like a new penny with Vaseline and maybe a little spit, just . . . dead . . . well, that kind of tragedy? That monstrous act? It sears the memory. Can't just shake off fresh news of the murder of four little girls any more than you can rub the black off a Negro's skin.

But then there was LoLo, who remembered that exact date for reasons other than the lynching of those babies—who, in fact, remembered September 15, 1963, because that was the day her own children were lynched.

The baby that made it to her belly was Bear's. That baby was not made in love. That baby's heart hadn't been beating even two weeks and already, it had had enemies. Clarette, burdened by a husband who fancied beating and sexing his teenage cousin, couldn't stand the thought of LoLo bringing a child into the house where she and her man had buried four babies her womb turned out before their time. She wanted LoLo's baby dead. The head nurse down there at the whites-only hospital—the one with the keys to the medical supply room and enough assists on the ob-gyn ward to know how to pull unwanted babies from bellies—wanted LoLo's baby dead, too. In fact, Nurse Betsy Mills had made it abundantly clear to whoever would listen—fellow nurses, her Wednesday evening Bible study group, guests at her Thanksgiving table—that, in her estimation, the only good nigger baby was a dead nigger baby. And so she did what she could to fulfill wishes when it came to the matter—those of the women who sought her out for her basement abortions, and those of the white community, who'd just as soon scrape out the insides of any nigger woman they could get on the operating table than they would pay their hard-earned tax dollars feeding, clothing, and otherwise supporting the results of the Negro's pathologies, feeblemindedness, and reproductive ineptitude.

LoLo, well, she laid herself on Nurse Mills's table and spread wide her legs because she couldn't see any other way out of the pain—out of being tied to a baby she couldn't bear to raise and the rapist who had planted it in her. It was a decision Clarette called herself helping LoLo to, but the teenager, broken, scared, would have found her way to it on her own, what with the nightmares that had taken over her dream state, all of them the same, all of them awful: Bear would call LoLo out of the fields and push her into the barn, make her kneel next to his pregnant prized sow. "Pull it out!" he would demand as he undid his belt and the buttons on his overalls. "I said pull it!" LoLo, on her knees next to the pig, just lying there on its side, swollen and panting, would cup her hands, bare and bloodied, to pull tiny piglets from the sow's nethers, one, by one, by one, by one, by one, by one, by one, until there were seven in all—two black with white spots, and a couple dark brown with tiny black specks, and two more, pink, like their mama. The last one, that one was hairless, with a reddish-brown tint to its skin—the color blending seamlessly with LoLo's trembling hands. When she turned its face toward hers to have a look at its snout, it screamed like a human baby.

"You feed it!" Bear would demand.

LoLo would turn to put the screaming piglet on the sow's teat but Bear would only scream louder: "You feed it!" LoLo, then, would look down at her own chest and see her breasts leaking with blood and puss and, just beyond them, that piglet, screaming and wriggling in her hands, wiggling its snout and rooting for LoLo's bloody, puss-leaking ninny.

What was in her belly was not natural. Not right. LoLo knew this just as easily as she did the reason her monthly didn't come down in July and then in August. Clarette would quickly come to the same conclusions not ten minutes after finding her sixteen-year-old cousin deep in the fourth row of cotton stalks, vomiting up the cornbread and buttermilk bowl she'd eaten as the sleepy pink and yellow sunrise shone its light on the horizon.

"What ail you, gal?" Clarette yelled as she stomped through the soil, her concern heavy, leaving a trail in the dirt where she shuffled toward LoLo.

LoLo tried so hard to stop her stomach from retching, but it felt as if someone was ringing it like a washcloth full of bathwater and dirt. The sharp smell of the fertilizer, the cotton sending notes of sweat and musk to her nostrils, exacerbated that feeling. "I . . . I'm . . . sor . . . ," LoLo began before heaving again, the chunky liquid spewing from her throat and nostrils and splattering far enough to sprinkle droplets on Clarette's shoes. "It won't stop," were the only words LoLo could manage.

Clarette stood there staring at LoLo and the ghastly scene splayed before her. Face crinkled, hand over her nose, neck, spine tight, she took in how LoLo bent over the cotton stalks, how the girl's face tensed as she heaved. How she kept grabbing at her belly. It took less than a wink for her to do the math.

"When's the last time you got yo' monthly?" Clarette asked. Her eyes narrowed into slits, but her voice, it was even.

"I . . . I can't remember," LoLo managed between heaves.

"Come here," Clarette ordered, simultaneously grabbing LoLo's arm and rushing herself and her young charge toward the outhouse.

LoLo held tight to her stomach as Clarette burst through the rickety wooden door and grabbed the basket that held the pieces of sackcloth the two used when their blood came down. Clarette had paid it no never-mind until that very moment, but the only somebody who'd been using those cloths over the past couple months was her. But now, the contents of this basket, along with LoLo's retching out in the field, were painting a picture—a pile of evidence that quickly, easily led to the obvious conclusion.

LoLo stared at the cloths as Clarette slowly put the basket back in its place. She couldn't bear to look at her cousin's wife in the eyes, knowing what was next. Knowing she would be the one to carry all the culpability and the shame—knowing that Clarette could never, ever reach beyond her own pain to put the blame in its proper place or be of any real use to this sixteen-year-old girl, who had managed not much more on her own than to survive her suffering.

Clarette, well, she did the unexpected: she poured her sweet sweet straight down LoLo's gullet. "I know you didn't mean for this to happen," she said simply. And then she got to it. "I know somebody can hep you," Clarette said, her tongue sugared—her lips, syrup. "I won't let you get rid of it alone."

Clarette was expert at sweet-talking because that is, inherently, what she was: sweet and good. She was the kind of woman who would fall for the first boy who picked sunflowers off the side of the road special for her and say "yes" to him before he could halfway stutter through the words "marry me"—the kind of woman who would hold on tight to that man and that marriage because that is what she wanted and what was required of a woman of God, too. Obedience. Bear told her the Bible said it and she supposed it was so because passuh said it, too, and so the first time Clarette saw Bear on top of LoLo, consuming her, blood rushed to pressure points all over her body—ears, nose, eyes, feet, wrists, ankles, temples—but she didn't say shit. Just watched LoLo squeeze her eyes shut tight and choke down her cries beneath Bear's grunts and threats and commands. "Shut the fuck up and take your medicine, you nasty bitch," he said, his words wrestling through his furled lips and gapped teeth.

Clarette quietly, quickly backed out of the doorway of the storage barn and fell to her knees out in the field, prayers rushing, mind racing. She knew it would be just a matter of time before that young gal, tall and pretty, would yield what Clarette never could. God, He say, "Let it go," clear as a bell, clear as her prayer and the skies she told it to, and so she did. She did. All of it. Sweetly let go of the anger, sweetly let go of the disgust, sweetly forgave her husband and the little hussy he brought into their home. Sweetly delivered LoLo to Nurse Mills, who would rid the girl's belly of that evil and any other evil that could come after that. That Sunday, when the church exploded and the flames took those four babies and their sweet dresses that fluttered about their knees and their Mary Janes and pigtails, Nurse Mills scraped all the evil right out of LoLo's body and made her new. Made the living easier for everybody, Clarette told herself—for LoLo, for Bear, for Clarette Loretta Franklin, who loved the Lord and her husband and refused to let any man tear asunder what God brought together.

LoLo knew she was getting rid of Bear's baby that day. She'd made that choice willingly. What she was completely unaware of when she slowly closed her eyes and counted backward from one hundred was the tacit arrangement her cousin had made with that nurse once LoLo got to about the number ninety-three and floated off into the quiet dark—an arrangement that would forever change any other choices LoLo had the right to, for the rest of her natural-born life.

"Make it," Clarette had sneered to Nurse Mills when she saw her husband's lover fall deep into her medically induced slumber, "so she can't never sin against God again."

Bear, he saw things differently. Truth came to light when he tipped into LoLo's room later that evening, looking for his pleasure but stumbling, instead, into a room pregnant with pain. There was LoLo, laid up, pitiful, doing her very best to swallow her moans, and Clarette, dutifully changing the dressings on the three incisions in LoLo's groin that, once healed, would be thick with scar tissue and black—a historical marker of the day, time all her babies were taken from her, and, later, an intimate coat of arms, too, for all the lies she told to the men with whom she laid. Their eyes would narrow first, and some would reach to touch and LoLo would find a way to block their fingers and follow the action with one of her untruths: "I fell off a horse when I was little and landed on spikes," or "Some bitch stabbed me, talmbout I was eyeing her man, even though I wasn't. You should see *her* scars," or "Terrible poison ivy accident—I scratched myself something awful and the scars never went away." Then there was the one that would eventually stick with Tommy: "I went swimming in a part of a creek that had jagged rocks—come all the way up near to the surface. I swam over one and it cut me wide open. I liked to died." They all believed her. All of them. Especially when she punctuated her lies with reassurances that beneath all that black and bulbous tissue and thick scar, where they planted their seeds, flowers could still bloom.

But for Bear, the wounds—LoLo's, Clarette's—were fresh and so there would only be the truth. Bear tripped over his fat feet, as his brain caught up with his eyes and he quickly backed up to the door. "The hell going on here? How she cut herself there? How that happen?" he asked, his questions tumbling.

LoLo, embarrassed, fearful, withered from Clarette's touch and the sound of Bear's voice. Clarette, she shook more iodine onto the rag and dabbed at LoLo's trembling belly.

"I said what's going on in here? You don't hear me, woman?" Bear said, more forcefully this time, but still immobile. Stuck in his place.

Clarette slowly turned to her husband and let the truth fall where it willed. "I am cleaning up your mess, Joe Nathan," she whispered, staring, first at his shoes, and then directly into his eyes.

"Wha . . . what you mean, 'my mess'?" he snapped, but not as confidently as his demand for the particulars.

Clarette took her time so that her husband could hear her good. "Hebrews thirteen, verse four," she said slowly, her eyes narrowed into slits. "'Let marriage be held in honor among all, and let the marriage bed be undefiled, for God will judge the sexually immoral and adulterous.'"

"Woman, what is you talking?" Bear asked Clarette as he slowly shifted his eyes to LoLo. LoLo dropped hers, tried to catch her breath. But it was of no use; panic was winding its way through blood and sinew, through organs and up into the esophogus and touching gullet. She desperately fought the vomit, her heaving stabbing the places where, just hours before, Nurse Mills's scalpel had attended. LoLo cried out in pain.

Clarette was unmoved by the two of them. She carried on with her points. "'Therefore a man shall leave his father and his mother and hold fast to his wife, and they shall become one flesh.' Genesis, two and twenty-four," she practically whispered through clenched teeth. "Proverbs five, eighteen through nineteen: 'Let your fountain be blessed, and rejoice in the wife of your youth. Be intoxicated always in *her* love.'"

"Okay, passuh, we in Sunday school? What this got to do with what all is going on up in here?"

"It's got everything to do with what's going on here!" Clarette yelled. "You gave this gal what was meant for us—what God meant for a husband and his wife." She jabbed her pointer finger at LoLo's belly. LoLo jumped at the sudden movement and screamed as her body responded in kind with a stabbing pain so intense she felt it in her toes.

"I don't underst—"

"You know exactly what I'm talking about, Joe Nathan," Clarette yelled, her voice a high-pitched siren. She was the only somebody, besides his mama and white folk, who ever called Bear by his full first name. Then, through pursed lips: "Don't worry none. I took care of it."

Bear's eyes stretched wide. "What you mean you took care of it? Took care of what?"

"Won't be no bastard babies in this house, Joe Nathan," Clarette yelled, each word a staccato, like she was spelling out a complicated word, with "Joe Nathan" stretched, melodic, like a song. "Baby gone. Won't be no mo', neither."

"What . . . ," Bear began, and then he fell silent, his face contorted as his eyes fell to LoLo's wounds, first, then LoLo's face.

"I fixed it," Clarette said. She dabbed more iodine on LoLo's wounds.

LoLo shook her head, sluggishly at first, then gradually faster, lending to a crescendo of nos and pleas and calling to the Lord. "OhGodohGodohGod-ohGod no no no no no!" she yelled.

"You hush!" Clarette yelled. "Don't you lay here after what you've done and call the Lord's name in vain. He ain't have nothing to do with your sin. Now. Won't neither one of y'all be able to commit that sin again. My God is a forgiving God, but He will have His vengeance."

"Clarette, how could you do this to that girl? What gave you the right?" Bear yelled.

"What give you the right . . . ," Clarette yelled back.

And it went on like this, the two yelling over LoLo and her wounds, blame landing like buckshot, their denial and anger as scorching as a sip of boiling tea on lip and tongue—both keenly aware and yet still blind to the devastation they'd wrought on a sixteen-year-old girl who, humiliated, ashamed, devastated, lay there with holes in her soil where seeds would be sown but flowers would never bloom. LoLo's sadness would be an ocean that crossed her continents, crashing waves of grief against her shores 'til the day her breath was no more.

And now here was Cindy, standing before her, belly ripe with fruit, looking to lay her body on that same line. "Cindy, don't do this. Colored women get on those tables and their whole insides end up on the floor."

"What you know about it, LoLo? Huh?" Cindy asked, angrily wiping a tear that rushed down her cheek. "What you know about being so desperate you'll take that chance?"

Off in the distance behind them, back in LoLo and Tommy's tiny, two-bedroom house, just beyond the back window that always got stuck in the up position when the humidity of the hottest summer days made the wood sweat and expand, Rae began to stir. She was so tiny—cherubic in the face but all wiry legs and arms—but her whines, especially the ones she released as the prologue to her more epic cries, carried weight. LoLo looked off past Cindy's shoulder toward the window and then back into her friend's eyes. The sadness, the darkness in them was an ocean.

"But you told us Tommy was the one who couldn't make babies."

"And what you think he would have done if he found out it was me all this time? What you think he woulda done if he found out they took my womb?"

"That man loves yo' dirty bath water. He ain't going nowhere."

"You don't know that, Cindy," LoLo said quickly. "Men—especially our men—measure their dicks by how many babies they can make. They want to know they planted some seeds on this earth before they pass on. Tommy ain't no different. He a good man. But he ain't no different. He was looking to plant those flowers."

"You make him sound like one a them Black Power niggas," Cindy said, emphasizing her words with a scoff. "Like he want to make babies to save the race or some shit."

"Tommy not walking around with his fist in the air, you know that. My husband is quiet. But he still got his pride."

"How you convince him something was wrong with his manhood, then? How he didn't figure it was you?"

LoLo was quiet; Rae, getting fussier by the minute, was working up a cry that, surely, would put an end to garden time.

"Most men don't care to talk about monthlies," LoLo said slowly, staring at the jimmied window. "And they especially don't want to see it."

"You still get your monthly after . . . after, um . . ."

LoLo dropped her eyes; her heart started racing. There wasn't much she hadn't told her best friends, but this—it was a secret shame that weighed heavy, like an anchor pulling her down, down, down past the surf and the creatures that lived there, beneath the ripples, away from the ring of light, into the darkest recesses, where there is no air. Just black and fear and no bottom. LoLo couldn't breathe down there.

"It's okay, you don't have to talk about this anymore if it's too hard . . . ," Cindy said.

Rae worked up some more whimpers.

"He thinks I still get my monthly," LoLo said. "I told him it couldn't be me because a woman who still gets her monthly can still make babies, and he believed me.

"I made a choice and somebody erased all the rest of the choices I could have made after that," LoLo continued. "But they couldn't take away my choice to love. I still got that. Somebody thought better than to get up on that table, and her decision, however she came to it, made it so that Tommy and me could still be somebody's mama and daddy." LoLo's eyes chased after her daughter's cries. She stared at that window. She searched for TJ, who was chasing his ball, giggly and oblivious. "It's hard, I ain't gone lie," LoLo added. "But this is our family. This is my life."

Cindy moved in close to LoLo and took her face into her hands. There they stood, forehead to forehead, and chest to chest, in a tangle of arms and tears, swaying under the August sun. Over the course of a friendship that would go on to span four decades, LoLo and Cindy would never speak of LoLo's womb again.

Finally, they pulled themselves apart and ran their hands over their clothes, straightening themselves—LoLo ready to tend to her garden and her kids, Cindy ready to tend to her business at hand. Cindy watched as LoLo pulled a weed from around the pole beans and tossed errant rocks too close to her plants' roots over by the fence, so they wouldn't tear up Tommy's lawn mower when he cut the grass low.

"I'm still going to do this," Cindy said. "I love Roosevelt, but I don't have room to raise a baby in that house with him. Not now. I can't let what happened to you drive that decision any more than I'm willing to let Roosevelt do it. This something I got to do for me."

LoLo picked another weed, tossed another rock.

"Just pray for me, LoLo," Cindy said. "Can you do that for your ol' friend?"

Rae finally let out the wail she'd been working up all that time. "Let me get in here and see about this little girl," LoLo said, grabbing her garden tools. "TJ. Come on, baby. Your sister up. Put your ball away and let's go see about her."

LoLo looked at Cindy one last time and headed into the house—headed to her children.

16

1971, in the springtime

Tommy was no one's headline. He'd refused to subscribe to the running narrative written with the blood of all the niggers who came before him and all those to come after him, too. The authors, well, they regularly, religiously whipped up fantastical tales about the Black boogeymen whose laziness, ineptitude, and criminal tendencies, they claimed, reigned terror down on the good and righteous and rightful citizens of God's America, robbing them of their most prized possessions: their virtuous women, their money, their property, their livelihoods. Their very lives. It was a claim so oft told, so carefully listed among the fabrics that make up Black men's beings, that even some colored folk actually believed those tales to be true. Tommy's pa was one in that number, and so from the moment his wife pulled their sons from her belly and Pa clapped his hands at the sight of the fleshy parts dangling between his newborn boys' legs, he expected—exacted—hard labor. Proof that his sons, that he, were all cut from a different cloth. Tough. Hardworking. Strong, with the might of the biggest, blackest buck on the field. Tommy hated his father for this, but he relished in that characterization all the same. He liked to be counted as the hustler—the one you could trust to always, always win at survival. At having and keeping his own.

LoLo knew this firsthand and she legislated herself accordingly—with an unwavering trust in who Tommy said he was. Her words, in this moment, confirmed such. But still, she knew her eyes betrayed her fear, her unsurety, all the same when Tommy slowly pushed open the front door not even a couple hours after he'd left for work and quietly explained why he was darkening the threshold of their home so early on a Tuesday. "They ain't tell us a thing, Tick. Not one word. We got to work and they had this great big ol' fence all the way around the building. Shut down. The whole factory was just shut down," Tommy said as he dropped his lunch pail on the small wooden cocktail table, slowly sat on the sofa, and buried his head in his hands. "They wouldn't even come outside to tell us what happened. Just sent the security guard out to tell us to get the hell away from the fence and they'd send us our last paycheck in the mail."

LoLo, unsure of how to respond to news that Tommy's paychecks, already stretched thin by the pull of low wages attached to colored bodies, would stop altogether, trained her eyes on Rae, who was sitting naked in the middle of the multicolored braided wool rug, tugging on her doll's hair. She said nothing.

Tommy's eyes followed LoLo's and wrinkled in confusion. "Why the baby naked?" he asked.

His words snapped LoLo out of her trance. She quickly popped off the couch and grabbed a blanket to wrap their daughter in, using it to cover all of the important bits that LoLo didn't want any man staring at, not even Tommy. Rae fussed when LoLo picked her up, but quickly quieted when LoLo bent back down to grab the doll baby and place it in her tiny grabby hands. "I'm potty training her," LoLo said.

Tommy wrinkled his brow. "In the middle of the living room floor? With no clothes on?"

LoLo smirked as she bounced Rae in her arms and patted her bottom to calm the wriggly baby. "I was out hanging her diapers on the clothesline and Skip next door came by the fence to say good morning. Told me that if I let her walk around the house for a bit without her clothes on, she would know to tell me she needs to use the toilet."

Tommy looked at the baby and back at LoLo. "I guess Skip would know something about it, with five kids and all, huh?" he said finally. "It work?"

"Don't know yet," LoLo said, kissing the baby's cheek and tugging at the blanket to keep her covered. "She ain't pissed or shit in the floor yet, so he might be on to something."

"Where TJ at?"

"Next door playing. Skip said he could go over and play with the kids over there."

"Hmm."

LoLo took Rae into her room and plopped the baby into her crib, handing her the doll when she fussed. Tommy appeared in the door as LoLo pulled a dress out of the drawer of the small bureau, and he stared at both of the girls in his life—the two he'd vowed to himself and his god he would always protect. Or die trying.

"Look, you know your man. Ain't no way I would leave you and the kids hanging. I'll get another job. That's what I do, you know that. I work hard, I get paid, I bring it home to you. That won't ever change." Tommy let his words dance on his tongue like a prizefighter bouncing on his feet, center ring. He said them with his chest.

"What we gone do in the meantime, Tommy?" LoLo said, closing the drawer and finally letting her eyes meet his. "We got enough for groceries and such, but the mortgage gonna be due in a couple weeks. The insurance. What we gonna do then?"

"We're gonna do what we have to do to make it," he said simply. "Look, I already got the line on a gig cleaning banks. It don't pay what I was making at the factory, and I'll have to be working in the evenings, but it's going to have to do until I can find something else."

"Will it do, though? How much they paying to be a janitor at the bank?"

Tommy dropped his head as LoLo pushed the dress opening over Rae's soft, coiled Afro. He didn't have to say it; LoLo had been clear from the giddyup that staying home with the kids while her man earned all the bread was a fool's bet for a colored man and his wife and it would be just a matter of time before she'd have to do what everyone else around them did: earn her keep. Tommy's idea of taking care of her was noble, but LoLo knew to have her running shoes ready for the rat race.

"You know, Mr. Deerfield down at the tailor shop, he really liked my work and he did say that if I ever wanted to come back, I should stop by."

"I don't want you working, Tick. I promised you . . ."

"We made promises to each other, but the biggest one we have to honor is taking care of these children. Those checks we got for them, they need to stay in savings. We can't go spending that money. We got things to do with it and buying milk and collard greens with it ain't what we had planned."

"Making my wife work isn't what I had planned," Tommy said quietly.

"I know," LoLo said, turning to her husband. She reached out her arms, inviting him to her—a display of affection she rarely initiated, but felt appropriate, needed, in the moment. Happy, Tommy folded his wife into his arms. "It won't be long, right? I'll work in the daytime, and you can be with the kids, and then I'll take over while you work at night. We can do this. And you know Freddy got that job working for that company what makes the airplane parts. Maybe I could ask him about a job for you."

"Your brother just got to town—just got that job. He's not about to go begging The Man on my behalf. Besides, you two barely cordial."

"That don't matter. He owes me," LoLo said. She narrowed her eyes.

"Naw, I can't do that. I'll figure it out," Tommy said, running his hands over his Afro, like he was trying to rub the worry out of his head.

LoLo never doubted that eventually, it would come to this, as she did not have the luxury to think otherwise. She'd known, after all, that this dynamic her husband had dreamed up—this live-action, technicolor *The Adventures of Ozzie and Harriet* fantasy he had of working a good paying job that could keep food in the refrigerator, shoes on the kids' feet, and his wife free to get down to the business of taking care of her man and their home—was a con. Wasn't too many colored folk who could pull that one off, no matter how many niggers squeezed their eyes tight, clicked their heels, and envisioned themselves easing on down the yellow brick road toward that particular utopia. Crackas needed bodies to do their grunt work and they didn't care if those bodies had dicks or poom-pooms, so long as the work got done and *they* could focus on playing Ozzie and Harriet.

LoLo, no stranger to hard work, knew how to play this particular part. But leaving her babies in someone else's care—well, being prepared for that was a whole 'nother matter.

"Hello?" LoLo called out before she got in the door good. It was a Thursday—pay day—and so she was struggling under the weight of the armful of groceries she'd bought at the supermarket where she cashed her check. The apples, at the top of the brown paper bag in her right arm, tottered as she struggled to take off her shoes. Usually, Tommy would be resting on the couch, half-sleep, half-not, the children close by, flitting about like little butterflies kissing flowers. Busy. Everybody would be happy to see her—Rae looking to be picked up, TJ, thumb in his mouth, grabbing a leg, Tommy, grabbing the groceries out of his lady's hand and kissing her on the lips, relieved that he was about to be relieved. It was a dance they'd been doing for close to a year. But on this day, there was silence. Awkward, gut-churning silence. Something was . . . off.

LoLo took the groceries into the kitchen and peeked out the back window, thinking maybe Tommy and the kids were out back, maybe getting some air, but there was no sign of them there. She beelined into the kids' room—nothing. Same for the bathroom. She found Tommy in their bed, sleeping hard, snoring so loudly that it was a wonder he didn't swallow the lining of his nose. No kids in sight.

"Tommy!" LoLo yelled, panicked. She reached across the bed and pushed his shoulder. He bolted upright and grabbed the collar of LoLo's shirt with one hand, while drawing back his fist with the other. "It's me! It's me!" she quickly yelled, narrowly avoiding being pummeled by her half-sleep husband.

"Oh, LoLo, hey," Tommy said, releasing her collar and rubbing his eyes. "I didn't realize that was you for a second there."

"Tommy, where the kids?"

"What?" he said, yawning and rubbing his eyes, still not quite awake.

"The kids! Where are the kids? What are you doing a sleep? Sweet Jesus!" LoLo took off for the front door, every doomsday scenario she could think of running like a reel through her head: *They ran out the house and somebody snatched them; they ran out of the house and somehow got out the gate and got hit by a car; the front door was unlocked and someone somehow figured that out and kidnapped them; they were in the yard playing by themselves and someone came along and kidnapped them and killed TJ to keep him quiet and . . . and . . . and . . . Rae . . .*

"Tick, the kids are fine," Tommy called out nonchalantly.

LoLo, consumed with fear and tasting bile in the back of her tongue, could not process his words.

"LoLo," he called out a little louder. She was down the front steps—

fast-walking toward the chain-link fence standing sentry at the perimeter of their small front yard. He moved to the window and called through the screen. "Delores! The kids are all right! They at Skip's place."

LoLo turned on her heel and looked toward where she'd heard Tommy's voice. "What?"

"Come inside, baby, they all right."

"What you mean they at Skip's place?" LoLo asked as she fast-trotted back to the front door. Tommy met her at the threshold.

"I needed to get a little rest, so I took them over to Skip's. He cool. He watching them with the other kids."

LoLo's eyes revealed her horror, but her words sliced like swords. "What the hell you mean Skip's watching them?"

"They over there playing," said Tommy, standing in the middle of the floor, naked save for his boxers.

"You sent our children over to a man's house? Our baby girl? By herself?"

"They not there by themselves," Tommy said slowly, a look of confusion crossing his puffy, still sleepy eyes. "Skip is with them." His words beat in staccato.

"But she's a baby. She three years old. How she gonna defend herself against a grown-ass man? Who gone stop him from doing something to her?"

Tommy reeled back. "What you talking about, LoLo? Ain't nobody doing nothing to that girl."

"You don't know that!" LoLo yelled, bordering on hysterical.

"I do know that because Skip and I been friends for years. He looks out for our kids like he does his own."

LoLo looked at Tommy, more confused. "What you mean he looks out for them? You've left them over there before this?"

"Yeah." Tommy shrugged. "I don't see why you all puffed up. He don't mind. What's another two kids in the house? His oldest, Yolanda, she twelve. She helps out, and I can get in a little time for myself before I head to work."

"That's what you doing up in here? Getting in time for yourself, sleeping and shit while our babies are doing goodness knows what?"

"I already told you, LoLo, they over there playing," Tommy said, exasperated. "I don't see why you all bent out of shape. It's under control."

But that was just it; LoLo did not feel in control at all. She was keenly aware of what happens to little girls caught in empty rooms and dark corners, where predators gnashed their teeth and dug in their claws. She cut one last eye at Tommy and wriggled her feet back into her shoes and rushed out into the cold evening air, through the gate, across the sidewalk, cracked and littered with all manner of pebbles and cigarette butts and such, and marched up to Skip's door. She knocked but didn't bother waiting for anyone to answer; she just pushed her way through the front screen door, which, to both her dismay and her gratefulness, was unlocked. She rushed into the living room yelling Rae's name, the shrill of her voice matched only by the clop of her shoes as she rushed across the bare hardwood kitchen floor. Silence and wide eyes greeted her in the entryway; there was Rae, sitting on Yolanda's lap in the middle of the floor, tousling with a doll's hair while she looked to see who was causing all the commotion. TJ was on the couch, sucking his thumb, alternately staring at the television set and a set of baseball cards two of Skip's younger sons were organizing on the cocktail table in front of him.

"Mommeeeeeee!" both kids screamed as they struggled to get up off their respective seats and make a run toward her legs, like defensive linemen rushing the wide receiver headed to the field goal line. In their exuberance, they nearly knocked LoLo over.

"Oh, hey, Mrs. Lawrence," Yolanda said as she stood up from her perch on the floor.

LoLo eyed the room. Skip wasn't anywhere in sight. "Where's yo' daddy?" she asked, trying hard to keep the bass out of her voice.

"Oh, he upstairs, fixing on the record player," Yolanda said. "You need me to go get him?"

LoLo looked around some more, trying to take in every detail for evidence that her children were, indeed, safe. Finally, satisfied, she picked up Rae, grabbed TJ's hand, and said, "No. That's all right. You tell him I said thank you for watching the kids, hear?"

"Yes, ma'am," Yolanda said.

Tommy was dressed in his gray, one-piece janitor's uniform, pulling the bread out of the grocery bags and rooting for the peanut butter and jelly by the time LoLo marched the kids back through the front door of their house. She was steaming, still, despite that, by all appearances, what Tommy said was happening over at Skip's was, indeed, happening.

LoLo stood in the kitchen, rocking Rae and watching as TJ grabbed hold of his father's leg. She wanted to yell—wanted to smash something, just thinking about her daughter's vulnerability outside of her watchful eyes, just thinking about how powerless she felt as a mother to protect this girlchild. Just thinking how mute she was—had to be—to traverse this high wire of secrets tied above her marriage, above Tommy's head. Instead, she kissed her daughter and rocked.

"Hey, say, listen, how 'bout this," Tommy said. "Why don't you make some sandwiches for me, you, and the kids and come with me to work tonight."

"What you mean come with you to work?"

"Y'all can sit in the car and have your dinner while I do what I gotta do, and hey, TJ can help with the garbage and whatnot while you hang back with Rae. It ain't exciting or anything but at least we'll be together."

"I don't know, Tommy, the kids need to go to bed soon. Do you really want them out in the street at this hour?"

"First of all, the sun is barely set, and you know Rae gonna fall asleep in the car anyway. Plus, TJ should see his old man making a honest living. Maybe pick up a thing or two," Tommy said. He walked over to LoLo and pulled her waist toward his; he kissed the baby's cheek and then his wife's lips, slow, deliberate. "I like it when my family is with me. I miss y'all when I'm away. I want you close. Even if it's just during the ride from bank to bank."

There would be no arguing about this; Tommy wanted what he wanted and LoLo wanted it, too—these snatches of togetherness that were perfectly imperfect, but small treasures that added up to a fortune, nonetheless. Riding with the baby in her lap, watching Tommy as he drove, as he gathered TJ's hand and walked up to the banks with his big, round set of keys, as he smiled at her through the grand picture windows while he rubbed the fingerprints out of them, as he laughed at TJ putting the garbage in the pails, that wide, boundless grin on his little face—all of these things made her giddy. Put her at ease. And when he came back to the car, his fist full of lollipops he copped from the bank's stash, and leaned into Rae's face and said, "Gimme some sugar and I'll give you some sugar," LoLo could squeeze out the parts of her that could only see darkness in the exchange, and saw them for what they were: a father bonding with his daughter, introducing sweetness into her life in a way that LoLo never got to experience—in the way she'd always dreamed for herself when Bear was having his way with her. Only then could LoLo allow herself to lean in.

Rae wrinkled her nose and giggled. "Daddy! That tickles," she said, pointing at Tommy's mustache. She put both her hands on her father's cheeks and pulled his face close to hers and kissed his nose. Then, she turned and repeated the movements, this time, holding LoLo's face. "Kissy!" the little girl said. When her parents, confused, didn't move, Rae yelled it this time: "Kissy!" she said as she put one hand on Tommy's face, the other on LoLo's.

The parents, understanding what was being asked of them, leaned in and pecked each other's lips, Rae in the center of it all, overseeing the whole affair. The three burst into laughter when the deed was done. LoLo stared into Tommy's eyes and then Rae's; the baby buried her head in the space between LoLo's neck and chest and LoLo squeezed her daughter so tight, so tight she couldn't tell which of their heartbeats belonged to one and the other.

Days later, LoLo put the kids into a local daycare. Yolanda or no, LoLo wanted her babies where, if their father couldn't or wouldn't be responsible for their care while she was at work, they could be consistently seen in the light of day. Tommy tried to fight it, at first. "We don't have that kind of money to be wasting on a babysitter," he tried to reason. "Not with Skip annem willing to help us out."

"And what if something happens to them over there?" LoLo asked. "Yolanda ain't but a baby herself. How she gonna protect our children?"

"Protect them from what? It's a house full of kids."

"And Skip."

"Who ain't some trifling nigga who don't look after his kids. I don't understand what the problem is, LoLo."

But eventually, Tommy came around, and even took it a step further, recommending a spot where little Rae could go for half days while LoLo worked and Tommy got in a touch of free time before heading to the banks. "They call it the Black Children Rise Daycare Center," he'd said before spooning a pile of pinto beans in his mouth. LoLo had made them just like Tommy liked them, with a small slab of fatback and onion, some brown sugar, mustard, and lots of black pepper. She'd made a big ol' pot on the fly, and a skillet of spoonbread, too, to go with the chicken Skip was barbequing out in his backyard on that warm, fall Saturday afternoon when he waved LoLo and Tommy over for an impromptu get-together. He said he just wanted to share his chicken. But his new old lady was there and what he really wanted to do was show her off.

"Where is it?" LoLo asked as she blew air on a spoonful of beans and deposited them into her daughter's waiting mouth. Rae, holding on to her mother's knees as she stood waiting for her portion, did a little dance when the sweet confection, rich enough to be dessert, hit the back of her tongue.

"That's good, ain't it, baby?" Tommy said, laughing as Rae wriggled.

"Stop all that prancing," LoLo said, popping Rae on the meaty part of her fat little leg. "Twisting your little butt for everybody to see."

Rae wrinkled her face and cried out, her voice like a siren starting quietly and crescendoing into a full-on wail. She caught her breath and near choked on it, beans falling every which way.

Tommy shook his head but said nothing. LoLo was in charge of raising those kids; his job was to back her up. That was it. Even if he didn't necessarily see eye to eye with her discipline tactics or even understand, really, why a baby couldn't dance.

"It's a good place—clean, the teachers got them kids counting and saying their ABCs just as nice."

Skip coughed hard, like he was choking on that bite of chicken he'd just taken into his already full mouth. "Sorry," he said, looking at Tommy. "Chicken went down the wrong pipe."

Tommy wrinkled his brow—tossed Skip a look of concern. LoLo blew on another spoonful of beans. This time, Rae stood still. "I can take Rae on down there for a couple hours in the afternoon, and you can pick her up from the center when you get off work."

Skip cleared his throat again. "'Scuse me, y'all," he said, shaking his head. "Food so good, I can't get it down fast enough, I guess. Hehe." He wrinkled his brow at Tommy—slow enough that LoLo noticed. She narrowed her eyes but swallowed her questions. "You know, I can help y'all out if you need it," Skip said, quickly slicing through the awkwardness. "I can pick up Rae and bring her back home, so you don't have to worry about rushing to get to her before they close," he said.

"You know about this place, too?" LoLo asked.

Now, Skip was a numbers runner who moonlighted as a cab driver, mostly as cover for his off-the-books business. He combinated bets all over town, even with the teachers at Black Children Rise Daycare, who whispered their dreams and pressed wrinkled dollar bills into his hands all the same, looking for their big piece of pie. He knew the place well. "I ain't heard nothing bad about it or nothing, if that's what you asking," Skip said. "Ladies seem nice enough."

LoLo didn't say anything else about it. It was settled. Tommy would get TJ off to school and drop off Rae while LoLo was at work beginning the following Monday, and when she got home, there would be her ready-made family, poised to do ready-made-family things. This is how it would go.

And that is how it went for months, just like it did for so many other families of the time, doing what needed to be done to keep cereal in the cupboard and a little fatback on the stove and some extra change for the milkman to bring what they needed to wash it all down. LoLo liked the daycare just fine and soon enough, trusted her baby was in good hands, too. She could see her growth—not just physically, but mentally, too. Regularly, she entertained LoLo with recitals of her letters and numbers, and the teachers, they said she was quiet but studious. "She a good baby," they'd say, grabbing Rae from LoLo's arms in the morning.

But then came a crisp day in fall, when somebody in that place determined that Rae was not, indeed, a good baby. It was Skip who told her about the teacher with the golden wig and the bulging pregnant belly who laid hands on the three-year-old, beating her with a paddle for stepping out of bounds at lunchtime. Rae's offense: she ate her ham sandwich before her pea soup.

"I . . . I hate to be the one to tell you, but I ain't feel right not saying anything," he said. It was a Friday night and he was standing in LoLo's door, fiddling with his hat, shifting his eyes between LoLo's feet and the kids playing on the living room floor.

"Say what, Skip?" she asked. "Come on now, I got some field peas on the stove and I got to get this rice going. Spit it out." Whatever he had to say, LoLo wasn't prepared for it to rock her; she was distracted, and besides she'd just kissed Tommy as he left for work not even five minutes earlier, and her babies were right there in the floor. That was her world. That's it. Nothing else really mattered.

"I was over at the daycare today doing my collectin' and, well, I walked in and saw one of the instructors, Miss Betina . . ." He hesitated. LoLo folded her arms and looked at her neighbor quizzically. He gulped. "I saw Miss Betina hitting on Rae."

LoLo reeled back her neck. "Miss Betina? Hitting on Rae?"

"Yeah, that was Miss Betina, yes," he said, rubbing his eyebrow.

"Wait a minute; she hit on my baby?"

"With the paddle. Shole did."

LoLo scratched her neck and adjusted her shirt—looked at Rae, who was parting the hair on her little doll's head and pretending to grease its scalp. "Rae, baby, come here," she said. "Come to Mama."

Rae dropped the doll and comb right where she was and dutifully presented herself like a little soldier in front of her mother. LoLo patted her down, inspecting every inch of her body she could gain access to—up under her sleeves, her shirt front and back. As much of her legs as she could see by hoisting up her little green corduroy pants. Her face and neck and hands. Sure enough, there was a welt on both her palms. "She beat my baby on her hands?" she asked, yanking Rae's palms to show them to Skip.

"That's about right. She kind of a stickler for order, you know, and well, look," he said. He took a deep breath. "You don't really want the kids around her. She ain't . . ." He hesitated again. "She ain't good for your chir'ren."

LoLo didn't hear anything else he had to say. Not another word. In her head, she already was down at Black Children Rise, raising holy hell. Skip walked out, quietly closing the door behind him, his neighbor staring off into the color red.

Of course, Tommy told LoLo not to make a big fuss. Of course, LoLo didn't listen. Of course, there wasn't anything anyone could say or do to stop her, including Tommy, who had to stay behind with the baby, seeing as his wife was giving herself extra time on this particularly crisp Friday morning to have words with a woman who tore up children's palms for eating.

"Morning, Delores," the head of the daycare center, Mrs. Nesbit, announced to LoLo's wake. LoLo wasn't there for niceties and so she didn't bother with a greeting. She marched all through the small center—in the reading circle area, the lunch area, over where the Legos and blocks stood sentry, waiting for sticky fingers to build them into magnificent cities. Finally: "Where the girl who call herself beating my child?"

LoLo, busy looking for an answer, hardly noticed the nervous eyes dancing about the room, searching for more eyes, wide, concerned. They'd known it would come to this. Always, it came to this.

"Delores, let me talk to you over in the reception area," Mrs. Nesbit said, gently placing her hands on LoLo's elbow to lead her away from mothers settling their children in for their day.

LoLo snatched her arm. "Don't you touch me. This the kind of establishment you running? Y'all beating kids in here?"

"I don't know what you're talking about," Mrs. Nesbit said as calmly as she could muster. "Please, can we step over here to reception and—"

"I'm not going over to no damn reception!" LoLo yelled, shrill enough to make everyone—the mothers, the teachers, the children—freeze in time. Only the outside was moving. "Now," she said through knitted teeth, "I'm not going to move from right here in this spot until somebody tells me why that heiffa beat my daughter and why you all stood around watching."

The squeak of the bathroom door popped the silence like a balloon. Everyone turned toward the sound and bathed Betina with their worries. Unaware of the waves of drama rushing toward her feet, she adjusted her sweater and picked lint off her maternity dress before rubbing her belly.

"Let me ask you something," LoLo said smoothly, finally capturing the woman's attention. Betina looked around, as if to get a read on the situation and, after seeming to make note of the closed mouths and wide eyes, clearly registered two things: there was trouble in the room and it was she who was on the other end of it. "What kinda nerve you gotta have to put yo' hands on a baby that got a mama and a daddy who love her? You must be some kinda fool to think you can get away with some shit like that!"

Betina opened her mouth, then closed it.

"What? You ain't got nothing to say? You can beat on babies but you ain't got no explanations or hands for a grown woman?"

Betina stared.

"You plan on beating your baby like you did mine?" LoLo yelled, blithely waving her hand toward the woman's belly. "Answer me!"

"What I do with my baby ain't none of your concern. Not yet," she snapped. "But keep on, hear? You gone mess around and get your little feelings . . ."

"Okay, okay, okay," Mrs. Nesbit shouted, slicing through Betina's angry soliloquy. Mrs. Nesbit shook her head in the woman's direction, and Betina hushed completely. But it was too late; LoLo lunged at Betina.

Mrs. Nesbit was quicker on her feet than her sagging jowls and gray wig portrayed. She grabbed LoLo by the arm. "Now, you don't want to do that," she said. "I'm going to need you to leave this place right now," Mrs. Nesbit insisted, as she pulled LoLo toward the glass door and pulled it open.

On the other side of that glass, where the world was swirling awake, LoLo stood paralyzed save for her screams, which, in LoLo's mind, bounced off walls in dark corners where little girls had no power, no reasonable defense. Nothing but torment—and their tormentors.

LoLo drove back to Penny Drive in slow motion, the buildings and houses and trees and road all a blur through her tears. So focused on her anger and sadness was she that she'd forgotten that she was even driving; her subconscious, a bit of God's grace, got her to the house. LoLo snatched the car door open and slammed it closed behind her; her long legs stretched quickly across the driveway and grass, up the stairs by twos; she burst through the side door, eyes frantically shifting from chairs to sofa to floor as she rushed past Tommy and the kids into the bedroom. She turned in circles, fanning herself as she drew in and then blew out quick breaths. When she finally stopped spinning, her eyes landed on her dresser. In two steps, she was standing in front of it, chest heaving as she snatched open the top drawer and dug through the neat piles of panties and her two good bras and her socks and pajamas, down to the bottom until her fingers touched what she'd been fishing for: Rae's pouch. LoLo rubbed her thumb against the white material and, after a few more tracks of tears raced down her cheeks, she pulled the pouch open to stare at its contents. Rarely did she do this; Tommy did not approve of keeping any evidence of their children's former lives. "That's our son, our daughter," he'd told the lawyer who handled the children's adoptions. "We a family. Anything that happened before they came to us don't matter." But that pouch, it did matter—its contents not only a connection between Rae and the person who loved her enough to petition on her behalf, but also a petition to the baby's new mama, too. LoLo opened the pouch and carefully unfolded the letter inside—mouthed the words as she read them. *A sweet, protected, prosperous life.*

LoLo jumped when she heard the knob to the door twist; she quickly stuffed the pouch and the paper bag letter beneath her pile of socks and slammed the drawer closed.

"Uh, everything all right?" Tommy asked, his voice tentative, as he peeked around the door. "What happened at the daycare?"

"It don't matter," LoLo said. "Rae won't be going back there."

"What you mean? Where she supposed to go, then, Tick? You won't let Skip watch her and now the daycare can't do it, either?"

"You okay with them beating on our baby?" LoLo asked, incredulous.

"You don't have no problems beating these kids at the house . . . ," Tommy said. He stopped himself mid-sentence, knowing what was coming next.

"They are *ours*. We're raising them. We're teaching them. We're responsible for disciplining them. Not some stranger with no self-control, beating them for no good reason!" LoLo yelled.

So busy was she yelling that LoLo hadn't noticed Rae clinging to Tommy's leg. The little girl smiled when her father rubbed his fingers against her curls but dropped her lips back to neutral position when she focused, again, on her mother.

LoLo smiled. "Come here, Rae," she said, beckoning with her hands. "Come here, baby."

Rae rushed over to her mother and buried her face in LoLo's knees as she hugged her legs. LoLo grabbed each of her arms and pulled her up into the air—hugged her baby's body against her chest and backed up slowly to sit on the bed. She took each of Rae's hands into her own and examined the welts in her palms, then leaned down and kissed each of them.

"My sweet girl," LoLo said, smiling. "That lady won't ever hit you again, okay? Mommy's going to protect you. Always."

Rae buried her face in LoLo's chest and wrapped her arms around her mother's middle, her fingers light like butterflies against her mother's sides, forever changing the shape of her mother's heart.

There was no end to the day that LoLo could have imagined that would be worse than its start, but here she was, rubbing the cramps out of her stocking feet that, for hours, had pushed sewing pedals up and down and up and down at her work, trying to make sense of what Tommy was proposing. Rather, telling. His words tumbled down his lips like rocks off the side of a cliff giving way to pressure. Nature.

"I already started looking for houses out there. Well, my brother Sam is helping, but I think I got the hook on one," Tommy said. "I can put this one on the market and we'll have the money for the down payment on the new house. And you and the kids, y'all won't have to want for anything. It's a good job. It's a good move."

LoLo kept rubbing her feet, paying close attention to the bunion on the right. It was throbbing, aching like a toothache. Like her heart.

Finally, she picked up her head and faced her husband. The decision had been made, really; the details didn't matter. Already, she was focused on the mourning.

"Where did you say we're going?" she asked, letting out a deep breath.

"Jersey. We're going to New Jersey."

17

1973, in the wintertime

There were white people everywhere. Tommy had apprised LoLo of this when he left to put a down payment on the modest, three-bedroom house in the small southern New Jersey town, but still, seeing them in the grocery store, at the mall, on their front porches, the worried looks betraying their alarm over seeing colored folk carrying on with the daily life of normal human beings—all of this was a shock to Lo-Lo's system. After all, she'd spent a lifetime corralled into neighborhoods that, though plagued with inequity and neglect, were a gumbo of Blackness, thick with Africa and seasoned by the South. Filling and flavorful with roots that couldn't be easily killed. Willingboro was tasteless and bland, made deliberately so just fifteen years before Tommy and LoLo settled themselves on Burlington Drive. Back then, every homeowner who bought into the township's new development had signed a figurative blood oath, drawn up by the architect of the Philadelphia bedroom community, to refrain from turning niggers into neighbors. They wanted to keep the suburb and all it had to offer—new schools, gleaming grocery stores, long winding roads full of spacious new bungalows and picket fences, and expansive lawns ripe for babies and barbecues and neighborly banter—pristine, neat. White. This was no place for the coloreds, and so it was written, and so it was said.

Martin Luther King's blood scratched out the ink on those covenants, giving Negroes the salve they needed to heal at least some of the wounds Jim Crow had carved into every inch of their collective body. But many knew, too, that salve was no cure for the actual disease that white folk had spread from the moment their first slave ships touched shores, and the Civil Rights Act would be no cure for what coldhearted, blue-veined white folk suffered. "Let me tell you something: crackas don't give a shit about no damn constitution. Not when it comes to us," Tommy's brother Sam said as he and Tommy sat with ice-cold cans of Schlitz in their hands, bent over a map of New Jersey. They'd been pinpointing towns where a Black family could put down roots without fear that white neighbors would poison the soil. The task felt Herculean. "They'll sell to who they want to, and you'll be living in the back of Woolworth's with them kids waiting on the constitution to make it so you can spend yo' money on a house next to them."

Tommy traced a circle with his finger around Willingboro and took a swig. He was a Southern boy, which meant he was well aware that he could never fold himself small enough to escape the wrath of white people, and so, in his mind, there was no use in trying. Still, he wanted—needed—to focus on what worked for him, for his family, and Willingboro would be that place. The neighborhood was only twenty minutes from his new job at a plastics plant, where he'd be lead mechanic on the wallpaper line; forty minutes south and LoLo, him, and the kids could have their feet under Theddo's kitchen table, inhaling the glorious scent of his sister-in-law's homemade yeast rolls while they laughed and tapped their feet to Marvin Gaye; and two hours north on I-95, and LoLo could be hugging Cindy, Sarah, Para Lee, and the rest of her friends on the front pews of their home church, a connection that was important to his wife. But it was the FOR SALE signs that won Tommy over—how they bloomed on the lawns like bushes of black-eyed Susans, signaling all the homes his wife could choose from. This was important. LoLo, after all, had agreed to move to Jersey, but under duress, knowing she was leaving all she'd come to know and love two hours north of this odd place where colored people were banned and then not. Of course, it never occurred to Tommy why all those houses were up for sale, why the white people were practically crawling over one another to escape the tiny town, like some blond-haired, blue-eyed All-American girl stumbling and running from some heavy-footed ax murderer in a horror movie. Of course, had he thought to ask the whys, he would have eventually stumbled on the hows of the imploding neighborhood—how the developer and real estate agents teamed together to shower the white townspeople with rumors of forced integration, declining property values, and the theft of their families' futures. To solidify their tall tales, they moved in colored families, told the whites niggers were about to defile the streets, then stood back and watched all the whites panic-sell to developers, who in turn resold or rented their real estate to coloreds at a steep markup. The scheme was diabolical. Tommy and LoLo were, unwittingly, the poison on the developers' arrows.

Neither Tommy nor LoLo knew anything about that, though, and really, Tommy wouldn't have cared if he did. Tommy wanted what he wanted and was busy playing big with that new job that paid him more money than he'd ever made in the whole of his twenty-nine years—the likes of which, LoLo knew, he had every intention of using to keep her eyes on him and their home. LoLo, well, she could work with this new life for now, holed up in those four pretty walls that shielded her from their prying eyes. Their judging eyes. She'd already had a long talk with herself about it and she'd decided. She'd decided that this was going to work, like she actually had a choice.

LoLo grabbed for herself some peace and even a pinch of joy, too, watching her babies rush into the house on move-in day, gleefully twirling all around their new rooms. "Mommy, you have a bathroom in your room!" TJ exclaimed, his words tumbling over and under and around his thumb, thick with spit and water-logged crinkles. Rae trotted in behind her brother, hanging on to his Evel Knievel T-shirt. It was the window, yet to be dressed with the navy-blue curtains LoLo sewed together just days before they piled everything they owned into a small moving truck, that caught her eye. LoLo couldn't help but to smile watching her daughter press her nose against the glass, her eyes washing over the lush Kentucky bluegrass that stretched from their vantage point to infinity. Rae giggled as she leaned deeper into the windowsill.

"What's so funny, lil' girl?" LoLo asked, moving closer to her daughter.

Rae, fixated, didn't answer. Just kept giggling. Staring. LoLo inched even closer to her daughter, looking for an in to what, exactly, had caught babygirl's attention, and sucked in her air when she finally zoned in on what it was: a swarm of orange ladybugs, a dozen or so, crawling around the wooden sill, the pane, and the glass itself. Rae let two of them dance on her fat little pointer finger.

"What is all this here?" LoLo asked, looking around the window frame and the window itself, confident she'd find some hole or crack through which they crawled—something maybe the house inspector missed. But there were none. Just ladybugs everywhere.

"Look, Mommy!" Rae exclaimed as three of the insects crawled onto her palm, which she'd laid on the sill. TJ rushed over to take a gander and whipped off his tennis shoe to kill them.

"No, no! What you doing, boy? You don't kill ladybugs; they good luck!" LoLo said. Then, to herself: "Maybe this is where we're supposed to be after all.

"Y'all come on," she said, grabbing the children's hands. "We'll ask your daddy to come put them outside. I want to show you something."

LoLo could barely hold on to the kids as she pushed through the back screen door leading out into the backyard, and she didn't much try once their sneakers sank into the lawn. TJ took off running, doing a cartwheel and somersault down the length of it before falling into the blades and rolling around, dirt and grass and all manner of ants and such clinging to his short, lopsided Afro. Rae bounced around a little bit, but then ran in a series of crazy circles, screaming in terror as a bumblebee lumbered lazily in the thick air surrounding her. LoLo laughed. "What ail you, gal? That bee don't want you!" she yelled as she bent her knees and spread her arms wide, waiting for her daughter to find safety in them. Rae settled immediately—smushed against her mother. "I don't like bees," she said.

TJ took off running in the opposite direction—toward the back of the yard, where a small, rocky creek separated their land from a forest of trees, pretty, but menacing.

"TJ! *Tee! Jay!*" LoLo yelled as her son raced full speed toward the water, which rippled just beyond a small cliff low enough for an adult to step into the creek with ease, but still high and steep enough for a child to hurt himself if he weren't careful. "Stop right there!"

TJ skidded to a stop, so close to the edge of that cliff that even he was a little turned about by how close he came to falling in.

Rae on her hip, LoLo run-walked to her son and snatched his arm.

"You listen to me and you hear me good: you bet not let me catch you in this water, or I will tear your little ass up, you hear me? Both of you!" she said, squeezing TJ's wrist to solidify her words. "You get in that water and something gonna bite you! You go in them woods and something worse gonna happen to you, if I don't find out about it first! You hear? Don't let me catch you down here!"

"Yes, ma'am," TJ said.

So busy was she chastising the kids and pulling them back up the hill toward the house that LoLo didn't notice her at first. A white lady. In her yard. Staring. Portly and gray-haired with icy eyes. She put LoLo in the mind of the nurse who'd scraped out her insides and any chance she had of having a baby of her own, of having her blood flow into the future. In LoLo's mind, that was what all white people did—they cut your air, sealed off your blood supply, starved you of your humanity, made it so they had everything and you, well, you with your black skin, you had little. Scraps. And they wanted those, too. *What this white woman want from me?*

LoLo stopped short when she locked eyes with the woman's icy ones, and instinctively grabbed TJ's wrist. Her legs, arms, nose, tongue, toes—all of them began to tingle as she stood there, with wide eyes and bile creeping up her throat. Where is Tommy? Sam? What this white lady fittin' to do?

Finally, the woman waved. "Hi! I'm Daisy. I live next door," she yelled, pointing at the brick ranch to the right of LoLo and Tommy's place.

LoLo waited. Said nothing.

"I saw the moving truck," the lady said, shielding her eyes from the sun.

LoLo waited. Said nothing.

"I, um, I just wanted to come and introduce myself and welcome you to the neighborhood," she said, her enthusiasm, unmet, still high.

LoLo waited. Said nothing. Only when the lady started walking deeper into the yard, teeth shining, the corners of her eyes crinkled in the same direction as the corners of her mouth, did LoLo's body shake itself loose of the acid that immobilized her. Rae, body weight leaning into her mother's side, compromising the hip LoLo had jutted to stabilize her child in her arms, wriggled down the length of her mother's body and started toward the woman but was quickly immobilized by her mother's grip of her shoulder. TJ, having never seen a white woman up close and beyond the square of the family's television set, didn't have to be contained. He took a step back and another right, landing himself just behind the only grown-up in the yard that he was neither scared of nor distrusted.

"Hello," LoLo said simply as the woman took her place before her, still grinning.

"It's so nice to make your acquaintance," she said, reaching out her hand for a shake. "Like I said, I'm Daisy, your neighbor. What did you say your name was, dear?"

"Delores," LoLo mumbled, allowing for only a feeble handshake of their fingers. "It's, uh, nice to meet you, too."

"Where are you all moving from?" she asked, just as casual, like it was her right to know LoLo's business. Like it was her right to know the answer. LoLo, having twenty-six years of living and mostly questionable—if not hostile—dealings with white people framing her interactions with them, knew that even in this moment, this woman standing on LoLo's grass, in her yard, in the back of the home her husband had purchased for her and their babies, just as easily as she asked for the information, this white woman could make the answer her right to know.

"Long Island. New York."

"Oh, Long Island. That sure is one fancy place, isn't it? I've never been, but I hear it's lovely all the same. Here I was thinking that's where people went to vacation. I guess it never occurred to me that people would live there year round. What made you leave paradise for little ol' Willingboro?"

LoLo hesitated, pulled Rae and TJ a little closer to her. *Paradise?* "Work," she said, croaking. She cleared her throat. "Pardon me, my mouth is a little dry. My husband got a new job out in Camden. We came so he could work."

"Oh, well, looks like you all picked a mighty fine place! Camden is just a hop, skip, and a jump from here. My husband, Steve, spent a lot of time that way while he was in the military. Guess you can say we moved here for my husband's job, too. Seemed like a good place to raise a family. We have five kids. The last of them graduates from high school in another year. Then we'll be empty nesters!" she said cheerfully, waving her hands in front of her like pom-poms.

LoLo waited. Said nothing.

"Well then," Daisy said, clearing her throat, and focusing her icy eyes on Rae and TJ, "who do we have here? Aren't you two just the cutest," she said, bending down and shaking Rae's chin. Rae giggled as she looked into the woman's eyes and then focused on her hair. Enamored by the new, Rae stealthily reached for the woman's mane—her fingers running the length of the woman's cropped, wavy 'do, equal parts fine, soft, and wiry in the parts that had turned from jet black to various shades of gray. LoLo slapped her hand away.

"Ah-ah—don't you touch!" LoLo said, grabbing the little girl's wrists. "I'm so sorry. She's only four; she doesn't know better just yet not to touch. I'm so sorry. That won't happen—"

Daisy cut LoLo off. "Oh goodness, don't you worry! She's just fine." Then to Rae she said, "How lovely to have a little girl in our midst! I have a little girl, but she's all grown up now. My oldest, Julie. She's twenty-eight with a husband of her own. I'm waiting for my grandbabies, but you will be perfect in a pinch, won't you, sweetie?" She patted Rae on the head. "You're such a beautiful child."

LoLo cleared her throat again, this time not because it was compromised, but because she wanted this white woman, this stranger she did not know, to get her hands off her child. Daisy, aloof and missing the racial dynamics crackling in the air between them up until that very moment, took the hint. She stood back up straight and took a deep breath. LoLo's would be the fourth houseful of colored on the block that stretched just shy of three miles from the corner gas station just down from the highway on one end, and the school and community swimming pool on the other. She was beginning to get used to their reaction to her, but their fear was still a shock to her system.

"Well then, I need to get back over to my place and get dinner on the stove. I hope you like chicken and dumplings . . . ," Daisy began. LoLo folded her brow and fought the urge to shake her head no—not because she didn't care for the dish, but because she knew what the woman was about to say. "I've been cooking for a family of seven for all these years, and it's hard for me to cook for just three these days, so I always end up cooking so much more than I should. I'll send my son Mark over with some of the extras. All that unpacking, I can imagine it'll be tough stopping to find the pots and pans and get over to the grocery store to figure out what to cook for dinner tonight. Everyone loves my chicken and dumplings." Then, to

Rae and TJ in a baby voice, she said: "You're just going to love them. I know you will." She gave the top of Rae's head another little pet and, with that, she disappeared back over into her yard, and up the steps to her back porch and through the back door, LoLo and the kids standing there staring into the wake of this energetic, talkative white woman who was kind for no other reason than that it was the neighborly thing to do.

LoLo, put off by the whole affair, already knew how the evening would end: She would find her pots relatively easy because, really, they did not have a lot of things and so there were not a lot of boxes to root through. She would pull out her favorite, the heavy-bottomed steel one with the burns on the outside, remnants from meals she'd cooked in it since the day she'd purchased that pot at Woolworth's, which happened to be the same day she and Tommy said "I do" and she moved into his house with nothing more than a suitcase, her sewing machine, and a paper bag full of material and patterns. She would fill that favorite pot with water and put in a half pack of franks, boil them up real good, cut them up into chunks, and add them to a can of pork 'n beans with a little brown sugar, some salt, pepper, onion. And when that white boy would come to the front door with chicken and dumplings made by Daisy's hand, she would smile and be gracious because that would be the neighborly thing to do, she guessed. And she would close the door and walk that pot directly to the kitchen, open the top to the plastic garbage pail there, and throw the whole affair in.

Because there were white people everywhere, and LoLo did not feel safe, and LoLo needed to do what she could to stay protected, LoLo fell to her knees every night and asked God to surround her and her family and that house at 283 Burlington Drive with the blood of Jesus because, beside niggers, only He knew just how precise a strike white people could mete out with their cruelty, especially when they were being kind.

This was the way the year passed, and then the next and a few more after that, too, with the days blending into the nights and LoLo, a speck of pepper in this bowl of salt, throwing away Daisy's food and sitting in the house on hot days and cold ones, too, and all the days in between, gorging on Argo starch and Diet Pepsi and *General Hospital* and *One Life to Live* and watching the kids tumble down the block to school and Tommy pull out the driveway heading to work and LoLo, all by herself, looking for something, anything, to busy herself. To not feel alone or scared of what the white folks might do if they noticed her there. To not feel alone or scared of what she might do to herself if she ceded to her loneliness. This was, by no means, an easy task.

And then came Suzette Charles and her four kids and no husband, wriggling the FOR SALE sign out of the lawn across the street. It was 1977. LoLo could see her Chaka Khan hair, big and expansive, all the way from Rae's window, its curtains through which she was peeking to see who all was moving into the home of the latest white family to take flight. She could see her ass cheeks, too, pushing out from under her shorts, tight and small, like her top. There was no man in sight. LoLo watched wide-eyed, absentmindedly shoveling spoonfuls of Argo into her mouth while she picked apart and judged the woman, who waved her cigarette in the air like a wand, orchestrating her boys—three in all, two teens and the youngest, the ten-year-old twin of the little girl—on how to unload the furniture and boxes from the small truck she'd backed into the driveway crooked. She was intriguing. Thin but buxom, like one of those girls on *Soul Train*—glamorous, even. And loud. LoLo could hear snatches of her "thank-yous" and her origin story and the names of her children as she chatted up Daisy, who slinked over there with something in a bowl before the woman even finished unloading the truck. "Hmph," LoLo said out loud, a little cloud of Argo escaping her lips as she rolled her eyes. She quickly ducked out the window when Daisy turned and pointed across the street toward her house, Suzette's eyes following her finger. "She's got a daughter about your daughter's age!" LoLo heard Daisy exclaim. "The lady of the house is a little quiet, you know, but you all should get along just fine."

"Is that so?" Suzette asked.

"Why yes, of course."

"And why is that?" Suzette quizzed.

Daisy let out an awkward laugh and looked to and fro as she used the back of her hand to wipe beads of sweat from her brow. "Well, she's a really nice Negro lady with two lovely children," she said nervously.

"So we'll get along because she's Black?" Suzette asked.

Daisy cleared her throat. "Well, I baked some cookies and thought your little ones might like some. They're working so hard. I'm sure they're working up quite the appetite."

Suzette smiled but said nothing.

"Okay, well, it was lovely meeting you . . ."

LoLo filled her mouth with another spoonful of Argo and giggled. She would introduce herself to this woman before week's end.

The kids and Tommy were already out the door and LoLo had an hour before her stories came on, and so she went out to the garden and picked the prettiest vegetables—the roundest, reddest tomatoes, the firmest, greenest peppers, a couple cucumbers, blemish free—and put them in a paper bag, smoothed down her jeans, retied the bow in her shirt, and headed across the street to meet this intrigue with the quick tongue and the Chaka Khan hair. Standing on the woman's stoop, her heart raced a bit. It had been a long time since LoLo made a new friend; Cindy, Sarah, and Para Lee were her tight girls with a friendship closing in on a little over twelve years. They grew into women together. It was natural. Standing on a stranger's stoop, peering into her screen door, trying to make hay of what she was about to walk into, that didn't feel natural to LoLo—more agonizing than anything.

LoLo saw Suzette circling in her kitchen and knocked, so as not to appear to be some weirdo peeking into a house that didn't belong to her. Suzette turned to the door and smiled when she saw her neighbor standing there, looking awkward with her respectable Black lady clothes on, hair coiffed just so.

"Well, hello, neighbor!" Suzette said, walking to the door with a smile spread across her dimpled face, a cigarette dangling between her fingers. "I was going to come by this weekend to introduce myself, but you done beat me to it! Come on in here!" she exclaimed, pushing open the screen door and stepping aside so LoLo could enter.

Her house smelled like incense and musk—like Africa and old things and little boys who washed only occasionally, and definitely only when threatened with a whooping. The scent fit. There were old velvet chairs and sofas, worn with time and many asses that had curled up on them with liquor and bongs, talking shit and plotting revolution that never came. Velvet pictures of naked couples with Afros adorned the walls, sitting above small tables displaying African statues and wooden Black Power fists that announced Suzette's politics louder than any megaphone could.

"These are for you," LoLo said, holding out the bag of vegetables.

"What we got here?" Suzette asked, tucking the cigarette between her lips so she could receive and open the bag. "Hey, vegetables. That's nice. That's real nice."

"They're from my garden," LoLo said, fidgeting uncomfortably.

"Well then, I'm Suzette," the woman said, unfazed by LoLo's discomfort. "I don't know nothing 'bout gardening but I sure do like me some tomatoes and cukes. Awfully generous of you to bring them by."

"You're welcome," LoLo said quietly as her eyes washed around the room. She couldn't help herself.

"I was planning on getting on over to introduce myself as soon as we settled in, but now is just as good a time as any, I guess. What's your name again? And can I offer you something to drink?"

"Oh, um, no, thank you, I . . . I just ate and had a Pepsi before I walked over. Delores is my name. My people call me LoLo."

"Well, LoLo, a drink maybe later, maybe not Pepsi," she said, smiling. "Come on, have a seat. Tell me what I done got myself into moving into this house."

"Well," LoLo said, smoothing down her jeans as she sat on the couch, "me and Tommy, that's my husband, been here for going on five years now. We got two kids, Tommy, Jr., we call him TJ, and my baby girl, Rae. She's nine now, and TJ is twelve, almost thirteen. I saw your babies walking to school this morning, 'round the same time as mine."

"Yes, that's Reggie, David, Malachi, and Felicia, my heartbeats," she said. "Mal and Felicia, they twins, same age as your Rae. Reggie and David, those are my little men, fifteen and sixteen."

LoLo nodded. "And your husband? I don't think I've seen him."

Suzette took a long drag on her cigarette and blew out the smoke, then waved toward a picture on the mantle. A man in an army uniform stared back, stoic. "That's my Frank," she said quietly. "He's, uh. He's gone."

"Oh goodness, I'm so sorry, I didn't know," LoLo stammered. "I mean, I didn't mean to bring it up . . ."

"There's no reason you would have known. It's all right," Suzette said, taking another drag. She tilted her head up and blew circles of smoke into the air above her head. "My man almost made it out. Those bastards came knocking on my door beginning of March 1975, long in the face, fake concerned. Told me he stepped on a landmine hauling sacks of potatoes to base camp. Ain't that a bitch? Died fetching some damn potatoes for white men in their white-man war. One more month. That's all he had left was one more month before he could come home to me and the kids. And then he was gone. Just . . . gone."

"I . . . I'm so sorry," LoLo said, reaching for Suzette's hand. "I am."

Suzette wiped a tear. Took another drag. "And they got the nerve to stiff me on benefits. Talmbout he didn't formally adopt my big boys, and so they only give me a little something for the twins. Like he wasn't a daddy to allem."

LoLo knew to let Suzette's words tumble. She knew what it was like to have no one but the four walls and God to hear her troubles.

"Been bouncing around, looking for work. Trying to keep a roof over our heads, some food in our bellies. Get stable for these kids, you know? I'm maintaining. Got no other choice."

"Yes," LoLo said, rubbing Suzette's knee. "I understand. We do what we have to do, don't we?"

"Yes indeed," Suzette answered. She tucked her cigarette between her lips and patted LoLo's hand, then stood up. "Well, this time I'm offering a drink, but it ain't Pepsi. Come on and have a lil' sip with an ol' girl."

"I, uh . . . it's kind of early, isn't it?" LoLo said, looking around for a clock. Her stories came on at one, and she'd given herself plenty time to say hello and get back across the street, which meant Suzette was suggesting a weekend evening drink be had just after noon on a school day.

"Oh, honey! It's never too early for our friend brandy!" she said, reaching into a cabinet in the kitchen. LoLo sat nervous, looking for an exit, a reason, as she listened to the liquid hit the bottoms of two coffee cups.

Suzette handed LoLo her cup and clinked it with hers. "To Franklin Charles. A good man. A good daddy." She bottomed her cup and so LoLo did, too. Suzette laughed big, hearty when LoLo lowered the cup, revealing her crinkled face. She slapped her bare thigh and laughed some more. "Wooooo-weee!" she said. "Only the good stuff for my Frankie. Come on, let's have another."

"I don't think that's a good idea. I have to get back over to the house . . ."

"Girl, you don't have shit to do. I see you out there in that yard, fiddling around. In ya house, sitting in that chair in the window, staring at the TV. The kids are in school, ya man is at work. Relax! I'll get you home safe."

And with that, Suzette gently pushed LoLo back down onto the couch. LoLo did some smooth talking to herself as she listened to the brandy splash, this time a heavier pour than the last. She stared at the brown liquid as Suzette pulled a record out of its jacket sleeve and dropped it on her record player. The Emotions' "Best of My Love" streamed from the speakers loud as Suzette popped her fingers and struck a pose, her hands in the air, hip swung to one side, ass tooted out. "Owwww! Oh oh!" she sang along with the explosive opening of the song, one that LoLo had heard on the radio in the morning while she got the kids ready for school but hadn't added to her collection of albums, which consisted mostly of gospel and a Stevie Wonder record or two.

By the time Suzette had her way with her, LoLo was three sheets to the wind, slow-dragging with a strange woman with a gang of kids and a dead husband whose benefits barely covered his wife's rent and food bill but was being stretched enough for copious bottles of brandy and a little weed. LoLo wasn't even sure what she was doing with her body smushed against this woman's, croaking through the Isley Brothers' "Footsteps in the Dark."

"I gotta go," LoLo finally said when the song ended and the needle scratched against the paper, the arm stuck in the position. She pried Suzette's hands off her waist and gently pushed away from her.

"Ohhhhh, stay!" Suzette begged. "The kids aren't home yet. Let's slice up your tomatoes and cucumbers and have us something to eat!"

"No, no . . . I gotta go," LoLo said, looking around, trying to find and focus on the front door. "Dinner. I gotta get dinner started before Tommy and the kids get here." She made a dash toward the screen door, stumbling through it and down the stairs, holding on to the railing as she felt her body move forward. Dizzy, with her stomach doing a slow roil to what for sure would be an emptying of its contents, LoLo looked at her house and then back down to the ground. She told herself to hold on to the car and the bushes. She considered crawling. She moved one foot in front of the other, knees buckling, trying to walk upright best she could so as not to call attention to the fact that it was only 1:34 in the afternoon and she was the drunkest she'd ever been in the whole of her thirty years.

She spent the rest of the afternoon contemplating her whole life and her choices that day and trying to pull herself together before those kids came tumbling into the house with their questions and homework and their needs. What would she say? How could she hide her midday drunkenness? How would she avoid Suzette and her profound sadness—its contagiousness? Her grabby hands?

LoLo didn't have any of those answers. What she did have, though, by the time she was heaving into the commode, laid her head against the cold ceramic, and collapsed in her recliner in front of *General Hospital*, was a clear understanding of this one true thing: she would remain profoundly lonely, even though a Black lady with Chaka Khan hair lived just across the street, and that loneliness, paired with a servitude she could not escape, was slowly killing her.

18

1981, in the summertime

LoLo wasn't particularly good at cornrowing hair. In fact, it was the running joke among her friends, who could not understand how a Black woman who had worked in southern fields was incapable of doing even the most basic of plaits across her baby girl's scalp. Knowing how to cornrow was, after all, practically a birthright; one submitted to the process while laid across laps or awkwardly bent between mother's or big sissy's knees as intricate parts were carved into enviable patterns on heads, and somehow, via some kinetic energy passed from the ancestors' fingertips to one's own, you did the same for your baby girl and she did the same for her baby girl and so on and so forth. This particular style was the mother of invention—on par with what the wheel was to transportation, what the cotton gin was to the pockets of white American men. Beyond the historical significance of the braided style, mamas with daughters who had that thick, curly, cottony hair with the propensity to stretch toward the clouds one minute and smush tight and viselike against scalps the very next, could get their daughters out the door in the morning with minimal fuss—could make it so they could have a little less dread about a hot, sunny, sweaty afternoon that, without the benefits of cornrows, could have one's daughter tumbling back through the door looking like who shot John. Saved them both from ridicule and judgment from other Black women who considered an unruly head an assured sign of motherly neglect.

LoLo was grateful for Sarah, who, every two weeks back in Long Island, would happily "borrow" Rae and, over the course of a couple hours, turn a series of small three-strand plaits into hairstyles worthy of some history book on African princesses, or an *Essence* magazine cover. But Sarah was there and LoLo was here and so she had to do to Rae's head what was achievable.

"Hold still now, and don't you move them fingers," she said to Rae as the little girl bent her body into the shape of a "C" between her mother's knees. Rae presented her kitchen for unencumbered access to both her mother and the hot comb, and tried to talk herself into being a statue, but still, she trembled. LoLo watched as the stove's flames licked the metal comb and, employing some kind of intuition, picked it up when she thought it was hot enough, and then pressed it against a folded paper towel. When she was satisfied that the comb was no longer hot enough to scorch that paper towel, she leaned into Rae's body and slowly blew a stomach full of air onto the child's neck as she glided the comb over the edges of her hair. LoLo knew how to deal with a hot comb. Curling irons, too. Every two weeks, she would scrub Rae's hair in the kitchen sink, comb through the kinks with her best Afro pick, blow dry it, and, finally, press and curl the girl's thick, kinky, curly mane into submission. The child didn't have but enough hair to pull into a couple short pigtails and some bangs during the weeks between washes, but those first few days, LoLo had Rae looking right.

"Mommy," Rae asked tentatively as she adjusted herself on the stack of thick yellow phone books, both she and her mother waiting for the flames to make the metal comb shine an orangey-red again.

"Mm-hmm," LoLo said, her attention on the stove.

"I had a daydream," Rae said.

"Oh yeah?"

"Yeah."

"Another daydream? Not a night dream?" LoLo asked, pulling at Rae's tight, coarse curls with the tips of her fingers.

"Yes, a daydream, while I was folding the clothes downstairs."

"Yeah? Is that why it took you so long to finish that last load? You were standing around daydreaming?"

"No, I was folding while I was daydreaming."

"Hmm," LoLo said, her eyes, mind, back on the hot comb, the stove. LoLo hadn't daydreamed in so very long she barely remembered Luna and hot pants and Warhol and her long legs in miniskirts twirling, twirling down runways in threads she conjured. That was a fanciful life about as tangible as a rocket trip to Xanadu—even in the recesses of her imagination. Some days, she was tempted to let Rae in on the gag, just how useless all those random daydreams she kept going on about were—that really, they were nothing more than little movies that had a beginning and a middle and an end, sans any kind of reality. On better days LoLo hoped big for her daughter—thought maybe she'd have a shot at escaping, maybe living out some of those daydreams she kept pestering her mama about.

"It was about you. You were walking in the creek, but instead of swimming in the water, it looked like you were trying to lay down in it."

"Is that so?" LoLo asked. She glanced at the window, the grass beyond it. Thought about the creek and the water and the hot comb.

"Do you know how to swim, Mommy?"

"No," LoLo said. "I don't know how to swim."

Rae was quiet. Then: "Felicia's taking swimming lessons at the community center," Rae said, legislating her words.

LoLo, her mind on the flame, was only half listening and so didn't immediately know where Rae was going with her transition from daydream to announcement.

"She's learning how to hold her breath underwater and how to kick her legs to move in the water and stuff."

"Is that so?" LoLo said, rubbing the hot comb against the paper towel.

"Uh-huh. And in a couple weeks, once she knows how to swim real good, they're going to teach her how to jump off the diving board."

LoLo leaned in and blew on Rae's temple as she ran the hot comb through her hair. The Afro Sheen hair grease she'd rubbed through the girl's tresses sizzled as the heat ran smooth over the tiny strands at the edge of the girl's scalp. Rae winced.

"Hold still and I won't burn you," LoLo said.

Silence.

"Mommy?" Rae said, shifting under her mother's hand.

"What, Rae?"

"Can I take swimming lessons, too?"

LoLo sat up straight in her chair and laid the hot comb across the flames, so she could give her full attention to her child. Her eyebrows folded into each other. "Oh, so because Felicia's down there at the swimming pool you think you should be there, too?"

"I . . . I just want to know how to swim," Rae said. "When I go to the pool all I can do is sit on the side and put my feet in the water."

"And? You're at the pool, ain't ya? With your friends."

"But I'd like to be able to get in the pool with my friends," Rae said quietly.

"You lucky I let you go down there at all."

Truth was, LoLo didn't particularly care for either one of her kids going down to the community pool—not in that neighborhood. Not with those people. A hole full of water and crackers was a stew that made LoLo anxious, and rightfully so; she'd read and heard enough firsthand accounts of the sheer terror white folk visited on Black children who dared strip down and dip their brown bodies in "community" pools that it was virtually impossible for her to get out of her head visions of angry pool managers pouring acid into pool water in which Black children frolicked—couldn't get out of her mind the horror show of white mothers tucking boxes of nails into their picnic baskets, intent on tossing them into waters where brown toes bounced. Of Tommy going crazy and careening down the street to fight the first cracker he saw that had anything to do with the mistreatment of their kids and what kind of retaliation that could lead to: a cross on the lawn, perhaps. A bottle of fire through the window, maybe. Somebody being shot or maimed or killed—that somebody being her Tommy.

But even the possibility of those very real modern-day terrors didn't hold the weight of the fear LoLo had for her daughter in particular, beyond what any white stranger could do. It was the enemies from within that made LoLo hold Rae close. LoLo remembered the first time she went swimming—in a watering hole Bear and Clarette liked to call their own, just down the way from their farm, at the end of a little trail on their land. It tended to be more mud than creek, but a good rain brought enough water for the adults to wade and children, depending on how slight they were, to float. Before they were saddled with a child neither of them wanted but were obligated to take in, Bear and Clarette used to steal away to that watering hole to do what was natural between a husband and his wife, in the midst of nature. He called the act "Genesis" on account Adam and Eve got to "know" each other in what God created, and he saw fit that he and his wife did what the Bible said married couples do, out in a place where he could feel equally free and a little wicked. When LoLo went to the watering hole in her panties and one of Bear's sleeveless white T-shirts, the act of being out in nature in that way became, simply, wicked.

"You don't need to be down there at the pool no way," LoLo said. She dug into the small glass jar of Afro Sheen, put a dollop of the blue hair grease into her palm, and smashed it between her hands before rubbing it into Rae's freshly pressed hair. "All this time I spent making your hair look pretty and you want to go down there and, what? Get it wet and come out the pool with a head full of nappy hair?"

"Felicia's mother braids her hair . . ."

"I spend all this time pressing and curling your hair to make it look nice. Felicia's mama don't care what her child look like. Clearly. Because every second of the day she got her walking around here looking like a little hobo tramp. Little scrawny, ashy ass."

LoLo watched as Rae's shoulders folded into themselves but continued charging through the line of attack anyway. Her point would be made.

"I ain't Felicia's mama and you damn sure ain't Felicia," LoLo continued. "Plus, she can get in the water and not be affected by all that chlorine and such. She light enough to where you can't see the ash and she can stand to get a little sun anyway. But you," LoLo said, leaning into her daughter and pulling the girl's head back so she could look her in the eye, "chlorine, the sun, they'll make you black. You don't want that, do you?"

Rae sank deeper into the pile of phone books on which she sat. "No, ma'am," she said, whimpering.

"That's right," LoLo said. "No, ma'am. You stick to cooling your feet in the water. Cover up, so the sun don't turn you into a crisp."

"Who's crispy?" Tommy asked, strolling to the refrigerator. He snatched open the door and grabbed himself a Michelob Light. "You not talking about my pretty baby, is she, baby?" he said, leaning down to pinch Rae's cheek.

"This girl trying to talk her way into a swim class."

"What's wrong with swim class?" Tommy asked, clearly oblivious to LoLo's concerns, mostly because they hadn't talked about them, but also because the coordination of extracurricular activities—what the kids did with their time outside of the house and inside of it, too—wasn't really any of his concern. LoLo was in charge of such things.

"Well, if you spent four hours washing, drying, pressing, and curling this child's hair, you wouldn't be fixing your mouth to ask that question, now would you, Thomas Lawrence?" LoLo said, aggressively pushing Rae's head forward. Rae sank under her mother's touch. LoLo made a part at the nape of Rae's neck and dragged the comb through the girl's hair while she waited for the iron curlers to heat in the stove's flames.

Tommy cracked open his can of beer and caught the foam bubbling up the metal top with his lips. He sucked a good deal of the liquid behind that, then raised his free hand in the air. "Hey. Listen to your mother," he said. "She knows best." Then, to LoLo he said: "Babe, Theddo's coming by in a couple hours to watch the game. You think you can throw some fish into the pan when you finish up?"

LoLo picked up the hot curlers off the flame and ran them across the white paper towel, looking for the scorch. She said nothing. When she thought it was cool enough, she tapped the hot iron on her wrist. Still, she said nothing. With a flick of her fingers and wrist, she maneuvered the hot curlers on the small patch of Rae's hair and twirled the contraption until the strands were a neat, uniform row of a most perfect curl. LoLo didn't care too tough for Theddo, particularly after he broke up his almost twenty-year marriage. The man never did see a skirt he wasn't trying to get up under, and he'd done so on enough occasions to produce evidence of his dalliances. Their names were Darius and Joy, two children he had with two different women—neither of whom was his wife. LoLo knew Tommy wasn't blind and, certainly, there were enough women out there willing to lay all their morals down by the riverside without much cajoling, but she couldn't help but to think that, like wolves, cheaters ran in packs. She didn't want her husband around a man who could leave his wife, his children so he could go lie with whoever was willing to spread her legs. "'Til death do us part" was just something Theddo said out loud when the pastor told him to repeat it. He didn't mean that shit.

What LoLo wanted to say—rather, scream—was that she was tired and she just wanted to sit down somewhere and have a smoke or two and steer clear of the kitchen and call Sarah or Cindy on the phone and give herself just a little time on this day to at least pretend, even for just a few minutes or so, that her very body wasn't being pulled every which way deeper into a darkness she was finding hard to shake as she melted, melted,

melted into the wallpaper and the linoleum floors, her needs tended to with just about the same voracity as a dog owner extended to an animal tied to a chain-link fence, which wasn't really any kind of care at all.

"Yeah, Tommy, I can fry some fish," LoLo said finally. Tommy did not notice her pupils growing big and dark—the way her shoulders slumped, same as Rae's. "But you got to go down to the market and get it."

Tommy took another sip of his beer and let out a little burp. "I can do that. What you want—whiting? Porgies? Perch?"

"Whatever they got fresh," LoLo said, blowing a cool breath on the curlers. "Head off, split."

"All right then, head off, split," he said, taking another swig of beer. His brogues scuffled against the kitchen floor tile as he walked over to Rae and bent down to look her in her eyes. "Your hair looks pretty," he said.

"Thank you, Daddy," Rae said, smiling for the first time since her mother shot down her swimming quest. There was a lot of this thing between Tommy and Rae, this easiness and understanding that daughter took willingly from father, as if she'd given up trying to wrest this kind of attention from her mother. This thing from Rae, this cuddly, quiet personality to her brother's brash and brawn, was new—a few weeks old. LoLo knew she had no one but herself to blame; she'd ceased greeting the kids at the front door after school and, instead, left them to shout their hellos through the thick wooden door LoLo had taken to shutting up tight in the afternoons. This was the only way she could buy time to dry her tears and climb down off the ceiling from the heart palpitations that had begun to knock her wind in the hours before the children were to arrive home from school and LoLo was to hop to, feeding and talking and showing care and concern and cooking and cleaning up after everyone and having to spread her legs wide for Tommy and all the while having to find ways to forget the orphanage and Bear and that nurse and the forceps and the scraping and the broken parts that no one saw much less cared about.

"Mommy?" Rae called out that first afternoon, when she and TJ stood on the other side of the locked front door. LoLo heard Rae tapping lightly and calling out in her sweet voice first, then her playground voice when LoLo failed to answer in a sufficient amount of time. TJ, that boy didn't have Rae's patience; he balled up his fist and pounded the door so hard, LoLo was convinced his hand was going to rocket clean through the wood, and then she would have to beat him again, maybe black his eye this time, feel even more remorseful than she did when she bruised his shoulder and dabbed alcohol on that gash on his thigh and blew on it gently so that the liquid wouldn't burn. Blew on it gently so that he could see she loved him and cared for him and just needed him to do right, to be quiet for a change and let his mother spiral into the still.

"TJ, stop!" LoLo heard Rae yell-whisper. "She's gonna get mad!"

"So!" TJ said, pounding the door. "She always mad."

Peeping through Rae's bedroom window, LoLo watched her daughter stare at her brother as he beat that door, her eyes narrowed as she studied his hand and wrist and then his wiry arm and the fresh blue-black bruise just to the side of his bicep—this one pounded into his arm when LoLo had discovered him a few days earlier eating peanut butter directly out the jar. TJ didn't know what the big deal was; it wasn't like LoLo was eating the peanut butter—or anything else, for that matter—and Rae didn't like it anyway so . . .

LoLo kept watching as Rae, likely convinced TJ was going to break the door down, picked up her book bag and ran around to the back of the house, no doubt to see if their mother had maybe left the back door open this time. LoLo hadn't bothered. She had, however, closed her bedroom window's curtains, mostly. Rae pressed her perky nose against the glass and squinted through a sliver of a view between the heavy material LoLo had pulled together hours before so that she could lay her body down on top of her covers, fully clothed in a church outfit, down to her pantyhose and heels, hands folded over her chest, like she imagined a funeral director might pose her had she been lying in a grand, white, satin-lined casket. She went back to her bedroom and assumed that position again. It was all she could muster. Out the corner of her eye, LoLo could see Rae quickly pull her face from the window when she caught sight of her mother's mascara making black tracks down LoLo's face, puddling on the starched white pillowcase. Rae, terrified by the sight, backed away from the window so quickly she stumbled over her feet and fell, landing in her mother's hydrangea bush, which tore the tiniest of holes in her school pants. Rae hopped up almost as fast as she'd fallen—looked down at that hole, knowing there would be no explaining it to LoLo. There was never any explaining.

Rae scrambled to her feet and ran off in the direction of Daisy's house.

LoLo suspected her child would fall into that white woman's arms, eat up her snacks. Maybe play in her hair. LoLo had told her about playing in that white woman's hair. Like it was better than theirs. Rae stayed over there long enough to give her mother some time. Time for her father to come home and make her mother act right again.

"Don't worry yourself 'bout swimming," Tommy said to Rae. "You keep them grades up like you do and you can grow up to be rich and buy four swimming pools of your own and a hairdresser at each one of them to fix your hair when you finish dipping under the water. Okay?"

"Okay, Daddy," Rae said, giggling as Tommy pinched her chin.

A couple hours later, there was Theodore Lawrence—everybody called him Theddo on account that's how Black tongues painted his name on the air— with his feet up on LoLo's couch, one hand wrapped around a beer from her refrigerator, the other holding a cigarette, sitting around waiting for food like he was King Tut. He called himself being a Muslim because that's what the rest of his family in Philadelphia was, but he'd never so much as darkened the doorway of a mosque, still smoked, drank, and cavorted with all kinds of women, white ones, too, and LoLo neither believed nor respected his denouncing of pork, so she put some fatback in the field peas all the same. She intended to do like she always did when he had his plate out and fixed his mouth to complain about the smoked, salty goodness LoLo used to season her vegetables, like any other self-respecting southern cook pouring her heart into a pot of soul food: "Don't put the meat on your plate, then," she'd say sweetly out loud, but like a grizzly deep on the inside.

LoLo stood over the fish, scraping down its scales. They never cleaned porgies to her satisfaction, so she always had her knife at the ready when she unrolled the brown paper wrapping under a stream of cold water in the sink. This batch was no exception; scales flew all around the metal sink, onto the Formica counters, a few into her hair. It was methodical, meticulous, this ritual cleaning; nothing ever made it to LoLo's pots without the extra care she employed to make sure the food she put in her family's belly was as close to pure as she could get it. Chicken got bathed in a solution of vinegar and fresh lemon juice, collards got soaked, washed, soaked, washed, soaked, and washed of their grit, black-eyed peas got picked through. The ritualistic cleaning—of food, laundry, every nook and cranny of the house, bodies—was certainly a throwback to her childhood, during which she was expected to, as a girlchild, maintain the upkeep of every place in which she took up space. Used to be that it was soothing, a way to clear her mind, lower her stressors. But slowly, she came to resent these routines and now, LoLo had begun to dread them, these albatrosses around her neck that squeezed her just so—just so that she had begun to hide from them, under covers, in her closet, behind the closed bathroom door. This when no one was looking. This when the kids were looking. This, when she slowly began to disappear from her very own eyes.

Just as she began sprinkling the salt on the flat pieces of flesh, her mind wandered to her garden—specifically the cornstalks she'd inspected only a few hours before. They were pregnant with ears climbing two and three to each stalk, the dark brown silk signaling that the kernels inside were milky white and ready for her pots. Fried corn, she thought, with the back of the knife run down the ears just so to produce the nectar that made her dish a sweet standout, would be satisfying with the fish. Maybe even make her see some light.

"Rae!" LoLo called out. She needed to tend to the fish and didn't feel like going out to the garden anyway. Rae, to whom LoLo was teaching the particulars of homemaking, cooking, and gardening, knew which ears were ripe and ready for picking. She didn't let TJ, clumsy and destructive, near the vegetables. She looked over at Tommy just as he jumped off the couch and yelled at the television set. "Come on, baby! Let's go, baby! You see that play?" he called out to the equally roused Theddo, clapping his hands for emphasis. They gripped each other's hands like they'd just made the shot. LoLo rolled her eyes. Tommy wasn't about to go out there. Rae would have to do.

The girl didn't answer.

"Rae!" LoLo called a bit more forcefully. Then, to herself, after having her yell be met with more silence, she asked, "What that girl doing?"

LoLo shut the water off and turned to the kitchen doorway, half expecting the girl to materialize in the opening. Nothing. LoLo shook the water off her hands and wiped the wet on her apron, her eyes never once leaving the kitchen entrance. The heat of her forehead rose commiserate to the dipping of her angry brow line.

"Rae!" LoLo yelled again. Tommy and Theddo, oblivious to LoLo's mounting irritation, jumped out their seats again and cheered as some basketball player took a victory lap around the court, dapping up his team-mates and making a mental note to watch his fete on the evening news' sports highlight reel.

Fed up with an errant child who had not hopped to at the sound of her mother's voice, LoLo stomped out the kitchen and down the hallway, anx-ious to see what her daughter was doing that was so much more urgent than answering her mother's call. She burst into the girl's room like she was the law, making a bust. "Didn't you hear me calling you, gal?" she asked as she pushed through the door.

There was no Rae.

LoLo quickly searched TJ's room and then the bathroom the children shared. Still no Rae. That's when her heart started to skip—when every worst-case scenario she could think of invaded, like some kind of cancer, every cell in her body. LoLo went from a trot going from each closet and un-derbed to a full-on frantic sprint as she ran into her own room, the last place she thought to look. There was Rae, standing in the master bathroom mirror, arms flailing about as she chanted some strange incantation at her reflection.

"I must . . . I must . . . I must increase my bust! I will . . . I will . . . I will increase my . . ."

"What in the hell?"

Rae jumped at the sound of her mother's voice, and immediately dropped her arms to her side. Her eyes were wide as good china.

"What you doing in here?" LoLo yelled. "Did you hear me calling you?"

Obviously stunned by both her mother's appearance and rapid-fire questioning, Rae said nothing. LoLo washed over the girl's body with her eyes—made note of the slight tremble in Rae's shoulders.

"I said what you doing in here, girl?" LoLo demanded, grabbing Rae's arm to whip her face to her own.

"I . . . I was reading a book."

"You gone stand here and lie in my face? You weren't reading no damn book!"

"I was, Mommy, I swear!"

LoLo raised her hand to the back of her own head and crashed it down with maximum speed for maximum impact across Rae's meaty cheek. Stunned by the force of her mother's hand, Rae's face contorted into a noiseless scream as she tried to catch both her breath and her cry.

"What I tell you about swearing?" LoLo yelled.

Rae, finally having caught her breath, cried out from the sting of the slap. Within seconds, Tommy appeared behind LoLo, his face contorted into a question. "What's going on back here?" is all he could muster to say as he stood watching LoLo, standing over their daughter like a prizefighter who was waiting for the referee's count to wind its course.

"I'm calling her name and she in here prancing and preening in the mirror and lying to me about what she doing," LoLo said between breaths, anger making her chest heave up and down and up and down. "And then she swore!"

"What you in here lying about?" Tommy asked, his words more gentle in their search for context—understanding.

Fear rang in Rae's eyes, but she answered her father all the same. "I was reading the book," Rae said.

"What book, Rae?" LoLo demanded. "Ain't no damn book."

"This one," Rae answered, placing her hand atop a paperback book that LoLo missed, lying right there on the bathroom counter.

"That's the book your uncle gave you?" Tommy asked, reaching for it.

"Yes, sir," Rae said, still whimpering and sniffling and shaking.

LoLo, glaring at her child, snatched the book and read its cover. "What this got to do with you chanting in the mirror?" she demanded of Rae. Turning to Tommy, she said, "She was in here with her shirt open, saying some kind of spell or something."

Rae vigorously shook her head.

"What were you doing, then?" LoLo asked, letting go of the book as Tommy took it back into his hands.

Rae was quiet, save for her sniffles.

"Answer me!" LoLo said, the force of her words making Rae jump.

"In the book, Margaret is doing an exercise to make her chest bigger," she said, practically mumbling the words.

"Make your what bigger?" LoLo asked.

Rae, embarrassed, whispered this time. "Your chest."

Tommy laughed and peeked around LoLo to get a good look at Rae. He stared at her chest. "Well, is it working?"

"That's not funny!" LoLo said. "What the hell kind of book is this telling girls how to get bigger chests?"

Tommy sighed. "It's just a book, Tick, that's all," he said, turning it around in his hands. He checked the cover and the age range listed on the inner page.

"This what your brother brings to my house? Books about how young girls can make their boobs bigger?"

Tommy shook his head and sighed again. "He bought her a book because he knows she likes to read, LoLo. Don't make that out to be a bad thing."

"I don't know nothing about this book, and something tells me he doesn't either. Got our daughter in here chanting and prancing in the mirror, focused on making her chest big," she said, seething. She turned to Rae: "Take your fast tail outside and get me some corn out the garden," she said. "Now!"

Rae scrambled out of the bathroom and practically tripped over her own feet as she rushed past her parents and out into the hallway, through the kitchen and the back door, into the yard, where the fireflies were starting to take flight and the corn stood at attention, brown, silky hair blowing in the evening breeze.

LoLo had noticed the little buds poking out of Rae's T-shirts, how they danced like little stone fruit seeds against the fabric as she rushed out the door for school in the morning. Breasts were coming, and her little booty was getting a bubble shape to it and soon, hips would come and thighs, too, and with that, a period, and with a period, questions she wasn't ready to answer and complications she wasn't ready to handle. How, after all, was she supposed to talk to a twelve-year-old—a baby—about having babies? That's what periods led to: babies. The very thought made LoLo's womb ache. Menstruation, sex—she could barely talk to Tommy about these things, much less a child. Wasn't appropriate. LoLo needed, too, to tuck the feelings that came with that discussion—her memories of bleeding and being fucked against her will and not knowing what any of it meant, including the consequences and the choices that were made for her, choices that tore every inch of her insides, her heart, to pieces. This was not something she should have been forced to reckon with after her first blood. This was not something she wanted her daughter to reckon with before her first blood. Little girls needed to remain little girls, at all costs.

It would not occur to LoLo that this very moment would be the impetus for her daughter's silence when it mattered that she talk to her mother—when she would need her to calm her anxiety and explain what all was really happening to her body, beyond the whispered conversations she'd been having with her friends about menstruation and blood. Not even two weeks from that day when LoLo had caught Rae fiddling with her chest, when LoLo finally relented and let Freddy pick up the kids and keep them at his house for the weekend, Rae would get her period. Rae would also keep that a secret. LoLo would find out about it only because she was busy with the upkeep of her own long-held secret about her own blood. LoLo had stood there, staring into the box of Kotex she kept in the closet as part of her elaborate, decades-long ruse that she still got her period. She ran her fingers over each of the pads, counting to herself—two, four, six, seven. What happened to the other three? LoLo shook the box, as if doing so would make the missing pads appear. She quickly stuck her head into the linen closet, adjusting her eyes to the darkness of the deep end of the shelf, eyes searching for the missing pads. Then, the shock bolted through her chest. She stood up and turned toward the trash can—focused her eyes on three mounds of wadded-up toilet tissue, one of them with a small trickle of blood seeping through it. And LoLo knew. She knew.

She practically flew to the phone and stuck her fingers in the holes of the rotary dial, spinning up Freddy's phone so haphazardly she had to smash down on the receiver three times before she got the numbers right. Finally, she heard the phone ringing on the other end, and then Freddy's cheery but succinct greeting, "Yeah, this is Freddy," and her greeting back wasn't a greeting at all, but more like sharp blades and knife points as she accused her brother, this man who'd asserted this sibling bond despite his sister was all elbows and quiet fury, of deliberately withholding that Rae got her period during the weekend visit at his place.

"I figured she'd tell you herself," he said into the phone. The timbre of his voice was mellow, but his face was wrinkled. He was in no mood for a fight, not after having spent the long weekend with his niece and nephew crabbing and watching bootleg movies on his VCR. Only reason he knew Rae had gotten her monthly was because she stopped up the toilet with bloody tissue she'd had wadded up in her panties all weekend long. It looked like a horror movie. He'd tried not to be angry about it; the girl was embarrassed and flustered as it was, and she'd been running around his house sneaking aspirin to soothe her aching belly. Still, that was as close to period blood Freddy had ever been and ever would be again if he had anything to do with it. Such things were for the women to work out. "I don't exactly run around getting in the middle of lady business," he'd told LoLo simply.

"She's not a lady. She's a little girl," LoLo seethed.

"You still haven't explained what that has to do with me."

"Are you too busy cavorting with all those tramps that you can't keep straight how to handle your twelve-year-old niece? She's a child. When things like this happen, you tell her mother!"

"First of all, don't you go policing what the hell I do in my house. I don't see you paying nan bill here."

"You a grown man. I would expect you to be able to pay your own bills."

"I know you do. And you sent them ungrateful kids over here with their hands out, with them same ideas. I was too busy feeding them and buying them shit to call you about lady business, Delores."

Hard as she and Tommy worked to tend to their kids, LoLo wasn't about to be chastised about their care and upkeep. Claims that she was dependent on others to care for them were met with swift derision. She didn't care if they ever spoke again. He, equally stubborn, felt the same. It was a small incident, so very insignificant in the body of their history— their separation, her abuse, his ultimately forging a relationship with their father after he was grown and their daddy had remarried and had another baby to add to the five he'd made with LoLo and Freddy's mama and so easily sent away. Freddy was good for that—for pushing all that pain, all that disappointment, that history deep into the recesses. It was the root of what made him find LoLo, insist on a relationship. What led him back to their father. Family was the beneficiary of his grace, generous, even, to those who were the stingiest of all. "That's family. That's blood," he'd say, like it was supposed to mean something to LoLo. Like she was supposed to forget. She could not. Her frustration surrounding the argument with Freddy over Rae's menstruation was like a little lump in a titty— buried deep down in the fatty part, invisible to the naked eye, but sore to the touch. Cancerous. Without medical intervention, terminal. Neither of them had the emotional aptitude or wherewithal to survive the disease of their blood. They weren't about to see eye to eye over Rae and her period.

LoLo pulled the phone from her head and put her mouth directly against the receiver. "Lose my number," she growled through knitted teeth before slamming down the phone. Chest heaving, she rushed back into the bathroom and looked at the wads of tissue one more time. Hard as she tried, she couldn't quite figure out what to say to Rae about this thing. So on that day, she said nothing at all.

But on this impromptu fish-fry day, Theddo got her words. All of them. LoLo stomped into the TV room, waving the book in her hand. She threw it with all her force at her brother-in-law, who, oblivious to the drama that had minutes before unfolded in the heartbeat of the house, jumped off the couch, half-surprised, half-mad. "LoLo! The hell?"

"Don't you ever give my child anything before clearing it with me, you understand?" she said, seething.

"What you talmbout, woman?" he said, rubbing the dull ache on his chest where the book had landed.

"You heard me," LoLo said through clenched teeth. "Do it again and see what happens."

"Come on now, Tick, he just gave her a book. It was a nice thing to do," Tommy reasoned.

"Oh? You think it was nice to give our daughter a book about how to make her titties bigger?" LoLo yelled. "What's a grown-ass man doing giving a book like that to a child?"

"I . . . I gave her . . . that's a really popular book," Theddo said, confusion contorting his face. "My girlfriend let her daughter read it and all her little friends are reading it, too."

"Your girlfriend, huh?" LoLo said. "The one who fucks married men? You take children's book recommendations from her?"

"Come on now, Delores," Tommy said. "Easy now."

"I expect you to have my back, Tommy. This is your daughter. If you don't want no extra babies around here, you don't want these menfolk looking at her like she a grown woman, you better start paying attention," LoLo spit through her teeth.

LoLo stomped back into the kitchen and turned on the water in the sink. She shook more salt on the fish and then black pepper and a smidge of cayenne and paprika into the cornmeal she would use for dredging. Through the window, she watched her daughter as she stood on her tiptoes to grab an ear of corn off the top of a large stalk, the shadow of which darkened the basket Rae used to collect the vegetables. Her movements as she picked the corn were slow, deliberate. Thoughtful. LoLo trusted the girl would bring back a most perfect bounty. LoLo was raising her to be somebody's perfect wife. Someone's perfect slave. She couldn't help but to do it. She didn't know how to help her baby girl.

Her heart broke in the place where it should have been puffed up—proud—leaving sadness in the slivers.

19

LoLo was twelve the first time she got happy, right there where the backwater slough met the sloping shoreline of Windlow River and the flutter of tree leaves in the southern breeze sounded to believers like God whispering in their ears. Pastor Charles and Deacon Claytor held on to either of LoLo's arms, warning her to step lightly as they waded through the water that, though sun-kissed, was always cool. Plenty before her had stubbed their toes on the trunks of the cypress that, decades before, a chain gang had sawed to the nub to make way for the river. Those underwater trunks, they were ghosts that held unspeakable truths about what happened on that land, before the water, before the large-mouth bass and white perch swirled in it—the kind of things that were unyieldingly callous and particularly cruel. Kind of memories old folk knew to hush up about. The good and righteous people of Mt. Nebo Church of God in Christ of Nazareth believed that in the still of the morning, if you listened real good, you could hear the clinking of the chains used to tether human bodies—skin ripped and bloodied, bones broken, limbs and appendages chopped or sawed off as punishment for whatever slight or for whatever whim—to those trunks. That made this particular stretch of water a sacred place. A place where God's name wrapped itself around tongues. Where mercy was promised to those who believed, even in their darkest hour. On baptismal days, the congregation made a habit of standing on the shore in their fresh-washed whites, smashing their metal buckets together and loudly singing their songs of faith in the Godhead to scare away the water moccasins, but also to quiet the ghosts. *CLANG.* "Take me to the water. Take me to the water." *BANG CLANG.* "Take me to the water, to be baptized." *BANG CLANG BANG.*

LoLo held on tight to the reverend's and deacon's arms. No matter her fear of the tree trunks and ghosts and even the water snakes, LoLo wanted to be in that river—to be crucified, buried, and resurrected in it. To come up . . . new. Deacon Claytor had laid out how all of this worked in LoLo's Sunday school class and Pastor Charles, he'd preached about it enough for LoLo to recognize and comprehend its significance, even if Bear's cynicism was for true and Pastor really was extolling the virtues of Baptism solely to gain new members and, of course, new tithers. At age twelve, even with very adult, very worldly problems stalking every day of her miserable life, LoLo was still young enough to hope, to have faith in Pastor's promise that going under that water could, would change things. That God and Jesus and Holy Spirit would deliver her from evil and goodness and mercy would hold tight to her hand and lead her out of the dark place, into the light.

"It's okay now, Delores, we're not going to let you fall in this water," Pastor Charles said as he and Deacon Claytor led LoLo deeper into the river. The water, gentle, rocked her as she settled into the men's hands. Her long, white baptismal robe looked like an angel's wings fluttering just beneath the river's surface. Confirmed for LoLo why she was there. "None but the righteous shall see God." *BANG CLANG CLANG.*

"Trust us," Deacon Claytor said. "Trust God."

When they arrived at their preferred spot in the water, the men gently lifted LoLo onto one of the taller stumps beneath its surface—one that made it so that her head and shoulders could sit comfortably above the water—and spun her around so that she could witness the congregation swaying and singing the Holy Spirit down. There was Bear, clanging his buckets, and Clarette, hands raised in praise, singing the top notes of the hymn's harmony.

Pastor Charles raised his hands and the voices and clanging immediately ceased. "This water has seen many sinners," he began.

"Yassuh," Deacon Claytor whispered.

"Many souls that needed to get right with God," Pastor Charles said, the last four of his words a staccato on his tongue.

"Yassuh," Deacon Claytor answered, louder this time.

"But when you show Him your heart, when you surrender to the Great I Am," Pastor said, "You, you, you become new."

"New! Yassuh," Deacon Claytor said, with gusto coloring his scant words.

"You give your mind and your body to the Lord, and He will bless you, oh yes He will!" Pastor Charles yelled.

"Yassuh! Oh, bless His holy name!"

"Come up out this water pure as snow!"

LoLo had stared ahead as the preacher preached on, absorbing his words, which really weren't that different from what he said most Sundays, but on this particular day, as the water swirled her robe and she rubbed her toes against the soggy wood grain, the words—the promises of redemption, of liberation—made the soreness in her nether parts fade. Made her light as air. Turned Bear into a lamb that she didn't have to fear anymore because when she went down into that water, she would be new again and God, He would take His place beside her because she was His child and He was her redeemer, the all-powerful Emmanuel, her healer, her supplier. Her protector. The pastor said it and it would be so. No more hurting. No more pain. No more shadows and dark corners. Only light.

"Little sister," the pastor said, pressing his wet hand to LoLo's forehead. "Do you accept Jesus as your Lord and Savior?"

"Yes," LoLo whispered as she stared at Bear.

"Do you accept Him as the one true God and promise to obey Him for the rest of your days?"

"Yes," LoLo whispered, closing her eyes so she could focus on the lamb and not the bear.

"Tell it to the Lord, then—shout out loud!" the pastor shouted.

"I love Jesus," LoLo said.

"Oh, you can do better than that, tell it to your Savior!"

"I love you, Jesus!" LoLo shouted.

"Again! Let Him hear you from across the waters all the way to Jerusalem land!"

"I love you, Jesus!" LoLo shouted over and over again, as the breeze moved the leaves and God whispered in her ears. She felt the vibration first in her toes. Then it skipped up her legs and to the pit of her stomach—burned her heart and set her insides on fire. She rocked and then a little jump—another, higher, and another still. "I love you, Jesus!" she said from her gut up into the sky, arms raised in hosannah.

"Praise God!" Pastor yelled as he and Deacon Claytor tightened their grips on LoLo's shoulders and pulled her backward into the river.

Under the water, the pain was gone. Under the water, there was nothing. Under the water, LoLo was free.

This was the regard she'd held for church, tipping down the center aisle in her finest accoutrement sewed special for the occasion, her good Sunday shoes crossed ladylike in the pew, prayer cloth across her knees, tambourine by her side. The Word at her fingertips. Those poems, the prayers—they were the key to her salvation when she was a teenager, fighting her way to freedom from Bear's tyranny. It had been on those early Sunday mornings, while the whole town attended to its collective soul, Bear included, that she'd been safe. Then he was an angel—a man of the cloth who was too busy playing right to do wrong. Merciful, even. "This here my little cousin," he'd tell the righteous of Mt. Nebo. "Po' thang ain't have nobody but God to look after her until we found her and brought her on this way. Saved her life. Now we got her here to save her soul."

"Amen," they would say, anointing LoLo's shoulders and forehead and shouting their "Ain't God good" proclamations.

Suffer the little children. The church couldn't save LoLo from Bear or The Scraping, but when she was about the age of sixteen, Pastor did order the passing of a collection plate when Bear and Clarette announced plans to send LoLo up north, to a church-owned tenement in Long Island, managed by a family friend. The couple had conveniently left out the part where Clarette demanded Bear get LoLo the hell out of her house not even two days before, when she found Bear on top of LoLo out in the chicken coop.

"What's taking you so long to fetch the eggs?" Clarette had demanded as she rushed up to the coop in a huff, having stood one moment longer than she cared to over a bowl of flour and sugar on the kitchen table, waiting for the missing ingredient she needed for the white cake she planned to present at Saturday night revival. Neither Bear nor LoLo had heard her as she breached the doorway—he, busy grunting and sweating and grinding, LoLo just lying there, eyes dead, thinking about water and cypress trees that hold God's whispers. As her brain caught up with what her eyes were taking in, Clarette stopped short and jerked backward, as if she'd run smack into some kind of wall. Her shadow caught LoLo's attention first; she slowly shifted her eyes until they found Clarette's, the two of them locked in a ringshout of anger and disgust and profound sadness. Oblivious, Bear scrambled himself off his little cousin's body, still sore and healing from The Scraping, only after his wife yelled, "Either you get her out of here or I will pack up my shit and leave you two at it!"

1964, in the springtime

Church was both ultimatum and threat in Ms. Ella's house, LoLo's first stop in New York. "You come on in here and set ya things down there in the basement," she'd said as she opened the door, before LoLo could get her big toe across the threshold of the two-bedroom ranch, every bit as prim and pristine as its owner. "Around here, you wake up before the sun do, you keep your space neat, you earn your keep, and Sundays is for the Lord. You abide by those rules and we get along just fine. You don't and there'll be some hell in the city, understand?"

"Yes'm," LoLo'd answered quickly, not to please Ms. Ella, but because her demands weren't demands at all. They made it easy for LoLo to tap into the very essence of who she was then. Who she'd been desperate to be in the now. Free.

1981, in early fall

"Yes, baby, that's how you do it. Just keep moving the cheese up and down the grater, like you scrubbing it," LoLo gently directed Rae, as she poured macaroni elbows into a big metal pot full of boiling water. "You got to hurry now; they gonna be here soon and we got just enough time to get the macaroni and cheese in the oven and cooking before your aunties get here."

LoLo was grateful Rae was in the kitchen helping her prepare dinner for Sarah, Para Lee, and Cindy, who were making a rare visit to New Jersey to visit LoLo—only their second since their beloved friend had moved three hours away from her friends, her adopted hometown, her job, her church, and everything that mattered to her beyond her man and her babies. But really, it was time the girl learned some kitchen basics anyway—at least that's what LoLo thought. Hell, she was wringing chicken necks and gutting fish before she got her first blood; she wasn't about to raise a daughter who couldn't find her way around the kitchen. LoLo wiped her hands on a dish towel and stood over Rae as the little girl scraped the cheese against the metal grater, more tentatively than LoLo would have liked. "Come on, now! Don't act like you scared to tend the cheese," she yelled, her voice making Rae jump, move a little faster. "That grater gone cut you right up if you scared of it. Just take your brain out of it and scrape it."

A couple hours later, and the two were standing over their handiwork, admiring the spread and slapping Tommy and TJ's hands off the table's bounty: macaroni and cheese, fried chicken, fresh string beans and potatoes, a southern lemon pound cake made from scratch. LoLo looked like some movie star, cheeks rouged, her miniskirt and collared shirt straight out the Sears pattern catalogue. Everything had to be perfect. Everything.

Tommy slapped LoLo's ass and said, "Mmph. We need to have company more often," as he circled her like some predator about to pounce on his prey.

"Oh, stop it, before the kids see you!" LoLo giggled before tooting her butt up for another pat. Tommy obliged. Their laughter, rare, flowed easily.

"They're here, Mommy!" Rae said, twirling in the curtains in the living room.

"Get out my curtains before you make them fall down!" LoLo yelled, more out of excitement to see her friends than any kind of worry about the curtains or her daughter's movements. She rushed over to the record player and ran her fingers through the crate of albums beneath the console. Stevie Wonder's *Songs in the Key of Life* would set the perfect mood. She blew on the disc, twirled it around in her hands, and dropped it on the turntable. Knuckles were rapping on the front door as she carefully placed the needle on the groove for "As."

"Who dat at my do'!" LoLo yelled through the wooden door in her best deep man voice.

"Chile, if you don't open this door! We done drove all this way and I got to tee tee!" Sarah yelled, giggles ringing her words.

LoLo snatched the door open. "Don't act like you drove all this way without a slop jar in the back of that ol' battle-ax of a station wagon, Sarah Johnson. You live in New York, but I know you ain't forgot them Alabama travel ways!"

"Me? Pee in a jar? In this dress?" Sarah said, falling into LoLo's embrace. "No, ma'am!"

"Plus, we got company," Para Lee said, tossing her chin toward her right shoulder. Just beyond it was Cindy and . . . a man. A man who was not Roosevelt.

"Heeeeeeeey," Cindy said, waving, with a wink. "This here Leo."

LoLo stepped aside to let Sarah and Para Lee pass, but then blocked the door again just as Cindy tried to step through the threshold. "Well," she said, with Para Lee and Sarah behind her, Sarah hopping from foot to foot, not wanting to miss the show. "And who is this fella on my doorstep? Ain't nobody tell me about an extra guest!"

"He's a surprise," Cindy said, sassy-like.

"For me?" LoLo asked, clutching the gold cross on her necklace. "Why sir, I'm afraid I'm already taken. I got me a man."

"Y'all let the man breathe!" Tommy said, hugging Sarah and Para Lee from behind, then pushing through to size up the gentleman standing on his stoop. "Come on in here, brother. These ladies will boss you into next week if you let them," Tommy said as he shook Leo's hand and waved Cindy and her new man through the door.

"Mmmmmhhhhmph!" LoLo said, looking Cindy up and down, cackling as she passed.

And just like that, just that easy, LoLo was whole again, fortified by the presence of the three women who gave her . . . air. Until they sat their feet under her dining room table, their plates filled with LoLo's soul food— her love letter to them all—she hadn't realized just how long she'd been holding her breath. How she'd suffocated under the weight of longing for the people, the things, she loved so hard.

"Oh, I got this—let me grab that," Leo said, pushing his chair away from the table and grabbing plates as LoLo began clearing the table for dessert.

"Oh, you don't have to do that, I got it," LoLo said, politely trying to grab the plates from Leo's hands.

"I insist," he said, refusing to yield. "Least I can do is wash up these dishes after you cooked such a fine meal."

LoLo shot a look at Tommy, who was knitting his eyebrows in confusion as he watched Leo walk the dishes to the sink. His brows practically touched his nose when he turned back toward the table, only to witness the women, heads cocked, eyes wide, watching Leo pour dish detergent onto the dirty plates and utensils and run water in the sink.

"Welp, the game is on," Tommy said finally. "It ain't gonna watch itself. Ladies," he said, tipping his chin as he pushed from the table and headed to his recliner—to exactly no one's surprise.

"Mmmm-hmmm, I'mma need me some details, Melissa," LoLo whispered, leaning in Cindy's direction the second Tommy was out of earshot. "Where did you bury Roosevelt? Because I know that nigga did not just step aside and make room for Mr. Perfect over here."

Sarah and Para Lee dramatically turned their bodies in Cindy's direction and waited for her to tell the juicy bits.

"I brought him because I thought you should see me happy for once," Cindy started. She looked at her man and sighed.

"She brought him because she finally got some act right about her and left that no-good Roosevelt," Sarah said, raising her palm for a high five. Para Lee obliged.

Cindy hushed the women, scared they'd draw Leo's attention, but he was oblivious as he dipped his hands in the sudsy water, alternately rubbing the dishes clean and peering over the breakfast bar to get a clear look at the basketball game blaring from the TV. He yelled, "Aaaaye! All right now!" when Tommy hopped out of his recliner to celebrate whatever was happening with the team for which he was rooting.

"She left Roosevelt because he finally gave her a reason she could get behind," Para Lee said dryly. "Tell her about that other gal."

"And the baby on the way," Sarah said.

"And don't leave out the part where he tried to convince you to stay with him and raise the baby with that other girl."

Para Lee and Sarah laughed heartily, but LoLo could see the creases in the corners of Cindy's eyes—the way her chest heaved up and down and up and down, betraying the labor of her breath.

"I left Roosevelt," she said quietly, "because he said he wasn't going to hit me anymore, and it finally occurred to me that he ain't nothing but a liar. He had a baby on me. Did that make me pack my bags a little quicker? Yeah. But I wasn't running away from Roosevelt. I was getting myself loose and free so that I could be ready to run to a man who's good to me, and that's when Leo came along." She looked over at her boyfriend as he stacked a pile of freshly washed utensils on the dish rack. "That man don't ask for nothing but my love. And he give me plenty of it in return. And don't none of it hurt."

LoLo reached for Cindy's hand—rubbed it with her own.

"Y'all don't understand what it's like because you're all happily married—to good men," Cindy said, addressing Para Lee and Sarah, whose jovial smirks were clearly overpowered by their friend's anguish—an anguish they'd leisurely dismissed after years of watching their friend succumb to Roosevelt's wrath. "All I ever wanted was to be loved—have a man care something about me like I do him. Took me a minute to figure out Roosevelt didn't have that kind of heart. Took me a couple mo' minutes to figure out mine was still beating."

Cindy looked over at Leo, who, feeling the energy flowing his way from the dining room table, looked over at his woman and smiled big. "You need anything, baby?" he asked easily.

Cindy rubbed the wet from her cheek and shook her head no.

"I'mma go catch the end of this game," he said, folding the dishrag over the side of the sink.

"Thank you for doing the dishes!" LoLo shouted after him.

"Wasn't a thing," he said, waving over his head and disappearing to the couch.

"See? I got me a good one," Cindy said, smiling hard. "He just like Tommy, LoLo."

"Like who?" LoLo asked. She folded her arms—tossed a quizzical stare in Cindy's direction and let out a little laugh.

"Don't act like you ain't got no good man," Sarah said, reeling back.

"For real," Cindy said. "Don't do him like that!"

"Hold your horses, now, I didn't say he bad. He is a good man and I love him for making this good life for me and our family," LoLo insisted. "But ain't nobody around here perfect, Tommy Lawrence, Senior, included."

Para Lee, Sarah, and Cindy answered her back with their eyes.

"Come on now, Para Lee. Sarah. Don't act like y'all don't know what marriage is. We got a whole, what, almost two decades of marriage between us. Y'all better shame the devil and tell this girl the truth."

"Hmph, it ain't easy, I know that," Para Lee said.

"That's right, it ain't easy," LoLo agreed.

"Well, what's hard about it?" Cindy asked. "I mean, come on now. Your men are good men. They not beating you, they keeping you and your babies fed. They not making babies with other women. LoLo, you out here in this great big ol' house in Jersey, living like Miss Anne."

"Is that what you think? I'm just out here eating bonbons and living the life?" LoLo snapped. "I'm out here in the middle of nowhere, sitting in this house by myself most days, just me and God until them kids come stomping across the grass. You think Tommy such a good man, what that good man do when he finished his supper?"

LoLo's friends didn't make a peep.

"I don't even have to tell you. You saw it. Your man grabbed all the plates. My man left his sitting right there on the table and went on in the room and put his feet up like he got maid service around here."

"Shit, my man do that, too," Sarah said. "I know Judge ain't busting no suds, is he, Para?"

"Naw," she said. "I don't think he even know where the dish detergent is." She looked over toward the sink. "You got Leo trained, huh? He just went on over there and handled them dish

"She got her a new model of a man," LoLo said, laughing.

"So, what you saying, LoLo? Something wrong with your model? Because from where I sit, Tommy sure look like a good man."

LoLo measured her words. "I didn't say he wasn't," she said slowly. "Tommy Lawrence is a good man. One of the best there is. Look like Leo is, too. Got him hopping up from the table, washing dishes and such. He ain't putting his hands on you. Nice-looking fella, too. But there's a difference between the man and the marriage."

"Hmph, I know that's right," Sarah said, practically whispering.

"You better tell it, LoLo!" Para Lee said, slapping her hands together, nodding in agreement. "Somebody need to say it."

"All I'm saying is love is love. It's pretty—sunshine. You lucky and it's just like Stevie says, hotter than the fourth of July," LoLo said, rocking side to side in her chair as she talked. "But marriage? Shit, that's the ants stomping all over your picnic. Eating all the sugar out your watermelon, floating in your beer. Every day, you got to pack your picnic, lay it out on the blanket, and fight them damn ants. Hope they don't ruin the picnic. Some days, they do. A lot of days, they do. You gotta make the decision every single day you can open your eyes to pack another picnic. Hope the sun come out and the ants stay the fuck in their hole today. That's a choice. A hard one. That's all I'm trying to tell you."

"Aye, LoLo!" Tommy called from the next room. "When you gonna cut that cake?" Then, to Leo, he said, "Man, my wife had this whole house smelling like Christmas this morning. You want some cake? Hey, LoLo, why don't you cut the cake? I'll take mine with a little ice cream."

LoLo trained her eyes on Cindy's as she listened to Tommy's subtle command. She shifted in her chair and cracked her neck, but kept her eyes locked with her friends. "You want chocolate or vanilla with that?" she called out to Tommy.

The boom of her voice made Cindy jump ever so slightly.

LoLo pulled open the accordion doors of the master bedroom closet and stood with her hands on her hips, staring at the wardrobe of dresses she'd hand-sewn exclusively for Sunday service. Walking down the center aisle of the Right Church of God and Fellowship back in Long Island, with her wide-brim hats casting a shadow over her eyes, long skirts swishing like sheets in a summer breeze, made her feel like somebody—like she wasn't just some seamstress who spent the majority of her days in a dingy, formless gray smock, sewing gowns she could neither afford nor wear anywhere elegant. Some Sundays, she would strut down the church's red carpet, head forward, eyes focused on white Jesus with his arms spread wide across the back wall behind the pulpit. Like he was beckoning her to sit at the hem of his long white robe. Other Sundays, she might give a little nod to her fellow parishioners—only the women, though, on account that some of the deacons were fresh and the rest were married, and LoLo didn't want any of that static. Always she would find herself squeezing somewhere between Para Lee and Sarah, sometimes next to Cindy if she didn't have to go to her second job or Roosevelt wasn't meting out his Sunday demands and she could actually make it to church. With peppermints on their tongues, they'd lick their fingers and flip through the parchment of their Bibles to the scriptures Pastor called, while they nodded and said, "Amen," or nodded in the direction of whoever caught their attention for whatever infraction to draw the trio's ire. "Loo-loo-loo-loo-look. To the right," Para Lee would yell-whisper and each of them would slowly turn into whatever direction they needed to witness whatever foolishness was going down. Sarah, she was the one with the voice. LoLo, who couldn't hold a note if it were gift wrapped and handed to her, loved her friend's voice—relished when the organist would play the beginning notes of "Jesus on the Mainline" and Sarah would spring up out her seat and take the lead—her gruff, heavy alto overpowering the harmony of the entire congregation. Para would be dealing with the tambourine and between the two, they would call Spirit down and LoLo, she would take off running and be filled. "Hah, gloray!" is how it would begin, and her body would constrict and the one arm would gun while her feet stomped out a rhythm on the twos and the fours. Para would push out her arms like she was stopping traffic, keeping her friend safe—their pew mates, too, if they were heathens and sitting there, unmoved. Sarah, she would keep singing down the walls of the sanctuary. After church, they would laugh and laugh and talk about the goodness of the Lord.

LoLo pulled her favorite hat from the top of the closet shelf and twirled it around in her hands. It'd been up there unmolested so long that the dust had caked itself to the felt, a fitting if not tragic reminder of just how long it'd been since she'd strutted down a church aisle, looking for her friends and the Good Word. God. Going to church close by wasn't any kind of option; LoLo would just as soon drool on her pillow another hour into Sunday morning than pull on her church hat and sit in the pews of a staid white church filled with stale hymn singing and a preacher who didn't know how to strike a fire up in her bones. And Tommy's Philly folks were Muslim. Which left LoLo longing—for her friends and her God.

Tommy shifted in the bed, turning over his pillow, trying to find the cool side. He reached out his hand to feel on LoLo, and found nothing but sheet, then opened one eye, then the second. "That hat always looked good on you," he said before pushing out a good yawn.

LoLo rubbed at the dust and held it close to her eyes for a more thorough inspection. "I miss wearing it," she said finally. "I want to go to church."

"Church, huh?" Tommy said, adjusting himself to rest his hand beneath his head. He sighed. "You might be better off driving to Philly. They got lots of churches out there, them holy roller churches you like."

"I don't want to go to church in Philly."

"Here? I don't know if they got what you looking for in Willingboro . . ."

"I want to go to church in Long Island. The Right church—with Para Lee and Sarah and Cindy."

Tommy adjusted himself again, this time sitting himself upright. "That's three hours away. You leave now and you gonna be a little late for service, ain't you?" he said, chuckling.

"I don't want to be here on a Sunday morning, staring at my church hat. I want to wear it to church. My church. In Long Island."

Tommy wrinkled his brow—was silent for a moment. "What's this all about?" he asked finally. "This about your friends visiting yesterday? What, you homesick or something?"

"I miss my friends," LoLo said. "I miss doing the things we used to do when we lived there—bowling and going to Para Lee's for barbeque and beer on a Saturday night and hearing Sarah sing on First Sunday . . ."

"Don't be like that. You acting like we don't have a good life here," Tommy said. His words tumbled out of his mouth fast and wrinkled. "Your friends come to town and now your life is for shit?"

"I didn't say that," LoLo said quickly. "Don't twist my words."

"If anything is twisted, it's this idea you have in your head that you missing something. Don't I make you happy?"

LoLo shut down. Always did when Tommy zeroed in on his replies rather than his wife's words—pleas.

"I take you and the kids out to the Ponderosa and we eat nice dinners, we got my family close by and they treat you like you blood, these kids don't want for nothing, you living in this pretty house, doing whatever you want to," he continued. "What's the problem?"

LoLo rubbed the hat once more and put it back up on the shelf. She couldn't answer his question in any kind of way that would satisfy, and didn't have the energy to, anyway. What she wanted to do was lie back down. Feet straight. Arms crossed on her chest. Chin up. Eyes closed. Maybe forever this time. "The kids are up," she said, closing the closet doors. "I'm going to get breakfast together."

LoLo could feel his eyes following her as she walked out the room, down the hallway toward the kitchen. She knew that though she'd caught his attention, she could hold it no longer than she could a firefly cupped in her hands; the light was compelling, pretty, but still, it was just a nasty bug slamming against her palms until she got disgusted—let it go.

The two didn't say much else the rest of the morning. They chewed on their fatback and salmon cakes while the roast beef and yams LoLo had prepared for Sunday dinner baked in the oven; the kids were oblivious to the tension, thick and putrid, that settled over the small wooden table.

"TJ, when we finished eating, go out to the shed and get out the lawn-mower and the gas, so we can cut the lawn, edge it up," Tommy ordered.

"Yessir," TJ answered quickly.

"When we done, I'll take you kids out to the dairy farm while your mama gets some rest."

The sun rose on Rae and TJ's faces, but LoLo's was still a cloudy sky. It didn't make Tommy any nevermind.

Tommy had butter pecan in a waffle cone, and TJ had chocolate in the same. Rae, well, she ate strawberry ice cream only, and even at age twelve, she still had trouble licking the creamy confection in a way that would keep it from dripping down the sides faster than it could on her tongue, so her blue T-shirt with her name spelled across it in rainbow letters had enough drips on it for her father to tell her to change it when they got in the house. Always, Rae did what she was told, so she was too busy hustling into the house to notice the commotion in the backyard. This was a good thing. LoLo didn't take into account, after all, how her young daughter would process finding her mother's body at the bottom of the creek, lying on a bed of rocks, the flowing water a sheet over her head. Only thing that was on LoLo's mind was getting up under the water and staying there, in the one place where she knew she could get free.

TJ heard the screaming first but dismissed it as the rebel yells of Daisy's

Seattle Public Library
Beacon Hill Branch
(206) 684-4711

09/21/23 01:17PM

Borrower # ****3

My darkest prayer : a novel /
0010107032459   Date Due: 10/
acbk

Razorblade tears /
0010103780804   Date Due: 10/12/
acbk

Blacktop wasteland /
0010100433613   Date Due: 10/12/
acbk

One blood /
0010106838450   Date Due: 10/12/23
acbk

TOTAL ITEMS: 4

Visit us on the Web at www.spl.org

youngest son, Mark, and his friends, probably out back playing football. TJ tried to join them once, but then quickly developed a myriad of excuses for why he couldn't play with them anymore. It happened the second he got tackled on either side by Mark's teenage man friends, who sneered, "Stay down, nigger," in his ears as they shifted all their weight on his thin, crumpled body. Hearing today's commotion, TJ quickly followed Rae into the house.

But Tommy, he could hear and decipher the screams out back; it wasn't a football game or some folly. A woman was out there, begging for someone to help her. Tommy shut the car door and jangled the keys as he swept his eyes over at the Daleys' front porch, looking to see if the neighbors were playing their usual position, rocking to and fro in their rocking chairs while they minded the neighborhood's business. The porch was empty. The screams grew more frantic.

Tommy creeped around the side of his house, still looking at the Daleys' porch, but following the pleas. Someone was yelling, "My God, somebody help me! I can't get her up! Steve, somebody, help! Please, somebody!"

Finally, Tommy picked up his pace. He could see only the top of a head bobbing frantically, but the straw-gray hair was a giveaway: it was Daisy down in the creek, hollering about something. When she looked at him and yelled his name, Tommy took off running. "Daisy, what's wrong? What's going on?" he yelled as he scuttled across the grass, almost tripping as he ran down the hill toward the creek. There, he found Daisy, tugging on arms, legs, begging, pleading, "Delores, honey, please! Sit up! You're going to drown in the water!"

Tommy deftly hopped down into the creek and splashed over the rocks, through the water as fast as he could. "LoLo! Baby, sit up! Get up! What are you doing?" he yelled. "Daisy, what happened? Daisy!"

Daisy's words tumbled as Tommy scooped LoLo into his arms, her body limp, deadweight. "I waved hello and called her name, but she didn't answer. She just kept walking like she could walk on water and air."

Tommy smacked his wife's face and shook her. "Baby! Baby! Come on, breathe. Come on!"

LoLo coughed and focused first on Daisy and then Tommy. "Why did you do that?" she said between gasps, struggling to get out of her husband's grip. "Why did you do that, Tommy? God is down there. He was setting me free."

Tommy rocked LoLo as she struggled.

"I want to be free."

This time, Tommy didn't speak. He listened.

20

1983, in the summertime

Tommy swished vinegar into the bucket full of water and swirled the liquid around with his finger as he smiled at LoLo. "That sho smell good, baby," he said as his wife dipped a basting brush into a small pot full of her homemade barbeque sauce and sopped it onto a row of chicken and hamburgers sizzling on the brick grill Tommy had made by hand, special for her. "Keep it up and even that racist cracka across the street gonna find a reason to come over here with a plate in her hand."

"Hmmph. She could try," LoLo said, pursing her lips. "All she get from me is my ass to kiss. She wouldn't know what to do with all this flavor anyway."

Tommy looked up from the bucket and narrowed his eyes—licked his bottom lip. "You right about that. You definitely got a whole lot of flavor, and I don't intend on sharing."

LoLo wrinkled her nose. "Hush! Before one of them kids come out here and hear you," she said, laughing and slopping. "You so nasty!"

Just then, Rae came bounding out the house with the vegetable basket, swaddled in a thick sweatsuit meant for midwinter, not the eighty-nine-degree Sunday that was hosting the family's impromptu, after-church family cookout. LoLo's wide smile turned into a look of puzzlement when she got a gander of her daughter's outfit. "You not hot in that?" she asked, waving the barbeque mop in Rae's direction.

"There's bugs over there," Rae said, jutting her chin toward her mother's garden, swinging the gathering bowl in her hand. Her contribution to dinner was to gather string beans and white potatoes for the pot, but she was still traumatized by the critters that showed up in the prior week's harvesting session, including two large beetles chomping away at the collards she'd been picking, and a small green garden snake the girl swore lunged at her ankles as she pulled weeds from between the pepper and tomato plants. Neighbors three houses over had heard her hollering, but, of course, nobody came to check on their neighbors because these particular white folk, mostly immigrants eating from the same American Dream pie as the Lawrences, could not be bothered with reaching across stereotypes to shake hands with Black people. In fact, LoLo said a silent "Thank you, Lawdy" that none had called the cops on them, which, by then, had happened no less than a half dozen times since Tommy and LoLo moved their family from New Jersey to a two-story home in a quaint, all-white neighborhood, walking distance from one of the territory's largest employers, a commercial bakery that sold its confections in supermarkets all throughout the nation. Tommy had two years as a line mechanic under his belt and already there was talk about him being a mechanic's supervisor because he was that good at fixing things. But that didn't change things for the neighbors, many of whom worked at the bakery, too, and saw the trail Tommy blazed there. Niggers were niggers, and there would be no distinctions. Not even in 1983.

LoLo shook her head and smirked. "Ain't none of them garden bugs and snakes studying you, girl. It's too hot out here for all them clothes and all that drama. Keep it down, hear?"

"Leave her alone, Tick" Tommy laughed. "My baby don't like bugs and snakes, she don't have to like bugs and snakes, ain't that right, baby?"

Rae giggled, tugging at the sweatpants hugging tight around her thighs and butt, which LoLo had watched in practical horror blossom into the shape of the bottom half of a Coke bottle shortly after Rae had gotten her period. The girl kept a wedgie in her bubble butt.

"You do your exercises today?" LoLo asked her daughter, looking her up and down as the girl shifted uncomfortably under her mother's gaze. She'd read in some fashion magazine that one could train the curve of her behind to lay flat by walking backward on the floor—useful information that the article said would help women fit into the stylish Jordache jeans that were all the rage. LoLo had adopted the exercise to help stave the womanly curves that had started getting her daughter the attention she wasn't ready for—the kind of attention that could get a fourteen-year-old girl into a world of trouble.

"I just did them," Rae said, shifting from one foot to the other.

"Good. Get on over there and get them stringbeans. I need to get them into the pot if they're gonna be ready for supper."

"Yes, ma'am," Rae said.

"Uh-uh—nope," Tommy said, raising up from the ground around the huge hydrangea bushes he'd been messing around with when his daughter tumbled out the back door. "Not until I get me some sugar. Your mama had you in church all day, and I can't get no sugar?"

Rae's thick lips spread across her face like butterfly wings in flight. She practically flew into her father's arms, stretched wide. "That's my girl," he said, hugging and kissing her forehead. LoLo smirked and sopped.

"You changing the colors on the hydrangea, Daddy?" Rae asked, peering into the bucket and then at the two large bushes, which were pregnant with a bounty of oversized, round flowers in various shades of blue, violet, and purple.

"Yep. I'mma turn one of these bad boys pink—something sweet for your mama," he said, winking at LoLo. "You like pink, too, don't you?"

"Yeah, I like pink. And the purple ones, too."

"Well then, good thing we have some purple here, for both my girls," he said. "Now go get them stringbeans. Your daddy's hungry and we don't want to keep Mama waiting."

Rae shined her teeth and bounded toward the garden, then tipped when she got to its edge, looking for bugs and snakes and a quick harvesting.

This is what LoLo had laid down in the water for. What felt like freedom. She'd fought for this right here: a home where she felt comfortable, with her church and friends—her community—close by. A little help. By now, they'd had time under their belt having moved back to Long Island— time for LoLo to have the environment and tools to feel like she had some control over her own life. Like she wasn't equal parts exotic accessory and potential menace standing in her own yard. Standing in her own bedroom.

Of course, moving to that particular community in Long Island presented its own challenges at first. LoLo loved the house and so did Tommy, and their concern for integrating the block was nil, considering they'd already successfully survived doing so in Willingboro. Besides, Long Island was familiar. Home. Still, Tommy took his shotgun and pistol out of the attic and put the former in the bedroom closet and the latter in his top side drawer the morning he arrived home from his overnight job to find a two-foot-wide burn mark in his prized front lawn. "What you mean y'all was just playing out there and it was an accident?" he'd yelled at TJ after his son finally admitted he'd witnessed the scorching of fescue not ten feet from their new home.

"They were just setting off firecrackers and the grass got burned a little bit," TJ mumbled as he, now seventeen, and his parents stood over the charred lawn. Of the three, one was awfully matter-of-fact about the incident. The two others, who'd seen firsthand the terror white folk with some wood, gasoline, and matches could rain down on Black people, didn't have to stretch too far to correlate the Long Island burning with a southern one and, therefore, were not about to easily accept it as anything other than a threat. Particularly after the neighbor across the street made quick work of erecting an eight-foot fence around the whole of her property not even a week after the Lawrences' moving truck backed into their new driveway, and, not even a week in school, TJ had gotten into a tussle with a white kid who thought it a good idea to tell a lunchroom table full of Black boys that he had the right to say the word "nigger" because it meant "ignorant," not NIGGER.

"Don't you ever let me catch them fuckin' white boys anywhere near my house, you hear me?" Tommy demanded. All three knew that if Tommy, who was not prone to cursing, pushed the F-word past his gold-capped teeth, he meant business. The firearms were cleaned and rotated later that evening.

Beyond that, LoLo was at ease—in a routine that was a salve for her spirit. Para Lee had helped her get a job at a big cosmetics factory, where she worked on an assembly line, snatching lipsticks off a conveyor belt and running the colorful wax under a Bunsen burner–style flame machine. A quick, deliberate flick of LoLo's wrist made it so that rich women from the Hamptons to Hong Kong could open the packages of their twenty-four-dollar lipstick and see a flawless shine on the overpriced colored wax they'd be swooshing across their lips. Her wrists hurt from the hours-long grind—the union made it so that she could take two fifteen-minute smoke breaks and a half hour to swallow down her Diet Pepsi and Spam and tomato sandwiches—but LoLo relished the time away from the house, a steady paycheck Tommy let her keep all to herself, and the haul of free makeup and perfume she got to take home every now and again as part of the company's employee perks. Not that she needed the cosmetics or anything; she wore only lipstick most days, save for Sundays, when she might swoosh on a little mascara before tugging on her church hat, and she favored the brown sugar and musk scent of Fashion Fair's body lotion over any of the overpriced perfumes she got from work. They made for good gifts, though.

Five days a week, this was LoLo's life: up at 5:00 A.M., wash face, brush teeth, get dressed, make lunch, leave meat from the freezer in the sink for Rae to cook for dinner, grab smock, be at work by 6:15 A.M., sit and have coffee and gossip with Para Lee and a couple other girls she didn't mind talking to, on the line by 7:00 A.M., back in the car by 4:00 P.M., sitting down to dinner by 5:30 P.M., in the bathtub by 7:00 P.M., under the bedcovers by 8:30 P.M., sleep by 9:00 P.M. Friday evenings were for the kids and Tommy (his overnight work schedule took him out of the house before LoLo got home from work in the evening, and brought him home after she'd already left for work at the factory), Saturdays were for Bible study and bowling with the church league, and Sundays, well, those were for God, first, and preparation for the week and rest. There was very little deviation, save for the occasional Friday night when LoLo granted Tommy sex and the Saturdays when bowling spilled into an impromptu gathering of friends at someone's house. Occasionally, LoLo hosted. But she loved most when they ended up at the 1940s split-level ranch of one George Ragland, a short, spunky lady from Alabama, named for her father and grandfather before that because she was the last of seven girls and her daddy wanted a child named after him and so she was it.

"I hope y'all got your Pokeno pennies together—I'm in the mood to take them all tonight," someone would call out as the lot of them tucked their custom bowling balls and shoes into their bowling bags and bragged on who got closest to scoring a perfect three hundred.

"Shhh, not so loud. Sister Shane might hear you," LoLo would say, giggling. "You know Rags don't want her feet under her table."

"Shole don't," Sarah would say.

"I'm trying to enjoy my chitlins tonight, shit. What y'all bringing by?"

"My money, so I can take all of yours."

And so that's how it went—LoLo surrounding herself with an easy group of friends who, like her, had gathered their roots and planted them in the fertile soil of New York's suburbs—an ecosystem of southern tradition, hospitality, family. Love. There they'd all be in Rags's kitchen, waiting for her to invite them to her great big ol' pot of chitlins, meticulously cleaned of all their fat and filth, steamed in a bath of onions, salt, pepper, and red pepper flakes.

"Whewwwww, Rags, when you gone come up off them pots and give us a taste of what you cooking over there?" Sarah called over from the small, four-seat kitchen table, where she, Para Lee, Cindy, LoLo, and their friends Tina, Lori, and Annette were crowded, sipping on cans of Pathmark soda. Rags had already set out two bowls of popcorn she'd shook and salted in the big pot she usually used to cook her greens, and all the husbands were in the living room, shaking Planters peanuts in their hands like dice while they screamed and hollered at the basketball game blaring from the small television console, but when them chitlins get to stewing on the stove, no amount of nuts and corn can keep stomachs from rumbling.

"You want your chitlins right, don't you?" Rags called over her shoulder as she took the lid off the pot. Steam wafted into the air, right into her face as she stirred and examined—smelled, put a little piece of meat on her hand to taste. She licked it off her hand and smacked her lips a few times—added in more pepper flakes and a scooch of vinegar. "Ooooh-wee! Won't be long, now," she said, gently placing the lid back onto the pot.

"We sho did miss you at Bible study this morning," Para Lee said. She absentmindedly shuffled the deck of playing cards they would use that evening for Pokeno, took a sip of her store-brand orange soda.

"Yeah, well, I had to run some errands today," Rags said. She wiped her hands on a dish towel and stretched her short frame and fingers toward the second shelf of her cabinet, stretching for her set of bowls like this time, she would actually reach them. She couldn't. "Kent!" she called out to her grandson. She turned her body toward the basement door and listened for his footsteps and, unsatisfied that he hadn't traversed the steps in the two seconds from the time she called his name, she yelled it out again. "Kent! Come up here, boy!"

Kent, a striking fifteen-year-old with a chiseled jawline and long legs, hadn't heard his grandmother the first time over the din of Rae and Medina yell-singing to Stacey Lattisaw's "Let Me Be Your Angel," but by the second yell, he took the steps three-by-three, the girls hot on his heels. All three were keenly aware that they need not give the Bible-thumpers upstairs any reason to question what all they were doing in that basement, as they, too, enjoyed the ease of Saturday night—of watching the adults drop their shoulders and laugh a little bit, get off their backs—and they didn't want to jeopardize that little bit of freedom. "Yes, Grandma?" Kent said as he appeared in the door.

"Reach up there and grab me them bowls," Rags said, pointing at the second shelf, which was beyond her reach but chest-level to her grandson. He obliged.

"How many, Grandma?" he asked.

"Y'all eating?" Rags said, peeping around her grandson, addressing the girls as they appeared in the door.

"No, thank you," Medina said, wrinkling her nose.

"You still won't try these chitlins, gal?" Rags asked. She turned to her friends and shook her head. "Who raising these kids to turn their nose up at this good food? This delicacy?" she said to no one in particular. The question set off a chorus of "Chile, they don't know" and "I'll take her portion" and "It's a crime and a shame!"

"I'll have some, Miss Rags," Rae volunteered. She stood by Rags's left hip and let her eyes dance across the pots.

"You know what chitlins is, gal?" Rags said as she scooped a spoonful into one of the bowls Kent delivered to the counter.

Rae brought the bowl up to her nose and inspected its contents with her nose and eyes. "No, ma'am," she said, taking from Rags the plastic fork she'd offered. She dug in.

Rags looked at her friends, cackling at the table and leaning into the action unfolding before them; she pushed a wry smile across her lips. "Hog intestines. That's what they push they boo-boo through. You still want 'em?"

Rae looked at the bowl and then Ms. Rags and her mother, who was sitting at the table with her arms crossed, amused. She shrugged her shoulders and dug her fork right into the bowl, no hesitation. "Can I have some hot sauce?" she said as she lifted a steaming forkful of the meat to her lips.

"That's my baby, right there!" LoLo shouted, her friends slapping her back and laughing easily as they watched Rae devour what so many refused with a grimace and turned-up nose. "She know what's good."

"That girl raised right!" Rags said heartily. "Here you go, baby," she said, shaking red liquid on Rae's bowl. "Go on back downstairs with 'em. This grown-folks' business up here."

And they ate quickly and laughed loudly and told their tall tales in fellowship, in the way that made LoLo's heart so very full. She wasn't thinking about the water, about those eight years stuck in that pretty hell and what it took for her to get out of it. Her friends, mostly they protected her from those memories because that's what friends are for, but occasionally, something would be said, done, to bring a pall over their rowdy room. Tonight would be one of those nights.

"What did I miss at Bible study today?" Rags asked as she pushed her seven dimes to the center of the table and straightened her Pokeno cards before her.

"Oh! We were studying Samson today—Judges thirteen to sixteen," Sarah said.

"It was a good discussion, too," Para Lee chimed in, tossing her money into the pot. "Ol' Samson didn't obey God and got his comeuppance, didn't he? Served him right, prancing around them womens. Especially that Delilah."

"We got into a really good discussion, too, on what it meant for Samson to knock over the pillars and kill everybody, himself included," Sarah chimed in. "Imma have to talk to Deacon Lewis about it because I'm a little confused about whether Samson still got to go to heaven, seeing as he killed himself on purpose."

The room got quiet; all of the other women shifted uncomfortably in their chairs, rolling coins between their fingers, adjusting their Pokeno cards, rubbing their brows and tossing looks at Sarah, who was oblivious to the growing thickness between them.

"I was taught that if you commit suicide, you don't go to heaven, because you violating God's commandment to not kill, and that includes yourself.

Can't ask for forgiveness when you dead, right? But Samson killed himself when he knocked over the pillars, even if it was in service of God and the Israelites. So did he go to Heaven, or . . ."

"Sarah!" Cindy called out. She shook her head and awkwardly tilted her head toward LoLo. The men screamed out in the other room and unleashed a symphony of high fives; downstairs, the kids were gyrating their hips and pumping their shoulders like Michael Jackson as they warbled along to the Jackson 5's "Lovely One." LoLo began to fold herself into herself but thought better of it. She sat up straight like someone had inserted a rod in her back, nose in perfect alignment with the earth's surface.

"It's okay, y'all," LoLo said finally. "We talking the Bible, right? What God wants from us?" Her friends were statues. "I think maybe we need to leave the explanation about Samson to Deacon Lewis tomorrow, because don't none of us really know the answers to that one, do we. Lotta things we don't know the answer to, right?" Para Lee reached over and took LoLo's hand in hers—rubbed it as LoLo searched for more words. Cindy focused her eyes on Sarah, the squint yelling, *Now look what you did!* "I don't have an explanation for what happened in Jersey, I can tell you that. I was wrong and I'm embarrassed, really."

"Ain't no such thing," Cindy said. "Don't you sit here and beat yourself up about it. We just happy you okay now."

LoLo smiled, looked down at her lap. "Me too. God saw fit to save me, didn't he? There but for the grace of God I go."

And the friends said, "Amen."

21

1999, in the springtime

LoLo told Rae not to marry that man. She knew when that girl called her from a pay phone in the bowels of the restaurant where he'd proposed that Rae didn't really want him. Heard it in her voice—that little quiver that bounced around in her throat when she was choking down a good cry. It was the same sound Rae had made that one time when some boy she'd dated in college called himself breaking up with her over the phone. LoLo was watching her shows before bed, only about a half hour away from getting on her knees and thanking Jesus for His perfect peace when the phone ringing hauled her right out of her wind down and straight into the middle of some secondhand drama full of wasted emotion. There was Rae, over there on the floor, phone cradled in her neck, pupils dilated and covered over with a pool of tears like some cartoon character, demanding an explanation—wanting to know what *she'd* done wrong. LoLo had watched her—listened with narrowed eyes and a tightening of her lips. Rae hung up the phone, finally. LoLo pounced with precision. "I know you not down there on my carpet, crying over some boy," she'd sneered.

"I . . . don't under . . . stand . . . what . . . I . . . did . . . wr-wr-wrong," Rae managed through gulps of air, tears and snot running their race down her cheeks and contorted lips.

"What *you* did wrong?" LoLo yelled as she struggled against her pile of pillows to sit upright. Her wrists, sore, swollen from the extra shift she'd pulled getting lipstick prepped for the holiday rush, had yet to respond to the anti-inflammatory she'd dry-swallowed at the top of the hour. The pain put extra sizzle on LoLo's words, but she meant, too, for them to be heard. Digested. Remembered. "Don't you ever let me see you crying over some boy ain't got sense enough to know he got the prize. The hell is wrong with you?"

"But . . . he . . ."

"I don't give a damn what he said on the other end of that phone or what he did. All that snotting and gasping won't change a damn thing, now will it?"

Rae used the collar of her robe to wipe her face as she seemed to fight to swallow her tears.

"It's his loss. That's all there is to it. Ain't no use in crying about it."

LoLo had come to regret that this was the extent of the relationship advice she'd extended to her daughter. Neither that nor her demand that Rae not bring any babies into her house until she had a college degree and a ring had saved her daughter from the decision she made to say yes to Roman Lister when he asked Rae for her hand in marriage. LoLo heard the tentativeness in her daughter's voice—recognized that tremble as she shared the news. "I don't know, Mommy," she'd said. "The ring is pretty, I just . . . I wasn't expecting this right now. I don't know . . ."

"What don't you know, Rae?"

Behind Rae's silence, LoLo could hear the restaurant breathing—women laughing out loud, the squeak of doors opening, closing, and rustling.

"You don't have to say yes," LoLo had said. "And you don't have to explain. 'No' is a complete sentence."

More rustling.

Finally, Rae had answered her mother. "I gotta go, Mommy. He's waiting."

Now, not even three years after the wedding, there was her daughter, belly swollen, little feet and hands pressing hard enough against her womb to make themselves seen through her tight, thin maternity top, posted up on LoLo's good couch, giggling as she tore wrapping paper off baby monitors and bundles of newborn diapers and more blankets than any one baby could possibly use. To everybody in the room, Rae looked happy. Ready as she ever could be for June 11, 1999, her due date. But LoLo knew her daughter. She knew Roman, too, this man with his charm and fancy credentials. On paper, he was impressive—went to one of those fancy colleges up north, made a decent living. Seemed nice enough. But he was four years Rae's senior, divorced. And his hands were soft. LoLo had felt them in her own the first time they pressed together their flesh, and she knew. Right then, she knew. His grip was significantly less than firm, which immediately made LoLo question what kind of household he came from—what happened to the one he tried to build with his first wife. What else his father failed to teach him about manhood, aside from the fact that limp handshakes and soft hands were a dead giveaway that their owners were weak. Prone to letting someone else do all the work.

Rae chose to ignore the signs, but to LoLo, they were bold and flashing neon. What kind of man quit his job not even three months before his wife was due to give birth to their first child? What kind of woman let him? If Tommy and LoLo had taught Rae anything, if only by example, it was that the most solid of marriages had very specific underpinnings, chief among them a husband who worked hard to make sure he could provide for his family. His babies. The thought of her grandchild coming into this world to be cared for by a daddy who willingly gave up a steady paycheck while his wife was pregnant made LoLo sick. Absolutely sick to her stomach.

Rae sipped her ice water and rubbed her belly while LoLo's friends cooed over her baby shower haul. LoLo appeared from the kitchen with a gorgeous handmade cake Para Lee had baked special for the occasion, with pink peonies and roses cascading every which way, proclaiming what a sonogram had shown a few months before: LoLo's grandbaby was a girl-child. LoLo's heart had beat triple time when Rae had called with the news. When Rae had stopped by with a sonogram picture and a recording of her ob-gyn visit later that evening, LoLo could hardly catch her breath when she put the mini cassette recorder to her ear and heard the warble of her grandbaby's heartbeat. "This baby's gonna be everything good," LoLo had said as she held the picture, rocking to and fro as if she could barely contain herself. LoLo believed that with every fiber of her very being— like she did scripture and the resurrection.

"Cake time!" LoLo shouted as she gently placed the pink confection on the dining room table. "Y'all come on over here and get you some of this good cake Para Lee whipped up special for my grandbaby."

"And for me!" Rae said, waving her hand.

"Aw, girl, you might as well forget anybody paying you any kind of mind," Sarah said, laughing as she watched LoLo slice the cake. "That baby get here and yo' mama gonna forget you even existed."

"Mmm-hmmm," Para Lee agreed. "Whole lot getting ready to change."

"Oh, you better believe it. Just leave my baby right at the door," LoLo laughed. "Now you'll see what it feels like when you and your daddy run around here like I don't exist."

"Now see? See how she's plotting to do me?" Rae said, laughing and pushing herself up from the couch. She rubbed her belly and grimaced a little. "We can't help it if you don't like boxing and don't want to hold hands and snuggle!"

"Mmm-hmm," LoLo said, pursing her lips. "Just wait."

"Whew," Rae said. She reached beneath her belly with both hands and massaged where her baby was trying to push her entire booty through her mother's skin. "This baby is stomping all over my bladder. Excuse me, I need to go to the restroom."

The women all cackled and clicked their teeth as Rae ran-walked to the bathroom down the hallway, the eyes of the women chasing behind her. LoLo shook her head as she plopped another piece of cake on a plate. "She ain't gone know what hit her when that baby get here," she said with a sigh. A chorus of "I know that's right" rose in the air, thick with judgment, a smidge of resentment. "These young mothers ain't built like we were."

"Right?" Para Lee said. "All we had was ninny and a clothesline to hang the dirty diapers on. Look at all that stuff over there," she said, pointing at Rae's baby shower bounty. "Expensive strollers and enough disposable diapers to cram a whole landfill. They don't know nothing about having a baby hanging on your titty while you washing out them dirty diapers and waiting for them to dry on the line."

"Or raising the kids and keeping house and going to work all at the same time, like you some robot superwoman," Sarah said.

"And a man that don't help you with none of that," Cindy chimed in between bites of cake.

"Well, at least she got a man who'll get that part right," Para Lee said.

"Chip in around the house and help with the kids. That's the way they doing it these days. The menfolk actually help now."

"What man you talking about?" LoLo asked, smirking. "You talking about that trifling ass don't even have a job? You think he gonna help with that baby? Hmph. I'd like to see it."

In what looked like some choreographed dance move, all of the women leaned every which way looking to see if Rae had emerged from the bathroom. This wasn't a conversation for the ears of children, even if those children were grown enough to have babies of their own. That's just the way it was with LoLo and her friends: they lived their lives in secret, a requirement if one were to maintain her dignity.

Upon confirming her daughter was, indeed, still in the bathroom, LoLo leaned into her circle of friends. "Now y'all know he quit his job," she whispered conspiratorially. "What kind of lazy-ass man is going to live off his wife's savings, let her go back to work, and then all of a sudden find it in his lazy bones to help with a baby? He still a man—I don't care what they talking about on these talk shows y'all catching on the VCR."

"You don't think he's going to help with the baby?" Para Lee asked. LoLo sucked her teeth. Sarah scraped pink icing off her slice of cake and smashed it onto the crystal plate LoLo always saved for the most special of occasions.

"She'll learn soon enough," Sarah said.

"She got her head stuck so far up his pompous ass, she gone learn that lesson the hard way," LoLo said.

"Wouldn't make her any different from the rest of us," Sarah snapped back.

"She ain't lying," Para Lee agreed.

"Here's what I know," Sarah said. "It don't matter what era you're in, what kinda degree he got, how much money is in his pocket, or how many hours he puts in down there at the job: men are going to be men. Every time, they're going to be men. Looking out for themselves first and maybe who they claim to care about after that. Always in that order. The question," she continued, "is when will she get tired of his shit and find a little joy for herself."

"Joy?" Para Lee snapped. "Oh, she won't be seeing any of that anytime soon. Not with a bunch of bigheaded kids running underfoot."

"It don't have to be that way," Sarah said, sitting back in her chair. She swirled her sherbet punch around in her cup, watching the neon-green ice cream melt and foam into the orange. She took a sip.

"Now Sarah, don't you start your shit," LoLo warned.

"Listen, you know where I stand on this. There's no reason to let these men run you into an early grave. Women could stand to get a little bit of that man-thinking into their brains. Go get them some happy."

"Cheating on your husband makes you happy, Sarah?"

"Getting away from the madness of my house and a nagging-ass husband and all those badass grandkids makes me happy, LoLo," Sarah said, exasperated. "And Reverend Greenwood? Well, he keeps me more than satisfied."

LoLo didn't care for this part. This wasn't the first time the ladies had discussed Sarah's infidelity; she'd been cavorting with the pastor of Friendship Baptist Church in Christ for years now, long before her children had found their own way—long before any of her friends began to remember that before their children, before their husbands, before they folded up their needs and desires and buried them deep beneath scriptures and commandments and rules made for them without their consent, they were women. Pastor Greenwood had a reputation for indulgence, and seven years into her affair, Sarah couldn't be sure he'd tamed his proclivities for church ladies and their sweet sweet. But she didn't care. She took what she could and left the rest for someone else to fret over. Sarah was good with boxes.

LoLo, well, she was not. Her stomach flexed whenever the subject turned to the goings-on of Sarah and her paramour. She didn't like being a part of this secret—the betrayal. Didn't want her name all up in it. She'd told Sarah time and again not to include her in such talk, but it would come up every now and again, always in the context of what each of them should be doing to get them a piece of happy. Sarah believed it was something you went out and got, like a dress out of a Spiegel catalogue or a pair of shoes off the sales rack at Macy's. LoLo's belief was fundamentally different; happiness, disappointment, anger, satisfaction, all of them were a stew in the big pot on the stove. You stir it up and take a bite, knowing that every spoonful had a little something different in it, maybe something you didn't like as much as the other, but the stew, it was still good. If it had love in it, it was still good.

LoLo didn't want any of what was slopping around in Sarah's bowl.

"Not everybody is out here thinking the only way they can be happy is to run around on their husbands," LoLo whispered, peeking around the corner to make sure Rae wasn't on her way back into the dining room. "Don't wish that on my daughter, Sarah."

"I'm wishing her a little bit of happiness," Sarah said. "From the sound of it, she's going to need it."

"No, see, what she'll need is to respect what she promised that man in front of God and you, me, and everybody she loves. 'Til death do us part. That means something to some of us," LoLo said.

"At some point you got to mean something to you, too," Sarah sneered.

"Now see, I'm not about to sit here in my own house and . . ."

"Okay, all right," Para Lee said, sticking a pin in the balloon that was fast filling with hot air. Ever the referee. "How about you and Cynthia clean up the table, Sarah, while LoLo and me get all these presents packed up. Rae's husband will probably be here soon to take her on home. She needs her rest." Turning to Sarah, she added, "LoLo, our gracious host, probably needs her rest, too, not all this here heated debate, huh?"

"Okay then," Sarah said simply. She pushed herself back from the table and headed into the kitchen without another word.

Para Lee shook her head, drew a deep breath, and took LoLo's arm into hers as they walked over to the present pile and surveyed what all they needed to pack up. "Just let it go," Para Lee said. "You know how she is. Just let it go."

LoLo had been so grateful for the quiet. She liked having company over, but she was much more comfortable—happy—in the stillness of her home. In her solitude. In their old age, she and Tommy had grown to understand they didn't need to be up under each other to prove they wanted to continue to be together after all those years. The most loving thing he could do for her, in fact, was to head down to the basement and watch his sports games and westerns on the big floor console TV from the comfort of his well-worn recliner—leave her to read her Terry McMillan novels and watch her shows in peace. She was partial to *20/20* and *Law & Order: SVU* and liked to watch them on the VCR on Saturday evenings, uninterrupted. If not for the damn phone ringing battering her repose, she may have even fallen asleep by now.

But this was not to be. The phone already had rung three times that evening; each time, LoLo's kind "Hello?" was met with silence, then a click, then a dial tone. Here it was, ringing again. Had Tommy not just left to visit his brother, she would have given him some choice words about the prank calling—would have told him, yet again, that he needed to identify just who the hell hated him so much down there at his job that they were making it their business to torture their family. Years ago, he'd told LoLo, TJ, Rae to brush off the calls—"It's just somebody on the line, mad I'm in charge," he'd insist when they'd complain. "Just hang up." Per usual, LoLo sucked it up. But on nights like this one, when she was desperate for quiet, for peace, she would remember she wasn't obligated to be nice about it.

"Listen, stop calling this phone or I swear, I will call the cops on your ass for harassment!" LoLo screamed into the phone.

"Ho, ho, ho—wait a minute: Harassment?" the voice questioned on the other end of the line. "You would call the police on your own brother for dialing your number?"

LoLo opened her mouth, then shut it again. Opened it. Shut it.

"Hello? Delores? You still there?" the voice, deep, asked. "It's Freddy. Your brother."

"H-Hey, Freddy," LoLo said tentatively.

The silence between them was thick and crusted over by a decade of misunderstandings, anger, loss, grief. Abandonment. Every argument ended with them clawing at each other's throats like some wild animals on a fresh kill, and all these years later, the wound was still oozing as if the captured gazelle's heart was still beating.

Freddy was sitting at his kitchen table where, only seconds prior, he'd silently cursed it for rocking and rumbling beneath his rough, calloused palms. He'd been meaning to fold up a wad of paper towel and glue it into the hole in which the errant table's leg had loosened itself and turned the wooden four-seater, a remnant somebody had trashed at the Goodwill the same day he came looking for something to replace the milk crates on which he'd been serving himself his dinners, into a most rickety affair. But after fixing on air conditioners and school desks and mopping up vomit and piss and every other manner of bodily secretion and being ordered around all day at his job down at the Archie Street Elementary School, he wasn't about to repair a damn thing when he got home. Really, all he wanted was his beer—a little quiet while he watched his shows. He was partial to reruns of *Martin,* especially the main character's little girlfriend with the round head. The light-skin one. She was pretty. Real pretty. Sensible, too. Freddy liked Martin's mouth—all those crazy sayings helped him keep up with some of the loud talk he heard the kids spewing in the halls when he bothered to listen. Most times, though, he returned the students' conversations with the same energy they gave him when they occupied a mutual space: he was the janitor and therefore invisible; they were a bunch of loud-mouthed children he ignored, like any respectable adult should, even when they ran through the halls screaming "Wazzup!" from the bottom of their guts.

But *Highlander* was where it was at for Freddy. Had a whole drawer full of VCR tapes of the show, which he watched like prayer. He was fascinated by the idea of immortality—all the ways one could move through the world among mere mortals, confident in his choices, clear that neither mistakes nor bravado, bad choices nor shitty luck could end him. That was living—something he hadn't truly done since being fired from Grumman a few years earlier. He missed those paychecks—how they made it so he could buy what he wanted to, live where he wanted to, dress like he wanted to. Lord, fuck who he wanted to. Then, he was a Black man working on airplane engines, making a mechanic's ransom—the kind of money that made the little dusty-ass, motherless boy from the bowels of South Carolina, who should have died under the weight of his sorry world, feel like he could do anything. Like he could live forever. But one shot of bourbon in his coffee—one little shot his supervisor could smell on his tongue—and it was off with his head. The coworker who dimed him, who worked under Freddy and just couldn't wrap his mind around answering to some nigger every day, put an exclamation point on the one true thing: Freddy was a mortal Black man after all.

On this particular night, mortality had grabbed hold of him. Freddy had rocked back in his chair as he licked his middle finger and ran his thumb over his sister's contact information. Used to be he knew it by heart, but it'd been a good decade since he'd actually called her phone. Nothing was the same after their big fight over Rae. He tried to make it right with his sister. LoLo, she would not have it. On this, the occasion of the death of their father, Freddy decided he had to be bigger.

"LoLo," he said finally. "Daddy dead."

"Oh," LoLo said simply. Emotionless. "What happened?"

"He, um, had a heart attack," Freddy said. "He died at the house in the living room. Brenda found him."

"He died alone, huh?"

"Yeah. Brenda and them getting the arrangements together now."

"That's good," LoLo said.

Silence.

"So, you going, right?"

"Going where?"

"To our father's funeral."

Silence.

"It's only right, LoLo. You gotta pay your respects."

"I don't have to do a damn thing but stay Black and die," LoLo snapped. She was not about to be guilted into attending the funeral of the man who had left her for dead and then let her decompose in the hands of her abuser.

"Look," Freddy said gently. "I understand. You know I do. All of us do. But that's still the man who gave us life. We blood."

Silence.

"Listen, you'd be the first one to throw out a Bible scripture at somebody if they refused to do like God say and forgive," Freddy said in earnest. "I think times like this is when He expects us to practice that."

"You quoting scripture now?" LoLo asked.

"I don't know a whole lot about the Bible, I'll give you that. But I know I won't feel right sitting here in Long Island while our father is being put in the ground in South Carolina. And you won't either."

Silence.

"We can fly down together. The two of us."

"Let me think about it a little, okay, Freddy?" LoLo said finally. "I won't take long. I promise."

"All right then."

LoLo sat in shock with the phone receiver to her ear, long after the dial tone began to drone; she put it in its cradle only after the harsh alarm signaling her to hang it up slammed her eardrum. She hadn't talked to her father in years, and back when she bothered, when he reached out through Freddy and Freddy reminded LoLo of the tenets of the fifth commandment and she reluctantly took their father's call, the conversation was superficial, curt: *Hey, you doing okay? . . . The wife all right? . . . The kids must be big now . . . I'm fair to middlin,' but my arthritis acting up . . . Silence . . . Okay then, good to hear from you . . . Take care, now . . .* was the extent of it before the two of them gave up. It was all, frankly, LoLo could muster. He wasn't about to fix his mouth to apologize. Wasn't even going to consider giving one. She could feel it deep down where her anger burned the hottest, where embers stood in her womb's stead. The very sound of his voice was a fireplace poker, jabbing, digging, moving around heavy logs and old newspaper jammed in the in-between, coaxing a roaring flame. Had she continued on, surely she would have burned to a crisp.

She'd wished him dead then. She felt no remorse now that he actually was.

Not even two minutes after LoLo hung up the phone with Freddy, it rang again. This time, she answered politely, thinking it was Freddy again.

"Hi. I'd like to speak to my father," the voice on the other end said. She sounded young.

"Who?"

"My father, Thomas Lawrence."

"Rae? That you?" LoLo quizzed.

"This is not Rae. But I am Thomas Lawrence's daughter, and I would like to speak to him."

LoLo pulled the phone away from her face and looked at the receiver, like she would be able to see who the hell was playing on her phone.

"Hello?" the voice said, a tinge of attitude ringing the greeting.

"I'm here. But I don't know what is going on. Who are you, really?"

"I just told you: I'm Thomas Lawrence's daughter. He is my father. My brother is his son. He came to see us today, but we weren't ready for him to leave."

Silence.

"Hello?" the girl said, this time with definitive attitude. LoLo could hear it in the girl's voice. And that put her over the edge. All she could see was black.

"And you thought today was the day to call this house to talk to him?" LoLo asked.

"He's my father and I call his house all the time to talk to him . . ."

"Let me tell you something," LoLo interrupted. Her tongue, having tasted death, sadness, anger, and betrayal all in the span of five minutes on what was supposed to be a peaceful Saturday night, was an ax. A freshly sharpened hatchet. "I don't care if Tommy is your father or not, you will never be who Rae Lawrence, his daughter, is to him. He has a family. Of that, I'm very clear and so is he. It would be best if you got that through your thick . . . little . . . skull . . . whoever you are.

"Now," LoLo continued, her words now sugar. "If you'll excuse me, I've had a helluva day. Don't call my phone, my home again. Whatever you have to say, you best save it for Tommy."

22

Used to be she would squeeze her eyes tight and imagine herself with someone else—a technique she'd employed as a child, when screaming and struggling just made Bear laugh and bear down his weight as he pounded inside of her, faster, harder, his sweat dripping onto her skin, hair, the dirt beneath them. Back then, she would see the black on the inside of her eyelids first, and then scroll through images that made her body go numb: the ripples on the surface of the lake; Booger, the neighbor's mangy dog, barking at cars passing by; Bible scriptures that made promises she expected God to keep. The images, like photos in a scrapbook, were armor. When she got with Tommy, her mind's eye got equal parts more creative and hardwired to images that were more practical for the task at hand: she was Pam Grier, straddling Richard Roundtree, or gyrating front row while Mick Jagger caressed his microphone stand and sang straight at her. She learned, eventually, to be in Tommy's moment. Couldn't remember when that happened, exactly. But when it did, finally, she understood the depth of Tommy's love and was able to return it in kind. He was the glue that held their family, patched from four separate ripples in an ocean of human sorrow, together. He was a good man. He was love. Her love. And she gave of herself fully in exchange for that love. She gave herself to her husband. No one else. Even in her imagination. Even in her dreams. And here was the girl ringing her line, announcing the betrayal. Announcing her blood.

Not even ten minutes after she hung up on Tommy's daughter, the rattling chain on the garage door was the bell in the opening round. Lo-Lo's heart was Jackie Joyner-Kersee as she raced around the room, throwing shirts and jeans and bras in her suitcase, listening for Tommy's heavy feet stomping up the stairs two by two. She was face-first in her closet, snatching dresses to and fro in search of her best good black dress when Tommy bounded into the bedroom. He stopped short like he slammed into a wall when his eyes found their way to his wife. He rubbed his hands back and forth over his freshly shorn scalp. "I told her to stop calling here," he said. "I told her I needed to tell you in my own way."

LoLo snatched more dresses across the clothes rod, but she kept her face in the closet. She couldn't look at Tommy. "Well, shame on her, huh? For not listening? She was really wrong for that, wasn't she?"

"Yeah. I mean, it was my story . . . ," he began excitedly, and then, more quietly, "my story to tell."

"So, what happened? The cat got hold of your tongue?" LoLo asked. Her question was met with silence. "How old is she, Tommy? She sounded grown. Using her big-girl words and everything on my phone. Our phone."

"Twenty-seven," Tommy practically whispered.

LoLo popped out of the closet and folded her arms. "What did you say? Speak up—I can't hear this story you have to tell. How old?"

"She's twenty-seven years old," Tommy said a little louder.

"And her brother?"

"Twenty-five."

LoLo pulled a few dresses out of the closet and tossed them on the bed. "I'm no mathematician, but if my count is right, she had to have been born right around the time you forced me to pack up our life and move to Jersey."

"I didn't force you," Tommy said, a little bass in his voice.

"Oh. I had a choice," LoLo said. "That's news. Definitely not the way I remember it."

"We moved to New Jersey because there was work there."

"And, apparently, a baby here," LoLo said, snatching her dress off the hanger and rolling it around her hands. She stuffed it in her suitcase.

"Whoa-ho-ho, what's all this?" Tommy asked, noticing the suitcase on the bed for the first time.

Silence.

"LoLo, you can't leave. Don't leave, baby."

"Tommy, the days of you telling me what I can and cannot do are over."

"I'm not trying to tell you what to do! I'm telling you this isn't worth breaking up our family."

"Family?" LoLo asked. "Which one? Are there any others I should know about? How many families, exactly, do you have?"

Tommy opened his mouth to talk then shut it. Opened it, shut it again. Then, finally: "You lied to me, LoLo," he said, his voice cracking.

"Lied to you about what, Tommy? What lie could you possibly bring up that's bigger than you making two babies with someone else while we were married?"

"You had me out here believing I was the one who couldn't make babies. All that time, you were running around here hollering about how it couldn't have been you because you get your monthly and that proved you could have kids and I was the problem. It wasn't me. I can make babies."

"So, you had not one but two babies out of spite?"

"You going to ignore what I just said?"

LoLo stopped fiddling with the dresses in her closet and held on tight to the clothes rod. Blood rushed to her head, making her temples pound and her nose sting. She didn't want to cry—didn't want her husband to mistake her body's reaction for a response to his "gotcha" or even to news of his infidelity. That wasn't what this was. She needed to steady herself to help fight her body's visceral reaction to remembering—to being put back in the moment, the many moments in which she struggled under Bear's weight and the times, too, when she didn't, and laid there, begging God to strike the very ground beneath them, the bodies on top of it. Every time Bear raped her, LoLo died. Every time she thought about him raping her, she died. As she held on to her clothes rod, being reminded that she couldn't have children and why that was so, she wanted to die. Her body wanted to just give in and die.

"I was raped," LoLo finally said, the words landing against the back of the closet wall.

"What did you just say?" Tommy asked.

"I couldn't have babies because my cousin raped me."

Tommy's body stiffened.

"He made a baby and his wife killed it and had me fixed, so he couldn't get me pregnant again," LoLo said, turning around to face her husband. "That's why I couldn't have babies."

The two stood there, an ocean apart, neither sure of what to say. Neither with the emotional acuity to say what needed to be said. When, finally, she felt like her legs wouldn't give way beneath her, LoLo turned back to the closet and pulled out more clothes—a blouse, two pair of jeans, a dress jacket—all the things she'd calculated she needed to get on a plane heading for the funeral of the man who'd given her life and then dispensed of it like a piece of chewing tobacco he no longer wanted to feel on his tongue.

"Don't go, LoLo. I love you. We can work this out," Tommy said finally as he watched his wife smash her clothes into her suitcase. He grabbed her wrists—as if to get her full attention. "I want to work this out. I don't want her. I want you. It's always been you. I made a mistake, but it's always been you."

LoLo wrestled her wrists out of Tommy's hands and turned to face him. Her eyes traced his—the flecks of black in his dark brown pupils, the red veins popping out of the white part, signaling his pain, fear. The corners were starting to wrinkle and beneath them was a halo of puffiness that seemed to linger no matter if he were tired or up and at 'em, angry or in complete peace, but all in all, he looked like the same Tommy to her. Except he wasn't. Nothing between them could ever get back to the beginning; they were too far gone.

"My father died," LoLo said dryly. She slammed closed the suitcase. "I'm going to South Carolina."

LoLo sank down into the old couch, the plastic covering squeaking beneath her as she adjusted her long legs to fit in the small space between the cushions and the dull edge of the glass and wooden coffee table. Her head was pounding out an ache to the rhythm of the air conditioner, which, even on full blast, was doing little to cool the room. Humidity and sadness hung thick in the air, like a cloud of black smoke—dark, rancid. LoLo's eyes were fixated on the small patch of navy-blue shag carpet that lay in front of the well-worn plaid recliner where her father had, apparently, spent a majority of his time. He'd taken his last breaths right there on the carpet, having fallen out of his chair, clutching his chest like in some Hollywood movie as he reached for the house phone, trying to call for help.

"He died right there," said Brenda, LoLo's half sister, pointing to the spot where she'd found her father. She used the insides of her wrists to swipe tears from her eyes. Just beyond the spot at which she pointed, closer to the front door, was a wide, crusty stain, lighter than the rest of the carpet, announcing Brenda's reaction when she stopped by with two large cups of coffee, light and significantly sweeter than they needed to be considering both she and her daddy had diabetes, and found him. He was lying there, eyes fixed on the ceiling, but seeing nothing. Brenda dropped the coffee where she stood and rushed over to her father, screaming, shaking him, slapping his face, begging him to wake up. He was already gone. The paramedics hadn't even pulled out of the driveway before Brenda got down on her knees with a small tub of vinegar and bleach, trying to get that coffee milk smell out the carpet. In the swelter of the summer heat, it still stank. In the three days since he passed, no amount of company, condolence casseroles, or burying herself in the minutiae of her father's funeral arrangements could soothe the heaviness of her heart, its weight more significant than that of Freddy and LoLo's. Brenda, the product of their father's second act, knew a different daddy—a version who was loving and tender. Present. Simple things—kissing her face in the morning, taking her to church on Sundays, being there for her graduation, putting a little something on her tuition—all of this was a cloak spread over his past. All Brenda knew—all she cared to see—was a loving husband, devoted father, upstanding Baptist deacon, hard worker, retiree. LoLo tried to let her have that—swallowed her anger whole at the door when a sobbing Brenda fell into her arms. But now, LoLo felt like she was going to choke.

"I, um . . . I don't feel well. Can I grab a glass of water out the kitchen?" LoLo asked as she struggled to stand up from the couch. Her palms were wet and slid from side to side on the plastic couch covering as she pushed herself up.

"Oh, of course, of course," Brenda said. "Sister, you don't have to ask. This is just as much your house as it is any of ours."

LoLo nodded and forced a half smile to her lips. Her eyes washed over the walls, the furniture, the family photos that froze happiness in a place and time that forgot her—happiness that wasn't hers to have. She wanted to be angry about it all—Brenda's college diploma hanging in the hallway between the kitchen and living room, the black-and-white department store picture of her and her parents, each of their hands resting lovingly on either of her shoulders—but mostly, LoLo was sad. This was supposed to be her life memorialized on the pale yellow walls. Who could she have been had she had the chance to go to college? To be raised rather than raided? To be loved?

LoLo grabbed a coffee mug from the pile of freshly washed dishes drying in a rack next to the sink and filled it practically to the brim with water from the faucet. She gulped down half of it and filled it again to the brim before heading back into the living room. A burp was stuck in her chest, but she held it in. She didn't want to be rude, not in this place. Not in front of Brenda and Freddy.

"You all right, sis?" Freddy said, returning to the living room from the bathroom. LoLo was rubbing her chest.

"I'm fine," LoLo said, her words clipped. Then, to Brenda: "Who all else is coming? Of the children, I mean?"

"Well, Charles said he can't afford the flight from Texas, so he won't be here," Brenda said. "And Franklin and Linda said they're not coming." She clicked her teeth—shook her head. Sighed.

"They have their reasons, Brenda," LoLo snapped. "It's not your place to judge."

"Oh, oh, okay—here we go. Here it comes," Brenda said, pursing her lips.

"Oh, come on now, let's not do this!" Freddy said, waving both his hands in front of him. "This ain't the time . . ."

"When, exactly, is the time, Freddy?" LoLo asked. "Tell me! Because from the way little sis is sitting here judging people, it sure sounds like airing it out right now wouldn't be a second too soon!"

"Look, I don't want to fight . . ."

"Oh?" LoLo interrupted. "What, you thought sitting here sighing over my brothers and sister not coming to their deadbeat dad's funeral wasn't about starting a fight? Do you have any idea why they might not want to be here? Did your daddy tell you what kind of daddy he was to us?" LoLo cleared her throat. A few beads of sweat formed on her nose and forehead. "He tell you about all those nights he left us right here in this house hungry, thirsty? How Freddy cried and cried so hard for his mama's ninny we thought he wasn't gonna make it? Oh, wait: he couldn't have told you any of that because he wasn't here to see it. He left us, Brenda. To die. Right here in this house, where he died."

"I'm not going to pretend like I know what y'all went through . . ."

"Good, don't!" LoLo said, trying to catch her breath. The air had gotten thicker. She unbuttoned the top of her blouse.

"Sis, what's going on? You okay?" Freddy asked.

LoLo trained her eyes on his mouth but could barely make out his words. She scratched her chest and tried to slow down her quickened breaths.

"Oh my God, what's happening?" Brenda yelled, hopping to her feet and rushing over to the sofa, arriving just in time to catch LoLo as her body shifted backward. LoLo's back seized, making her involuntarily raise her hips toward the ceiling. She tried to catch her breath. It proved elusive.

"Call an ambulance!" Freddy yelled as he crashed onto the sofa next to his big sister and pulled her face toward his. "LoLo, baby, what's going on? Talk to me. What's happening. Breathe, sis. Breathe!"

She wanted to tell him but she couldn't. She wanted to tell Freddy she was angry. She wanted to tell the two of them that she loved her husband and her children, but she wasn't any kind of wife and mother she could have been. She wanted to tell them why that was. She wanted to tell them that she needed her mama and her daddy. She wanted to tell them that Bear had hurt her. She wanted to tell them that her insides were empty— that she had nothing to give to this world. She wanted to tell them she tried anyway.

She wanted to tell them that her heart was broken.

THE BOOK
OF RAE

1999–2004

23

Rae did not share her parents' DNA, and that was about as irrelevant to her as the color of the liquid that ran through her veins. Blood was red, Delores Lawrence was her mother, and Thomas Lawrence was her father, and that's just what these three things were to her: indisputable. They clothed her. Fed her. Saw to it she got a good education. Took her to church most Sundays. Put the fear of God in her, too. Loved her. She had her own room her daddy painted pink because that's what he thought girls liked and Rae certainly did, not because she was a girl but because she rode shotgun in her daddy's Eldorado to the hardware store and pored over all the rectangle paint swatches that had any kind of pink on them looking for the color that was most divine, and really, it didn't matter to her that it had a little too much red in it and favored Pepto Bismol more than it did Bazooka bubble gum: her daddy had picked it special and it, like he, was perfect. The papers, they didn't change any of that. Couldn't. Wouldn't. The words screamed the reality—*It is hereby certified that an order of adoption was duly granted by the Surrogate's Court dated the 6th day of May, 1971, whereby the petition of Thomas Lawrence and Delores Whitney Lawrence, his wife, as adoptive parents for the adoption of the child to be known and called by the name of Rae Lawrence was granted*—and Rae read them and wept great big ol' tears all alone, splayed across her parents' carpet, the contents of the secret metal box they kept hidden under their bed emptied all about her wiry, ashy brown knees, and still, once the initial shock of it all infused itself into her then twelve-year-old system, once she finished

276 • DENENE MILLNER

sneaking looks at the papers and her parents for clues about who they were for real and searching the mirror to figure out who she was for real and pored through all the family photo albums to confirm that her mother, indeed, was right there, frozen in time on a boat, with a stomach as flat as the deck she was standing on just two months before she was supposed to have given birth to her daughter, Rae was good. She didn't care that she was adopted or that her parents hadn't told her. Her adoption was LoLo and Tommy's secret and so she would keep it. If it meant that much to her parents, she would keep it.

Tasheera had no such precept. She stood in the hallway at the top of the stairs, watching as mourners filed into Tommy and LoLo's house with their peace lilies and pans full of overcooked baked chicken, their sorrow-filled eyes and black outfits announcing what they came into the room to do. Some said "hello" and she nodded. Others hugged her like she was family, like she was supposed to be there. Tasheera stiffened under their embrace. She had no sweetness to give—just truth. Her truth. The house in which she stood—this lovely two-story home filled with all these fine things that, piled high, would be a mountainous shadow over the modest apartment she'd grown up in with her mother and brother—was a testament to the need. These people, with their kind words and unwanted hugs, deserved to know just who Tommy was. Today she would announce, practically over his dead body, that she, Tasheera La'Nae Brown, was Tommy's little girl. The real one.

Rae had seen her first at the church, staring. At TJ, her mama. Her. A church full of people she'd known most of her life—this small circle of friends LoLo had collected over her decades of marriage who loved her Tommy, too—and here was this one girl Rae didn't know, on the receiving end of TJ's awkward wave, watching her. Rae was used to such things; people tended to train their eye on celebrities, no matter how bright or dim their starlight shone, and Rae, well, she was certainly that among her parents' circle. They were proud of their own, this girl their community raised and sent off to do big things working as a producer for a popular show on MTV. Still, on this day, because they knew Rae for real and they loved LoLo, wasn't nobody thinking about MTV or which celebrities Rae rubbed elbows with on her high-profile job; their hearts ached for Rae and LoLo and TJ as they each took turns kissing Tommy's face that one last time before the deacons slowly closed the casket and adorned it with a modest spray of pink hydrangea LoLo picked special from the bushes Tommy had tended just for her. When Sarah stood and sang "His Eye Is on the Sparrow" and Rae wailed, they, too, wailed for this fatherless child, who was saying her forever goodbye to the absolute love of her life: her daddy. The people who cared for Rae, they were focused on the mourning. All of them except that girl.

And now here she was, walking around Rae's parents' house, standing around, trouble written all over her. Rae, seven months pregnant and, just, worn out from the grief, the suddenness of her father's death, everybody telling her that her daddy was in a better place, had nothing left—not a thing—and so it was her intention to kiss her mother's cheek, hug her brother, tuck into her purse the small cardboard box of her father's jewelry her mother set aside for her, and leave everything else behind.

But this one, Rae was compelled to watch.

Rae searched the kitchen cabinet for a plastic container and a matching lid and made her way to the repast bounty her mother's friends and church elders had cooked, watching through the makeshift breakfast bar her father had built by his own hand in the wall between the kitchen and dining room. The girl, who looked only a year or two younger than Rae, was walking from one person to the next, shaking hands, saying a few words, then moving on, leaving dropped jaws and hushed talk in her wake.

"Okay, the car is all packed up," Roman said, rubbing Rae's shoulders. So focused on the girl was Rae that she barely heard her husband. She dug a serving spoon into a bowl of macaroni and cheese sitting on the fringe of the massive dining table repast spread and almost missed dropping the heaping spoon of decorated pasta into her plastic tin. "I, um, thought you didn't like eating other people's mac and cheese," Roman said, eyes creased as he watched his wife fumble the food.

"What?" Rae asked as she kept scooping and watching, her question more a placeholder than a plea for clarification. She was a statue with the spoon in one hand and the container in the other as the girl made her way to yet another set of her mother's friends—this time, Sarah and Cindy, who had been perched together on the double-wide chair Rae loved to nap in when she visited from college. Before that, LoLo had forbidden the family from lounging in her formal living room; the sofas, that double chair, the glass cocktail table and étagère that housed mementoes of LoLo and Tommy's life together—all of them were collected under some invisible shroud that was off-limits except for cleaning and entertaining LoLo's most special guests. Rae's pursuit of a degree—she was the first in her family to do so—earned her a perch on that chair, where she studied, read. Slept off the rigors of college life. Now, judging from the looks on Sarah's and Cindy's faces, what was meant to be a place of peace was anything but.

Just as the girl began to speak, TJ rushed over and grabbed her by the meat of her arm and led her away from the two women, away from the living room, down the stairs, and out into the warmth of the sun, Rae's eyes boring a hole in her back until she could see it no more. She stood there, hands full, mouth agape, unsure of what, exactly, she had just watched, and clear, too, that she needed to get to the bottom of it. Every eye in the room was either downcast or turned in awkward angles to avoid her own. This was personal. This was bad.

"Babe, I thought you wanted to go," Roman said, slightly whiney, as Rae dropped the spoon and dish on the dining room table and headed for the stairs. Roman wasn't a fan of funerals or the theater that followed them, but even more, he disliked being in the confines of the Lawrence family and its orbit, this group of religious, blue-collar Southerners with whom he could not relate. The back wall in his father's study displayed college degrees from family members dating back three generations, announcing the ambitions of the Lister family: Howard, lawyer. Howard, engineer. Xavier University, nurse. UPenn, PhD. And still, Mrs. Lawrence looked down her nose at Roman, as did her husband, God bless the dead, as if Roman missed the target on whatever standard they'd had in mind for their daughter. As if his soft, callous-free hands were some kind of measure of his manhood—his ability to make a home for Rae, take care of their young, growing family. Roman usually met their displeasure, wrapped in stiff hugs and insignificant conversation, with a slather of indifference, bowing out of their boisterous Pokeno games and raucous communal recollections of "the good ol' days," when country niggas eschewed books and pencils and instead focused on shooting things and lifting heavy shit and struggling to feed six and seven and eight mouths at a time on land they either owned or died trying to buy. This wasn't Roman's type of struggle; he had no desire to relate. Usually, he'd simply tuck himself into a corner somewhere and read until a reasonable enough amount of time had passed for him to stretch, yawn, and say, "All right now, it's probably time we hit the road back to Brooklyn." Rae was never ready to leave. But today, after her white rose and a handful of dirt chased her father's casket into the ground, she pulled herself away from her mother's shoulder long enough to whisper, "We not staying at the repast for long. I need you to get me out of there as soon as you can." It was the most reasonable request Rae had made all day.

And now, here she was, making it hard on a brother.

Rae, hardly ever oblivious to Roman's itchiness, would not be consumed by his needs in this moment. She wasn't about to leave until she understood why a pall had fallen over the room and what the stranger girl had to do with it. Rae tipped past the downcast eyes and double-timed down the steps, straight through the screen door, past the crepe myrtle tree her mother had grown from a clipping she got during a visit to her sister's house in South Carolina years before, and down another set of stairs that poured her at the foot of the garage, where all that was left of her nuclear family stood, shifting from foot to foot, waving hands excitedly in the air even as the volume of their voices rushed out in hushed tones. Rae locked eyes with Uncle Theddo first, who, in turn, stopped whisper-arguing in mid-sentence, which, of course, signaled everyone else staring at him as he spoke to turn and see what he was looking at.

"Oh, hey, darlin'," Uncle Theddo said, sounding nervous. "Come on over here and give an old man a hug."

Both LoLo and TJ stared at their shoes, sneaking peeks at Rae and the girl as Uncle Theddo stretched his arms for the requested embrace.

"Hey, Uncle Theddo," Rae said, her voice tentative. She let him hug her tight but remained on task. "I'm about to head out, Mommy," she said to LoLo, but Rae focused on the girl.

"Yeah, baby, all right. It's been a long day," Lolo said hurriedly. "It's probably best—" was all she could muster before the girl interrupted.

"Hi," she said quickly, offering her hand. "I'm Tasheera."

"Oh, hey, nice to meet you," Rae said. Just as she primed her lips to ask Tasheera how she knew her father, TJ butted in.

"Yeah, uh, we were going to introduce the two of you. This here is Theddo's daughter," TJ blurted.

Rae caught how Tasheera snapped her neck in TJ's direction when he made the introduction—saw how LoLo shifted from one foot to the other, narrowed her eyes. How Uncle Theddo's shoulders deflated as he dropped his head, cleared his throat. Tasheera pulled back her hand from Rae's and cleared her throat, too.

"Uncle Theddo's daughter?" Rae questioned.

Now, Rae was nosy and so there wasn't a whole lot the grown-ups could get past her big ears when she was younger. It wasn't until she got older, though, that she actually understood what was being said and why, and once she put together her adult understanding of things, many of the abstract conversations she tried to make sense of as a child formulated into concrete comprehension of just how fucked up the adults around her actually were. Uncle Theddo, who had enough "spare" children outside his first marriage to fill a bench at a pickup game, was probably the most fucked-up of all. That there was a damn-near grown woman being introduced to her as a first cousin nobody knew about until this day wasn't at all odd to Rae. Just par for the course, though she did wonder what Uncle Theddo's kids by marriage thought of this newfound sibling—if they'd been introduced at all.

"Mmm-hmm," Uncle Theddo said, nodding, his eyes never really leaving his black Stacy Adams oxfords, shined up just so, like their owner was trying to be respectable at a funeral. Or catch the attention of a woman.

"Hey, it's, uh, good to meet you, cousin," Rae said.

"Yeah, um, I can't do this," the girl said.

"Hey, hey, not here—not now," LoLo interjected, reaching for Tasheera's arm.

"What you mean not now?" she snapped, snatching her arm from LoLo's grasp. "You ask me, there's no better time than right now!"

Rae reeled back. "Whoa, watch it," she said, looking at her mother's arm and then at the girl. "That's my mother." Her voice, normally sparkles and light, was a bass boom. "Time for what?"

"*Not now*," LoLo repeated, this time through her curled lip, more forcefully.

Tasheera narrowed her eyes but said nothing. She instead reached into her purse and pulled out a small slip of paper—the flap of an envelope—

and shoved it in Rae's direction. "I, um, I wrote this down for you," she said. "I thought you should have them."

Rae took the paper and held it close to her face. On it were two names, scrawled in red cursive, followed by phone numbers.

"The top one is my number, and the bottom one is my brother's," she said. "I thought maybe it's time you get to know your siblings."

The paper felt like fire in Rae's hands—the names and numbers danced like flames on the page. She looked at LoLo first, then TJ as he shook his head and muttered to the sky, "You wrong for that."

"Siblings?" Rae said, cocking her head, her eyes slowly panning from the girl's shoes to her eyes. "What you mean 'siblings'?" she asked, with more bass than curiosity filling the space around her words.

"I mean exactly what I said. My brother, Mikey, and me, we got the same daddy as you."

"What daddy?" Rae asked, still angry but also still confused.

"Thomas Lawrence is our father, too," Tasheera said simply.

LoLo, still recovering from the minor heart attack she'd suffered just a few weeks earlier while traveling to South Carolina for her father's funeral, rubbed at her heaving chest as she took in huge gulps of the humid air. Rae grabbed her mother as she watched her brother walk away, throwing both his hands in the air and then running them through his short Afro. "Oh man," he said and sighed. "I told you to make her go home! Now look," he said, tossing his chin in Uncle Theddo's direction. Uncle Theddo stood right there—said not one more word.

Turning her attention to her brother, Rae said, "You knew about this?"

Tasheera answered for him. "Yeah, he knew. Everybody knew. Your uncles, your brother. Told your mom, too, several weeks ago. Sorry she didn't let you in on the—"

Rae didn't give Tasheera the satisfaction of saying the word "secret." Rae figured the girl had already done enough talking—enough disrespecting her parents' house, her mother, her family. Her father's name on this girl's tongue, she would not stand. Not here. Not in front of her parents' home. Not on this, the hardest day of her thirty years on this earth—the day she put her daddy in the ground. Rae would not allow this. She simply would not.

She was right-handed but it was her left hand that she balled into a fist, a trick her daddy had taught her one Saturday evening when she was a kid, sitting on the floor next to his recliner down in the basement, yelling at the TV as some welterweight annihilated his opponent in a televised boxing match. Rae loved watching boxing with her father—that and his aggrieved New York Mets, the NBA, the NFL. This was by no means any indication that Rae was some kind of sports enthusiast; in fact, she rather disliked sports except for the Knicks and that was only when she could watch them in person and see John Starks's cute ass up close. But really, outside of that, especially when she was a kid, watching sports wasn't so much about cheering on her father's faves as it was about spending time with her dad—laughing with him, eating a whole pint of Häagen-Dazs butter pecan ice cream guilt-free, gleaning lessons, love, from time well spent. And then there was the one night that she revealed to him that she was scared of some girl named Laurie. Laurie was a tough one who, despite being the center of all the boys' attention in their seventh-grade English class, was full on jealous that Tony turned to Rae for help with an assignment and for that, she thought Rae deserved a beating. Passed word of this all around their class, all around every lunch table—across the yard where the buses lined up. Rae was petrified. She was neither a lover nor a fighter—just a nerd who made straight As and was asked by some boy if she could help him with social studies. It was a service she didn't mind providing, but not for the price of having her ass whooped.

"See? See? Watch him, baby. Watch him right here," her father had said, jabbing at the TV and leaning in. "He got him on the ropes but Hagler gonna bring that left hand up and give him the hammer straight to his gut. Watch."

Sure enough, Marvelous Marvin Hagler's opponent was no match for that southpaw. "See, they expecting you to hit 'em with the right because that's what most people are: right-handed," Tommy had said as he sat on the edge of his recliner, shifting his body toward the huge wooden TV console parked on the floor next to the equally large stereo and speakers. "They looking for your right hand. Got their eye on it. And that's what they train to duck and counter. But you pull out that southpaw, and boooooyyyy," he said, huffing and grinning, "they don't see that coming."

Tommy had stood up, balled his fists, and got himself into a fighting stance. "Okay, stand up here and do like this," he'd said. Rae complied.

"Now, she come at you this way, she gonna pop just like this," he had said, raising his hand slowly toward Rae's face, "and then she gonna drop her arm and duck this way, expecting you to hit her back with your right. She do that, and she gonna lean right into your fist. You gonna swing with the left, pull that power from your right leg and your left hip. Throw your whole body in it, you got me? Now put your hands up."

Rae didn't let Tasheera finish her sentence. She punched that girl straight in her filthy mouth with the intention of making it so that whenever Tasheera so much as thought about Delores and Thomas Lawrence and secrets, she would quickly stop herself and conjure something—anything—else but the parents of the girl with the mean southpaw who knocked her so hard across her right cheek she literally saw a flash of stars and would spend the next thirteen days borrowing her mother's Maybelline to cover up the bruise Rae's left knuckles painted across her face.

It took TJ, Uncle Theddo, Sarah, and a couple more hands that Rae neither saw nor remembered to get Rae off that girl and into the house, into the basement, onto the couch, where they held her while she said all manner of nasty, foul things that the good church folk neither approved of nor wanted to hear. LoLo just stood there in the driveway, in a daze. Everyone quickly filed out of the house past her, with their quick waves and their "I'm so sorry for your loss" mumbles, their respect for Tommy and LoLo's home surmounting any desire they may have had to watch the Black-ass theater playing itself out before them. Tommy wasn't even cold in the ground. To them, all of this was a damn shame.

This is how they did. Lives, histories were experienced on the hush, buried deep—so very deep into the recesses of memory, in the marrow of the bones. The Lawrences, like most Black people who had been through some things, were deeply private—held their stories to their chests like holey undergarments, never to be seen in the light of day. The roots of their reasons for hiding were fed by embarrassment, shame, fear. Wasn't nobody going to tell about Uncle Jed having his privates sliced off and laid at the base of the tree from which he got hung by a bunch of drunk peckerwoods with nothing better to do on a Tuesday night; the law didn't give a damn about such things and those same peckerwoods, pissed about accusations and indignant about even the prospect of finding themselves at the end of a nigger's pointed finger, could always come back and do the same to Uncle Jed's brother, son, mama, pregnant wife. Anybody who sought retribution. Fear kept your mouth closed. Embarrassment worked the same way; a family's dirty laundry—the losses, the missteps, the lies, the secrets—could never see the light of day. All of it needed to be buried with the caskets, six feet below the rest of the dirt.

Rae wanted no part of this. She was naturally curious and a journalist, to boot—someone who appreciated a good story and knew how to tell them, too. Bigger, though, was her yearning to know and understand her family's origin story—the good, the ugly, the complicated, all of it. If she was to have her own origin story hidden from her, if she was to know nothing about a mother and father that could give her away, who she looked like, from where her bloodline actually flowed, if the birthday on her birth certificate was even real, the very least she should know was all of these things about the family that claimed her, raised her, enveloped her into its own. These things meant something to her.

Neither Tommy nor LoLo could bare themselves in ways that suited Rae. She made it hard for them to do so. Too nosy. Too loud about it. And much too sensitive for them to want to divulge. Something big would happen and everyone would hide it from Rae, whose first reaction to most tough discussions, she would be the first to admit, usually elicited some kind of emotional response: tears, yelling, brooding silence while she figured out some things. Her mother couldn't stand it, though it occurred to neither LoLo nor Rae that the mother was the architect of the daughter's reactive outbursts. It had racked her daddy with worry. But in Rae's mind, asking questions, examining information, expressing emotion was the purview of normal people: you heard or experienced something that was hurtful, upsetting, and it was perfectly natural to have a demonstrative emotional reply—a release that was every bit as necessary to one's recovery and ability to plow through the problem at hand as hot, wet air was to a steamboat's movement. It never seemed to occur to any of them that hiding what cut them didn't spare any of them from feeling the festering wounds. It infected the family in ways they could not and were not willing to name, but Rae had come to understand that her tears, her questions, her constant digging, gave those wounds fresh air and light, the kind necessary for healing. Even if ripping the Band-Aids off those wounds made them hurt.

Still, that type of vulnerability made her mother, father, brother, everyone uncomfortable, and that made them masters at hiding from Rae. Little things, big ones, so many secrets they kept from her—for her protection, they'd insist. "Now, now—you too busy to be dealing with all this here," Tommy would say whenever Rae stumbled on the details of something gone wrong—the broken refrigerator he and her mother couldn't afford to repair, TJ getting his girlfriend knocked up and needing just the precise words to convince her to have an abortion. Tommy had even debated and taken his time telling her that her mama had a heart attack while in South Carolina to attend her father's funeral and had been just moments away from following her estranged daddy through death's door.

"Hey, baby, what you up to?" he'd said just as easy, like this was some ol' regular summer Sunday afternoon, warm and quiet.

When he called, Rae had been in bed for only about twenty minutes, alternately dozing and wincing at a cooking show hosted by some Italian lady who kept licking her fingers while she prepared a lemon curd she intended to serve to guests. Rae was grateful that Roman had gone off somewhere with his boy to play some form of tennis-meets-handball that she'd never heard of and the baby had finally stopped wrapping her toes around her mother-to-be's ribs, settling into a nap of her own. Peace for the young TV producer was rare, especially since she'd been counting down the days to maternity leave. Still, when she saw her parents' phone number pop up in the caller ID, Rae answered the phone, holding back a yawn. "Nothing, just sitting here watching TV. Your granddaughter finally settled her little fast tail down," Rae said, giggling and rubbing her belly.

"That's my girl. She's not fast—just busy, like her mama," Tommy said, his laugh hearty. "It's gonna be something else watching you trying to keep up with a little you."

"I'm tired just thinking about it," Rae said.

They must have bantered on like that for a good fifteen minutes before Tommy finally seemed to find the words and the guts to share the news. "You know, LoLo is in South Carolina."

"I know, Daddy. I talked to her yesterday. She said Auntie Brenda was trying to talk her into getting her eyebrows done. I'd pay good money to watch that. You know Mommy doesn't like pain. This place plucks."

"Yeah, well, today she's in the hospital," Tommy said.

"The hospital? What, they finishing up arrangements for Grandpa? I thought he would have been in the funeral home by now."

"No, he's laid out at the funeral home. Your mother is in the hospital because she's sick."

"Sick?" Rae asked. She sat up a bit on her elbows as if doing so would help her hear and understand a little better.

"She's, uh, in intensive care."

"What do you mean, Daddy? What is she doing in intensive care?"

"She had a heart attack, sunshine."

"What?" Rae said, clutching her own chest.

"They, um," Tommy's voice cracked, "they're working on her, baby girl."

"Don't say that to me," Rae said, her eyes welling with tears.

"Baby—"

"Don't say that to me," she repeated, this time, her voice cracking.

"Rae, don't you start all that cryin'—"

"Don't you say that to me!" she yelled. Her nose burned as adrenaline rushed to her head, making it pound with pain.

"Rae, stop it! There's nothing you can do and all that crying isn't going to change anything."

"Where is she? I need to see her! What hospital is she in? We have to get over there—I need to see my mother!"

"There's no need for all of that," Tommy said flatly. "Ain't no use in you calling over to the hospital; there's nothing you can do for her. I'll get it sorted out."

"But Daddy—"

"I said I'll get it sorted out. Where's Roman?"

"What? Roman? He's . . . he's out playing tennis or whatever . . . ," Rae said, hardly intelligible.

"You best let him know. I'll call you later tonight."

And just like that, Tommy hung up on his daughter. By the time Roman took the C and then the F train from Manhattan back to Brooklyn and hoofed it the four blocks from the subway station to their Fort Greene apartment, Rae had already spoken to a nurse at the hospital where her mother lay. "Oh honey," the nurse had said. "We're doing everything we can." Her voice was pound cake—sweet but sturdy and full of things no one needed. Things Rae was sure would be the death of her.

It was a tough discussion that Rae, with only two years of marriage under her belt and a baby bouncing around in her belly, just wasn't ready to have, but she knew she had to have it, even if her father wasn't convinced she could handle it. What choice did she have? Her mother, this woman Rae loved like she did air but feared to her very depths, had been, just a few days before, kissing her cheek and rubbing her pregnant belly, whispering, "Gamma loves you, little one. Come on out here so I can see you!" And now, just as her mother was beginning to reveal this tenderness that was unfamiliar to them all, she was lying in a hospital in another state, her heart, suddenly filled with light, also significantly weaker. Rae needed her mother. Needed her to be strong. Needed her to come home and show her how to be a mother to her own daughter. She needed to tell her that.

"Call back this evening, sugar," the nurse said sweetly. "We should have some more information for you by then."

Rae would never get the chance to make that call. Instead, just a few hours after finding out about her mother, she would get a second phone call, this time from her brother. Unlike Tommy, TJ was one for neither subtlety nor gentleness nor dallying. "Rae, Dad got into a car accident on the way to the airport to go see about Mommy. He's dead."

Now, after all that tragedy, Rae sat on the couch in the basement of her parents' home, alternately staring at her swollen ankles and her brother's lips, trying to make sense of the information she'd just received in the driveway. Trying to make sense of how her father, this kind, beautiful man who loved his family, could have created a second one in secret. Made it so this girl could stomp all up into their home and try to claim all that Rae had left of her daddy—all the good.

"I told her not to come here," TJ said.

"Wait, I don't understand. You know that bitch?"

"She's not a bitch," TJ said. "But what she just did, that was definitely a bitch move."

"TJ. Stop playing with me. Who is that girl? What does she mean Daddy is her father?"

TJ swallowed hard. "Well, she's not lying about that. She is Daddy's

288 • DENENE MILLNER

daughter. She got a little brother, too, and he's Daddy's son." Rae stared at TJ, his thick lips, as if doing so would help her better comprehend the words coming out of his mouth. He continued. "They're just a few years younger than us; she's twenty-seven, he's twenty-five. They live with their mother a couple blocks away from Uncle Samuel."

"How do you know all of this?"

TJ was uncharacteristically quiet. Then: "I was with Daddy when he would go see them—check on them, give them money, make sure they were good."

Rae scrunched her whole face into a ball of incredulity. "Wait, you what? You knew all this time?"

"Yeah," TJ said quietly. "Dad would tell y'all we were going to see Uncle Sam, but I knew getting in the car where we were really going."

Rae's chest began to heave as tears worked their way to her ducts. The baby shifted and kicked, drawing Rae's hand to her. "Mommy . . . Mommy knew all this time?"

"Well, that's the thing. Tasheera used to call the house when she thought Dad was home. He told her to hang up if any of us answered the phone. But this last time Tasheera stayed on the line. She told Mommy everything."

Rae angrily swiped at her tears. "She what?"

"Yeah. Everything."

"When was this?"

"Right before she went to South Carolina. The same day Grandpa died."

"You mean to tell me this girl called our mother's phone and, like, talked to her?"

"Yeah."

"How do you know this?"

"Mommy called and told me."

"Called and told you what?"

TJ took a deep breath. "She said Tasheera called her and told her she was Daddy's daughter, just like that. And Ma said she put her in her place."

"What do you mean, 'put her in her place'? What does that mean?"

"She told her she didn't care who her daddy was or how hard she tried, she would never be his real family and she could never be Daddy's little girl because he already had one."

Rae swiped more tears from her cheeks and was working her way to full-on bawl when she heard the front screen door slam. She listened for her mother's unmistakable footsteps—heavy, slow—down the thick carpeted staircase. Their eyes met.

"I meant that, too," LoLo said. "She could never take your place."

Rae burst, her throat a fount of sobs. She struggled through them as she stuck out her right hand and pushed herself up off the couch; TJ hopped to help her stand, and his and LoLo's hands were on her arms, back, everywhere, supporting her as she stood. TJ pulled a handkerchief from the breast pocket of his suit jacket and tried to use it to wipe his sister's tears. Rae snatched away her face.

"Aren't I lucky?" she sneered. "I watched my father be put in the ground and gained a sister and a brother all in the same day." And then, still staring deep into her brother's eyes, she yelled, "Roman! I'm ready to go home!" Her breath and spittle were hot. She stared for just a beat longer, then shimmied between her brother and mother best she could, her stomach brushing against her mother's, her butt against her brother's leg. She knew the two were watching as she disappeared up the stairs and out the front door, her anger, sadness, confusion a thick stew on which her mother and brother choked. This is why they hid truths from her. This is why they kept their secrets.

24

The needle to her spine, the contractions, the way that stupid machine kept beeping a rhythm counter to Donny Hathaway's "A Song for You" playing on repeat on the CD player—all of it induced the type of pain in Rae's body, deep down to her spirit, that, in the moments when she could actually catch her breath, made her question exactly what had been going through her brain when she gave Roman a heavy pour of cheap white wine, kissed his lips, and said, breathlessly, "We should make a baby." She always knew she wanted to be a mother, back before she could begin to fathom, even, how a woman technically became one. Her own mother had damn near beaten the black off the meaty part of her thighs when she caught her, at age eight, prancing around the basement with her Rub-A-Dub Dolly doll smooshed beneath her nightgown, the centerpiece in Rae's earlier pregnancy fantasies. "Get your little fast ass in bed!" LoLo yelled, chest heaving as she held Rae's arm in the air, forcing her to dodge and dance her slaps like a clanking wooden puppet on the end of a marionette. She had no idea what she'd done wrong; Auntie Para Lee had a bump on her belly and everybody got excited when it moved and rubbed on it and said their coochie coos while Para Lee sat there fat and jolly and giggling. The first day Rae laid eyes on Para Lee's newborn, she thought she was a doll—went to bed that night thinking about how the baby curled her little fingers around her pinky, how her head smelled when she snuck and rubbed her nose on it. Rae wanted a baby. She knew that from straight away. That urge grew stronger still after Rae found her adoption papers and realized, for the first time, that all the branches on all those family trees she'd created for school projects over the years were as fake as the maple leaves she'd meticulously fashioned out of green construction paper; no matter how many different ways she cut them, the names of the people she claimed were relatives by name and decree only. She wanted what truly belonged to her, too. She loved her parents, her brother, and she wanted her a real branch with its own roots. Her womb would be the soil, her happiness, her wanting, the fertilizer that would assure her own family tree would bloom.

But now this baby that she'd dreamed about since she was but a baby herself was coming—mere moments from gulping her first breath—and nothing was right. Rae lay in a hospital room with her legs splayed, a room full of strangers staring at her private parts and poking at her belly and arms and vagina as an entire human being whacked its way out of her body, and there was not an ounce of joy. In typical Rae fashion, she'd read every "how to have a baby" book she could get her hands on to prepare for what was to come—had memorized, considered, practiced, and prepared for every second of what would be. Braxton Hicks contractions. Water breaking. Having a packed suitcase ready to go. Having a plan in place at the hospital and eyeballing the maternity ward. Meeting every doctor in her ob-gyn practice. The importance of swallowing those horse pills. What would happen as the baby made her way out—the pain, the bearing down, the shit, the ring of fire, the tearing, the placenta, the colostrum, the skin-to-skin bonding, the bleeding and immobility after it was all said and done, everything that could go right, everything that could go wrong. But none of those bitches had said word one about what to do when your daddy, your hero, cheated on his wife, created and supported a whole 'nother family, and died trying to get to the woman who worked herself to the damn bone taking care of and loving him, only to have that man break her heart.

Rae couldn't find the joy because she was angry. She felt bamboozled. All the things LoLo had demanded, exacted from her in order for her to be the perfect woman—all of it was bullshit. *Bullshit.* Get good grades, keep your legs closed, go to a good college, get a good career, marry a good man like your daddy, have some kids and be a good wife, mother, and homemaker—that's what LoLo had drilled into Rae, what she had insisted in both word and deed was necessary to be the virtuous one, the successful one, the one who would be picked, cared for. Make it through the gates. And how did that work out for her mama? She poured every ounce of herself into raising kids, keeping house, cooking, cleaning everything with precision, down to Tommy's dirty drawers, which she worshiped, too, and now her man was six feet under, and all her mother got for her troubles was humiliation. *Is this it?* Rae questioned when it was just her and her thoughts. Is this the price for a man's devotion? Even that of the good ones?

Rae squeezed tight to the sides of the hospital bed and screamed. This was a most exquisite agony—the pushing of a human through a tiny hole at the end of her loins, trying to center her thoughts on this baby and what her face would look like, and not the way her father's face was scrunched as he lay in his casket, his hair greasy and flat from all the Afro Sheen the funeral director slathered on his thin, misshapen Afro. Nothing Rae'd learned in months of Lamaze classes—all that leaning back into Roman's chest and heavy breathing through pretend contractions—made any sense. There was the casual ripping of one's nails off her toe beds, a slow waltz across white-hot coals, and then there were contractions and grief—no difference between them. Another contraction hit and Rae literally lost feeling in her feet and the backs of her knees. "Oh God, oh God, oh God!" she yelled, her words curdling in her throat, on her tongue.

"Stop all that screaming!" the nurse said curtly. "It's not going to get the baby out any faster. Focus on breathing and pushing when we tell you to."

"I . . . can't . . . help . . . it . . . this . . . shit . . . hurts!" Rae snarled at the nurse as she writhed.

"Baby, baby," Roman said, leaning in, running his hands over Rae's braids, puffed up at the roots and edges from all the sweat. "She's just trying to help you. Come on, breathe with me," he added, grabbing Rae's hand. "You can do it."

This is what Rae could count on from her husband—an unwavering devotion to making his wife believe she was the star of every story, that as easily as the sun rose in the morning, so, too, could she. For a woman programmed to let self-doubt flood her every thought, decision, such things were important. Roman was the muscle who shut off those valves with a simple "Don't listen to them, you're right about this" and "They wish they could do what you do" to remind his wife that she did not have to suffer the indignity of an elbow to the very backbone of her spirit—that chin up, shoulders squared was a soldier's stance. "You're my soldier," he would say. "You got this." It is what made her love him. It is what made her love herself.

Roman blew three big, exaggerated breaths through his thick, puckered lips and then pushed a long fourth hiss through his teeth. Rae nodded her head and repeated the breathing pattern. "That's it. That's my girl."

Rae watched his face as he leaned toward her spread legs and peeked beyond the sheet draped over her knees. She could tell he was trying to keep his face neutral, like he was unbothered by what he was witnessing, but Roman was a terrible actor; worry, fear, distrust, anger, each of these emotions would slather themselves across his face, no matter the words he was peddling from his mouth.

"What?" Rae said, breathing heavy as another contraction began its crescendo of pain at the base of her pulsating belly.

Roman fake yawned, another telltale sign Rae had come to learn during their two years of marriage, three years of living together, that whatever words followed would be lies. "Nothing," he insisted. "Nothing is wrong. It's all good. Everything is beautiful. It's all going to be fine."

But it wasn't. Beyond her father dying, beyond learning of his betrayal, there was the matter of Roman being out of work and not looking. He was a copy editor by trade but fancied himself a novelist—a dream he'd conjured and nurtured from childhood, when the extent of his understanding of publishing involved ditto paper, a couple Bic pens, and a stapler. Before her heart attack, LoLo questioned if his understanding had grown at all. He'd quit his day job as a copy editor at a national magazine when Rae was but six months pregnant, because, as he put it, he wasn't "passionate" about his gig anymore, and could afford to pursue what did make his soul fly because Rae had saved up enough money, vacation time, and maternity leave for the two of them to live comfortably for a year—a justification that wasn't any kind of sound reasoning at all in LoLo's book. "What you mean he quit?" she'd practically screamed at Rae when she delivered the news via a phone call—just one day after an in-person visit to her parents' house, when she was to divulge said plans but knew how her mother would respond and, therefore, was too embarrassed to bring it up.

"He wants to be an author, Mommy. He's not happy."

And this much was true. Countless mornings, Rae would wake to the sharp buzz of the alarm clock snatching her out of a deep slumber, and, upon wiping the slimy, cottony remnants of a fairly restful sleep out of the corner of her eyes and rubbing them into focus, she would turn her head to the side and always, there was Roman, his two pillows propped up against the wall behind their headboard-less bed, a pile of printed papers and note-books spread all about the mattress and his bedside table, his dream, pas-sion, marching in printer ink and hand-scribbled notes across the pages. The morning he chose himself over his family, Rae had stretched her bones and let the yawn push from stomach to throat as she greeted her man: "Hey, you," she said, whispering so as not to crash his concentration. In-stinctively, she reached for her belly. "Good morning, little one," she said, accenting the greeting to their unborn child with a gentle rub.

"Hey, babe," Roman said, half smiling and tossing a glance Rae's way as he struggled to get onto the pages the last of his thoughts until he'd have to stack the sheets like a deck of cards against his lap and lay them down until the next time the story would call him out of his sleep.

Only after he'd gingerly placed his work on the table and turned his thin but muscular frame toward her did Rae speak.

"Look at you, getting it in. While the rest of us sleep our lives away, you up with the farmers, feeding the beasts."

Roman laughed. "Early bird gets the worm, or something like that," he said as he scooped Rae into his arms.

"I'm really proud of you, going after your dream. There's a whole lot of people who say they want to write books, but look at you, actually doing it. Putting in the work."

Roman squeezed Rae's body tighter. "Yeah, I guess," he said, burying his head into the crook of her neck. They sat like this in their solitude, lis-tening to the sounds of Brooklyn yawning itself awake. The garbage men crashed empty metal cans against the curb as the oversized truck screeched up the block.

"What do you mean, 'I guess'? You're doing it, full stop."

Roman squeezed tighter. "I just wish I had more time to really go hard, you know? An hour here, two or three there, isn't really getting me closer to producing the kind of work I need to get published. I mean, this job . . ."

Roman hesitated, dug his face a little deeper into Rae's neck.

"What?" Rae asked.

"That place," Roman started, before going quiet again. Rae could feel his heart pick up its beat against her back. "It's soul-crushing, babe. The white boys, they just steady climbing and I'm sitting at the same desk, circling mispellings and reminding them of the Oxford comma, like that's the beginning and end of my writing career, and they're out there getting all this love off stories that are mediocre at best, you know? Brett Van got a book deal yesterday, based off a story he wrote in the magazine a couple months ago. I saw that story raw. He's not good. But here he is, off to live my dream."

Rae cradled her belly—let the first of her thoughts slide down her gullet. This was a different version of the same story he'd begun to tell of late. The pivot. From the very beginning, he'd told her she was his dream—that making babies with her, making a life with her, that was all that mattered to him. This was to be the source of his content and so it was hers, too. The nestling down, the preparing of arms spread wide, ready to welcome new life. Their family. But six months into the pregnancy, it felt to Rae like restlessness was altering the dreamscape for which the two of them had yearned. Pride and envy were broad, sloppy black strokes across their sweet and simple sky. *But don't we make you happy?* is what she wanted to say to him. *Aren't we your dream?* These were things she would never say out loud. Better to choke on those words than throw water on a man's ambitions. This is what was expected of her. This is what she knew. This was the Pavlovian response required of a Black woman who wanted to keep the peace—to keep her man.

"I been thinking," Roman continued. "What if I just left that place and, you know, focused on this book?"

Rae shifted her body, pulled away from her husband's embrace ever so slightly, leaning into her belly. She rubbed. "What do you mean? Leave your job? Like, quit?"

"Yeah," Roman said, nodding, stretching the word into multiple syllables. "We have enough saved for both of us to be off-grid when the baby gets here. I could use that time to finish my book, and by the time you need to go back to work, I'll have a fat book deal to add to the pot. I can always get another copyediting gig. But this might be the one opportunity to make this book-writing thing work. You feel me?"

Rae hesitated. "Ye—um, yeah. I guess that cou—that could work," she said, her feelings about this thing every bit as unsure as the sound of her stuttered response. Roman did not notice. Roman did not notice a lot of things. His ambition, which she'd loved about him in the beginning, which she had compared to the callouses that served as evidence of a lifetime of hard work right there on the palms of her own daddy's hands, was morphing into an albatross on Roman's neck. Hers, too. That ambition, she would come to find, was the source of his repute. In time, it was all that seemed to matter. Not Rae, not the baby. *His* happiness.

LoLo saw right through it from the beginning and now, here came her daughter, six months pregnant with a no-count husband opting to be a bum on her baby girl's couch. Because working hurt his feelings. "Well shit, who says you need to be happy when you're earning your keep?" she'd said when Rae shared his book-writing plan. "What does he think, he's supposed to get a damn parade every day he goes into work? What kind of man quits his job when his wife is pregnant with their child? And you just gone let this happen? I can't believe . . ."

Rae had taken the receiver from her ear and smashed it against her sore, swollen breasts; she knew this was how her mother would respond to the news of Roman quitting his job to write a book, because her mother was a stickler when it came to a man's responsibility to his family and believed deeply that if there was any one person in the house who should be pulling down a paycheck, it was the man, and, deep down, Rae felt the same way. But she didn't need the lecture. Rae needed to focus—figure out how she was going to manage juggling a job that required her to be in the office, some days stretching well beyond ten hours, while preparing her body and her home for a baby with a husband—a Black man—who needed her support, her encouragement, not her skepticism, even if she had to grill up her own doubts and fears and eat them with Sunday dinner to make their marriage, this family unit she craved, work.

"Okay, Ma . . . Mommy . . . Mama, I got to go, I got to get back to work," Rae had said, interrupting LoLo's rant. "I'mma try to call you back tonight when I get in, if it's not too late," she'd added, knowing full well she had no intention of doing so. Everything, she'd told herself, would be fine.

Roman yawned again as he took another peek. "Wow, that's um, whew." He turned his entire body away from the show happening between

Rae's legs and gripped her hand a little tighter. "Everything is okay. Um, it's okay."

"What? What's wrong?" Rae said, alarmed by the look that had settled on Roman's face.

"Come on, focus," the nurse said, rubbing Rae's shoulder.

"What's wrong? Is . . . is there something wrong with the baby?" Rae said between pants, her voice getting higher the more distressed she grew.

"Everything is fine," Dr. Hazel said quietly as she pulled back from between Rae's legs. "The baby is crowning, so I need you to look at me."

Rae squeezed Roman's hand but focused on her doctor.

"Remember when we talked about the ring of fire?"

Rae nodded.

"That burning you're feeling, that's what that is."

Rae tried to swallow down her tears but there was no use. Her whole body felt like it was being torn apart; she could barely hear words, much less concentrate on the ones coming out of Dr. Hazel's mouth.

"Listen to me. Do not push, you understand. Let your uterus do its job. I'm going to massage your perineum to help with the stinging you're feeling right now, okay? And when that contraction comes, I need you to breathe through it, but let your body do the work. Do not push."

This is how the next twenty minutes worked—Rae breathing and crying, Roman looking away from it all, the nurse shushing everybody—until the doctor caught that pretty little baby and wiped the blood and thick, pasty white film off both her scrunchy, puffy little face and the poof of curls sitting on top of her scalp and took her over to the corner to poke and prod and measure her then, finally, put her safe in the crook of her mother's arms. Rae stared at the little being in equal parts shock, awe, and a fear as immense as her love. Her devotion to this baby was immediate.

"Hi, little baby," she said, straining the words through a gulp of tears. "Hi, Skye."

"Skye?" the nurse asked, scribbling the word on a piece of paper tacked to a clipboard. "How are we spelling that?"

"It's S-K-Y-E Tommie with an 'ie,'" Roman said, squeezing Rae's shoulder as he spelled out the baby's full name.

"The middle name—that was my dad's name," Rae said, this time unable to contain her sobs. "He's gone now."

The nurse balanced the pen on her clipboard and patted Rae's other arm. "He's still here, baby," she said. The woman handed Rae a small piece of paper with Skye's birth measurements scribbled beneath ink prints of the baby's feet and hands. "Believe that if you believe nothing else, hear?"

Rae stared at the sequence of little lines swirling in perfect patterns, barely taking up space on the page, but so big—mighty—to her eye. Rae turned her attention to little Skye, taking in her cheeks, nose, the way her lips puckered as she turned her head toward Rae's breast and rooted for her mother's nipple. She was so bright—not at all near Rae's dark brown complexion—and, let the tips of her ears tell it, she wouldn't be getting much darker. A few shades, maybe. But nothing like her mama. Rae wanted her to open her eyes—look at her. So she could examine for herself and believe it to be true that this was her child—that her beautiful blood would look like her, too, so that when the world looked at Skye, they saw a reflection of Rae and knew that she had done this thing, that she was not all alone in this world.

Fresh tears poured.

"It's okay, babe," Roman said, bending down to kiss both his girls' foreheads. "She's here. You did so good and our daughter is here."

Rae stroked the baby's cheek and wished her mother and father were there to do the same.

"Excuse me, nurse? Excuse me!" Rae called out to the woman who'd walked in and out of what, to Rae, felt like some kind of herding area for new mothers. It was a room with ten beds, each of them occupied by Black and Latino women in various stages of post-birth—some cradling their little ones, others struggling to sleep, one hand on the tiny plastic cribs connected to their beds, others, still, having just arrived, waiting for their newborns to be brought back to them. One woman sat in the corner bed by the window, empty-handed, angrily swiping away tears as she stared out the window, occasionally sneaking peeks at the other women and their children. The room was a putrid yellow with baby-blue curtains marking off a small area for each of the new mothers on the floor. Large flower stickers of varying sizes and colors were stuck haphazardly on either wall; several large, tattered posters screamed in bold letters LOVE SHOULDN'T

HURT, with directions for how to seek help for domestic violence. The room, it felt heavy, as if joy was more the afterthought than the point.

This hadn't been a part of Rae's birth plan. She'd visited the maternity ward twice—once with Dr. Hazel when she was but four months pregnant, a second time when she was six months along and signed a contract and a check that guaranteed her a private room and a special dinner she could share with Roman as they celebrated their new family. "And my parents, they'll be able to come see me, too, right? No restrictions?" Rae had asked.

"Yes, yes," the hospital's maternity coordinator had assured her. "Private suites are allowed guests until ten P.M. That's one of the best features besides the lobster dinner and champagne. You're not getting any of that in the semi-private rooms."

"Well then, sign me up!" Rae had said enthusiastically.

Rae tried her best not to stare at the other women and focused on her feet, which still looked like fat sausages poking from brown balloons. Anything to keep her mind off the fact that her baby was not in her arms.

"Excuse me!" she called out again.

Finally, the nurse, on her way back out the room with her nose in her clipboard, looked up and in Rae and Roman's direction. She narrowed her eyes. "He can't be here," she clipped, jutting her chin at Roman.

"I . . ." Rae began, fixing her mouth to ask where her baby was, but thrown by the nurse's proclamation. "What do you mean?"

"He can't be here. Only blood relatives of the mother or the child are allowed in the semi-private rooms. He has to go."

Rae digested the woman's words, trying, in her fog of exhaustion, to make sense of what all she was talking about. Inferring. "He's my husband," she said simply. "Can you tell me when I'll have my baby back? And when we'll be switched to the private room?"

"Huh," the nurse said, staring at Rae, then Roman, then Rae again. A second nurse walked into the room and, upon seeing the first nurse's stance, stood next to her to see what theater was unfolding today on what they called "the Ward." Without looking in her colleague's direction, she addressed her, not caring at all that the person about whom she spewed her next words could actually hear them. "She say this her husband," the nurse said, her words tinged with a bit of laughter, a bit of incredulity.

"Husband?" the second nurse said. "You're married?" she asked of Rae, without even looking in Roman's direction.

Rae did look a good decade younger than her actual thirty years, especially with her hair in thin, shoulder-length braids popular with the kids off whom the likes of Janet Jackson and Brandy had cribbed their glamorous-but-youthful looks, but no matter what anyone thought of her age in the moment, the shiny diamond on her ring finger, plus her actually saying, "Hey, this is my husband," should have sufficed for confirmation that she wasn't just some kid popping out babies and breaking rules.

"This is my husband!" Rae said, her voice an octave higher and a few decibels louder than appropriate for a room full of tired new mothers and their little newborns. Roman squeezed her arm.

"I, uh, think what she's trying to say is we've been waiting a minute to see our baby and we're wondering if she may have been taken to the private room we paid for?"

The nurses looked at each other, more incredulously. "Y'all paid for a private room? I didn't see that on your chart anywhere."

"I don't . . . I don't know what to tell you. I paid for it a few months ago? I have the paperwork in my bag if you need it." To Roman, she said, "Babe, can you get the folder out the bag?" Back to the nurse, she continued: "I just want to get my baby and get settled in is all."

Second Nurse, after getting a glimpse of the paperwork as Roman handed it to the first nurse, quietly left the room and, shortly thereafter, arrived with baby Skye in tow. Rae hadn't realized that she was holding her breath until, her baby finally back in her arms, she released it. She kissed her forehead, each of her cheeks, her lips, her tiny fingers gripping on her own, and sighed as she took her in—all of her. Her face was losing the post-birth puffiness and her eyes—finally, her eyes—they were open. They were round and black—expansive. Only three hours old and already, she was the center of the universe and all the stars in it. She looked like a new little person, with these long, spindly arms and skinny legs to match. Rae held her hand against her little feet; they measured the length of her pinky finger. She giggled until she saw it and then didn't giggle anymore.

"What's this prick on her foot?" Rae said, drawing her baby's foot closer to her face. A trickle of blood was stuck just beneath the skin on Skye's left foot.

The nurse, flipping through the paperwork and receipts Roman had just given her, looked up casually and then back down at the paperwork. "Oh, that's nothing."

"What . . . what do you mean nothing? I don't understand. Why was her foot pricked?"

Second Nurse, arranging a blanket in the crib in which she'd wheeled Skye into the room, barely lifted her head from her work. "That's from drug testing," she said.

"What?" both Roman and Rae exclaimed.

"Oh, it's nothing. It's administered randomly. We just take a little prick of blood to make sure the baby doesn't have any drugs in her system, in the event that the mother uses. It's so we can treat the baby."

"What about me makes you think I take drugs?" Rae asked, a look of horror darkening her face.

"Look, it's random, okay? That's it. We can't tell who in here may be on drugs and who isn't. This is about the babies, not your feelings," First Nurse snapped. "Now I see your papers are in order. If you don't have any other questions, I'm going to go and see to it that the room is arranged so we can move you into it."

"And the dinner, too?" Roman asked. "A brother is starving."

Both nurses looked at each other and walked on out without another word, as if Roman was not even there and his words were not even heard.

"I . . . I can't believe this," Rae said.

"Let it go," Roman insisted. "I get it, but let it go."

"But what gives them the right to just do that?" Rae insisted. "How is that okay? How is any of this okay?"

Rae held tight to her baby—laid her chest against her own and listened for her heartbeat, scared, angry. Feeling small. Powerless. She wasn't about to let this baby go, not knowingly, wittingly, as the hospital conspired to stamp her baby, her family, from its very inception. Even in the private room, where there were no more prying eyes and blank faces and the nurses forgot all about her and her child, stopping by only to drop off a goody bag of formula, baby powder, and a gang of coupons for baby items already overflowing in Skye's room back at their Brooklyn home, Rae held that baby tight, watching her breathe and sigh and sleep until she could no longer hold open her own eyes.

That's a pretty lil' baby.

And there was Tommy, standing in front of his closet at their family home, dressed in a new, elegant black suit, an equally debonair black duffel bag by his side. He'd always dressed up for travel, believing deeply that flying on a giant bird that soared through the heavens was a miracle—a luxury fashioned by the ingenuity of man for the enjoyment of those privileged to afford it. When he presented his airline ticket to an agent and boarded a flight, he meant to be seen. Respected. Invited in. And so, he dressed as such for the occasion.

Daddy?

I'm all right, baby. That's what you been wondering, right? I'm okay.

Where . . . where are you going? Rae asked, her eyes shifting from her father to the duffel bag and back to her father.

There's peace here.

Where? Daddy, where are you?

I'm right here. My grandbaby—she gone be somebody special. Like you. Give her sugar, and grits with butter. Take some for yourself, too. You gonna need them for your own journey, hear?

But I don't understand.

That's okay; you will. Now feed the baby.

Tommy pulled the folding closet doors shut and picked up his bag, and blew kisses at his daughter, cupping his hand in a way that made the sound of the series of kisses particularly pronounced.

Don't go, Daddy, please. Please, Daddy. Please don't go, Daddy. Come back. Come back! Come back! Rae said again and again, tears racing down her cheeks.

Her father's kisses grew louder, drowning out her pleas.

Skye wriggled and began to fuss, moving her head back and forth as she panted and whined. Rae felt that movement first, then a pulsating tingle in her nipples, but it took her a couple seconds to register her mother's lips on the side of her face, repeatedly and loudly kissing her by her ear—the same way she'd showered her with kisses since she was a little baby. Finally, Rae opened her eyes—confused about where she was, what was going on, why her face was wet, why her nipples were pulsing, why her mother was kissing her like she was a six-year-old.

Rae startled awake.

"Whoa, whoa, you got a baby on board," LoLo said quietly, resting her hand on the baby's back to steady her while she writhed on Rae's chest. "Be easy now."

Rae shook her head and blinked, trying to get her bearings. She saw her mother and TJ first, and then her baby, and then Roman, sitting in the same place he'd been sitting hours earlier, when she'd finally passed out from the excitement, work, and worry that came with pushing a human out of her loins. Slowly, it all came back to her. She was somebody's mama now. And her mama, she was there but her daddy was gone. The tug and pull of her heart made Rae's temples pound—like the whole of her insides were breaking.

Skye wailed. Rae did, too.

"Mommy," she called out, the sole word she could force between her sobs.

"I'm here," LoLo said. "I'm right here, daughter. I'm not going anywhere."

25

Rae stood outside the fourth-floor bathroom door at the Work Room Studios with her electric breast pump, the motor and components as big and cumbersome as a small but overstuffed carry-on suitcase. It had been a good three weeks since she'd been back to work, and nothing—none of it—felt right. Every day she kissed Roman and Skye goodbye and rushed out the door to catch the subway into Manhattan, weighed down with that machine and her guilt, her soul crushed just a little bit more with every step toward Park and Twenty-Third Street. She needed more time to love on and bond with Skye, to get used to this new life—this demand on her every waking hour and even the ones when she should have been asleep but couldn't get past the REM stage because sleeping deeply was a most impossible task when every one of her senses was beating to the rhythm of Skye's heartbeat. She was hungry and cried out for her mama's breast, and Rae was there. The baby peed or pooped or got a little gas trapped in her belly, Rae was up. She turned over in her crib and whimpered out just a little as she adjusted herself, and there was Rae, standing by the crib, rubbing her back, bouncing her in her arms, rocking her in the slider, singing "Ribbon in the Sky" until the baby fell back off into a deeper slumber—until thirty minutes or, if Rae were lucky, another hour or so passed, and Rae was there, rocking and singing and feeding and burping and shushing and saying, "There, there, now, baby girl. It's okay," until the night slipped into the day and the day became another mountain crest casting shadows where there should have been sun.

Rae had no choice in this matter. At least she didn't feel like she did. Every dime she'd saved up for what she'd thought would be a six-month maternity leave had to be put toward her father's funeral, a cost no one was ready to bear, and the only one in her house who actually had a steady paycheck to go back to after the baby was born was Rae and so back to work she went, hating every single thing about every moment of it: how she felt breastfeeding her baby in the morning, only to burp her and leave her; hating to pull out her checkbook at the end of the week to pay a babysitter to do what she should have been doing; hating to stand outside the fourth-floor bathroom holding that heavy-ass pump, her breasts pulsing and dripping milk, filled with anguish that she had to collect her baby's food in a room where people pissed, shit, farted, vomited, smoked; hating getting home, only to find that another woman had bathed her baby and rocked her to sleep and laid her down; hating that walking into her house after a long day at work felt like she was checking into a second and third shift at home, between getting dinner to the table and straightening up and laying her head down, finally for rest, only to wake back up every couple hours to feed Skye.

Rae fought back tears as she stood, exhausted and leaking, in the hallway in front of the bathroom, which was just across the hall from what was lovingly referred to by her colleagues as "The Bud Hut." It was a plush, well-appointed room filled with comfortable leather sofas and chairs, a coffee machine, a parade of posters of their show's hosts—all white boys save for one white woman—lining the walls and, of course, enough ash trays to accommodate every smoker from the Hamptons to Westchester.

"It blows that you don't have a dedicated place to get your baby's food together, but there's a whole-ass room dedicated to those fools killing themselves with cancer sticks," Rae's coworker Nimma said as she gently rubbed Rae's back.

Startled, Rae jumped and, realizing who had touched her, quickly wiped her tears. Nimma was a senior producer with seven years on Rae's four in the gig and, though they technically worked for different segments of the same show, Nimma was, for all intents and purposes, Rae's superior. In fact, it was Nimma who'd first interviewed Rae for her position, a job for which she'd been referred by a mentor she collected while working in one of the country's most coveted internships for minorities interested in television production. Rae thought her focused work in college—her producing prowess on the school's television news network had won the university equivalent of an Emmy every year except her sophomore one—was what got her that internship. It wasn't until she was sitting in front of Nimma, arguing about whether a television show with a Black host should celebrate what was considered "white" music, did she find out that her internship with Dale Studios wasn't as respected as Rae had thought.

"We used to clown the Dale program back in the day," Nimma had said matter-of-factly, right to Rae's face. She shuffled some papers on her desk then leaned back in her desk chair. "I mean, how good a program could it have been when it was only created to remedy an affirmative ac- tion lawsuit? Anybody who came through it was considered a mercy hire." Nimma leaned back toward her desk and took into her hands a piece of thick-stock paper—Rae's résumé. "You been on the move, though. Your work is impressive—definitely a head over the rest."

"Thank you," Rae said, unsure if she was being complimented or dissed.

"So, we're looking to shake things up a bit—hire a Black or Latina woman host and have her lead a new show that breaks outside the bounds of what we expect in a minority veejay. Basically, what I'm helping to de- sign is a show that celebrates 'the culture'" she said, making air quotes, "but that focuses on more than just rap and R&B. I'm talking a celebration of, say, Gwen Stefani and, like, Courtney Love, who I think are every bit a part of the culture as, say, Mary J. Blige and, like, SWV. How do you see yourself advancing that mission?"

Rae wrinkled her brow. "I don't," she snapped. She didn't mean to be so brash; Rae appreciated tact, more so than her young contemporaries, who tended to think showing up to an office dressed provocatively, be- friending celebrities, and throwing a good party that found its way to *Page Six* equaled a magic carpet ride to a top-floor office. Rae wasn't that girl; she worked hard, she kept her head down, she never mixed business with pleasure—not that she had time to anyway with a husband and a baby—and she could be a little corny, even, with her sensible clothes and comfortable shoes. The way she saw it, she was going to work, not the club, and her abilities—particularly her laser-sharp focus on highlighting the stories and cultures of marginalized communities—were an asset for any organization that would hire her, not something to be used to give more shine to the biggest stars in the entertainment universe.

"I'm sorry?" Nimma had said. "So, you don't see any use in a show that celebrates Gwen Stefani and Mary J.?"

"Actually, no," Rae quickly answered. "Gwen Stefani and Courtney and them are cool and all and I see the appeal, but so does everyone else—on every show on the MSK network. They already get coverage. Lots of it. I just think that if you're going to have a Black show, let it be a Black show, not another way to celebrate white artists wearing our culture like a coat they can put on when the temperature changes and take off when they don't need it anymore."

The two spent another ten minutes arguing back and forth on the topic before Nimma abruptly ended the interview with a curt, "Okay, um, so, we're looking to make this hire quickly. Someone will get back to you, I guess."

"Oh . . . um . . . okay," Rae said. She picked up her things and dragged herself out of that office with her head hung low, sure she'd talked her way right out of a good job. But not two days later, Nimma called her with a package in hand. Rae would later find out that her mentor stood in the gap, pulling the coattails of Nimma's boss—warning him that he was "about to lose the best young producer your deep pockets can buy." That guy turned around and told Nimma that if she couldn't convince Rae to accept the job, she was fired. Rae started working there a month later.

The intensity between the two dissipated just as quickly as it had built; such was life in a work office where four out of some thirty employees were Black, and one of the four cleaned the toilets, while another answered the phones for the executive producer. Rae and Nimma quickly figured out how to get along.

"Come on, Rae, get your head in the game," Arthur, her supervisor, said at the pitch meeting, Rae's first. His voice was slightly elevated; he paced back and forth in front of a huge dry-erase board on which he was scrawling in navy-blue marker the names of guests he agreed were worthy of being interviewed on the show. Rae, overprepared, anxious, had spent fifteen minutes in the women's bathroom, practicing her pitches in the mirror while flipping through color-coordinated Post-it Notes in a pile of *Vibe, XXL, Source,* and *Essence* magazines she'd marked up as research for what she planned to pitch. She couldn't concentrate while she studied, though—not really. Images of her boss, standing in front of a white piece of paper, tapping the word "TLC" with a marker kept creeping into her head. Now, here he was, standing in front of a white board, with a blue marker in hand, yelling at her. Rae sat gape-jawed, just shy of the middle of the conference table, which stretched thirty seats deep in the glass room referred to as the "Fish Bowl." Nimma and she were two specks of pepper in a cauliflower stew. All eyes were on her.

Rae cleared her throat and adjusted herself in her seat. Arthur didn't like Brownstone. Noted. But how was Jodeci a miss worthy of a verbal clap? What was wrong with an in-depth look into why TLC, one of the biggest girl groups in history, was running around claiming they were broke? Rae ran her finger down her notes and flipped through her magazines, her mind blank, a little weirded out by the déjà vu doing a shimmy in front of her eyes.

"Anyone else?" Arthur asked gruffly, throwing his hands up in frustration.

"Actually, I think the TLC story has legs," Nimma chimed in, swiveling her chair toward the front of the room to look at Arthur directly as she took him on. Rae stopped shuffling her papers and cocked her head to the side as she stared at her colleague. On the inside, she was all cartwheels and pom-poms, excited, grateful Nimma was going to run the ball. On the outside, she was pulling her button-down shirt a little tighter around her chest and fumbling with her pen, wondering why this woman was throwing herself on a sword clearly meant for a woman she didn't seem to care for. "They're loved by a whole generation and not just urban Black kids," Nimma continued. "They're pretty, they make good music that really sells. And they have some real heavyweights in their corner. Their bankruptcy is the talk of the industry right now. We can pull video, get their manager and some of their celebrity producers to talk about the music, talk about their personal relationships, their financial decisions. Lisa and her explosive choices. You know I don't really listen to R&B, but the TLC-going-broke story has legs."

Nimma smiled at Arthur. Turned her head and gave a quick wink to Rae, who answered it with a nod and a small smile.

"Hey," Rae called out to Nimma as the group filed out of the Fish Bowl almost two hours later. They all looked like a ragtag army unit that had employed hand-to-hand combat in a battle they weren't meant to win and barely did. "Thanks for that back there."

"No sweat. It was a good idea," she said. "I don't even like TLC like that."

"So, what do you like?" Rae asked. "I mean, you really all Team Gwen Stefani and Madonna?"

"What, I don't look like I should like their kind of music?" asked Nimma. She followed Rae into the bathroom and stood in the mirror as she pulled a scrunchy out of her pocket and tied her shoulder-length braids atop her head in a messy bun. Her skin, a deep brown with red undertones, was smooth and pretty, even more so when she smiled and her ultra-white teeth shined against it.

Rae shrugged and chuckled.

"*Yo soy Dominicana*," Nimma said. "Born in D. R., raised in the Bronx. "I'm all about the merengue; I like rock, pop, a little jazz. I just love music."

"But just not Black music," Rae said.

"I like all music," Nimma said gently. "Listen," she said, turning to face Rae, "I know we didn't get off to the best start in your interview, but we all we got up in here. You're a good producer. But you won't get anywhere with Arthur if you don't mix it up a little. You can't give him a plate of collard greens when all he wants to eat is burgers, *tu entiendes?*"

Rae wrinkled her brow.

Nimma laughed. "You understand?"

"Yeah." Rae laughed. "I get it."

In the four years that she'd been at WRS, Rae and Nimma had become a team of sorts, strategizing on how to game the system to get what they wanted, but doing it in such a way that would guard them from accusations that they'd formed some kind of Black alliance against their white counterparts. Any allusions of such would have been a fool's bet they could never win, and they both liked their jobs and eating too much to lose either. Still, they looked out for each other.

Nimma was doing just that when she saw Rae fiddling in front of the bathroom with her clunky breast pump in her hand, hesitating to venture in.

"It's . . . it's okay. I'm just going to get in there and be quick about it. Spike's script is pretty much done; I just have a few more things to add, but I need to, um . . ." Rae looked down at her Notorious B.I.G. T-shirt, and shifted her Adidas sweat jacket just a smidge. Breast milk was leaking through two breast pads and her padded maternity bra, straight to Biggie's forehead.

"Nah, I get it—don't apologize. I pumped in my car back when my baby was first born," Nimma said. "Right out there in the street. Everybody got a show, but it was better than gathering baby boy's milk in that funky-ass bathroom."

Rae wiped another tear and hung her head, feeling guilty for pumping in there rather than employing the same kind of ingenuity for her own child.

"I know a better place," Nimma said, smiling and rubbing Rae's arm. "Come with me."

A quick elevator ride and stroll down a series of halls on the sixth floor led to an empty conference room with a small side office, replete with an old school projector, a couple piles of random boxes, and two chairs. It smelled like weed.

"I know it's not fancy, but this used to be the 'Bud Hut' until a couple guys from the mailroom got busted getting high in here during their break. Nobody comes in here anymore. Just close the door and push a couple boxes against it to be sure. Definitely cleaner than the bathroom."

"Mos def," Rae said, looking around. She pulled the chair closer to the electrical outlet and swiped the seat with her hand.

"Okay, let me let you get to it," Nimma said, clapping her hands together and shifting herself to the room's entrance. "See you back downstairs, okay?"

"Nimma," Rae said. "I appreciate you. Thank you."

"It's all good," she said. "We moms gotta stick together, right?"

LoLo had taught Rae that when one is desperate, you look past what is ugly, what needs fixing, what isn't quite right, and instead focus on the bones of the thing: How do you make this habitable, pretty, even? How do you make this work? LoLo was a master of such things—of turning nothing into something. Where Rae saw a tattered scrap of fabric, LoLo saw the possibility of a new pillow cover for the living room sofa; where Rae saw Tommy turning up his nose at the price tags of the fancy grills favored by their neighbors, LoLo saw a pile of bricks in the construction aisle and, on the back of an envelope she pulled from her purse, she designed a monument to fire, charcoal, and smoked meats that she convinced Tommy he could build all on his own. "We can make our own fire, baby," she'd told him, tapping her rudimentary drawing with her pen. "Cheaper but better."

But LoLo didn't suffer fools, and she was quick to cut, which always seemed to leave Rae equal parts fascinated, inspired, and deeply embarrassed. Take, for instance, Carolyn, this girl at church who'd spent her fifteen years coming up on the rough side of the mountain and taking out her displeasure with it all on Rae. The girl didn't like "Goody Two-shoes," and Rae, well, in Carolyn's mind, had a closet that runneth over with the things Carolyn found most offensive: good grades, academic accolades, leadership positions in both school and church, admiration of adults. So, every chance she got, Carolyn made Rae suffer for it—pinched her through her choir robe as they made their way up the dark stairwell leading to the choir stand behind the pulpit, repeatedly tripped her as the two made their way to the hamburger table at the church summer revival and festival, so she looked like a fool in front of Len Bethencourt, the boy Rae fantasized about when she was all alone with her thoughts, down in the basement, singing Whitney Houston songs into the turkey baster, pretending she was singing to him. Carolyn knew Rae's weaknesses and preyed on them, satisfied only when she coaxed a quiver from Rae's bottom lip, or, even better, watery eyes. She got away with her bullying for the longest time, too, until the one day when LoLo just happened to be on usher duty, standing at the precise angle just beyond Carolyn's right back shoulder to give her full view of Carolyn kicking the shit out of Rae's legs under the church pew.

"Carolyn Sheff," LoLo whisper-yelled, low enough to keep from disturbing the reading of the church announcements, but definitely loud enough for everyone within a two-pew radius to shift their entire bodies in the direction of LoLo's voice. The tone made clear that somebody—that somebody being Carolyn—was in big trouble. "Come here," LoLo continued, the anger in her eyes matching the sternness laying all over her words. "Rae, you, too," she added.

Carolyn sucked her teeth and took her time pushing herself up from the pew, a wooden affair that groaned when she stood on account that it had been built by the hands of St. John's Baptist Church's forty-three original members some eighty years before. She pushed right past LoLo, grazing her chest as she headed toward the double-doored vestibule, her mouth twisted all up on the side of her face. Rae stood daintily, quietly. "Excuse me . . . I'm sorry . . . Excuse me . . . ," she begged as she stumbled and stepped on her fellow parishioners' feet, moving toward the side aisle. She crunched down on the inside of her cheek, but, alas, it couldn't hold back her tears, which grew hot behind the thought of what awaited her in the basement.

LoLo rushed both girls down the steps, down the hall, past the kitchen, and back toward the bathroom—where Rae especially didn't want to go because rough things went down at the hands of Black mothers in public bathrooms and LoLo was no exception to this practice: you could get threatened through furled lips, pinched, slapped across the face so hard the smacking sound would make a sick acoustic bouncing off the tiles. Rae had seen it plenty enough times, as TJ stayed getting hauled to a bathroom. But Rae, she wanted no part of it—especially on this day, as she did a death march behind her bully and her angry mother.

"Let me tell you something," LoLo said as she corralled Rae and Carolyn into the three-stall bathroom. It smelled of Pine-Sol and bleach, like it had been scrubbed by ten deaconesses and the ancestors. LoLo whipped Rae around and pointed at her white tights; on the calves were two brown dirt marks, looking like skids across Rae's legs. The marks matched the dirt beneath Carolyn's shoes. "What you won't ever do again is put your feet on my child, do you understand? I need you to really roll the words coming out of my mouth around your head, hear? Because if I ever see you kicking, slapping, touching, or even looking at Rae again, I will pull you in this bathroom and beat your ass. And I'll tell your mama exactly why I did it so she can get you, too."

Carolyn stood, defiant. LoLo, pissed but controlled, leaned into the girl's face. "Am. I. Clear," she said. It wasn't a question.

"Yes," Carolyn mumbled.

"I didn't hear you," LoLo snarled.

"Yes, ma'am," Carolyn said, more loudly, her eyes downcast. She looked remorseful, but Rae wasn't convinced, having been on the receiving end of that girl's bullying since the day LoLo, excited to be back at her home church, made Rae join the Sunshine Choir. She and Carolyn were altos.

"Now get on back up there to the sanctuary and get you some Jesus," LoLo said, as she watched Carolyn scoot through the bathroom door.

Rae stood there, waiting for LoLo to direct her attention to her, half expecting to get, at the very least, yelled at for allowing Carolyn to kick and torture her and just taking it. But LoLo, perhaps feeling the spirit of the Lord and maybe a little guilt for threatening a child in His house, shared a lesson instead.

"She's a good person, she just angry at the world because her daddy ain't home and her mother is struggling with all those kids," LoLo said as she picked at Rae's curls and adjusted the collar of her dainty white church sweater. "Some people got things going on that make them act out and become someone other than who they really are. I'm not telling you you have to put up with their shit, but I think Jesus would want us to make room for people's broken pieces."

When grown-up, Jesus-learned, LoLo-raised Rae walked back into her house after nine long hours on the job and a forty-minute subway ride home, her breasts so full of milk it felt like she was carrying small boulders on her chest, she wasn't thinking about anybody's broken pieces and what was the catalyst for the breaking points; Rae just wanted to get through the front door and bury her nose in her baby's neck.

But there was the nanny, posted up on the couch, arms folded, scowling as she stared at her three-year-old twirling in circles around the living room floor. Skye was in the bassinet close by, fussing and working her way to a cry, the sound of which made Rae's breasts let down. The milk spilled into the already soggy breast pads that had been catching Rae's breastmilk all the day long. Roman was nowhere in sight.

"Listen, it was a long day and I'm mad emotional right now," Ronica said as she tapped her foot. She didn't bother getting up from the sofa, much less grab the baby while Rae put down her things. Rae moved a bunch of dirty dishes and a pack of thawed chicken to one side of the kitchen sink so that she could wash her hands.

"Oh?" was all Rae could muster as she watched Ronica's rambunctious little son whip across the wood floor. Rae was unclear why the little boy was in her house and not with his grandmother, who, for the five weeks Ronica had been caring for Skye, kept the boy while his mother worked.

"Hmmhmm. I got word today that Cordell's daddy got himself a side girlfriend and wouldn't you know she work down at the bank just down the way," Ronica said, waving her hand in no particular direction. "I asked my mother to drop Cordell to me for my lunch break, so that I could go over and let the girl know he already has a family he's responsible for. He ain't got no more time for her to be prancing in his face."

Rae eyeballed the chicken and dirty dishes as she unbuttoned her shirt. Skye cried out. Rae's breasts were a milk fountain.

"Now, let's see what she thinks about that the next time she tries getting with somebody's man, somebody's daddy," Ronica said, standing up and wiping wrinkles out of her linen top.

Rae picked up Skye and kissed her face as she headed to the glider in the baby's room. Ronica picked up her son and followed behind her.

"Look, uh, I'm going to need to come in a little late tomorrow, and I'll need to bring my son when I do come in," Ronica continued. Cordell watched as Skye whined and hungrily rooted for her mother's breast before finding the nipple and latching on. Rae was too tired and her baby was too hungry for her to reach for a clean diaper to drape over her exposed breast, but she was uncomfortable, nonetheless, with the way the little boy was fixating on the whole affair. It took Rae a minute to actually hear what Ronica had just put down. "So that's okay, right? Because I have to run my mother to the doctor for a medical procedure and she won't be able to watch Cordell. She's gonna need to rest and I don't have a backup plan."

With one boob relieved, Rae could finally focus on the words coming out of Ronica's mouth. "I, um . . . did you talk to Roman about this?" she asked. And then: "Wait, where is Roman?"

"Oh, he, uh, went out to the park or something to write," she said, as Cordell struggled from her arms and shimmied down her leg. He scooted himself over to a basket nesting atop a wooden toy chest at the foot of the queen-size bed that had been the centerpiece of the room before it was converted into a nursery and filled with all the things that colored Skye's world—Black baby dolls, a mound of books, a wall border of black-and-white photos of all the people who love her, a free-standing closet full of fancy little dresses and lace socks and shiny baby shoes, so much of it picked special by LoLo's hand. Cordell promptly pulled down an entire basket full of CDs.

"Cordell!" Ronica yelled, the shrill of her voice startling Skye so badly she stopped slurping and breathing. The baby's scream-cry, which quickly followed, was a siren, low in the beginning, a crescendo to screech at its most robust. Ronica, oblivious to Rae and Skye but laser-focused on Cordell, raised her right hand high and swiped her child; he slammed down onto the floor and went flying a few inches across wood. "Girl, let me get out of here," Ronica said, grabbing her son by his arm and swooping him upright. "If you could tell Mr. Lister I'll be late, that would be great."

Her hands full with a crying baby and a fountain of milk literally spraying from her breasts, Rae said not a word—focusing, instead, on calming her baby and getting her breast back into the child's mouth, for both of their relief. She most certainly heard Cordell screaming all the way down the hallway, though. And just when she got the baby settled and back into the rhythm, Roman slammed the front door upon his arrival, giving Skye and Rae another start that led to another fit.

"Hey!" he said cheerily, walking into the room with his work bag slung over his shoulder. He bent down and kissed the baby's cheek and then Rae's and stood there as the two fussed and struggled to get settled again. As Rae adjusted the baby onto her second breast, Roman reached down and gave the flesh of Rae's unencumbered breast a little squeeze.

"Roman, come on," Rae said, annoyed, as Skye slurped.

"What? Come on, now, those were mine before they were hers. Can you blame a brother? They just sitting up right."

"Can you focus on being helpful? How about you give me a cloth diaper from the basket under the changing table."

It wasn't always this way. Used to be she'd have to shift in her seat a little to settle that thing that made her body vibrate at the mere thought of Roman's touch. He was sexy and confident, interesting and interested, and Rae was eager to please—satiate. Her enthusiasm was met with equal passion, and together, they would feed, any time, any place. This is what young love bred—lust, hot and fresh and sweet. The two were always hungry. The two always ate.

And then there was the baby, eating what had been her parents' portions. Roman had begun to starve. Rae had no more food to give.

"Hello, Roman, how was your day? Oh, it was good. I went to the park and made some headway on my book outline and came up with two stories to pitch to *Time* magazine," Roman said, holding with himself the conversation he seemingly wished for—nay, expected to have—with his wife.

Rae rocked in the glider and patted Skye's bottom as she suckled. She just didn't have it in her to argue with this man—not today. Not after the day she'd had. Not after the day her baby had had. "I'm glad you had a good writing day," she said quietly.

"I did. Getting out of the house and writing in the park shook up some things, you know? I just took a sandwich and a couple sodas and got to it."

"Wait, so you weren't here when Ronica took her lunch break?"

"Nah, I was writing," Roman said as he rooted around the basket for the cloth diaper. "I was in such a groove. She doesn't mind taking her lunch with the baby. Skye was probably sleep anyway."

Rae wrinkled her brow and dropped her jaw as the picture slowly unfolded: while Roman was in the park, communing with nature and scribbling notes on his legal pads, Ronica had Skye in the middle of her mess.

"But that means she took my baby with her to the bank!"

Roman, having secured the cloth diaper, walked it over to Rae. "Okay," he said slowly. "Aaaand? She had an errand; she took the baby with her."

"It wasn't just some errand, Roman! She just told me that she hauled her kid to the bank to pick a fight with some chick having sex with her son's father."

"For real?" Roman said, half laughing. "Wow. Ronica's wild!"

"That's all you have to say? 'Ronica's wild'?"

"What else is there to say, Rae? She was on her break. I can't control what she does when she should be eating a sandwich."

"But you can control being a father to our child and watching her while the nanny takes her lunch break, which, might I add, is her right and a part of her agreement for babysitting while you hang out in the park all day," Rae yelled. "Let me ask you this: What if the girl at the bank got into a fight with Ronica, and our baby was there in the middle of all of that? What if she would have gotten arrested for causing a scene or threatening that lady and the police had to take Skye to the police station or called child services? Why would you allow her to take our kid into the middle of that madness?"

"I didn't allow anything, Rae!"

"Oh, right. Because you were in the park writing the outline for the next great American novel. Roger that."

"What's that supposed to mean?" he yelled.

Rae could not answer him because at that precise moment, the baby chomped down on her nipple. Hard. So very hard. The way she'd always done when the breastmilk flowed across tongue and down throat, through belly and all the rest, and she got this demonic look in her little eyes and grunted and, like some miniature volcanic eruption, pushed out a poo that defied the boundaries of her diaper, spreading up her onesie, up to the folds of her neck and the curls on her nape and all over Rae's jeans and Biggie shirt.

"Fuck!" Rae yelled as Skye latched back onto her breast and resumed slurping.

"Oh wow," Roman said, moving closer and peeking over the mound of baby on Rae's lap to get a bird's-eye view of the explosion.

"I just . . . ," Rae began.

"Here, let me get you some more diapers."

"I don't need diapers, I need help!"

"I am helping," Roman said simply.

"You call giving me a diaper to clean up help?" Rae yelled. And that's all it took—that one declaration, matter-of-fact and devoid of emotion, much less understanding, piled up on top of the dirty dishes in the sink, the uncooked chicken sitting on the counter, the mess of stuffed animals and CDs splayed on the floor, the crazy nanny she paid almost 40 percent of her salary to put her baby in danger so that her unemployed husband could do what he wanted to do, the warm baby poop showered all over all the things—to break her. Rae burst into tears and reached for the closest thing her hands could touch—a little lamp on the side table next to the glider—and slammed it against the wall. "Fuck!"

"Are you out your mind?" Roman asked, his voice still even-keeled, calm.

Roman was a decent guy—smart, engaging, handsome, loving, with potential. Those good bones. Rae had picked through his flaws to get down to the meat, and over the course of the four years they'd been together, this is what she focused on. Loving those parts. But his broken pieces—all of the broken pieces—were becoming too heavy for Rae to bear, especially as she struggled with her own.

26

1979, in the summertime

There was a little TV on the thick, circular, wooden kitchen table—played cartoons at breakfast time, the stories on summer afternoons, and the news and game shows, mostly, at dinner time. That was Rae and TJ's company growing up—*The Transformers*, *General Hospital*, and *Live at Five*. There were no family meals, not even on Sundays. LoLo would come in from work and cook dinner and fix the plates, sure, but it wasn't lost on Rae that always, after she'd stood over that hot stove and made miracles out of franks and beans or a little piece of fatback with a salmon cake or two and a scoop of buttered grits, LoLo would pour herself a Diet Pepsi with a whole lot of ice, break off a little piece of paper towel, and take herself and her plate back into her room, back where she could be alone with her television shows and her uninterrupted thoughts. There was no help with homework; she wasn't about to solve for X or run anybody through the periodic table of elements or read some history paper on some dead white man who robbed and pillaged and was being celebrated on the page. She cooked, she ate, she watched a little TV, she took a hot bath, she popped a few pills to help her deal with pain and get to sleep, and it was door closed, lights out by 9:00 P.M., every single night, no exceptions.

Rae took this personal. She wanted her mother—wanted to sit and talk to her about everything and nothing, to lay herself at her mother's feet and get to know her not as the lady who cooked the food and jogged for Jesus every Sunday and tucked herself into the back room during meals, but as a person, a human being, a woman. LoLo guarded that part of herself, though—made Rae believe she'd have to traverse a rickety footbridge, swim an alligator moat, and fight a fire-breathing dragon to truly see her, to truly lay eyes on her heart. At some point—Rae couldn't really put her finger on when, but it was relatively early in her childhood—she'd even come to the heartrending conclusion that her mother didn't really like her, didn't really like kids at all. It was a tough realization for a child to bear, even as an adult who was slowly coming to understand the challenges of being Black and woman and wife and mother and all the other things that picked humanness down to the quick.

If he wasn't working and at the house, Tommy would take his plate and a Schlitz downstairs where some manner of sports would be playing on the TV. TJ, well, he would bury his face in his plate and scarf down whatever was there, never once lifting it until the black-and-white-flecked ceramic dish was damn near licked clean. "Take human bites!" Tommy once yelled at TJ when he happened to witness the carnage. But TJ, he was undeterred. His sole goal was to shovel as much food into his mouth as could fit as quickly as time would allow, so that he could move on to other things, like riding his bike or chasing after some girl—anything but getting caught sitting at that table when LoLo came back into the kitchen, her own plate empty, ordering whoever she saw first to put away the leftovers and wash up the dishes. "I cooked," she'd say. "I'll be damned if I'm cleaning up this kitchen, too—not with two big-ass kids in this house." Somehow, though, it was mostly on Rae's shoulders that the duty fell.

Some of it—especially the part where LoLo began grooming Rae for kitchen duty—Rae didn't mind. She'd be tucked away in her room, nose deep in some book she hauled on her weekly mile-and-a-half walk to the library, and LoLo would get to slamming those pots against the counters and the gas stove top and the smell of chopped onions and ham hocks simmering on the stove would get the house smelling like Sunday and next thing, Rae was peeping around the kitchen corner, looking. At what was in the pots. What was at the end of her mother's fingertips—her big, sharp knife and some yams, perhaps, or a box of Mueller's elbows being poured into a cauldron of boiling water with just a tip of vegetable oil. If she was in the mood—and she usually was—she would invite Rae to join her, but not in a bossy way. In a "come spend time with Mommy" way, which always, always, made Rae a little tingly.

"Go on 'head and get out them blocks of cheese," LoLo would say, tossing her chin toward the refrigerator. She never smiled, but Rae felt her mother's warmth all the same. She'd learned to read LoLo's moods by the timbre of her voice—where her shoulders sat in relation to her ears. Rough, sharp LoLo with the shoulders grazing her signature hoops was the mommy Rae cowered from—the one who made Rae seek out quiet corners, her daddy's arms. Smooth, light LoLo, with shoulders anchoring waving hands announcing her excitement, her want to be in this room at this time, was the mommy Rae liked to watch, for this mommy was rare and only revealed herself in front of girlfriends and Bible scriptures and hallelujahs in the front pews—the one who inspired the best parts of the little girl who looked up to her mother. Flat, smooth LoLo with the relaxed shoulders, that mommy was Rae's favorite. She let Rae in.

"Here you go," LoLo would say, reaching down into the bottom cabinet for the cheese grater. "We gone make some macaroni and cheese for tomorrow's supper. You remember how to do it, right?" And she'd grab one of the hunks of cheese—cheddar sharp, cheddar extra sharp, cheddar mild—and scrape it across the metal, bearing her weight down, pursing her lips, sometimes biting the bottom one as she concentrated, her movements deft, deliberate. "Now you try."

Rae would take that hunk of cheese into her hands, smaller and fatter than her mother's, whose were gnarly and thin with long nails that were solid and hardly ever broke, and she would try to move quickly, deliberately, too. She'd even try to do her mouth like her mother's. But she never could move as swiftly as LoLo. Rae didn't mind, though. Neither did LoLo.

"Now come over here and let me show you how to do the roux," she'd say. Like she hadn't shown Rae a thousand times already, but this, Rae didn't mind either, because a teaching LoLo was a kind LoLo, too. "Crack your eggs in there and whip 'em around, but not too much," she'd say, handing Rae one egg and then another and a few more until the yellow globs filled the bottom of the bowl. "Now, you take your milk and you pour it in," she'd say, watching close as Rae measured out the liquid that would make up the base of the creamy goodness all up and between the macaroni elbows. "That's enough. Right there, you see?" LoLo would point. "That's enough for that size pan," she would add, pointing at the eleven-by-nine-inch ceramic dish she favored for her mac and cheese. "Now shake your salt and your pepper on in there."

"How you do this so easy?" Rae would ask as she whipped the fork in the liquid, just like her mother taught her to do that time and the time before that and before that, still. Her whip never incorporated all the ingredients like her mother's did; there would be whole eggs floating to the top of the milk, big patches of pepper, slimy and stubborn.

"Been making it for a long time," LoLo would say, gently taking the fork from Rae's hands and perfecting the mixing. "You do it enough times and it gets as easy as brushing your teeth or folding a towel. Your hands just know what to do."

"Your mommy taught you how to make this?"

LoLo's silence would hide behind the whir of the fork against the glass bowl—behind her front teeth, biting down on her lip. Finally: "I missed out on learning a whole lot of things from my mama because she died when I was little. But I remember how to make her macaroni and cheese. Her lemon pound cake, too—you know the one. You got to be quiet while it's cooking or it'll fall down and get hard on you. I remember that."

"Did she cook on Sunday mornings like you do?"

It would go on like this, Rae asking her mother questions. To get information. Clarity. Most of all, engagement.

"My mother cooked every day. She made good eggs in the morning. Scrambled, sometimes with a little piece of ham or some fried fatback. I liked the eggs most of all."

"I like it on Sunday mornings when I'm dreaming about your food," Rae said. "Sometimes, I dream that I'm running through the woods with a wolf, looking for meat. And then I wake up and you're in the kitchen cooking roast beef. I smell it in my dreams."

"That's a really specific dream," LoLo said.

"I have a lot of dreams . . ." Rae hesitated, then added: "They're like that. Like a dream but real, too."

"Hmm," was all LoLo said. She was distracted, floating off somewhere distant as she conducted this orchestra of boiling pots and pouring ingredients and the chopping of things. Rae, recognizing the retreat, would stand by, taking the orders, completing the tasks. Grateful for this version of her mother and whatever she was willing to give.

By age twelve, the responsibility of cooking the family meals on weekdays when LoLo worked became Rae's in its entirety. "Take that chicken out the freezer" was almost as standard a final message from LoLo as her good-byes as she descended down the stairs to go to the factory. Rae knew better than to forget and learned quickly that her mother expected dinner to be on the stove and almost complete by the time she walked back up those stairs in the early evening.

By thirteen, Rae was doing the family laundry, too—washing, folding, ironing, lugging the clean clothes up to everyone's room. TJ managed to skirt this responsibility quite cleverly one Friday night when it was his turn to iron his parents' work uniforms, fresh and still warm from the load of lights he'd laundered after school. Jimmy "Superfly" Snuka was on the TV, center ring with some man's neck wedged between his knee and the crook of his arm; Rae was perched on the couch, reading *A Little Princess* for the fourth time, but completely enthralled like it was her first. She sniffed, wrinkled her face. Sniffed again, looked up. Caught sight of TJ mashing the iron into the lapel of their mother's light blue work smock, just to the right where her name was embroidered in fancy script beneath the words ESTÉE LAUDER, a reminder that it was and always would be corporate over employee. Steam rose from the fabric. So, too, did smoke.

"Ooooooooooooooh!" Rae sang, her voice a crescendo against the announcer screaming into his microphone about the whooping Snuka was putting on his opponent. "You're burning Mommy's uniform!"

TJ kept staring at the television and then turned his gaze to his sister. He left the iron on the lapel as his eyes shifted, long after Rae announced his mistake, and then looked down at the uniform as he pressed all his weight into the fire-hot metal pushing into the scored fabric, signaling that what he was doing wasn't a mistake at all.

By this time in her short thirteen years on earth, Rae had grown beyond getting scared for TJ when their mother entered the room. Used to be she'd see LoLo beating TJ in her dreams and she would smell something rancid in her nostrils—what, when she was littler, she imagined death must smell like. Whenever LoLo got a hold of TJ, little Rae would crumble under the weight of being a witness—would think that, surely, this time, her nightmare would be real and not just something that had rang the death knell in her dream, and TJ would be gone from here and their mother would be in big trouble. Bigger Rae thought TJ had it coming. On the occasion of his ruining LoLo's work attire, Rae didn't even flinch this time when LoLo rushed down the stairs, saw a massive brown and black flaky burn mark on her uniform, and slapped spit out of TJ's mouth.

"What the hell you doing, boy? I got to pay twenty-five dollars to replace that. Is you out your mind?"

"Sorry," TJ said through his fingers, which were rubbing his offended cheek.

"And why the hell is my blue smock damn near pink?" LoLo asked. She grabbed the smock off the ironing board and spun around in circles, looking for the load from which it came. On the second sofa, over on the back wall beneath the window, there it was, haphazardly folded, the lot of the pile of yellow, light blue, light green, and off-white clothes with a tint of pink to them, no doubt inked by the red sweater TJ had added to that load of wash.

"Boy, get the hell away from my clothes," LoLo said. She popped TJ on the back of his head as he rushed past her. The smirk he tossed in Rae's direction was unmistakable.

The older the two got, the less complicated was the math in the division of labor between them; TJ's sole responsibilities were to take out the garbage and make sure his room was clean. That was it. Rae, meanwhile, had mastered dusting, vacuuming, fluffing, mopping, and sanitizing the bathroom and such by age fifteen, in addition to all prior responsibilities, and her mother wielded Rae's work ethic like a sword against her; every weekend, LoLo would declare that Rae couldn't go to this party or hang out at the skating rink with her friends until her chores were completed. Her chores were never completed. "After you finish wiping down the furniture, come get this mop," LoLo would yell from her bed, where she'd be lying, legs crossed, remote in hand, pillows fluffed. "After you finish mopping, come in here and straighten out these drawers."

The chores also never were TJ's responsibility—just as they were never Tommy's. All things house—those fell on LoLo's shoulders, and Rae, well, she carried them when LoLo didn't feel like it, sending a singular, powerful message: this was women's work.

Rae didn't question it then. And she hadn't questioned it when she and Roman first started dating and, later, living together. In fact, she took pride in being the homemaker of her friends—the one who stuck by that old "the quickest way to a man's heart" adage and scored the guy. It worked for LoLo. She got a great guy. Oh, how Rae squared her shoulders and smiled all prim the first time she showed up to Roman's apartment with an armful of groceries and a bottle of champagne and made her way to his kitchen.

"You just sit down and relax," she said, dropping the bags on the counter.

"How can I help?" Roman asked as he deposited the champagne into the refrigerator. "Don't get it twisted: ya boy can make a mean bowl of angel hair with clam sauce."

"Mmm . . . that's not what I had in mind," Rae said, giggling. She puckered and leaned into Roman's lips, slipped him tongue. Wrapped her arms around his neck and pressed her body close to his. Closer.

"Whoa, now this is my kinda cooking!" Roman said, pulling back his face just enough to get out his words.

"Oh, don't you worry. I do enjoy your dessert," Rae said, wiping her lipstick off her boyfriend's lips. "But first . . . ," she said, turning to the grocery bags and tapping them with her palm, "chicken. Gotta make sure my man is fed."

"All right now. You won't get any arguments out of me. I like chicken."

"I know you do," Rae said, laughing.

Everything she needed to complete her dinner of fried chicken, rice, and fresh, country-style string beans was in the bag, and in no time, she was massaging the legs and thighs with seasoning salt and garlic powder and flour and snapping the string beans and washing the starch off the rice. And when she dropped that chicken in the hot oil and it got to sizzling and the smell of that skin browning rose up to the heavens and filled that house with what Rae counted, surely, as love, Rae knew. She knew.

"Damn, that smells so good, babe," Roman said, kissing her on her neck as she flipped the chicken in the pan and poured a tip of bacon grease into the string beans. "My house ain't never smelled like this before. It's Thanksgiving on a Tuesday up in here! My mother's gonna love you."

"Oh?" Rae asked, turning from the pan to press her chest against Roman's. "Is this me getting an invitation to meet the lovely Mrs. Lister?"

"She's definitely pushing to put the face to the name. There's only so much more I can tell her about you before she books a flight and comes to see you for herself," Roman said.

"You've told her about me?"

Roman's kiss was a pillow. "I talk about you to her all the time," he said. "She knows a good one when she sees one."

"Do you?"

"Hell yeah," Roman said. "Gloria Lister taught me."

"What do you mean?"

Roman buried his face in Rae's neck. "You know my parents been married for almost fifty years," he said as he carefully placed soft pecks on Rae's skin. "That's Jim Crow, the Civil Rights Movement, a couple wars, the Wu-Tang Clan. Their marriage survived all that. They're taking 'for better or worse, 'til death do us part' real serious, and that means something to me, too, you know. My mom holds it down. Dad's a good dude, but when it comes down to it, she's the one who made the family work. I respect that, and it's something I think I'm ready for. I see that in you."

"The Wu-Tang Clan?" Rae asked. She just laughed and laughed.

"Got 'im," she later told her homegirls Treva and Mal. The three of them were no different from every other twenty-something their age, weaned on Terry McMillan novels, living out their *Love Jones*/Nina Mosley fantasies, looking to let somebody be the blues in their left thigh and the funk in their right.

"What you mean you got him?" Treva asked, looking up from her menu to survey the surrounding tables at The Shark, the popular haunt they and every other young, single Black woman with a decent career and a deafening ticking biological clock went to see and be seen by the city's most eligible Black bachelors. Per usual, the tables were full of girlfriends, scant on what they all were searching for: handsome men, dressed nice, about something, looking to make some kind of connection beyond a simple, effortless sexual encounter.

"I mean, I threw it on him," Rae said, smiling as she took a sip of wine.

"Let me guess, you cooked for him," Mal said, adjusting herself in her seat.

Rae laughed.

"You know she did," Treva said, laughing. "What you cook? You did the fried chicken, didn't you? These Negroes are defenseless against it, I promise you that. She be in the kitchen cooking like somebody's church aintee."

Mal rolled her eyes and took a sip of her cosmo. "I know it. She done fed every Negro from Flushing to the South Bronx, and what she get beside a sink full of dirty dishes?"

"Hey, I like cooking," Rae insisted. "I grew up watching my mother feed my daddy and I know he appreciates that she takes care of him, and he returns the favor by taking care of her. They been married almost thirty years. She must have been doing something right to get that good man. That's all I'm saying. It's the fried chicken and the mac and cheese," she said, giggling. Rae put her hand up for a high five and Treva happily obliged.

"I'm just saying, what's special about this dude beyond that he likes your food?" Mal asked, folding her arms as she waited for an answer.

Rae sighed. "God, why you so negative?" she asked, shaking her head. "Roman is a good guy. He's got a good job, he's educated, he's sweet to me. I'm just saying, if you want a good man, I don't think it's a stretch to show him what you have to offer. That's how my mom kept her husband. I saw that up close."

"Let's see: so, he's got a good job and an education and he's nice. That's all it takes? That's all we want in a dude? Sounds like the bare minimum to me."

"What else is there?" Rae asked, getting a little annoyed by the conversation, which had started to feel like a broken record among her and her friends and, hell, everybody who was overly concerned with the love lives of Black women.

"Oh, I don't know, living your own life?" Mal said. "Being content with the fact that you can be your own woman, having what you want and deserve without being tied down to some dude?"

"Some dude? Tied down? That's what we're reducing relationships to?" Rae asked. She looked at Treva and chuckled. "Marriage is not some weight that stops us from flying. Tell her, Tree."

"And you know that how, exactly?" Mal asked, sitting back in her chair.

"Oh, I don't know, every freaking statistic about how couples thrive when they commit?" Rae said, tossing her hand in the air for emphasis. She ticked off The List. "Married couples have a better chance of building wealth, they're healthier, their kids have better educational outcomes. Everything our community needs is tied up in Black men and women getting along and building a life together."

"Goals!" Treva said, raising her wine in the air.

"Oh, now you one of those Black love experts, huh?" Mal interrupted. "You sound like a parrot. You sound like one of those niggas that be on the radio talking like strong Black families are on some superhero shit."

"I want my cape," Rae said, laughing. "Shit, I don't know what you talking about. I'm trying to be in that thirty percent of the community that's Black and married with kids. I'm trying to be a part of the solution, not the problem."

"You keep talking about what everybody else gains when they get married," Mal said. "But what you gonna get out of it?"

"Love!" Rae shouted. "Love, Mal. I want to be in love. I want to have babies. I want the kind of marriage my parents had. I want my man to look after me like my father looked after my mother. That's a good man right there."

"Mr. Tommy's a good dude, I'll give you that," Mal said. Treva vigorously nodded her head in agreement.

"I'm just trying to do my part. I'mma find my man and build my family and do good by all of us. I want to be a good wife and mom. Not gonna apologize for that."

"What you need to do is see if he got a friend for her ornery ass," Treva said, giggling. "Since you saving the community and all."

"Whatever, bitch," Mal laughed. "Here's my thing," she said, leaning in toward Rae, so she could hear her clearly. "When do we get to the part when we stop acting like the men are the prize? You over there frying chicken and making the good mac and cheese, trying to bag this guy. Why is it always about what we can do to show them that we'll make good wives? I think what would work for all of us is if these men proved that they'd be good husbands to us. I swear, don't let these books and TV therapists keep getting it twisted. Don't you want more than average?"

"I just want to be happy. A pan of fried chicken and a pot of string beans is a small price to pay for that," Rae said quietly.

2001, in the fall

And now here she was, four years into her marriage, a two-year-old on her hip, a dishrag in her hand, calculating just how much she'd paid for this happiness, which wasn't really happiness at all. It hit her on a Saturday, after a long week of demanding work at the production studio and a series of interactions with Roman that left her feeling like she would never realize a return on her investment. She stood there, shushing the baby, who was sleepy and hyped all at the same damn time. Roman squeezed his foot into his socks and then his sneakers, oblivious to the daggers his wife was throwing with her eyes, directly at the nape of his neck.

"I guess I'm having a hard time understanding why playing squash for four hours on a Saturday afternoon is a priority when there are so many things around the house that need to be done before work on Monday," Rae said, bouncing Skye as she paced the living room floor.

"Saturdays is the only time Rob can play. I don't know why we have to keep having this particular argument, Rae," Roman said as he pushed himself up off the sofa and smoothed out his shorts.

"How about Saturdays is the only day you can spend with both your girls!"

"Rae, there are twenty-four hours in a day on Saturday. You choose to spend a good four of them scrubbing toilets and polishing furniture that looks just fine and doesn't even need it."

"I choose to clean up? That's what you think this is?"

"The house is clean, Rae," Roman argued. "Look at it. You got a dishrag in your hand, about to wipe down stuff that doesn't even look dirty. Come on, man, why we having this argument when I'm walking out the door?"

"Because you're walking out the door!"

Roman didn't bother answering to that. Instead, he picked up his bag of rackets and balls, kissed the baby and Rae on the cheek, and headed for the door. He yawned. "I'll see y'all later this afternoon."

Rae's eyes followed Roman out the door and watched as he closed it behind him. She stood there, rocking back and forth, stewing, sure, but also coming to some hard conclusions. There were certainly times when Rae was a little girl, before her mother transferred her "skills" to her daughter, when Tommy would pile his baby into the front seat of his Cadillac on a Saturday afternoon under the guise of "running errands." He'd saddle up next to the drive-thru at the Chemical Bank to cash his check, then run to Macy's and Sears to pay his bills, maybe hit up the hardware store to buy a bit for his drill or a new hammer or something for his tool shed. "I got a taste for pizza," he would say, rolling the window down and adjusting his shades. "No, ice cream! Let's go sit in the mall and have a cone. What flavor you want, baby?"

"Strawberry!" Rae would say, struggling against the edges of the seat belt. She was so little, and the edge of the strap would always cut across her neck, irritating it. She wouldn't dream of complaining, though. She was just happy to be out of the house with her father. And happy, too, to have escaped buffing the wooden breakfront and vacuuming the staircase, the chores her mother entrusted to her early on, when she was grooming her for the cleaning takeover.

"Aw, strawberry?" Tommy would say, wrinkling his whole face in feigned disgust. "When God made butter pecan special for the sugar cone?"

"But I like strawberry, Daddy!" Rae would say, giggling.

Tommy would mock a sigh. "Tell me you'll at least get some sprinkles on that. Some peanuts. Something. Life's too short to be just a boring strawberry cone."

Always, they would arrive back home just in time for her father to walk back into a house that was white-glove clean. He'd pull out of his neatly arranged clothes bureau his freshly washed and pressed bowling shirt—tossing it in the laundry basket was the extent of his involvement in getting it clean—gather his bowling bag, and stand by the steps, waiting for LoLo to pack away her cleaning supplies, gather herself and her bowling gear, and hustle to the car. She always seemed tired, sitting up in the front of the car, slumped in the seat, staring out the window, her conversation clipped.

Little Rae wished her mother was strawberry ice cream with sprinkles. Grown Rae could see more clearly. LoLo, she'd decided, was tired. And angry. She was starting to understand why her mother took her plate into the back room, why she insisted on soaking in hot baths and curling herself up and watching her shows and laying herself down, eyes closed. Alone. Silently giving herself a second at the end of her long days to be . . . human.

Rae didn't quite know how to arrange this for herself—not with a husband who wasn't an earner, not with a little baby who still hadn't quite learned how to put her shit in the toilet instead of her pants, not with a full-time job and a house to keep up all on her own because the other grown-up in their home thought it passé to shower in a clean tub and cook in a kitchen that was neat and swept. Treva and Mal had both warned and advocated. "Girl, I don't know why you cleaning up after a grown-ass man when you can pay someone to do that for you," Mal had said during lunch a few months before this. It would be the only time she'd have to see her friends, unless they came to Casa Lister, and that rarely happened because Treva didn't really care for babies and Mal didn't really care for Roman.

"Who can afford a damn maid?" Rae had asked between bites of her tuna hero. "Between the bills and the babysitter, I don't have the cash to pay a stranger to come into the house and scrub a toilet. I know how to scrub a damn toilet."

That gnawing, desperately unsettled, perpetually unsatisfied, I'm-totally-failing-my-baby-and-at-life feeling of juggling her demanding but wanted job, a new marriage, and a new baby all at the same time had Rae feeling like she was treading water at the deep end of the pool, with legs that were too weak to keep her head above the surface. She stood there staring at the door with the same look LoLo had on her face riding shotgun in the Eldorado.

Skye wriggled some more and whined a little. She wanted to get down off her mother's hip.

"Okay, okay, baby," Rae said, putting her daughter's feet on the floor. She took off running, Rae watching her scoot off to her bedroom. The baby went straight to her closet, pulled out her sneakers, and plopped into the middle of her floor; she struggled to stuff her foot into the pink and yellow glittery affair. Rae laughed. "Where you going, baby?"

"Out!" she said.

"Oh! We're going somewhere?" Rae asked, her mood lightening a little. Skye was an insistent baby; Rae lived for her directness, which she brought with her from the womb.

"Out!" Skye yelled.

Rae looked around the baby's room and saw all the things that were wrong with it: the laundry hamper was overflowing; the diaper basket needed refilling; there were books and stuffed animals everywhere; the bed linens needed changing. But the baby, she wanted out.

So did Rae.

"Okay, baby," she said, bending down to put Skye's sneakers on the correct feet and tie them up. "Out. Let's go out."

Three hours later, winded from chasing behind Skye at the park and getting her amped up on a strawberry ice cream sugar high and then carrying the exhausted baby and the stroller up two flights of stairs to get to their apartment, Rae pushed open the door and walked straight into that heaviness again—that feeling of being in this alone. Roman was still out playing games. Skye's room—and the rest of the house, for that matter— was still a mess. Rae was pissed again. She was tired of being pissed again.

She laid the baby in her little bed and kissed her cheek, then popped up and put her hands on her hips. She didn't want to feel this—didn't want to fight with her husband and be mad during what little free time she had over the weekend, especially knowing that Roman would employ that blasé attitude of his to dismiss whatever was making her upset. She didn't have any more fight in her—didn't have the wherewithal to inhale the gaslighting that Roman was sure to walk directly into any conversation Rae would launch about her own needs and his shortcomings. So, she did what she always did to self-soothe, which also happened to be one of the very things of which she wanted—needed—Roman to be more conscious. She cleaned to get calm.

Rae walked into the tiny master bathroom, no bigger, really, than the handicapped stall in the executive restroom at work, and surveyed the counters, cluttered with skin creams, Roman's beard-grooming essentials, toothbrushes, and makeup and various other sundries that made navigating the sink near impossible. The white porcelain and countertop were full of little hairs her husband had left behind after his morning shape-up; she'd been brushing her teeth when he lined up his beard and she was watching as he used the side of his palm to haphazardly swipe the tiny hairs into the sink. She stared, bug-eyed, at the mess and then at him and then back at the mess, but he was oblivious. He simply dried his fingertips and walked on. Rae sighed at the memory and shook her head, then turned her attention to the shower: the tiles were screaming for a spritz of mold and mildew cleaner; the mirror was dotted with toothpaste droplets. It looked like the beginnings of some knockoff Lichtenstein.

Rae sighed again, rolled up her sleeves, and got to it, deciding that she would organize the cabinet beneath the sink to make room for the things on top of it. Simple enough. She kneeled to the floor and, without really looking, swiped at the first items her finger touched: a bottle of shampoo, some hair oil, her portable hairdryer, all slung around like they'd been dropped into the cabinet in a hurry. On top of the counter those went. She reached in a second time—again without looking—and swiped at a bottle of conditioner, a tin of bobos she kept for Skye's hair, and a small toiletries bag in which Roman kept their condoms, and those went up on the countertop, too. On the third reach, her hand hit something kind of slung farther to the back—something that was neither a bottle nor a bag nor anything that felt familiar for an undercounter. Rae scrunched her face and leaned into the counter a bit, her knees creaking as she readjusted her balance, the top of her shoulder and the side of her face hitting the furniture as she tried to get her whole hand around it. It was nothing for her to assume it was one of Roman's T-shirts or maybe a do-rag he'd slung down there in a rush to be done in the bathroom and get back to whatever it was he wanted to do next, but she was young and hadn't quite gotten around to understanding the consequences of assuming—how much more hurt one's feelings got when they hadn't prepared themselves for the awful. Rae got a good grip on the silky item and pulled it toward her.

It was a bra.

It was not her bra.

Rae knew this because she wore sensible brassieres—the affordable ones that stayed on sale at Macy's, on the rounder next to the five-for-$25 panties bin. A 34B, the cup size she'd graduated to after breastfeeding Skye for just shy of eighteen months—a change that came with considerable glee after she'd spent an entire lifetime praying to the *Are You There, God? It's Me, Margaret* saints for a little something to pop off her flat, president-of-the-itty-bitty-titty-committee chest. Until the size change, she'd worn mostly tight sports bras, like the girls from TLC, except she kept her belly covered and a sweater tied around her waist—a fruitless effort to try to hide her thick thighs and booty, which, because she was so small around the middle, never fit properly in pants that always seemed to stretch awkwardly across the hip and gap at the waist. Rae had grown up self-conscious about her shape—LoLo saw to that. "Big as you is on the bottom, you don't need to be focusing on making your little chest bigger," she'd told Rae one evening when she busted her doing the "I must, I must, I must increase my bust" exercise she'd read about in her then favorite novel. Rae's heart, chased by Rae's fear of having been caught worrying about breasts, had pumped so hard she got a little light-headed. She quickly dropped her arms and her eyes. "From now on, the only exercise you need to be worried about doing? Sit on this here carpet and walk backwards. That'll help stop that booty from growing so damn big."

LoLo had said it like having a round bottom was a crime and a shame and so that's the way Rae regarded it—regarded her body. Like it needed to be hidden. It tracked with the message she'd received her entire childhood; she was from the generation that had spent its most formative years—those critical moments when self-esteem was beginning to set—being told that the pancake asses in those Jordache jean commercials were the standard. That calling Black girls with bubble butts "fat"—not to be confused with "phat"—was the standard. That swimming in oversized T-shirts over your bathing suit and tying thick sweaters and lumberjack shirts around your waist to hide your donk was the standard. That wearing skirts that hiked up in the back and stretched across the hips was the standard. That wedgies were the standard. That exercising to get that weight off, even when the scale said you were actually underweight, was the standard. Bubble booties were to be covered, not coveted—worked off, not worked with. And no amount of Sir Mix-a-Lot's "Baby Got Back" homages or ass smacks from Roman could pull Rae out of that three decades of self-hate.

So, no, that sexy bra Rae had pulled from beneath her bathroom sink—it wasn't hers.

Come to find out, Roman wasn't either.

And that is when Rae learned that her husband was betraying her. That is also when she began unloving him.

27

*T*here was Rae, sitting on her father's childhood front porch on one of those old-school sofa gliders—the kind made of metal, with basket-weave squares and a powder-coat finish. It was baby blue and matched the sky and faced it, too, and on summer nights, when it was hot and cumulus clouds felt like showing out, that bench was the front-row seat to the most glorious of sunsets. The same ones Tommy watched when he was little, and his mama, too, and her mama before her—right there on their land that Tommy's grandmother owned outright and built a house on, where she caught all her little grandbabies with her own hands. Back then, they called it Lawrence Alley, on account of all those Lawrences who owned all that land over there and lived on it, too. Walked it. Tilled it. Raised children on it. Built businesses there, too. Sustained themselves for generations. All that dirt, those trees, that grass held the Lawrence story—the roots every bit as colorful and grand as those summer sunsets. Tommy met his daughter where he knew. Where he ran away home.

Now, here was Rae, smiling as she watched her father pick dandelions one by one off his lawn and hold them in his granddaughter's face. "Wish!" Skye demanded. Tommy closed his eyes and smiled and whispered something only he and the breeze could hear, and then he yelled, "One, two, three, blow!" over and over again, because two-year-olds are always *Team Do It Again* and grandfathers are always *Team Whatever My Baby Wants* and Skye and Tommy were no exception so this went on for quite some time before Tommy snuck a look at Rae and saw shadows where there used to be the sun. "Okay, baby, Pop Pop is tired," he said. He balanced one hand in the grass blades, the other on his bended knee and precariously pushed himself up to his feet. "You tired? I know you are."

"No, Pa Pa, blow!" Skye said, scrambling to pull another dandelion from its root. "Wish!"

"Yes, baby, wish," Tommy said. He scooped the baby into his arms and turned to his daughter: "I wish to see the sunshine on my Rae's face again," he said and smiled.

Rae shifted on the bench—the metal tugged at the skin on her thigh as it peeled off the bench's surface. She winced, but not at the pain emanating from the back of her legs. It was the pain of hearing her father ask for what she was not ready to give.

"How 'bout we go into the house and wish up some peanut butter and jelly sandwiches. You like peanut butter and jelly?" Tommy asked Skye.

"Mmmmm, Pa Pa! Peanut jelly sammich?"

"Yes, peanut butter and jelly. But you gotta come inside the house now to get it. Come with Pop Pop," he said, holding out his thick hand. She tucked hers into it and giggled as he and she skipped to the porch and he swung her up each step until she was standing in front of Rae, who did her best to fix her face for her two favorite people in the whole wide world.

"Come on inside, darlin.' Let me fix us some lunch," Tommy said, holding out his hand to help her up from the bench. He opened the door and put his hand on the small of Rae's back as he helped the baby and her walk safely across the threshold. It was a small gesture—that feel of his hands moving and shifting and gently guiding her away from danger. It always tickled Rae that her father opened doors and pulled out chairs and walked out of the elevator first to take the brunt of any danger if there was some on the other side of the door and moved her entire body away from the street side of the sidewalk, where it was safer. Where she was safer. It was that old-school charm—the gentleman who knew how to treat a lady, yes, but also the gentleman who understood that Malcolm was right about Black women being unprotected and disrespected and neglected, but not this one. Not his daughter. Not on his watch. With him, Rae felt valued. Priceless. Delicate and precious and worth taking a bullet for. It was what she needed on this day—that feeling of a strong Black man's hands on the small of her back. But her heart, it needed more. The broken bits were shards slicing through everything she ever knew, everything she ever trusted about her father, her husband, her relationship with the two.

"You deserve sunshine, Rae," Tommy said as they crossed the threshold. He gently guided Rae's body so that it faced the outside. "Look at it. I know you're in the storm now, but baby, look toward the sun. That's how you get free. That's how you bloom."

Tommy pointed toward the sun standing sentry in a cloudless, aqua-blue sky, Skye's eyes following her grandfather's pointer finger. "Bloom," he said. His voice was soft but deep and round, like a gentle thunder. Skye laughed big, from her little gut, her sweet voice growing louder as Tommy repeated himself. "Bloom." Sweet baby laughter. "Bloom." Baby laughter. "Bloom!"

Rae slowly opened her eyes and shifted herself in the big, cushiony chaise in her parents' living room as her blurry vision slowly came into focus. There was LoLo, balancing Skye on her hip, digging her fingers into the little girl's side, Skye doubled over, giggling uncontrollably. Rae rubbed her eyes.

"What time is it?" she asked as she stretched. "How long was I sleeping?"

"Long enough for my grandbaby and me to get good and hungry," LoLo said, nuzzling Skye and rubbing her nose with her own. It was a tenderness Rae watched with equal parts curiosity, envy, and a small measure of disbelief. Affection was Tommy's province, not LoLo's. "Come on into the kitchen and get you something to eat. I made sandwiches."

Rae stretched and headed for the bathroom to freshen up; by the time she entered the kitchen, LoLo had three sandwiches laid out on the table, plus a cup of milk for the baby and two sodas for the grown-ups. Rae was appreciative, but the food tasted like sand and glue on her tongue. She hadn't eaten since sharing ice cream with her baby the day prior, before she discovered the bra and her husband's infidelity, and hurriedly packed up a suitcase of clothes and went to Long Island, away from Roman, away from his lies. She didn't even bother waiting to tell him she was leaving—just sent him an email letting him know that she felt like her entire world was caving in on itself and she just didn't have it in her to try anymore.

"You gotta eat, Rae," LoLo said, looking at her daughter's plate. Skye absentmindedly wiped her mouth with her napkin, putting more crumbs on her face than she actually took off, and pointed at the potato chip bag. "Chips, Gamma?"

"Oh, yes, baby, here you go."

"No, no—no more chips," Rae said gently, giving her mother the stop sign. "You've had enough. It's time for you to get ready for your nap."

"Nooooo," Skye whined as she shook her head. "No nap, Mommy."

"Skye, it's time, sweetie," Rae said gently.

The little girl slid out of her chair and rushed over to her grandmother, a barrage of no's leading the charge. She smashed into LoLo's leg and buried her face into Gamma's thigh. LoLo picked up Skye and cradled the little girl in her lap, smushing her head into her chest. "It's okay, baby," she said tenderly. "Sit with Gamma for a little while."

"You getting a little easy in your old age," Rae said.

LoLo smirked. "I was easy when you kids did what I said do," she said. She kissed Skye's head and laughed. "I was hard when I needed to be hard."

It was a simple statement, pregnant with both truth and lie. LoLo had, indeed, been the hard one—easily offended, quick to slap when a talking-to would have sufficed, her hand judge, jury, and hammer in childhood trials that began and ended within seconds of the slightest of transgressions. Young Rae wanted to love her mother and she did, but their relationship was powered by fear—a fear so intense that Rae took to tiptoeing around her mother, convinced that if she let her feet all-the-way touch the floor, attention would be drawn and fault would be found and then would come the rage. "Go get the belt!" "Go get a switch!" "Get in here, right now!" Those words dangled from LoLo's lips like cigarettes. Rae had to be hit only once or twice to understand the rules and the consequences of break-ing them; doing as she was told and tucking herself away was every bit as much about survival as it was a behavioral trait.

TJ, though, had been a habitual line-stepper—stayed in trouble. He valued his freedom so much more than his physical well-being, and almost happily took the beatings, knowing that once it was over, he could and would just go on back to doing whatever it was he'd gotten hit for. When she got old enough to recognize the pattern, Rae couldn't understand why LoLo didn't catch on, either. Soon, though, she came to believe that maybe her mother was hitting to soothe herself, rather than correct her brother. That discovery is what scared Rae the most. For months after that, she suffered debilitating nightmares in which she witnessed her mother killing her brother—beating him to death with a chair, pushing him down a flight of stairs, his body crumpling into a heap of broken pieces at its bottom. LoLo walking away, a look of satisfaction smeared across her face like Maybelline. For the longest time, Rae couldn't sleep. Was scared to.

Tommy mostly did not hit his children, but he never defended them from LoLo's wrath, either. Rae's anger about this part was posthumous, as intense as her disgust at his infidelity. She didn't want to be mad at him, but here she was, feeling like her father had fallen down on his unspoken promise to protect her. From LoLo. From Tasheera. The only other time she'd felt that way was the one time Tommy had slapped Rae across her face.

"You remember that time Daddy hit me?" Rae asked LoLo as she held a quarter of a sandwich, crusts off, to Skye's lips. The baby took a bite.

"Now you know you need to stop telling that lie."

"He did! You don't remember that?"

"I remember us trying to hit you a couple times and how you always took off running and hollering like somebody was going to kill you. It made Tommy laugh so hard I guess he figured he would leave you alone. It wasn't that serious." LoLo laughed at the memories. Rae did not.

"But there was the one time," Rae said.

They'd still been living in New Jersey, so Rae probably hadn't even hit double digits yet, but there was her father, tall and hulking and shirtless and sleepy, with dried spit on the side of his face, standing over her menacingly. Neither Rae nor TJ knew he'd pulled a double shift that saw him walk through the front door close to two in the morning; they just knew to be quiet while he slept and hoped that he would stay that way long enough for TJ to get all the way down Burlington Road to the 7-Eleven, so that he could buy some candy. Rae hadn't been thinking about sweets; she was on the kitchen floor, playing jacks, specifically practicing picking up the fours. But here came TJ, talking about grape and cherry Now and Laters and Razzles gum. "All you gotta do is keep your mouth shut," he'd said. "If Daddy wakes up, just tell him I'm in the back in the shed. Do that and I'll bring you back the candy, okay?"

Rae didn't question it—didn't make any inquiries into where he'd gotten the money to buy the candy or why he couldn't just wait until their father woke up or their mother had gotten back from the mall; Now and Laters were involved, and that's all Rae really needed to hear to agree to be an accomplice in the procurement of said sweets. But almost as soon as TJ left the house, Tommy walked out the master bedroom with puffy eyes and questions.

"Rae? Come here," he'd said. All of her insides felt like they'd gathered in her chest and made the collective decision to exit as a group via her throat. She slowly picked up her jacks and the bouncy ball and dragged herself out the kitchen, through the dining room, past the living room, and down the hall that was suddenly the length of an airplane runway. She wished she could fly away.

"Yes, Daddy?" she'd said sweetly, forcing as much innocence into her voice as she could muster.

"Where's your brother?"

Rae hesitated ever so slightly, but then dove headfirst into the lie. "He's out in the back in the shed," she'd said.

On the long walk to her father, she'd contemplated the consequences of lying: he could believe her, a best-case scenario; he could give her a good talking-to, a punishment that would certainly hurt her as she hated to disappoint her parents, but her bodily integrity would stay intact; he could punish her for real, maybe tell her she couldn't play with her dolls or watch *The Six Million Dollar Man* for a couple weeks. But never did she consider the form of discipline Tommy chose.

He backhand slapped her with the meaty part of his right hand, right across her lying mouth.

"You gonna stand right here in my face and lie?" he'd yelled.

Rae, so shocked that her father had chosen violence as his form of discipline, stood wide-eyed and silent; a cry worked its way up from deep in her belly, but got stuck somewhere around where all of her insides were bunched up—right there next to her heart. Eventually, it managed its way through the tiny cracks and up through her throat and across her tongue to her mouth. When she finally got a hold of her breath, the noise chased after it.

"That was the one time he hit me, and he told me he did it because I lied," Rae said. She fiddled with her fingers, looking at them instead of her mother.

"Hmmph. I don't remember him hitting you, but I do know he didn't like liars," LoLo said matter-of-factly.

"But he lied to you, Mommy. He lied to us. All those years, he lied to our family."

LoLo was quiet. Skye sighed and snuggled into her grandmother's chest and blinked over and over again, trying so hard to keep her eyes open. Finally, sleep won out. LoLo kissed her granddaughter and wrapped her arms a little tighter around the girl's body, but more to comfort herself than the baby.

"You don't think I know that?" she asked finally.

"I don't understand how he could hate lying but live a lie all those years. He broke my mother's heart."

"He lied because he was trying to protect your mother's heart," LoLo said quickly.

"Mommy, respectfully, I don't understand that," Rae answered back just as quickly. "He had two children with another woman. How was that protecting your heart? He cheated on you. You were the love of his life, and he cheated on you. I'm standing in your shoes right now, with my heart in pieces because the love of my life stepped out on me. I know what it feels like. It doesn't feel like protection. It's not protection."

"Listen, there's a lot you don't know or understand, Rae . . . ," LoLo began.

"Daddy's lie showed up at his funeral. And she did that not more than a few weeks after she told you all the ways you'd been lied to. You weren't protected, and neither was I. Why in the hell are you defending him?"

Rae braced herself for what she thought would be her mother's terse reaction to her cussing, but LoLo said nothing at first. She rubbed the baby's back and sat in contemplation. Finally, her voice just above a whisper, she said: "I lied to your father first."

Rae reeled her neck back, like she did the day her father popped her in the mouth. "What do you mean?" she asked. Something was building inside of her body—fear? Anger? Disgust? Dread? Whatever it was, she wasn't sure she was quite ready to walk this path with her mother—if she was ready to discuss this level of detail, of her parents' personal history. But now, here was LoLo, putting her hand on the small of her daughter's back and leading her to a version of truth.

"I had your father believing in the beginning that he was the one who couldn't make babies," she said. "I could tell he was scared, but he went on ahead to all these doctors and got poked and prodded and things. Nobody could tell him why he couldn't have kids. But I told him I got my monthly real regular, and that meant there wasn't nothing wrong with me, so it must have been him, and he believed me."

Rae stared, wide-eyed, wanting to hear the story but also not.

"There was a lot of stress. A lot of stress," LoLo continued, shaking her head as she rocked the now-sleeping Skye. "He just wanted a family and I knew that. But I just wanted him. I . . . I couldn't tell him," LoLo said. She swiped at a tear as it escaped from the pool of water that had gathered in her eyes, an action that sent a shock through Rae's stomach. Aside from her father's funeral, she had never seen her mother's emotions on this speed. Without even realizing it, Rae grabbed hold to the sides of the seat of her chair.

"Tell him what?" Rae asked slowly.

LoLo inhaled deeply and ran her thumb over her sleeping grandbaby's tightly coiled curls. She planted her nose into Skye's hair—sucked in more air.

"I love the way she smells, even when she comes in from outside," LoLo said. "She still smells like a little baby to me, like a bundle of joy and goodness. That's what she is." LoLo rocked Skye and squeezed her a little tighter. "I never knew I could love another human being so big like this. Grandbabies, they're like a present that comes in the prettiest package and you unwrap it and it's exactly what you wanted. What you needed, too. But they don't make you think of lack. Just joy, big and round and full. First time I held her, I thought, now this is what love is.

"This baby brought the light into a world of darkness," LoLo said, finally looking her own daughter in the eye. "And I'm not even talking about the darkness that came when your daddy died. She made me understand not just what I lost, but what I managed to find despite it."

"I don't understand, Mommy," Rae said. Now her eyes were filled with water—a blurry vision of this softness about her mother that Rae had never before seen.

"When I was sixteen years old, I had to have an abortion. My cousin raped me and we made a baby that I couldn't keep," LoLo said, keeping her words simple, to the point, to get them out of her body. "The nurse who took the baby, she took all my babies. She made it so I couldn't ever become a mother."

Rae gasped and covered her mouth with both her hands, like she was the close-up shot of a character in a horror movie witnessing something grotesque. LoLo continued, a spigot of information pouring. Rushing.

"Your daddy wanted babies so bad. So bad, Rae. Back then, if you couldn't have no babies, men didn't see much use for you. I came to find out during our marriage that he really loved and wanted me, but in the beginning, for years, I was afraid he would leave me if he knew I couldn't give him children. I had to convince him it was him, you see? And then show him we could have a family a whole 'nother way."

"And that's how you came to adopt me and TJ," Rae stated. She wiped her tears with her wrists and clasped her hands in her lap. "I found the papers when I was twelve, you know. You didn't do a good job of hiding them," she said simply. She almost laughed. All those years she'd hid knowing—swallowing her questions, tucking the secret in the recesses of her life and her parents', too—were an uneventful reveal next to the discovery of her father's secret life. Finally, here was the needle popping the balloon, but there was no sound. Just air, quietly flowing where the needle pricked.

LoLo shook her head and laughed a little. "Yeah, well, uh, that's something," LoLo said, digesting that this part of her secret wasn't a secret at all. "And you never said a word about it."

"I was scared to say anything about it. I was scared about what it meant to be adopted, especially when I was a kid. Like, I remember thinking that maybe if you got mad enough, you would give me back."

"Rae! What? I would never . . ."

"Mommy, you were always angry," Rae said, cutting off LoLo's words. She felt emboldened enough to brave telling her mother the truth now, after all those years of pushing the feelings deep into the recesses, past thick skin and blood and heart muscle—memory, even—to become the very fabric of the Lawrence clan. To be indispensable. "I did everything you demanded. I tiptoed around you and sometimes I even wished I was invisible so you wouldn't look across the room and yell about something and make me feel like this time, my time with you was up. I remember thinking," Rae added quietly, "that maybe you didn't want us. And if my birth mother didn't want me, and you didn't want me . . ."

LoLo hugged Skye tighter—took her time finding the right words. The truth, the secret she and Tommy had kept for thirty-two years. "You were wanted, Rae. Someone left you on the steps of an orphanage down there on Canal Street, in the city. We came by four days later, looking for a little girl. I was upstairs, and your daddy went looking downstairs. He said it was so dark down there, he could barely see into the cribs. There was no light. But then there was you, over in the corner. Tommy said you sat up and looked at him and giggled. That same smile you got today. Caught hold of his heart then, held on to his heart 'til the day he passed on. He said he knew you were our daughter the second he laid eyes on you."

LoLo reached out to touch Rae, her fingers brushing lightly against her daughter's arms. Rae flinched, and only then did she notice that she'd folded her entire body into itself—arms wrapped around waist, ankles crossed, knees, calves bent in an impossibly awkward position beneath the chair. LoLo pulled back her hand as if she'd touched white-hot fire.

Rae tried to stop them, but tears escaped in tracks down her cheeks regardless. "I know he loved us, Mommy. But what about you?"

"What about me?" LoLo asked quizzically.

"Did you love me? TJ?"

"How you gone question that?" LoLo asked.

"Look at the way you are with Skye, Mommy," Rae answered quickly. "You didn't hug or really kiss on us like that. Sometimes, most times, it felt like you didn't want to be around us."

"I was a good mother to you," LoLo countered. "I may not have been touchy-feely or saying it all the time, but I kept you fed, you had clothes on your back, a roof over your head. Who taught you to love and fear God? Don't you sit here and act like I wasn't no kind of mother to you. You had everything you needed and even some of the things you wanted. All of that I did for you because you are my daughter. *My daughter.* When my mama died, my daddy wasn't no kind of father to me. He just left me there to die, and in some ways, I suppose I did." Then, in an almost whisper, she added: "Maybe I didn't say 'I love you' enough, but I sure showed you I loved you. That counts, Rae. That's my kind of love."

LoLo kissed Skye's head and then reached out for her own daughter's hand. Tried again, for Rae's sake. For her own. This time, Rae let her mother rest her hand on her shoulder. This time, she looked her in her eyes.

This time, she saw a woman. Not her mother. Not her father's wife. Not the mean, angry, abusive housewife, but a woman who had lived a hard life and who had sacrificed and protected her family with a fierceness that hurt not only her children, but her own self. Rae saw a simple, simple woman who'd survived an extraordinarily sad, complicated life.

28

Rae should have known not to ask LoLo this question—should have anticipated her answer. She'd had, after all, two years of evidence that LoLo had become a different type of mother with respect to advice, too, eschewing her penchant for being Rae's marionettist and, instead, stepping back and encouraging her daughter, this woman, mother, wife, to make her own choices and hold firmly to them, no matter what anyone else had to say about them. The first time LoLo defended Rae's choices out loud, Rae was shocked into silence, unsure if she'd actually heard her mother's words correctly. "Y'all leave her be," LoLo had told her friends. Aunties Sarah, Cindy, and Para Lee had piled into LoLo's house on the occasion of her wedding anniversary to soothe and console—take LoLo's mind off of the tragedy of what all she'd lost so that she could focus on a bit of the good. The ones tucked in her memories. LoLo's friends, they were good for that—a Voltron of sisters who used their powers to uplift, encourage, counsel. Rae hadn't realized it when she was little, but her mother's best friends had curated valuable lessons for her—lessons on how to be. Watching them, she'd learned the value of friendship, creating safe spaces for children, and laughter. She lived for her aunties' hugs, their approval, their truth. And they gave it—in spades. But on this occasion, Rae just wanted them to back off.

The brouhaha began the second Rae struggled up LoLo's stairs, her then eight-month-old baby wriggling in her left arm as she balanced a dia-per bag and a haul of Skye's toys, plus gifts for her mother in her right. Skye, fussy and squirmy, was clawing at her mother's T-shirt, smashing her lips against her mother's breasts. "All right, all right, all right, it's coming, little one!" Rae insisted as she dropped the bags in the upper foyer and headed straight for the cushy chair in the living room, just next to the couch where her mother and aunties were sitting. Photo albums filled with pictures pasted between cardboard and plastic and the lives they lived together were spread out all across the square cocktail table in front of them, on their laps, too, wide and open like their laughter.

"Ohhhhhh, here she is! Hand me my grandbaby!" LoLo said, her arms outstretched, fingers waving Rae and the baby in her direction. The aun-ties' joyful greetings filled the air.

"One second, Mommy, she's so hungry she's going to have a fit if I don't feed her, like, right this second," Rae said as she lifted her T-shirt and un-snapped her maternity bra. In an instant, the room grew quiet. Skye gave a couple more whines as she rooted for her mother's breast and then at-tached lips, tongue, like a suction on her mother's nipple, slurping, breath-ing hard, her eyelids wet and heavy from want, then satisfaction.

Auntie Para Lee went in first. "How old that baby?" she asked.

Rae reached for Skye's fingers and rocked her body, her baby, as the child suckled. "She just turned eight months. I can't believe how fast time's mov-ing," she said. "She's getting so big! It's like I see a new child every week."

Rae, focused on the task at hand, missed Auntie Para Lee shooting eyes in Auntie Cindy's and Auntie Sarah's direction, first, then over to LoLo.

"She's almost a year old and you still giving her ninny?" Auntie Para Lee asked, her brows creased. "She got enough teeth to eat a steak at this point."

"She can at least gnaw a piece of meat that ain't her mama's breast, that's for sure," Auntie Sarah chimed in.

Rae's smile slowly faded; she shifted uncomfortably in the cushioned chair, wilting under her aunties' gazes. In her head, she preached a fiery sermon—ran down the history of breastfeeding in the Black community and the harmful effects of formula on a baby's delicate stomach, ticked off all the statistics on just how smart and strong and healthy breastfed babies are and all the advantages they reap feeding off their mamas' milk and questioning how they could be perfectly fine slurping liquid squeezed from a cow's teats but bothered by her baby getting nourishment from her mother's breast. Out loud, Rae did nothing more than hold her lips tight and take the verbal lashing.

"I don't know what y'all talking about," LoLo chimed in. "Look how healthy my grandbaby is. Her mama doing something right. A lot of things right if you ask me." LoLo's friends stopped clucking. "Skye doesn't get colds; she hasn't had any ear infections. Look at them fat little legs," she added, reaching over and pinching her granddaughter' thighs. "Her hair is thick and curly—"

"You not going to put any barrettes in her hair?" Auntie Sarah interrupted. "Seem like with all that hair, you might want to comb it and put it in some pigtails or something. That Afro looks dry . . ."

"Sarah, ain't nothing wrong with that baby's head!" LoLo said. "Her Afro cute as a button. Y'all leave my grandbaby alone, now. That's Rae's baby and she doing a good job raising her."

"Looking a little nappy if you ask me."

"But nobody asked you, though," Rae snapped before she could catch herself. She instantly regretted it; her mother had raised her better than this. This time, more gently, she blew some cooler air into the situation, which had grown white hot. "I'm just choosing to do things differently, that's all. There's all these benefits to breastfeeding a baby for at least a year, and it's not hurting anybody for me to feed my baby with the milk nature makes just for that purpose. I don't tug and pull on her hair because she's tenderheaded and I like her Afro anyway," Rae said. "I think it's cute."

"I do, too, Rae," LoLo said, reaching over to rub her daughter's leg in solidarity. Rae looked at her tenderheaded mother's hand and then at her mother, trying hard to contain her surprise at it all.

Later, when everyone had had their fill of food and cake and fellowship and went on back to their own lives and LoLo and Rae laid down in LoLo's bed to watch a show while the baby drifted off to sleep, LoLo explained her newfound positioning. "Don't nobody have the right to tell you how to be," she'd said simply. "That's your baby. You raise her the way you see fit, hear? Nothing anybody else has to say about it means anything if it isn't what you want. Remember that."

This LoLo was a shock—unintrusive, a hail Mary, full of grace. Had Rae not been vibrating from the implosion of her marriage, she may have leaned into understanding, embracing her mother's easy turns around the hard curves. But what she needed more in this moment was LoLo's flashlight—the insight that would help her navigate this darkness and find her way back to normality, where husbands earned their keep and enjoyed spending Saturdays huddled up with their favorite girls and actively chose family over everything.

It had been three nights since Rae left her husband, and she was no closer to figuring out her next move than she'd been the moment she packed up their baby and piled her and everything she could stuff in a duffel bag onto the Long Island Railroad train headed to her childhood home. She sat at the kitchen table, sleepy, frustrated, sad, annoyed, running off only a few hours of sleep that had been repeatedly interrupted the night before by baby elbows to her nose and little feet buried in the small of her back, and memories of being a teenager in that perfectly preserved room, on that perfectly preserved bed that, more than two decades prior, she'd laid in doing homework, reading, listening to Frankie Crocker play love songs on her little plug-in alarm radio, wishing her mother would stop locking her away like some chocolate Rapunzel that needed to be protected from some evil world. Here she was, all those years later, thirty-two with a baby, still stuck in the tower, with no clear plan for how she could find her way out or even if the prince was worth the climb.

LoLo whirled around the kitchen easily, occasionally shouting out the answers to the questions Alex Trebek calmly posed on the night's episode of *Jeopardy!* as she prepared a quick dinner of fried pork chops, steamed broccoli, and applesauce. She was oblivious to Rae's growing agitation as she sat at the kitchen table, a sleepy Skye straddled across her lap.

"What am I supposed to do, Mommy?" Rae asked finally.

"Do about what?" LoLo asked as she set two prepared dinner plates on the table. She kissed Skye and smiled. "Oh, sleepy baby," she cooed.

"My husband cheated on me. On our family. What am I supposed to do? Do I stay with a man who slept with another woman? Do I stay with the bad guy, for better or worse? My daddy is my hero, but he's also a bad guy, too. Does his cheating change that? Is Roman's cheating supposed to change that I still want to be his wife? What do I do?"

"I can't tell you what to do, Rae, and I won't try. That's your marriage, that's your life. What your father and I had was what I wanted, but it wasn't perfect. It wasn't nothing to put up on a pedestal and say 'Do it like us.' I tried to be what the world thought a woman should be and it damn near killed me. You gonna have to decide what's right for you, no matter what you witnessed elsewhere. It don't matter what anyone else wants. It's about what you need. You understand?"

Rae wiped her tears. Nodded. Looked at her baby. "She's knocked out, huh?" Rae said, forcing a smile to her face.

LoLo looked down at Skye, who'd settled into Rae's belly like it was her pillow. "Yeah, she's out," LoLo whispered.

"Let me go lay her down," LoLo said, taking Skye from Rae's arms. "Be right back, okay? Why don't you eat your pork chops? You gotta eat something, keep up your strength."

Rae watched her mother cradle her granddaughter in her arms, the little girl's feet dangling down to her thighs. LoLo was knocking on fifty-five years of life, but still lithe and lovely. She'd made a good life for herself outside of Tommy—had become someone . . . new. Even the house was nothing like the abode the Lawrences had established in Long Island; growing up, LoLo had insisted all the rooms in her house be white, as she believed deeply that color was meant for sofa pillows, bedspreads, and tchotchkes on étagères, never walls. She also insisted that living room furniture was for company, not for grubby-handed kids or adults prone to just lying around. Mostly, everyone retreated to their own corners of the place; it was LoLo's house, LoLo's tastes, LoLo's rules.

But in this house she lived in without Tommy, the walls were a shock of red, gold, and baby blue, and, the living room, once off-limits to anyone but company, was now the place to be, whether family or guest, friend or foe. It was there that LoLo held court: she served snacks and drinks there, held Bible study there. She'd even bought a new TV and positioned it so that she could fold laundry there or nap while watching thrillers and old westerns. She was the ringmaster of her single-woman circus; she'd found her own way of living, her own way of entertaining, her own way of being, without Tommy. It was a delicious sight to behold.

Rae turned herself around in her chair to get a better look at the kitchen wall on which LoLo had hung all the family pictures that once stared out at the family from glass shelves in the living room. In the center was an old picture of Tommy, in a plaid suit and green turtleneck, LoLo in an almost-matching pencil dress, the two of them staring off into the distance like subjects tended to do in those old-school Sears photographs, with the colored background and the extra glossy finish. Rae thought LoLo was so beautiful—so very beautiful. Tall and lithe, like a model. She remembered plenty times sitting in the dressing room at the department stores LoLo frequented, watching her mother slip into outfits that always seemed to be cut perfectly for her long body. LoLo favored long dresses with belts at the waist and shoulder pads that made her already square shoulders look like a hanger and her already tiny waist look impossibly, freakishly small. She hated to show her legs, though, something Rae couldn't understand, as they were the most perfect legs—long and shapely. Nothing like the short, thick legs Rae had to fight into pants that never fit properly. Rae remembered sitting on the benches in the fitting rooms of Macy's, wishing she were shaped less like a Coke bottle, more like her mother—pretty and perfect. So very pretty and perfect.

Rae felt the sting in her nose first, and next, her eyes. She missed her daddy but she ached for what he did to this woman, how he piled on to her pain. The second she came back into the kitchen, Rae decided, she was going to tell her how pretty she was and how she looked up to her and was grateful for her, too. Grateful that she came and got her and made her her own. How she didn't deserve what Tommy did to her, to their family. How she wanted to be mad at him but couldn't figure out the space between the anger and her intense love for her daddy—a love that knew no bounds, but was even bigger now that he was gone on from here. She wanted to tell her mother that though she didn't understand her pain fully, she knew she was hurting and she would be there for her. Her mother, this woman whose blood she did not share but loved deeply all the same.

And then, Rae smelled him. Her daddy. Just as sure as if he were standing right there in her face, like in her dream. The scent was distinctive—the aftershave Tommy had splashed on his cheeks, chin, and neck, practically every day, no matter whether he'd just ran the razor over his face or not. He loved the scent. It smelled of neroli and bergamot, with a back of rose and persimmon and a little patchouli. Sensual and Black. Like, when-you-walk-into-a-barbershop-or-a-Black-man's-bathroom-on-a-Saturday-afternoon Black. Would stink on a white man.

"Mommy," Rae called to LoLo, so quietly mother almost didn't hear daughter.

Rae rubbed her tears with the back of her wrists and pushed herself up from the chair. The second LoLo crossed the threshold into the kitchen, she stopped short, as if she'd run into an invisible barrier, and closed her eyes—inhaled so deeply she almost coughed from taking in so much air.

"You smell it?" Rae asked. "It's been a while since he came, but he's here again. For you and the baby. Maybe for me."

"You used Daddy's aftershave?" LoLo asked, completely misunderstanding what, precisely, was happening.

"No, Mommy," Rae said gently. "That's Daddy's scent." Rae looked into her mother's eyes, her pupils piercing—her pupils saying exactly what LoLo needed to understand.

"He comes to you? Like this?"

"Sometimes it's his scent I smell—the aftershave," Rae said. "Sometimes he comes to me in dreams. Once I woke up on a Sunday morning and smelled calf liver, plain as day. I jumped out of bed and raced into the kitchen and it was quiet and empty, everything in place. But it smelled like he was standing right there over the stove, cooking liver with that gravy I like, and rice. His favorite.

"I didn't tell you," Rae added, "because I thought . . . I thought you would think it was something evil."

"You know I don't believe in that hoodoo stuff. It's not in the Bible and God's word tells us not to worship false idols."

"Mommy, I don't have any control over this. I see things in my dreams all the time—have since I was little. I just never told you. I thought maybe I was evil or sinning against God because that's what you raised us to believe. But you smell him, too. How can Daddy's presence be evil?"

"Let me finish, Rae," LoLo said, raising her hand to shush her daughter. "I have something I need to show you. I'll be right back," she said.

LoLo disappeared back down the hall and reappeared just as quickly, with a small white pouch in her palm. She ran her thumbs over it slowly and stood there, her feet stuck to the linoleum Tommy had laid with his own hands when Rae was just a kid, dancing around on the other side of the kitchen threshold, regaling her father with a recap of her favorite book, *The Little Princess*.

"This is yours," LoLo said simply. She pressed it into Rae's hands.

Rae looked quizzically at the pouch, then pulled it open. Her fingers touched the lock of hair first. She pulled out the bundle and her body tingled, like some electrical current gently shocking her system awake. She laid it on the table, and then the rabbit's foot next to it, and then the pipe. She gasped when she pulled out the handkerchief and saw the blood-stained material between her fingertips. That, she dropped on the table, this time involuntarily, her hands shaking as she cocked her head to one side and then the other, washing over it with her watery eyes.

"There's one more thing in there," LoLo said quietly.

Rae hesitantly reached back into the pouch and pulled out the folded brown paper bag square. She slowly unfolded the paper and read its contents.

"What . . . what is this?" she asked, finally looking up.

LoLo searched for the words that fear—of what Tommy would think of this thing, of what God would think of this thing—had kept her from uttering over the past thirty-three years. Standing there, her daughter's heart open wide, LoLo found the courage to pour in. "Your daddy didn't want me to show this to you, but . . ." LoLo paused.

"Mommy. What is this?" Rae asked again, her heart racing as she rubbed the paper between her fingers and stared at the letters.

> *This baby*
> *This baby*
> *This baby*
> *a sweet, protected, prosperous life*

"That was in the bag they found you in at that orphanage." LoLo's words, which she'd swallowed whole almost three and a half decades earlier, gushed from her throat. "I think your birth mother left it for you. See what this is?" she said, pointing to the circle of words on the paper. "It's a wish, like a prayer. But the way they used to write them down in the old days, back in the South, when they believed in haints and roots and such. It's a petition."

"A . . . a what?"

"A petition. A prayer—for you, Rae. I think from your mother, asking for your protection," LoLo said. "I think she wanted this to be with you. I think that's what she hoped for you. Protection.

"Your daddy, he was your protector. He was my protector," LoLo said. She rubbed Rae's shoulders as she talked. "That's all I required of him and he did that. He protected us. He found you in that basement and he is the one who made sure you were okay, even when it was me who was hurting you. He didn't want me to give you this, because as far as he was concerned, we are your family and you were born the day we brought you home. We are your parents. Nothing else before that mattered to him. But this paper, this petition, he did what it asked of him. His presence here, right now, tells me he still is."

Rae, overwhelmed by the idea that her birth mother wished the best for her, that she was holding her hair and blood in her hand, that her dead father was taking up space in the room in which she and her mother stood, just down the hall from where her baby was laying her head, took off running—out the kitchen, down the hall, to the bathroom, the scent following her as she moved. Rae slammed the door and slid down onto the bathmat, still wet with the water she'd just bathed her daughter in not an hour earlier.

Over the years, Rae had used her imagination to fill in her birth story with color and light and grace: *Maybe my birth mother was young and scared and couldn't fathom raising a baby on her own,* was the first of her thoughts. Sometimes, the story had villains: *Maybe she was forced to leave me on that stoop by a family that refused to support her and her child* or *Maybe she was in an abusive relationship and feared her baby would get swooped into the violence.* The stories, they would be as varied as the books she'd tucked on the top shelf in her childhood closet. Always, though, Rae's birth mom was the hero. Afterall, there were so many ways that life as a little, defenseless baby could have ended badly for her. But this woman, she earned her place on the pedestal Rae had tucked away in her heart and forever stood there, still, immovable, innocent, like the tiny ceramic angels LoLo kept on her glass étagère.

Now, her mother's blood between her fingertips, her own baby just down the hallway, Rae regarded this woman as so much more than an inanimate object or some made-up fairy tale gathering dust on a shelf. Rae understood her humanity. Her decision, as far as Rae was concerned, was beautiful, selfless, steeped in pain, heartbreak, and yes, love—a love that she could now understand because she, too, was a mother who had carried her own baby in her womb and couldn't fathom the strength and courage and resolve it must have taken for her birth mother to leave her child, her blood, the very beat of her heart, on a stoop for someone else—LoLo and Tommy, who loved her deeply—to have. To Rae, it was the ultimate sacrifice. A miracle, no different from the miracle of conception—what it took for sperm to meet egg and egg to attach to womb and for womb to maintain the absolute perfect conditions for new life and for new life to find its way to loving arms. The pouch was proof to Rae that she was exactly where she was supposed to be.

Rae held the paper to her heart and inhaled her father's scent. "Daddy, I miss you. I love you. I love you. I love you and I miss you and I love you," she said.

And then, for her mother, the one whose blood ran through her veins, she wailed.

29

Rae struggled down the center of the train's aisle with Skye hanging from her hip and both her purse and diaper bag, full of juice boxes, Pull-Ups, books, toys, and all manner of finger snacks LoLo had shoved into the folds, talking about how she needed "all that junk to go with the baby because it can't stay here and make me fat." Skye was being fussy; she wanted to walk on her own. But Rae couldn't stand the train and especially hated the Queens train station, that nasty bastion of germs traveling from every corner of New York and depositing themselves in the fabric, the walls, the very air in that stinking place. She didn't want the baby touching any of it.

"Skye, baby, let Mommy just carry you, honey," Rae said as she adjusted the little girl on her hip. The diaper bag, which she'd slung on her shoulder, shimmied down to the crook of her elbow, tugging her arm down and both bags, which were heavier than they really needed to be, after it.

"Walk, Mommy!" Skye whined as she wriggled and thrashed and went limp to free herself from her mother's grip.

"Skye, baby, please, work with Mommy."

Rae stopped abruptly to try to gather herself—gather her baby, her things—a sudden stop that didn't play well with a few of her fellow passengers, who didn't take kindly to also having to adjust themselves to accommodate this woman and her bags and her whiney kid, whom, by their exaggerated sighs and eye rolls, they'd deemed were taking up entirely too much space. The white man who'd sat behind them on the train, this massive brute who was as wide as he was tall, who gave not even a second's thought to helping the diminutive Rae lift her heavy bags, quite literally, over her head to get them into the train's bin before they pulled out, and watched with exasperation as she wrestled, too, with getting it back down upon their preparation to exit, had had enough and was now vocalizing his exasperation with Rae's toiling.

"Come on, lady!" he said, stopping short, his brows pushed together at the center.

Rae, embarrassed and frazzled, tried her best to get out of the way, to make herself, her baby, their belongings, smaller. To accommodate. To not be a burden. She'd already had two hours of all eyes on her: the white man; the white lady who'd shared their row and flinched and turned her entire body toward the aisle when Skye, curious about the buttons on the seats, touched her hand as she reached for the little knobs; even the Black woman, young, stylish, sitting across the aisle one row up, who kept looking back at Rae as Skye acted her age during the ride, with a face full of . . . disgust? Disdain? All of them, all of it, made Rae's head pulse—made her want to draw down. It was but a small taste, she thought, of what life would be, ultimately, had she to navigate the world as a mother, alone, with her baby and all her baggage, struggling to keep it all together while the world gave her that look and shook its head and muttered as it pushed past her, annoyed, like she, this Black woman with a baby and no man, was the problem. The scourge.

This kept her up each night while she was at her parents' house, as she considered her mother's words and even all the reasons a woman would stay with a philandering man—or any man, for that matter. She was sure her mother had loved her father, her family, but now, here was her mother, admitting that she'd held up her end of the marriage in exchange for a currency she and women like her deemed more valuable than love—a pact that was much more about financial stability, physical protection, than it was some fairy tale. She wondered if things had changed much. If the same logic applied to why she should stay with a cheating husband who had asked her nicely to come back home and said please again and again and re-iterated that he is the father of her daughter and daughters need their fathers in their lives, a fact that was indisputable in Rae's eyes, and made her actually listen to Roman's "Please, come home, baby; I miss you, I need you, I want my family back" begging and roll it around in her heart, yes, but also in the parts of her that processed logic and statistics and social currency and such. By the time she did all the math, she figured it would be better for her to take her baby back to Brooklyn and make things right with her husband than it would be to move through the world Black, and woman, and mother, and alone. And so, that's what she did. What was happening on that train—how all the people surrounding her and her baby, disgusted by her taking up space rather than sympathetic to her struggle, settled her decision.

"Excuse me, so sorry," Rae said as she scrambled out of the way. "Skye! Stop it!" she yelled, snatching her daughter's wrist and shaking her a little. This she did in the moment to get the baby's attention, sure, but later, when she would sit in her solitude and eventually take an accounting of her relationship with her daughter and the way she loved her, the way she treated her, the way she held and regarded her, she would recognize that yelling at her little baby in that train aisle in front of those people wasn't about her little baby at all, and she would feel like a Judas for betraying her child and herself, for submitting to the laying of the crown of thorns on her head. On her baby's, too.

Some forty minutes later, having collected her belongings and Skye's car seat and stroller and piled them all out onto the curb, Rae stood there, stewing and observing—bothered that Roman hadn't thought to arrive early enough to park the car and meet her inside the station to help with the baby and the bags. Roman was not that kind of guy—considerate, chivalrous. He didn't open car doors or go through the revolving door first or even insist on walking closest to the street to protect Rae from oncoming traffic and such. It only occurred to him to help with the groceries when Rae asked for it. In the mornings, he'd even taken to making up only his side of the bed—like, literally arranging his pillows and pulling up the covers on the one side but not the other where Rae slept. Rae noticed it early on and she furrowed her brow over it a couple times in wonder. Now such things angered her. "Why are you only making up half the bed?" she'd asked him, the question part curiosity, part "What the fuck?"

Roman had shrugged. "I didn't even notice I was doing that."

Pointing it out didn't stop the behavior. The behavior was curious and didn't much matter to Rae, until it did.

But at the train station that day, Rae was content to wait for Roman there on the curb, with her baby and her bags, watching the people collect their people. Of course, she recognized that New Yorkers came with a patina on them—a gruffness that left them gray and worn and hard, with lines carved into their exteriors. Pleasantries weren't a thing shared between strangers; time, after all, was as short as tempers and interactions were as flammable as attitudes, and so strangers just pushed past the other strangers in a huff and rush, concerned only with point A and point B and not much else.

Retrieving someone from the train station—it seemed like that would look like a different matter, though. Like a person who would endure New York traffic and travel all that way from wherever to the curbs of the train station did so not just out of obligation but maybe, too, out of love for the person who climbed on a big piece of metal hurling down miles of tracks so that they could get to them. To their arms. But it looked like to Rae a string of more curious acts—a bunch of hard people incapable of malleability. Car after car weaved themselves to the curb and screeched to stops in front of their charges and greeted them with about the same emotion and regard as a cab driver would picking up a fare. Mothers barely grunted "hello" to their children, arms hanging stiff to their sides rather than wrapped around their seeds; wives handed their suitcases to their husbands and climbed into the front passenger seats, lips pursed, while their men slammed closed trunks and took their places behind the wheel, as solemn as a funeral procession, their hellos more perfunctory than warm, genuine. They barely looked at one another; their necks were stiff as rods, heads faced forward, bodies moving only with the jerk of the car zipping out into the traffic, ferrying their cargo off to their corners, to their lives.

Rae wondered if any of them—if anyone at all—was just . . . happy. Whether this was just the way families were—men and women who at some point had a mutual attraction and maybe even love for one another but let it all get crusted over by hard truths about who they really were down to their cores, when the shine finally wore off and everybody took their eyes off wants and trained them on all the other things. The kids. The house. The job. The needs. The living. Rae wondered if this was now her lot. She wondered if she could be as strong as her mother—if she had what it took to survive her marriage.

Finally, she saw the hood of Roman's red Toyota Corolla creeping toward the curb, sliding in just as a stone-faced couple in a Ford Escort pulled away. He announced his presence with a light tap of the horn; Skye, who'd finally settled down beneath her blanket and purple stuffed puppy, shifted a little in her stroller but kept on dreaming, as if the world were clear blue skies. Rae forced a stiff smile to her face.

Roman hopped out of the car and moved swiftly, arms wide, to hug his wife. "Ayyyye, there's my girls," he said. Rae was a rod in his embrace; she didn't want him touching her with those same hands that had likely unsnapped the bra she found in their home, and she certainly didn't want to send the signal that her coming home meant they didn't have problems. They did.

"Hey," Rae said curtly, moving with the same coldness and urgency as all the other passengers who were hopping into cars before her. The way her mother had greeted her father, TJ, her, so many years before.

"Look at my girl—she knocked out, huh?" Roman said, pulling the cover of the stroller back so that he could see their daughter. "How was she on the train?"

"It was fine. She was fine," Rae clipped.

"Okay, let me get the seat situated. You want to get her out the stroller?"

They spent the next few minutes working in silence, their movements fluid as Roman attached the car seat to the seat belt harness and then turned to retrieve Skye from her mother's arms. The baby, deadweight as she slumbered, snuggled into the seat the second her father dropped her in and fastened the seat belt over the baby's shoulders and between her legs; he quickly moved out of the way to allow Rae to cover her with her favorite blanket, topped with her purple puppy, and then hustled herself into the front seat. Roman hopped into the driver's seat and put the car in gear and pushed the gas practically before his door was closed. Neither spoke; she couldn't find the words to say, and so the radio did the talking. Ella, Billie, Sarah, Abbey, each one of them spinning half truths and big lies on Roman's behalf. Always, this is who he turned to—the music he chose to bury himself in—when his heart was heavy and awry. Rae knew it well; it was this playlist—a never-ending stream of old jazz CDs he'd had piled high on his floor stereo—that he kept in heavy rotation around the time that he and Rae met, just as he was working hard to get over the breakup with his first wife.

"Why you always listening to all this old man music?" Rae had asked him when, finally, she'd been out with him on enough dates and to his place a few times and had enough of a rapport with him to ask the question. There was a lot about him that she liked, but there were a few things that took some getting used to—namely that he was slightly older than her, by four years, which, to a then twenty-six-year-old, felt grown grown. Borderline old. He was not helping his case with the grandmotherly tunes.

"What, you don't like the jazz greats?" he'd asked. "Ella, Sarah, Ms. Abbey Lincoln. This music is timeless."

"It's so, so . . . glum. Their voices are beautiful, don't get me wrong. But nobody sounds happy."

"They made happy music. This is just what I'm into these days is all. The music fits my mood."

"And what mood is that?"

Roman had fallen quiet while he contemplated the right words. "I thought I'd be good and married by now and starting a family. That's what I want, you know? To have a good woman by my side, some kids. My dad always says he's a better man because he had a good woman. My ex and I are over, and that's the way it should be. We aren't right for each other. But I guess I'm still feeling a way about not having what I really want."

"And what's that?" Rae had asked.

"A love of my own."

Rae and Roman had sat in silence as Abbey Lincoln sang her coulda beens, woulda beens, him shifting and squeaking on the leather of his chesterfield sofa, her, body still but heart aflutter, eyes closed, listening as she zeroed in on her mission to give this man what he had wanted. What she had wanted. Not much longer after that night, he said "I love you," and though it was fast considering they'd been together only a short while, Rae had thought he meant it. She said it back, and eventually, she meant it, too.

Roman eased his foot on the brake pedal as red taillights yawned a red pattern across all four lanes of the highway. As the car slowed, so did the rustle of the wind against the car exterior, a silencing that made the music louder, crisper. Rae recognized this tune: Ella Fitzgerald's melancholy "In a Sentimental Mood." Roman reached over and lowered the volume.

"Rae, baby, I'm so sorry . . ."

"Don't," Rae said, holding up her hand. "Not in the car. Not in front of the baby."

"She's sleep, babe. And we need to talk about this. Clearly, you got things you need to get off your chest."

"I'm not the one who did anything wrong here!" Rae yelled. She quickly settled her voice. "I think what I have to say about that won't really be any big revelation and I'm not the one who should be taking the lead in this conversation anyway."

"That's why I'm apologizing," Roman said. "Baby, listen to me: I know I fucked up."

"The baby," Rae said through clenched teeth. "Don't curse in front of her."

Roman took a deep breath. "I messed up, okay? But that shouldn't be the end of our family. It doesn't mean that I don't love you, us, this," he said, waving his pointer finger around in the air, "us."

"You sure got a strange way of showing it."

"For the record, I didn't sleep with her."

Rae turned her whole body toward her husband and narrowed her eyes. "So, on top of it all, you gonna sit here in this New York traffic and call me a dumbass to my face, too?"

"I didn't say you're dumb."

"I found a bra that did not belong to me in . . . our . . . bathroom. *Our bathroom!*" Rae yelled.

Her voice soared above Ella's, traveling in a circle around the inside of the car, dancing on the sound of the traffic and wind around them, and floating directly into the baby's ears. Skye's eyes popped open and, because she was unsure where she was, where her mama was, what was happening around her, why the air was thick and severe, she burst into tears.

"Oh, baby, baby, Mommy is right here," Rae called out as she reached around the headrest to touch her daughter's leg. "It's okay, baby."

Skye was unrelieved. She whined and took in a series of deep breaths through down-turned lips, the precursor to a full-on cry.

"Hey, baby, Daddy's here, too, honey," Roman said, reaching his right hand behind him to touch his daughter's leg, too. "It's okay."

Skye looked down at the hand touching her shoe and trailed her eyes up the fingers to wrist, to arm, and finally to the side of her father's head. She smiled, even as tears made tracks down her plump cheeks.

"We're going home, little one," Roman said. "You want to go home?"

"Yes," Skye said pitifully. She rubbed her eyes.

"Okay, we're going home, honey. Daddy's gonna take you home."

Rae cut her eyes at her husband and turned toward the passenger window, tucking her body as close to the car door as possible without being on the other side of it, as far away from her husband as she could get without jumping out onto the Van Wyck Expressway. When she left her parents' house, it had made sense for her to go back to her man. Now, she wasn't so sure.

It annoyed the fuck out of Rae that whenever she left the house—whether to go get her nails done or catch a flight out of town—she'd have to spend just as much time leaving detailed instructions on the care and upkeep of the baby, her schedule, what needed to be done around the house, as she would getting her own self ready to travel. It was an exhausting endeavor, planning out what she had to do when she arrived to wherever she was going, and planning, too, what needed to happen while she was away. Roman never cared to take any responsibility for what he considered minutiae, but that's exactly what made Rae want to fight him coming and going: just because he didn't care about the details and how they were assembled didn't mean they weren't important—necessary. In need of execution. And no matter how much work she'd done to leave the house clean, organized, thoughtfully arranged to minimize the disaster that would arrange itself in her absence, she'd walk right back into a cloud of chaos—as if Roman had invited Axl Rose and a merry band of his most loyal heavy metal fans back to the crib for an after-concert party that had gotten totally out of hand.

Rae, already on one from the conversation in the car, stood behind Roman, the baby in her arms, as he fiddled with the apartment door lock, attitudinal. Exhausted. Bracing. On the other side of that door, she stood shocked, a little light on her feet, pleasantly relieved.

"I know you always get on me about not straightening up," he said, dropping the suitcases in the foyer. "I wanted you to walk into a clean house, so that we could focus on us," he added, taking the baby out of his wife's arms and leading Rae by the hand deeper into their living room. Standing sentry on the cocktail table was a large vase pregnant with calla lilies, the flower she'd carried in her bridal bouquet four years earlier when they said "I do" and jumped over the broom that now hung above their front door as a reminder of their love. "I got you some flowers," he said, spreading his arm toward the bouquet as if he were showing Rae to a seat. "Why don't you sit down and relax a bit while I get Skye into her pajamas. I know both of you are tired. I bought that wine you like so we could sip and talk. I'll be right back."

Rae sat on the couch and took in the spectacle. She was not impressed. She slurped down a half glass of pinot and decided to tell her husband just that when he finally came back into the room, sans the baby.

"How's the wine? I got it from that little spot you like, over on DeKalb," he said as he poured himself a glass and gulped a mouthful and then another. "I know you like pinot, so . . ."

Rae nodded.

"So, let me just start by saying that I'm glad you're home, baby. I missed you. I missed my girls."

Rae nodded.

"Like I said, I know I hurt you, but I want to fix that. I want to fix us."

Rae nodded.

Roman twisted his head and looked at his wife from the side of his left eye. "So . . . you don't have anything to, um, say?"

"What is it that you're expecting me to say, Roman?" Rae asked, her breath betraying her exasperation.

"I mean, I want you to acknowledge that I'm trying."

"What do you want, a parade?" Rae asked, leaning forward.

"You don't have to be an asshole."

Rae shook her head and chortled. "So, I'm an asshole now? Because I'm not impressed enough for you?"

"I didn't do this to impress you. I did this because I love you."

"Don't sit here and tell that lie. You didn't do this because you love me. You did this because you want to change the conversation. You want me not to be mad at you."

"I mean, I would prefer that you accept my apology, so we can move on."

"You think it's that easy? Just lay out some flowers and wine and make your voice soft when you say 'sorry' and I'll just—poof!—forget you had a bitch in our house?"

"I'm telling you, nothing happened in the house," he said. "I promise, babe. I wouldn't disrespect us like that."

"Being with another bitch isn't disrespectful to your wife, so long as you do your dirt somewhere other than where your wife and baby lay their heads?"

"Stop twisting my words, Rae!" Roman said. This time, it was he who raised his voice.

Rae shut her mouth tight. Gave him dead eyes.

"I'm sorry. I'm sorry for yelling," Roman said. He reached over to lay his hand on Rae's. She flinched. "What I'm trying to say is that I think we need to go see somebody. A couple's therapist. Somebody who can help us work through this."

Now this was typical of Roman's family, and so it was not really a surprise to Rae that this was Roman's big idea. His mother had been studying to become a psychologist when she got pregnant with his older sister and had to drop out of school to work and save up for the baby while her husband was out doing . . . well, Rae still wasn't quite clear what he did for a living back then, beyond not really being present for his family. Eventually, with the help of her own mother watching the kids, Roman's mom got back to school, but focused on nursing—a quicker pursuit than psychotherapy. But you couldn't tell the woman she wasn't a therapist; she stayed in everybody's business and lectured often that having a good therapist on speed dial was "just as important as your ob-gyn, honey." And maybe Rae could have come around to that belief more quickly if Roman's family wasn't such a mess, or her own family didn't teach her different—that airing one's dirty laundry in the street was a low-down affair that signaled weakness rather than a genuine chance to get under the hood and fix things.

"A therapist? I don't need a damn therapist. I need you to keep your dick in your pants," Rae said.

"Listen, we have problems . . ."

"No, you have a problem," Rae snapped.

"You're just perfect, huh? You think you're the only one who's unhappy?"

"What in the hell do you have to be unhappy about?" Rae asked.

"Are you serious right now?" he asked.

"Dead ass, Roman. You have your dinner placed in front of your face every night, your house is clean, all your clothes down to your drawers are washed and put away without you having to think about any of those things," Rae said, her voice raising with each task she listed. "Hell, you don't do anything with the baby but kiss her good morning and good night, unless I actually ask you to do something specific, and you even drag your feet doing that. And I find that really curious, Roman, because you don't even work."

"See? That's it. Right there."

"What? Am I lying?"

"I'm pointing out that you don't respect my work, Rae. You don't respect me."

"Of course I respect your work, Roman. Why else would I have agreed to bring in the money so that you could write your book or whatever it is you're doing?"

"You don't get to say you respect my work and then dismiss it like I'm not out here trying," Roman said quietly. "This is what I mean. I don't feel like my wife supports my dreams."

Rae opened her mouth to speak but closed it again without another word. Her hands were tingling—from the fingertips straight up to the wrists. Her head, light. An ambulance roared past the huge picture window that introduced the neighborhood, the sun, and the moon into their brownstone every day—a noise so piercing in the midst of their uncomfortable silence that it should have shaken them both. But it is impossible to shake what is immovable.

The two were frozen, staring at the thread that would slowly unravel their marriage.

30

2004, early fall

It was a spot just above Rae's right ankle, not quite her calf, and every time she stepped down on that foot, it felt like someone had a vise grip digging directly through her skin and past veins and cartilage and down to the bone. It was but a small cramp the night before—a dull ache that got progressively annoying as she watched Roman watch her hustle fried fish and grits to the dinner table, then scrape the plates, then grease Skye's scalp and flat-twist and wrap her hair in a bonnet, then get her in the tub and out the tub and read two books—no, three—then check under the bed and in the closet for that monster that would stay away only if Mommy issued a very specific threat, and tuck in the child a good three, four times after fetching her water to quench her thirst and rubbing her back to help her settle and loosening her bonnet because it was giving her a headache and then, finally, settling her own self down to review show notes for the following day's taping. It wasn't the second shift she was pulling that had her tense; it was seeing Roman fall right back into the pattern couple's therapy, for a short while at least, had rearranged. "Baby," he whispered when she finally laid down and pulled the covers up over her shoulder. He'd rubbed her arm first, and then smushed his body against her back, his erection pulsing against the meatiest part of her ass. His kiss, which he'd aimed at her cheek, landed on her ear.

"Babe, I'm exhausted," she said.

Kiss, smack. Kiss smack.

"Roman, not tonight, okay? I'm just . . ."

Kiss, smack. Kiss smack. He tugged at her shoulder with enough gentle force to pull her body onto its back. "You don't even have to do anything, baby. Just lay back and relax."

When he collapsed back onto the side of his bed—sweaty, satisfied, oblivious—Rae slow-walked to the bathroom and wiped herself down and massaged that sore spot in her leg until her mind finally quieted and sleep had its way.

But that spot on her leg, sore from the severity of the cramp the night prior, was starting, again, to dull thud with each step she took toward Skye's kindergarten class—a walk that, after a shaky first few days, had become easier, pleasant, the sunny sliver in even the cloudiest sky. Both mother and daughter had come to rather enjoy the time, with mother filling daughter with platitudes and hype—"You're gonna be great today!" and "You be the sunshine, I'll be blue skies so today will be perfect!"—and daughter making discoveries that made every day feel new again. On this day, though, there were only lip quivers and near tears.

"I don't want to go, Mommy," Skye said.

"What do you mean, baby? You don't want to go where?"

"I don't want to go to Miss Carey's class."

"Oh, come on, Skye Boogie, you love Miss Carey! She gives you high fives in the morning and teaches you your letters and how to write your name. Don't you want to practice writing your name? And play with the crayons and see your friends?"

Skye got quiet and focused her eyes on her maroon patent-leather Mary Janes. "I don't have any friends," she said finally.

"What do you mean you don't have friends? All those kids in your class? There's sixteen friends you get to see every day!" Rae said, her daughter's displeasure still not really registering.

"They didn't let me sit with them yesterday," she said. "I don't want to sit by myself today."

The bell rang. "What do you mean you don't want to sit by yourself? When did you sit by yourself, Skye?" Rae asked, her steps becoming slower, more measured, to match her daughter's. She hadn't realized 'til that moment that she'd been practically dragging her daughter as the little girl heavy-stepped behind her.

Babygirl dropped her head, and her bottom lip slowly, surely pushed past the top. "Yesterday," she answered.

Rae stopped short—took both her daughter's hands into hers and bent down to get right into her face. That spot on her leg, sore from the severity of the cramp the night prior, was starting to pulse with sharp precision. "Tell Mommy what happened, sweetheart."

Rae braced herself. She and Roman, understanding the stakes of a Black child in the hands of the American education system, had taken such care to get their baby into the right school, into the right classroom. Simply surrendering Skye to the neighborhood school and trusting the adults to handle the child—this pretty little chocolate girl with cherub cheeks and a mass of Afro puff piled high atop her head, who knew her numbers and letters and already was reading cereal boxes and *The Snowy Day* and the names of some of the simpler flavors at the local ice cream shop—well, that was not an option. Rae didn't want to practice the same mostly hands-off approach to her daughter's schooling that her parents had employed. To Tommy and LoLo, minimally educated, busy with work, intimidated by those little chairs and teachers and their clipboards, completely trusting of an educational system that simply did not have the same challenges as the segregated one in which they struggled, the neighborhood school in their little piece of northern utopia was more than fine. But for Rae, being in it from day-to-day was torture; she was constantly having her intelligence questioned, challenged, by teachers and counselors who remembered when little niggers knew their place and stuck to more sensible pursuits— carpentry, factory work, maybe a gig down at the post office. None of this required As, advanced classes, leadership positions in school clubs and such that would make prestigious colleges open wide their doors and hand over a spot meant for a white student looking to excel in life to a Black student who, in the eyes of Rae's teachers and counselors, could never. There was only one time Rae could recall when her mother came to her rescue— that time when the school counselor, Mrs. McCarthy, refused to release Rae's transcripts and secure the principal's signature for a scholarship to which Rae had applied. That scholarship, which would pay full tuition to a local college that had a comprehensive television production curriculum and provide four years' worth of internships at NBC's production studios, was the difference between Rae getting a degree and a good job in her field and bagging groceries at the neighborhood Pathmark. "Your grades aren't really high enough for you to win that scholarship, sweetie," Mrs. McCarthy had said, tapping Rae's application—thirteen pages of handwritten essays and answers to questions about her coursework and extracurricular activities—on top of her cluttered metal desk. "I don't think you or I should be wasting the principal's time with this application. Why don't you fill out the application for Suffolk Community College if you're so set on getting a degree? I'm sure with your grades, you'll get in."

"But that's not where I want to go to school," Rae had said. "My parents can't really afford tuition anyway. I promised them I would try my best to pay for it myself."

"Well, you're a hardworking girl—industrious. I'm sure you'll figure it out," Mrs. McCarthy had said matter-of-factly, holding out Rae's application in front of her.

Rae had rushed out of that office broken, feeling like focusing on her lessons, like LoLo had insisted, working hard to earn her way into college, like Tommy had insisted, was all for naught. She dug deep down to the bottom of her bookbag, fished out a quarter, and pushed it into the slot of the pay phone in the hallway just outside the offices that housed the school administrators. Not more than fifteen minutes after Rae's teary phone call to her mother, who happened to be home on sick leave recovering from a bad rheumatoid arthritis flare-up and slightly hopped up on painkillers, LoLo was stomping into the principal's office. "Sit right there and don't you move," she'd told Rae as she opened the office door. To this day, Rae isn't quite sure what LoLo said or whose feelings she hurt to make her point; all she knows is that LoLo had walked out of that office with Rae's signed application and transcripts tucked neatly in a prepaid FedEx envelope. "Go on back to class," she had said as she hugged her daughter. "I'm going to drop this off and get back in the bed."

It was the one time Rae remembered her mother up there at the school, squaring her shoulders, talking to whoever was in charge. LoLo neither cared for nor understood how to work the system, but she understood money. She understood fairness. She understood that each of these things were due her daughter. Everything else, Rae had to tend to all by herself.

Rae would not have Rae wither under that same weight. She simply would not.

"Miss Carey switched our seats so we could make new friends, and no one chose me to sit next to them, so I sat at the table by myself," Skye said.

Rae gulped a mouthful of spit and fluttered her eyes, trying hard to compose herself. To keep from cursing right there in the street, right there in front of her daughter. "Let's get you to school, baby," she said. "I'll talk to Miss Carey, okay? You won't be sitting by yourself ever again, you hear?"

Rae wiggled her right foot and spun it around in circles, trying to loosen up the muscle, which was slowly constricting around that problem spot that had quieted but now was yawning itself awake. Ten minutes later, she was in Miss Carey's face out in the hallway. Rae did not see children. She did not see teachers passing by. She did not see all the cheerful colors and letters and stick-figure and flowery artwork decorating the hallway walls. All she could see was Lorraine Carey's face—specifically her lips—as she fixed them to try to explain why Skye, the only little Black girl in her kindergarten class, was sitting all alone when the specific assignment was for all the kindergarteners to kick it with someone new.

"Listen," Rae said, interrupting Miss Carey's mumbling explanation, which didn't sound like much of an explanation at all, "I don't want my daughter sitting by herself in your classroom ever again. Frankly, I'm deeply disturbed that the grown-up in the room didn't notice the optics of leaving a little Black girl to sit by herself much less understand how hurtful that could be to a five-year-old."

"Miss Lister, that's not the way it happened. There wasn't any more room at the tables, and she ended up sitting alone because there was nowhere else to sit," she said. "I . . . I can't believe you're turning this into a racial thing," Miss Carey said quickly and loudly.

"I didn't turn it into a racial thing. It is a racial thing that *you* created when you left my daughter sitting by herself. I don't care what the seating arrangements were; you should have made room for my daughter. Now we can do one of two things: I can either escalate this and take it to the administration that I pay tuition to and see if this aligns with the 'child-centered values' I pay twenty thousand dollars a year for, or you can apologize to my daughter and sit her in the middle of these new friends she's supposed to be making instead of leaving her to be ignored by her fellow students. I don't think the latter is too much to ask, but I need you to know that I'm very capable of the former."

"I . . . I understand," she said. "It won't happen again."

"I trust that it won't," Rae said. Still staring into the teacher's eyes, she yelled Skye's name. The baby, who had been ear hustling by the door, rushed to her mother's side.

"Yes, Mommy?"

"Miss Carey is going to show you to your new seat next to your new friends today! Isn't that exciting?"

Skye giggled and swung her arms in excitement.

Rae looked at her watch and hopped to; if she left the building right that second and ran to the subway station, she still had a chance to catch the express, which, if it was truly operating like an express, could get her to the crosstown line that would deposit her five blocks away from the office. If she skipped picking up her daily order of coffee and a lemon poppyseed muffin, she just might slip into her desk chair without her supervisor noticing she was late. "Give me some sugar," she said, bending down to press her lips against her daughter's. "Mommy loves you. What are you going to be today?"

"Fabulous!" Skye said.

"And why are you going to be fabulous?"

"Because who am I not to be?" she said, repeating her five-year-old understanding of the Marianne Williamson text her mother borrowed from to pour into her child each morning.

"That's right, honey. Now go in there and be great today so you can tell me all about it tonight, okay?"

"Okay, Mommy!"

And with that, Skye ran in her direction, and Rae hobbled off into her own.

The scratchy red fabric on her desk chair wasn't even lukewarm from her presence yet and here was Jeremy, standing over Rae, waving the copy she'd written for next week's taping in her face like a flag on the play. "Heeeeey, Rae," he said with this slow, sing-songy rasp he employed to drag out his words—something he did when he was uncomfortable, which he usually was, for some reason, whenever he engaged with Rae. It was not Rae's intention to make him feel any kind of way; really, she just wanted to get her work done, do it well, be paid for that work, and maybe get a little recognition when she did a particularly good job. Maybe even a shot at a promotion. Rae didn't think it was too much to ask. But here she was, sitting in her desk chair, her leg literally pulsing like it had its own heartbeat, having to answer to this white boy who, despite being five years her junior and with only a couple months of production under his belt compared to Rae's nine years, was hired over her for this supervisory position. He would say he was just doing his job, editing scripts, making sure the words, the stories, the build danced off the hosts' lips and pop-locked through the screen to the viewers. But Rae knew better. That contempt, those assumptions, the belief that this Black woman was taking up space meant for another more worthy, more male, more white, was a stench that wafted off his tongue every time he trained his voice in her direction. If he felt anything, it was her response to that.

Rae inhaled deeply but released silently. "Hey, Jeremy, what's up?" she asked, forcing a close-lipped smile to her face.

"I just wanted to go over your Jay-Z script," he said. "You mind coming back over to my desk?"

This time, Rae shined her teeth. "Sure, happy to," she said, even though she most certainly was not. She hobbled to his desk, the cramp in her leg balling up like a tight fist ready to strike. He tapped the back of a rickety chair he'd pulled up next to his own, and had her sit there, like she was some puppy he was going to pop on the nose with a newspaper and then teach a new trick.

"Good job with the script—lots of gooooood infooooo here. I think it still needs some woooork," he said, dragging his words. "Jay-Z is a fascinating guy, and you captured some of his maaagic, but there's a bunch of irrelevant information that bogs it down. Ummmmm, you need to work on getting to the point of the points you're trying to make and making those points universal."

"I, um . . . I don't understand," Rae said quietly, gently. The last thing she needed was another note in her file saying she didn't take criticism well. The cramp hit her with a combination punch.

"Well, like here," he said, thumbing through the pages, which he'd marked up with red Sharpie. "You name-drop a singer nobody's ever heard of."

Rae leaned into the page and focused her eyes on the words in the center of the big red circle at which he was pointing. "That's Donny Hathaway," she said.

"I know, sooooooo, nobody really knows who he issssss."

Rae cocked her head to the side and narrowed her eyes. "Everybody knows who Donny Hathaway is," she said slowly.

"No, everybody doesn't. I don't."

"'A Song For You'? 'Little Ghetto Boy'? 'To Be Young, Gifted and Black'?"

Jeremy shook his head no and shrugged.

"'This Christmas'! You know 'This Christmas'!" she said, snapping her fingers. He gave her nothing. Rae wrinkled her eyes again. "Come on, you know this song, J! 'Hang all the mistletoe, dah dah dah dah dah dah . . . thiissss Christmas . . .' It's the Christmas song! That comes on the radio and you know you better get your list together!" she said, adding a chuckle in an attempt to lighten the mood.

"Yeaaaaah, I don't know that one," Jeremy said, shrugging. "That's what takes away from the piece. You're name-dropping an artist that the audience won't know. That's not helpful in telling the story and helping the viewers get to know the subject."

"Well, Jeremy, this is a music show. Knowing Jay-Z's musical influences is important to the story."

"Heard. But we should stick to the influences that we know matter."

"Are you saying Donny Hathaway doesn't matter?" Rae asked.

Jeremy laughed. "I mean, he's not Jimmy Buffet, Elvis."

"Who's Jimmy Buffet?" Rae asked. Of course, she knew, but if he was going to say some disrespectful shit about the artist whose voice soared in her parents' house when they were young and loving and willing to let the music take them over despite their children were watching them slow-drag, she might as well say some disrespectful shit right on back.

"Rae. Jimmy Buffet? Seriously?"

"Seriously."

"He's only one of the greatest entertainers to ever grace the stage."

"I would say the same thing about Stevie Wonder, who was a direct influence on Donny Hathaway and vice versa, and definitely appreciated in houses like Jay-Z's and mine and, oh, I'd say pretty much anyone who's going to tune in on Thursday to see our profile on their favorite rapper."

"Look, I don't want to argue about it," Jeremy said. "You have your opinions, clearly. But it's my job to do what's best for the show. Donny Hathaway comes out. I made some more notes on the script. It would be great if you went through them and keyed in the edits. I'll need it back within the hour."

Jeremy unceremoniously swirled his swivel chair back toward his computer, leaving Rae to stare at his back. In her head, she deftly snatched the Fiskars scissors off the pile of clutter on his desk and plunged them into his ear, to fix what was obviously broken seeing that he didn't know good music, despite that he sat in a supervising producer's position on a music show. In real life, Rae pushed herself up from the chair and dragged herself and her leg back to her desk, and quickly edited every ounce of color and light out of her script and sent it back through the office's computer system to Jeremy—a bland compilation of talking points for a bland-ass supervising producer, intent on commodifying Blackness in a junk food meal as devoid of salt, fat, pepper, ginger as he.

Rae was hobbling through the hall, headed for the bathroom to swallow two Advil she'd scrounged up from the bottom of her purse when Nimma came rushing out of her side of the production room. She slowed and then stopped and stared at Rae's leg as Rae tipped on one foot and dragged the other behind it.

"Whoa, what's going on with you?" Nimma said, jutting her chin toward Rae's cramped leg.

"Oh, hey," Rae said. She kept hobbling. "This cramping thing. It's nothing."

"Doesn't look like nothing," Nimma said, rushing to open the bathroom door for Rae.

"I'll be fine. Just gonna take this medicine. Hopefully it'll loosen up this knot."

Don't follow me, don't follow me, don't follow me, Rae wanted to scream. She needed a minute to compose herself, shake off the day, swallow the things with the school and Jeremy and get her body to act right so she could make it to the end of her shift.

Nimma followed her.

"But where exactly is the pain in your leg, though?" she asked, staring down at Rae's pant leg.

Rae pointed and winced as she settled her body against the row of sinks.

"Mind if I take a look?"

"What, you a doctor now?"

Nimma smirked and raised both her hands in surrender. "It's your business, sis. I'm just saying, I had a cousin who passed from a blood clot. Thing started with a pain in her leg that she ignored and next thing you know, she was gone. Just like that."

Rae dropped her jaw.

"Oh, oh—I'm not saying that's what's going to happen to you," Nimma said. "Damn. My bad. I'm just saying I get really extra sensitive about leg pain. You really should go get that checked out."

"I don't really have time for that," Rae said, ripping open a packet of pills and pouring them into her hand. She turned on the water and cupped one hand under it.

"There's a doctor right around the corner—Dr. Wei. Her mother practices ancient Chinese medicine downstairs, and upstairs, the daughter practices western medicine. She's good. I went to her once for an emergency when my primary wasn't available and I needed to get somewhere quick and close, and she was so good I switched to her. I can give her a call for you."

"You're not going to leave me alone about this, are you?" Rae asked.

"Not while you're walking through the halls like somebody needs to amputate, no," Nimma said. "Besides the fact that I'm the union OSHA rep and I'm responsible for making sure we have a safe work environment for all of us employees, personally, I would much rather you go and find out why you're hurting. Go take care of that."

"Fine," Rae said.

The walk to the doctor's office was only three city blocks—light work for the average New Yorker—but for Rae and her knotted leg, it was a painful trek that took double the time. She spent the entire walk wincing and wondering how good this doctor could have been if she was able to take in a new patient within a half hour of a cold call for an appointment, and registered silent but serious concern when she walked through the office door into a bomb of red paint and incense. A huge sign, replete with an arrow and words written in both English and Chinese, directed Dr. Wei's patients upstairs. Rae stood at the bottom of the staircase and asked sweet baby Jesus in the manger for the strength and will to traverse the eighteen steps, particularly considering she wasn't convinced there was any real help up there beyond a doctor who would give her a couple Tylenol and tell her to rest her leg.

Upstairs opened into a more traditional American doctor's office— sterile white walls, row chairs covered with nubby, itchy blue materials, posters that warned patients of their duty to check their blood pressure regularly, eat healthier, be prepared to settle their bills for medical services before they're seen. Rae had barely sat down after checking in before the nurse called her name, her voice bouncing around the patientless room.

Rae had barely finished struggling herself up onto the examination table before a sharp knock on the door made her jump and a diminutive young woman in a white doctor's coat stepped into the room. "Hello, I'm Dr. Wei," the physician said as she checked over a clipboard with Rae's vitals and medical history. "So, what brings you here today?"

"It's not a big deal. Nothing a little Tylenol shouldn't be able to fix, really. It's just a bad cramp in my leg," Rae said, reaching over the side of the table to rub the sore spot. "My coworker was worried and insisted I come and have it checked out."

"Mm-hmm. When did the pain begin?" she asked.

"Uh, it's been working its way into a knot for a couple days now—since Saturday? But it started hurting much worse yesterday, and this morning, it was starting to affect my ability to walk."

"But your coworker had to convince you to come."

Rae said nothing.

"Tell me about your medical history," the doctor continued. "You didn't fill out any of those questions in the patient intake documents."

"I'm adopted, so I don't really have anything to fill in for those parts," Rae said curtly.

"Oh, I see. Well, I'd like to run some blood tests to check out a few things while you're here."

"I, um . . . I'm fine. I just have a pain in my leg," Rae stammered. She hated needles, about as much as she hated having to explain her ignorance on what lurked in her blood—all the ways relatives who were strangers to her swirled their conditions into her DNA, all the time she spent worrying about how, eventually, she would suffer, completely un-aware of what diseases could seize her body and take her away from here. Her anger over that lack of information was particularly acute when she stood in the pediatrician's office, repeating over and over again that her daughter, too, would have only half her family medical history—that of her father's. To be born without record—it made her feel ashamed. Incomplete.

"Yes, I know, but while you're here, we might as well do a full workup to make sure that we're not dealing with anything serious. It's good for you to have that baseline."

For what seemed like an eternity but what was more like just a couple minutes, Dr. Wei squeezed, pressed, poked, and pondered Rae's sore leg, which, coupled with the shame, coaxed tears to Rae's eyes. A gentle smile lounged across the doctor's lips as she leaned into her patient and took her hand into her own.

"My mother works downstairs. Back home, she's a respected physician. I grew up at her knee, watching her, learning medicinal traditions passed down from generations—ancient practices. They are the traditions of the East, but so many of them have found their way into western medicine, though their origins are hardly acknowledged. I'm sure you can say the same about health practices from your own culture. The American South was full of wisdom passed down from ancient African cultures," she said as she patted Rae's hand. "Granny midwives were extraordinary healers for their time, for instance, but their practices have been overrun by the medical system."

A chill made Rae shake almost violently.

"Well," the doctor continued, "I'm not going to prescribe any medication to you, and I want you to stay away from the over-the-counter painkillers. I'm going to show you some exercises that will alleviate the pain and loosen up the muscle. I suspect that this pain is your muscle's reaction to stress."

"Stress?" Rae asked. A small bit of water was stuck in the corner of her right eye. She wiped it clear. "Stress can make a body part hurt like that?"

"Oh, certainly. My mother treats this kind of thing in her acupuncture practice, and I've seen it as well. Tell me about what's going on in your life. You mentioned you work nearby. Full time?" the doctor asked as she gently pushed Rae back and massaged her leg.

"Yes. I'm a producer for a TV music show," Rae said through winces.

"Stressful?"

Rae huffed. "It can be, but that's just the job. That's what it is." She winced again.

"And what about home? You have children?"

Rae smiled. "I have a daughter, Skye. She's five."

"Oh, well, that can certainly be a handful. Husband?"

Rae pressed her lips. "Yes."

The physician balled her fist and knocked it into Rae's leg. "Your toenail polish is pretty," she said. "You do them yourself?"

Rae let out a yelp and grimaced. "No, I go to a nail salon not far from here."

"You should really stay out of nail salons. They're full of germs, particularly those sinks you put your feet in. Teeming with bacteria."

"Doc, you were just telling me that this knot is stress-related, right?"

"Yes, stress."

"Getting my toenails done is pretty much the only thing I do for myself that relieves stress. And now you're telling me that's bad for me?"

"The salons are dangerous. The act is not."

Rae wrinkled her brow. The pain had subsided; the knot had all but disappeared.

"What I am saying is that you are young, but as an African American woman, you are also vulnerable to a host of illnesses triggered, in part, by stress. You wear it on your body, but it also affects what happens *in* your body. That's why we're going to take blood today. But my doctor's orders for now are that you do some things that will relieve some of this stress, and you do the exercises I give you to keep your leg muscles from contracting."

"That's it? Exercise and do something nice for myself? That's going to keep my leg from becoming one big knot?"

"Destressing can literally save your life."

31

Rae would go to her grave remembering the first time she washed her daughter's hair—how she'd swaddled her up tight in that baby-soft pink and white blanket and gently laid her in the cradle of Roman's massive palms as she waited for the kitchen sink's faucet stream to warm. The boiler in the building was finicky and so the water was always much too cold when it was first turned on, and then after a short while, scorching hot, so one had to be patient, darting fingertips in and out of the surge until it was not so hot, not so cold, just right enough for the task before them—the washing of dishes, hands, hair, and the like. When the water had run lukewarm across her fingers, Rae grabbed the shampoo bottle and gave Roman a nod; gingerly, he extended his arms, positioning the mohawk puff of soft curls atop the baby's head directly beneath the stream. Rae had expected the baby to bawl when the water hit her scalp; after all, she'd cried holy hell when the nurse sponged her shortly after she wormed her way out of the birth canal, and the little girl didn't seem to take too kindly to the washups she was getting since arriving at home, either. She would fuss and bang her arms and thrash about the baby tub, which was too much of an oblong plastic bucket for her to feel comfortable. But Skye was altogether different when the gentle stream had begun running over her scalp; she stared directly into her mother's eyes as Rae massaged and smiled and spoke love into her little girl. "Look at you, you beautiful baby. You are so very perfect. Does that feel good, honey? Yes, it does. I know it does, yes, I do! Yes, I do!" she'd cooed. Rae reveled in how content Skye looked, this little wonder, so at peace that she relaxed her body into her father's big hands and, never breaking her stare into her mother's eyes, boxed and bobbed and weaved sleep until, finally, she couldn't hold her eyes open any longer. Like she was at some fancy hair salon. Like fingertips were magic. Like she was in love with her mama. That's how it began with Skye. How it would forever be. She'd sit just as quiet and sweet when Rae did her hair. She loved getting her hair scratched out, washed, twisted, tended to. Rae loved doing it. The proof was right there on Skye's scalp—evidence of her mother's attention and adoration, measured in the complexity of the style and the time it took to tend to the kinky, curly garden atop the little girl's head.

Rae could not claim that childhood experience with her mother. She had spent many a Saturday night perched on a stack of thick yellow phone books, crouched at some ungodly angle between her mother's knees, trying desperately not to flinch beneath the heat of the fire-red hot comb as LoLo dragged it around the edges of Rae's thick mane. The cool of LoLo's breath on her neck was little solace; greater was the fear of being burned—certainly of being popped with the giant, wide-toothed Afro comb if Rae didn't hold perfectly still or screamed out in pain while LoLo tried to straighten what she'd default refer to as "naps." Rae loved wearing a fresh press-and-curl, but the process of getting her hair done never felt like an act of love between her and her mother; it was a burden, something that hurt, something that was done not in any way to fortify or enhance Rae's beauty, but done more for practicality's sake. Hair got dirty. Hair needed to be washed. That was it. LoLo did not allow her daughter to harp on her looks, and so Rae didn't, though secretly, she wanted to be the pretty one for once—wanted the boys to notice her and whisper to their friends when she passed by, sure, but even more, wanted her mother to spin her around after one of those grueling Saturday night hair sessions and say, "Look at you! You wearing them curls, witcha pretty self!" LoLo's silence underlined what the world conspired to tell little Black girls—that something was wrong with their kinky hair and juicy lips and dark skin and their piercing brown eyes and their bubble butts and thick thighs and Black girl goodness. Rae simply wasn't strong enough, savvy enough, mature enough to guard herself from the tsunami of magazines and TV shows and popular radio and movies and the rest of pop culture that whipped Black women and girls for not being white. LoLo let it happen. Rae wore the scars. Even with a husband, a baby, friends literally holding mirrors to her face and demanding she see the beauty that they saw in her eyes, her cheekbones, her mass of thick curls swirling around her round face full of flawless skin smooth like polished ebony, Rae still wore those scars.

But Rae took one look into her daughter's eyes that first wash day and then so many days after that and saw . . . herself. Saw her own face staring back at her. A lighter-skinned version, but still her high cheekbones, her slender, button nose, her almond-shaped eyes—a marvel. Some days, the baby would just be talking to her mother about nothing in particular and Rae would look up and catch a glimpse of her child and her little girl's beauty would literally take her breath away. It would take some time, but slowly, Rae stopped picking the scabs—started thinking about how to let those scars heal. She was healing too fast, however, for Roman's tastes.

"Where you going again?" he asked, posting up against the bathroom doorframe as he watched Rae lean into the mirror and smudge a nude pinkish-brown lipstick—the only actual colored lipstick she owned—across her lips and cheeks.

"It's an album release party, remember?" she said. She picked up her earrings and squinted in the mirror as she inserted them into their holes.

"Right. And you're going dressed like . . . that?" Roman asked.

"Like what?" Rae asked, standing back from the mirror to look at herself in totality. Mal had let her borrow a dress—a little black number, a little clingy, a little curve hugging, beyond her usual style. "This is our night out," Mal had said when she showed up to Rae's workplace unexpectedly and shoved the outfit into her friend's hands. "I refuse to have you out at this event looking like the long-lost fourth member of TLC."

"That dress is, uh . . . ," Roman began.

"You look really pretty, Mommy," Skye said.

"Awwww, thank you, baby," Rae said, reaching for her daughter and pulling her close. "I feel really pretty. Almost as pretty as you!" she said, tapping her daughter's nose with her pointer finger.

"What time you gonna be back home?" Roman asked, glancing at his watch.

"I'm not sure. Definitely after Skye's in bed." To her daughter, she said: "It's going to be you and Daddy tonight, Skye! Isn't that fun? It's Daddy-daughter night!"

"Yay!" Skye said, hopping from foot to foot. Roman half smiled.

"Okay, I gotta go. Treva said she'd be downstairs to pick me up at six thirty sharp. I don't want to be late, traffic to Manhattan is going to be a bear."

She pecked Roman on his lips. Hugged the baby. Pushed past them both.

"I can't believe we got this bitch out the house!" Mal yelled, holding up three fingers to the bartender and jabbing her finger at a bottle of champagne.

"Right? She damn near had to die to get out the house," Treva said, holding her hand up to high-five Mal.

"Whatever," Rae said. "Who said I'm dying, anyway?"

"Listen, working at the pace you do, with a man and a baby?"

"Two babies if you ask me," Mal mumbled, pursing her lips.

"Hey!" Rae protested. "I heard that."

"What she means is, you got a lot going on and you need a break." Treva said. She grabbed two glasses and handed them to her girls, then picked up a third and raised it in the air. "To destressing!"

"And shaking that monkey off ya back!" Mal added.

Rae snorted. *Monkey?* she mouthed. She shook her head and laughed, took a sip of champagne. Let her eyes wash over the lower Manhattan restaurant the record company had taken over to introduce their artist to media and tastemakers in the industry. Rae hated these kinds of events—had avoided them all her career, telling herself and her superiors that she could excel at her job without being in those dog and pony celebrity networking events, where everyone pretended they had more cultural capital, more sway, than they actually did. Her superpowers were in her Rolodex, which held the phone numbers of some of the music industry's most powerful publicists and producers; they were the ones who held sway over the celebrities—who could get them to an interview on time or convince them to do an appearance on one show over the other. Getting drunk at an industry party and then heading back to your junky, barely-can-afford-it studio in Chelsea was not how one got to the top, as far as Rae was concerned. But there they were, in their too-tight dresses, their overpriced Js, talking too loud, laughing too quickly at each other's jokes, trying so very hard to be seen, selling something that wasn't worth nearly what they thought it was. Truth was, Rae wasn't sure if being out on this night, attending this party, listening to some future one-hit wonder try to pump up his debut album as if it were the next *Ready to Die* would make her feel any less stressed. Any more free. But here she was.

"Hey, you! Look who's out!" Nimma said, coming up behind Rae, rubbing her arm to get her attention.

"Oh, hey, Nimma!"

"I thought you didn't go to industry parties. You a Moore Payne fan like that?"

Rae laughed. "Uh, no. I'm here because the doctor you referred me to thinks I need to 'destress,'" she said, making air quotes, "and my two knucklehead friends here think drinking champagne at an industry party is going to help out with that. Nimma? These are my friends Mal and Treva. Y'all, this is Nimma. She's a supervising producer at the Work Room Studios."

"Nice to meet you," Mal said as she and Treva held up their glasses.

"Ooh, that's my song!" Treva exclaimed when the beat to a popular Method Man track dropped. "Let's go dance!" she said, disappearing into the equally euphoric crowd on the dancefloor, Mal on her heels.

"She's right, you know," Nimma said.

"Who's right? What do you mean?" Rae asked.

"You keep letting people stress you out, it'll kill you dead."

Rae sighed. "I mean, it's easier said than done, isn't it? I have to work—answer to Jeremy. I have to deal with my husband, my kid, run a household, all these things that wear us down. What choice do I have? What choice do any of us have? You mean to tell me you can just sit down somewhere and watch your whole world fall to shit and tell everybody you're letting it happen to keep your leg from falling off?"

Nimma laughed. "I get it. I get it. I promise. But when do you take moments for joy?"

"What do you mean 'take moments for joy'?"

"Like, what brings you joy?"

"My baby, she brings me joy," Rae said without hesitation. A gentle smile worked its way across her lips.

"I meant outside of what everybody tells you should make you happy. Take away the husband, the career, the kids. Those are the things society says we women should be happiest about. Like we should be grateful for stiff dicks when we're not in the mood, and getting smacked in the face at two in the morning when your kid pees in the bed for the third night in a row, and your job keeps you an extra two, three hours a couple times a week to do extra work you're not getting paid for because you're on salary and a team player. Whew—happy happy joy joy, right? But strip that down. What really makes you happy?"

Rae stared slack-jawed. All around them, people were drinking, cackling, swaying to too-loud music that was damn near drowning out every attempt at conversation. Was she as fake as them? Was she pretending she was happy, that what she was doing had meaning, value?

"Okay, okay, how about this: You know what brings me joy? Going out onto the fire escape and watching the sky at night," Nimma said.

"What, you just go out there and stare into space?" Rae asked, eyebrows furled. "You're a space cadet? You got time to just sit around staring at the stars?"

Nimma smirked. "I make the time," she said. "Because it brings me joy. I'm not out there all night. I catch the sunset. Or, if it's late and the sun has already gone down, the moon suffices. It's beautiful. Calming. You should try it."

"Staring at the moon?"

"Yeah," Nimma said curtly.

"Just . . . stare at the moon."

"I got one better," Nimma said. "Later this week, it'll be a full moon. Get yourself a piece of paper and jot down the things you want to let go of. Whatever that looks like. Worries about money, anger at your husband, lust for Jeremy . . ."

"Oh, girl, no. His old red-faced, pasty-faced, pot-bellied ass."

"I kid, I kid," she said, laughing. "But seriously, maybe you write down, 'I no longer let Jeremy make me feel less than my worth.' Write all that down on a piece of paper, put it in an ashtray, and burn it under the full moon."

"So now I'm setting fires, too?"

Nimma stared at Rae, the corners of her lips no longer curved up. She glanced over at Treva and Mal, who'd found their way back from the dance floor and now were listening in. "I'm serious. Try it. The moon is also a star, and it's okay to wish on them every now and again. It has the power to move oceans, gives the world its rhythm. Surely it could help little ol' us, right? Give it a try. Joy is your right. You might as well get you some.

"Anyway, I'm going to do a quick lap and get out of here," Nimma continued. "To be clear: this place does not bring me joy."

Rae watched Nimma disappear into the crowd—kept her eyes trained on her until she couldn't see her anymore. It was in her silence that she realized her whole body was vibrating—head, hands, heart, gut. She was not herself.

"Hmm," Mal said. She swallowed a sip of her champagne. "Sounds like some idolatry mess if you ask me."

"Yo' ol' heathen ass would know," Treva said, chuckling.

Mal raised her glass. "Cheers to that. Ain't nothing wrong with a little heathen behavior now and again."

"Y'all some fools," Rae said, her laughter nervous. She put down her champagne glass and ran her hand across her décolletage.

"See? Good girl Rae can't even finish a glass of champagne," Mal said. "Gotta maintain control at all times."

"What you mean? I . . . I can finish a glass of champagne. It's just warm in here. Y'all not hot?" she said, fanning herself. "And looking at the moon, wishing on a star, enjoying a good sunset ain't got shit to do with being a heathen," she said. "Y'all know I'm no Jesus freak, but if God made the heavens and the earth, he shouldn't have a problem with us admiring his handiwork, right?"

Mal leaned to her right and looked over Rae's shoulder. "Now the God that created that handiwork needs to be thanked for his goodness. Mercy."

Without thinking, Rae turned to see what was in her friend's sight line, just as the man—tall, chiseled, black as dark oak wood and solid like it, too—looked in her direction. Their eyes locked. Nothing in Rae's thirty-five years of living, of breath, could prepare her for the vivacity, the revolution he would bring to her life—the rapture that his very existence would set in motion. There would be him and a crown of thorns—a cross to bear. But this man, he was to be her savior.

"You having a good time?"

Rae delivered a half smile, hesitated. "Uh, yeah. Yeah."

"You don't sound too sure about that," he said.

"No, no, it's a nice event. It's just, um, a little warm in here."

Rae watched as his eyes washed all over her body and back to her eyes. "You're hot, huh?" he said, nodding his head. "Let me get you some water." He raised his hand to get the bartender's attention.

"No, no . . . it's okay. I'm okay."

The bartender leaned toward the man. "Yeah, can you get the lady some water? She's, uh, hot."

"Sure thing," the bartender said.

"She sure is," Mal said. She reached past Rae to offer her hand. "I'm Malorie. This is my girl Treva," she said, pointing behind her. "And this is Rae."

"Rae. Like sunshine. Nice to meet you, Rae," he said. He shook Mal's hand and then offered his hand to the one for whom he had eyes. "I'm Diego."

"Pleasure," Rae said. She watched as he reached for the glass of water and handed it to her.

"You should hurry and finish that up so you can come dance with me," he said.

"Oh, no, um, I'm not, uh . . ."

"What? You don't like Mary J. Blige?" he said, bopping his head. "Be Happy" pumped from the speakers as a crowd of partygoers danced on a makeshift dance floor created by a strategic removal of the restaurant's tables and chairs.

"She loves Mary J. Blige," Mal said, cocking her head to the side and giving Rae owl eyes.

Rae swung her gaze in Mal's direction, furrowed her brow, then turned back toward Diego with a fake smile spread from one cheek to the other. She sipped her water. "I do like Mary."

"Well then, let's get to it," he said, grabbing Rae's hand.

She looked back at her girlfriends as he led her through the crowd and shook her head as the two giggled and whispered to each other while they watched, goaded. *It's just a dance,* she told herself. This time, her eyes washed over his body—this magnificent specimen who was a good six-three and, from the looks of the way his button-down fit into his slacks, muscular, fit. He looked like a tall Tyson knockoff.

When they reached the dance floor, he turned and took both her hands into his, pulled her close to him. Rae, nervous, vibrating, let it happen. He smelled of vetiver and lemongrass. Earth. She liked it—loved her a good-smelling man.

He leaned in. "You from New York?"

"Born and raised," Rae said. "I grew up in Long Island."

"Long Island is New York?"

Rae gave him a playful punch in his stomach. It was hard. He laughed. "I kid, I kid. I'm from the Bronx."

"And you lived to tell the story!" Rae said.

"Ah, the lady has jokes!"

They laughed easily, and then Rae dropped her smile. "The lady is also married," she said. She lifted her hand to show off her ring finger.

"I gathered. Back at the bar."

"And yet you still asked a married woman to dance?"

"I asked a beautiful woman to enjoy a good song with me," he answered. "Nothing wrong with enjoying a song together, right?"

Rae looked down, said nothing. She didn't know what to say. She never knew what to say to men—could never gather herself in the face of flirtation and compliments.

"Maybe we could enjoy a meal together sometime," he said.

"Married women don't usually enjoy meals with men who aren't their husbands," she said quickly.

"You don't have to belong to someone to enjoy their company," he said. "Maybe it's okay to just reach out and take a little joy for yourself. You know—get yourself something good to eat."

Rae turned her back to him and let the rhythm take over her body as Mary sang from the depths of her shattered heart, laying bare how the worst kind of love crippled her, landed her square in the middle of an existential crisis that required—demanded—recalibration. Some kind of change that would make survival possible. "Be Happy" was sad Mary's prayer—an appeal for some sweet sweet in her life. Diego pressed his body against Rae's, and she did not resist him as Mary's prayer grew more urgent. Diego rested his hands on Rae's hips as she twisted and grinded against him, and she did not move his fingers. Mary moaned. Diego interlocked his fingers with Rae's and her chest heaved. Mary called out her plea to the sweet Lord up above and Rae sang out with her from her gut—sang out Mary's freedom song. Petitioned for some of that freedom for herself, too.

32

As it turns out, the dance floor happens to be a most perfect space for half truths and bold lies, particularly if you let the liquor tell them. Tall tales spin between the pound of beats bouncing off walls as hips, lips tempt, plot. Diego told Rae she was beautiful. Rae pretended she believed him. Diego said she was fascinating. Rae kept on with her stories, kept on acting as if telling a man what she wanted was ordinary, routine—that getting it was a given. He was turned on by this. She was turned on by him. And on this night, on her quest for joy, Rae would be bold enough, brave enough, to be who she needed to be to have what she wanted. To get to her joy. She screamed her phone number into that stranger's ear and told him that if he could both remember and use it before week's end, she would let him take her out. Came to her senses in the car ride home. Walked through the front door and found Roman masturbating to a magazine at the dining room table while their daughter was fast asleep on the couch. Argued with Roman again. Got mad at herself for expecting more from her husband, knowing it was a fool's bet. Went to bed hoping Diego would remember. Was excited when he did. Lunched with him. And then lunched again. Another lunch after that. Then dinner.

"So let me get this straight: You've never talked to your sister and brother?"

Diego had said he felt like eating a good burger, the best of which he insisted was in a secret hamburger joint tucked in the basement of a luxury boutique hotel in Chelsea. Rae was nervous that someone she knew would see them sitting close, drinking from the same bottle of beer, rubbing shoulders as they told more of those tales—more truths than lies this time. The kind that landed like spells. That felt like the kind of energy that made possibilities flood the brain. The loins. Drove desire.

"They're not my sister and brother," Rae said as she dragged a potato wedge through a sludge of homemade ketchup she'd poured onto her plate. She said that with bite.

"But they're your dad's kids, right? And you're his kid, right? That makes you their sister."

"That makes them his kids and not my problem," Rae said. "I don't want to have anything to do with them."

Diego nodded, got quiet. Then: "Respectfully," he said, "it feels like you're holding them accountable for something they didn't have any control over."

"Respectfully, the girl broke my mother's heart, and she disrespected my daddy by telling business she had no business to tell the day we buried him, in my mama's house," Rae said, her voice raised an octave.

"You're right, you're right. She didn't have the right to do that. But she does have the right to be recognized, doesn't she? To take her place in the family?"

"She's not my family," Rae said. She was getting annoyed. She saw no need to hold it back, playing nice, being typical, go-along-to-get-along Rae. This Rae had decided on the dance floor that she would say what she felt without care for what Diego thought about it. Because he didn't know her to be any other way, and she was obligated to be nothing more to him than free. "You know what? Why you so invested in me making nice with those people?"

"I don't know. Maybe because I'm those people," Diego said. He grabbed the beer bottle and took a long swig.

"I don't understand."

Diego sighed, rubbed his brow. "My father has two families, too. There's the family he took care of, and the family that he left behind in Dominican Republic." Diego raised his hand. "Me and my mom were the ones who got left. They got his love and attention. We got the struggle, in the DR and later when we moved to the Bronx, but I never wanted his money. What I really needed was . . . I don't know. I needed my dad. I needed us to be his family, too. I'm just saying, your sister—"

"She's not my sister," Rae interrupted.

"Your father's daughter probably just wants her family," he said. "I don't know. Maybe it's not such a bad thing to think about what it would mean to be the bigger person here."

"Respectfully?" Rae snapped as she wiped her fingers on her napkin. "I've been the bigger person all my life." She heaved a sigh from the gut. Diego sat back in his chair and stretched out his legs. He said nothing, and Rae was grateful for that—grateful for his willing ear instead of a fast mouth. "You get to feel the way you feel about your father, right? And so does my dad's daughter, even if I don't agree with the actions she took to express them. Why should I have to lie there and let everyone tap-dance on my feelings on the matter? Like, why is it my responsibility to make her comfortable and welcome her into my world? I'm adopted, Diego. I've been looking out for everyone else's feelings my whole life, and the world I live in has always felt fragile."

"I don't . . . I don't follow," Diego said. He sat forward this time, concentrated on Rae's words.

"My parents never told me I was adopted. I'm guessing that's because they didn't want to have to deal with their child one day announcing she was going to find her 'real' parents," Rae said, making air quotes with her fingers. "I kept their secret. I am their biggest lie. To perpetuate that lie requires a suspension of belief, right? All of us had to buy into this idea that we are family, even though technically, biologically, we are not. The price I have to pay for that, every day of my life, is gratitude. It's the first thing anybody thinks of when you say, 'I'm adopted.' How lucky we are, how we should be grateful our adopted parents found us and made the sacrifice to raise us and devote themselves to us, right? I'm just saying, I made sacrifices, too. I've lived their lie my whole life, to protect them—their feelings—even on the days when I really just . . ." Rae let her words trail off. It was hard for her to say out loud what she'd repeatedly swallowed, even knowing that each time, doing so would make her feel like she was choking. Like if she took one more big bite, she wouldn't survive it this time. She spun herself around in her chair in search of extra napkins, got up to grab one. She turned her back to Diego so she could dry her tears, but he knew. He knew.

"You think about your birth mom?" he asked, finally, after Rae sat, composed.

"Every day," she said without hesitating. "Sometimes I wonder what she looks like. Some days, I wonder where she is. If I have a brother or maybe a sister. If I have their eyes, the same fat cheeks. The same smile. My baby has my face. I wonder if my birth mom gave that to us. If she's even alive. If she ever thinks about me. But I'm not allowed to say that out loud, because, you know, those are the kind of questions that could make my parents think I'm capable of loving her more than them."

"Are you?" Diego asked in Rae's silence.

"Love is infinite. There's room in my heart to love all of them in equal parts. But I am devoted to my parents. I don't ever want to hurt them. To prove that, I've kept my questions and my own feelings about it to myself, so I don't hurt them."

"Even though it hurts you."

"That's right. You get it. So you'll have to excuse me for not giving a fuck about *her* feelings."

"Do you think you'll ever, I don't know, put your feelings first and try to find out who your real mom is?"

"My mother is my real mom."

"You know what I mean."

"No, you need to understand—my mom is my real mom. The other lady, she's my birth mom. I'm grateful she left me because I got to grow up a Lawrence. I wouldn't mind knowing something about my birth mom, though. Knowing her is knowing myself. Right now, my daughter is the only person on this planet I know for sure carries my blood. For now, that has to be enough for me, because I don't want to hurt my parents or, well, my mom."

"I feel that."

"Do you, though?"

He reached over and took Rae's hands into his. They were soft but strong, big. "I do."

"So then no more questions about the other daughter. She's not my business, not my concern. But she comes 'round me and I'm popping her. On sight."

"Who you gone beat up?" he said, playfully pushing Rae's shoulder. "Lightweight."

"I got hands," she said. She punched his shoulder; he feigned injury and reached over in retaliation, but instead of punching, he extended his fingers and dug into her soft spots—stomach, underarm, neck, ear. Rae giggled loudly, whisper-yelled "stop" as he tickled her and alternately grabbed her wrists to fend off her retaliation. Then, quick as a wink, without warning or permission, Rae pulled Diego's face to hers and kissed him. A light, gentle but intentional peck on his thick lips. He did not pull away. He did lean in. The air was thick—pregnant with the sounds of the restaurant workers flipping their burgers, taking orders, fellow diners chewing their meat and conversation, oblivious to the love story playing in technicolor at table forty-two. But Rae, she intended to be seen. Intended to feel.

"It's a Tuesday night, right? Wonder if they have any empty rooms upstairs," she said, tossing her chin toward the ceiling and forcing herself to look him straight in his eyes. *Don't blink, Rae. Hold him right there.*

Rae never did the picking. She always got picked, and she was just now starting to understand the implications and personal cost of such a thing—how ceding her freedom to choose was akin to cutting her own breath. Roman had not one problem being the one to hold his hand over her nose early on, when they were supposed to take their time turning "like" into "love." He'd rushed it because he wanted to be the bigger nigger.

Indeed, Roman told Rae he hadn't intended to invite her to live with him that night, but when she came down to the front door of her fourth-floor walkup in nothing more than a T-shirt and panties wadded up between her thick, bulbous cheeks, drunk after a night out with another man, the suggestion dripped easily from his lips. This had not been Rae's intention, either. Moving in with Roman would dead the arrangement he and Rae had to keep their dating casual, open, pregnant with possibility, and she couldn't say for sure if she was ready to change that, not after enjoying her evening out with Marques, a friend of TJ's whom she'd had a crush on back from when she was a wiry, corny teenager who'd never been kissed.

She'd spent so many Friday nights down in her parents' basement, fingers wrinkled from chores, pressing the "play" and "record" buttons on the family stereo while Mr. Magic and DJ Red Alert spun all the hits whose lyrics every kid in her high school knew better than they did their lessons. Rae couldn't dance a lick, but there she'd be each week, pretending she was at one of the many house parties her mother had barred her from attending, dancing loose and free, maybe even with a boy who would lean in and insist on what she didn't see for herself: "You pretty, you know that?"

No one had ever really told her such a thing, and LoLo, well, she'd insisted these things weren't important anyway. "Pretty ain't nowhere near as necessary as respect," LoLo had yelled at her daughter after having busted Rae smuggling a tube of lipstick in her school backpack. That Rae had swiped the makeup from the work stash LoLo kept on hand for gift-giving to friends on birthdays and other special occasions was bad enough, but when LoLo twisted the base to reveal that the tint Rae chose was a red "meant for sinners," she laid into her daughter something fierce. "All this red on your lip won't do nothing but have people looking at you like you a fast ass. That's what you want?"

"No," Rae murmured, her head hung low.

"What you say? I can't hear you," LoLo said, cupping her right ear and leaning into her daughter's face.

"No, ma'am," Rae said more loudly, her head a little higher.

"You smarter than this, Rae. Take your head off them boys and stop trying to keep up with those lil' fast-tailed girls at your school and focus on being the smart one. You gone thank me when you grown."

Rae wasn't concerned with what would happen when she was adult; she wanted to know what it was like to be wanted—to have a boy look at her the way Jose did Desiree, and Larry did Stacey, the latter of whom bragged about how the two of them had parked in the alley behind Pathmark and climbed into the backseat of his little rundown Dodge and kissed and rubbed on each other until she told him to stop. Rae found her way to the basement every Friday night and imagined doing the same thing— imagined that a boy, he didn't even have to be all that cute, invited her to his backseat. Or that he rubbed on her booty while they danced in dark corners at the houses where the cool kids partied. Or that some special boy, it really didn't matter which one, "heard" her when she lip-synched Whitney Houston's "How Will I Know" into a turkey baster and stepped out from the shadows to announce to her, "I'm yours."

Marques wasn't her first crush, but he was the first boy to pay Rae any mind. There she was, a junior in high school, looking like a loser in her mom's basement, in the middle of the floor like she was really on somebody's stage, lip-synching that twenty-eight-second-long note Teena Marie holds in that violin-heavy music break in "Casanova Brown"—eyes closed, hump in her back, one hand waving in the air, the other wrapped around the turkey baster. And there was Marques, standing in the window, staring at the whole affair. When Teena and she sang, "Didn't mean to make you cry," Rae opened her eyes and saw two eyes staring back at her. Marques smiled, pointed at the door. Mortified, Rae stood there like an asshole, stiff but wanting to run.

"Is your brother home?" he yelled through the window, cupping his hands over his mouth.

Rae nodded.

"Can I come in?" he yelled again.

Rae nodded and walked slowly to the door, trying not to trip on the way over there because that would have been just the icing on the cake—get busted lip-synching and then look like even more of a fool stomping on her own size-seven Converse to stand face-to-face with the boy she "sang" that song to in her raging teenage hormone fantasies.

Rae unlocked the door and stood back to let Marques in. She couldn't bear to look in those big brown eyes, set so perfectly on his oval face, on either side of his slender nose, which anchored his chiseled cheekbones and square jaw, looking like the living, breathing male form she studied in her Drawing 2 class. Most nights, she imagined counting the mahogany freckles dotting his light brown skin—fell asleep imagining what his lips would feel like on top of hers. If she would be able to survive it. To breathe.

"Yo, you lip-synched that better than Teena Marie did on *Soul Train*," Marques said with a chuckle.

Rae dropped her head.

"That's one of my favorite songs."

Rae smirked.

"What?" he said, crossing his arms.

"That's Teena Marie. Like, I thought guys would rather listen to Rakim or LL or something."

"I like them, too," Marques said. "But Teena Marie, Luther, Stevie Wonder, Shalimar—that's good music, too. When you wanna cool out and just, you know, chill. It's a toss-up between 'Casanova Brown' and 'Portuguese Love.' I really like those. But probably my favorite song of all time is 'Ribbon in the Sky.'"

"What? That's my favorite song of all time!" Rae said. She instantly regretted saying it so excitedly. But Marques reveled in it and answered in kind.

"That whole album is, *whew*! But the lyrics. Yeah, Stevie did his thing with that one."

TJ bounded down the stairs, interrupting the conversation with the clomping of his feet and his loud "What up, Marq, you ready?" and his awkward stare when he realized his little sister was in his friend's face.

Marques coughed and backed up off Rae a pace. "Yeah, let's get it," he said. He cleared his throat. "See you around, Rae. Maybe we could compare record collections one of these days. You got good taste."

Every once and again, Marques would stop by to link up with TJ, spend a little time talking to Rae. Just enough to give her fantasies color. Just enough to make her think maybe he liked her back. He even hinted, one time, that he had some business to attend to with TJ, but maybe the two of them could finally make good on that trip to Tower Records. Rae took him at his word—spent a whole week and a half planning what she would wear, how she would fix her hair. What she would talk about. How not to sound like a dummy. When that day finally came around, Marques stopped by, and Rae was ready for him, but they didn't go out. Marques let her down gently. "Maybe another time. I got something I need to tend to and can't make it today."

Later in the day, when LoLo would inquire why Rae was slinking around the house with her "lips poked out," TJ would interject—provide the context that would sit with Rae for years beyond that very moment.

"She just mad because Marq found somewhere else to be. She thought he was going to take her out," TJ said. "Real friends don't date little sisters." He scrunched his lips and glared at Rae. And that was that.

Later that evening, TJ went out with his friends. Tommy went to work. LoLo took her bath and turned off her bedroom light. And Rae went to the basement, dusted off her *Original Musiquarium I* album and gently placed the needle on "Ribbon in the Sky." She held the turkey baster tight in her hand as Stevie's words soared higher and higher more. As his voice slid out that last "for our love," Rae wrung the turkey baster in her hand. The rubber bulb was in her left, the liquid holder in her right. She slammed the two of them against the carpet with all her might. No one heard the crash. No one heard her crying.

Years later, while she and Roman were dating, Marques would be bold enough to stop by the Lawrence house to catch up and also to ask about Rae, how she was doing, what she was up to, and LoLo would pass along Rae's number to the computer whiz, who was now some junior executive at some fancy tech firm, and drop a not-so-subtle hint that her daughter was still single but fail to let him know that there was a guy and their relationship seemed to be more serious than casual, at least to her, and he better go get his woman not now but right now, before it was too late.

Marques made haste. So, too, did Roman. Rae let the latter do the choosing because that is what she thought she was supposed to do and plus, Roman had been there longer. It seemed rational, to Rae—breathing with diminished air.

He offered to have a bottle of wine sent up to the room. Rae politely declined; she wanted to be fully present. She wanted to feel. She watched him sit on the foot of the bed, a king-size affair appointed in crisp whites and paisley silvers and grays, and watched, too, as he watched her, standing there, slowly twisting buttons and undoing snaps, bottom lip between sharp teeth, chest beating its eager rhythm. One foot out of the pool of fabric at her ankles, second foot followed. One arm out of the pool of fabric at her shoulders, second arm followed. She let all that soft peach jersey drop to the wooden floor—stood there in the berry lace corset and matching crotchless panties like some kind of statue, some kind of prize. She practiced this pose in the dressing room of Frederick's of Hollywood just that afternoon on her lunch break, where she'd made the purchase. Where she'd made the calculations. Where she'd plotted her joy. Mirrors capturing her thighs, supple breasts, shoulders, square like a hanger, her ass, round and high. Balancing on her black stilettos with the dangerously pointed toe, she tugged, pulled, tied, cinched, and sucked herself in until she was tucked and satisfied. Until she was convinced Diego would look at her and see not mother, not daughter, not wife, but woman. *Woman.*

"Damn," Diego said. His eyes washed over every inch of Rae's body and she stood there, still, fighting the urge to cover up, to hurry this along, to remove herself from his gaze. To slip into the familiar—a quick peck or two, a submission to the licking of breasts, vagina, missionary in the middle of the bed, moans expertly wired to activate the "off" switch. Get it over with. This feeling, of standing in front of a beautiful man and being devoured, yes, but also of being confident in her body and articulating her desires, asking for and getting exactly what she wanted—all those things she wanted to last.

"Come here," she said so quietly he barely heard her. Rae's visual cue— the come-hither look, the beckoning of her index finger—got him to hop to. He stood directly in front of her, she looking up at him, he looking down at her, shoe tip to shoe tip, breath to breath. *Hold him right there, Rae.* One hand on his neck, the other on his cheek. She looked at his eyes and let hers slowly wash down to his lips, back up to his eyes—leaned in closer, closer still. Licked his bottom lip. Then his top. Tilted heads and tongues intertwined, heaving chest to heaving breasts, his hand in her braids, pulling, neck exposed, his greedy tongue on her neck, flicking in her ear. "Mmmm, that's my spot," she moaned, and it was, but she had stopped letting Roman lick her there because she was more disgusted by the trail of spit he left whenever he licked her than she was in love with the way it felt, so she denied herself that small pleasure and so many others, too, and instead focused on the performance. On getting it over with. She did not want Diego to stop.

"You like that?"

"Yes," she said breathlessly.

"What else you like?" he said, lightly flicking his tongue, getting a rise at how her body writhed to his rhythm.

Rae was taken aback by the question. She knew what she did not like, and she knew, too, the power of sexual deceit—how faking it through a man's touch assured he would enjoy having sex with her, which, in some weird, perverted way, made her feel wanted. But for her troubles, that's all she ever really got out of the act: being desirable, the same as, say, a blow-up doll or a squeeze of lotion in the palm of a hand. Getting no more than the bare minimum. Never did she have a partner who verbalized caring about what she needed, wanted.

Rae answered slowly, deliberately. "Fuck me like you mean it."

Diego pulled back from Rae's ear. Looked her dead in her face and smirked. Tugged her hair to gain full access to her lips, neck, eyes. The way he looked at her made her nipples tingle. Her breath was heavy with anticipation. He spun her around so fast she grabbed the wall to balance. It was how he wanted her. He cupped her breasts as he dropped down to his knees, then used his hands, the crooks of his elbows to spread her legs and lift her ass to his mouth.

He gave her exactly what she wanted.

33

"What are you doing right now?"

It was Mal, calling Rae's phone, asking dumb questions, knowing that on most Saturdays at 6:30 in the evening, she could find Rae standing over the kitchen stove, preparing a hot meal for Roman and Skye. Mal was usually the first one to clown Rae for this. "You are the most homemaking-est Black woman I know outside my granny," she'd say, poking fun at Rae's Saturday night ritual. "Saturday nights are for takeout. Better yet, date night."

"Saturday nights," Rae would huff, "are for me spending time with my daughter, who deserves something other than chicken nuggets and yogurt when her mother is able to actually sit at a dinner table with her. You know weekends are the only time I can make that happen."

This Saturday night was no different; Rae was trying not to let the rice burn while she rinsed the salad and basted the chicken thighs roasting in the oven. Skye was sitting at the table, grumpy and completely over the pileup of worksheets her teacher had sent for weekend homework. She absolutely did not want to write "me," "he," and "we" ten times on those fat lines when there was a copy of the new *Cinderella* movie sitting in the DVD player. Her gamma had sent her the movie starring a Black girl with a round, brown face and long braids just like hers, and the Cinderella gown and slippers were going to complete waste sitting in the kitchen when there was so much space in the living room to twirl and dance and "lose" her slipper so the prince could find her.

"I'm making dinner, Mal," Rae said. She held the phone in the crook of her neck while she tapped her pointer finger on Skye's homework and gave her daughter a look, then headed back to the oven to drop lemon wedges into the roasting pan. "Go ahead, make fun so I can get off this phone."

"Where's Roman?" Mal asked quickly, barely letting Rae finish her sentence.

"I don't know—he rushed out of here earlier to play squash, and in typical form, he'll saunter in here whenever. I'm telling you this much, a bitch is hungry tonight and Skye and I got a hot date with *Cinderella,* so he may be eating by his damn self . . ."

"Listen to me, Rae," Mal said.

Her words—clipped, urgent—made Rae pause. She slowly closed the oven door. "Mal, you okay? What's wrong?"

"Where is your cell phone?"

"What?" Rae asked. "I don't understand . . ."

"Your cell phone," she yelled. "Where is it?"

Rae jumped at the sound of her friend's frenetic, high-pitched voice; only then did it begin to click that something was wrong. She looked over at Skye, who was fidgeting and rolling the pencil on the table between her little hands, and then turned her back to the little girl. She whispered into the receiver of her cordless phone. "Malorie Victoria Height, what's wrong?" she whisper-yelled into the phone.

"Listen to me," she said. "I got an email from Roman about an hour ago. He was going off on you, calling you all kinds of cheap whores and a cheating liar who ruined his family. It came with an attachment. Rae, he got a hold of the text messages between you and Diego and downloaded them somehow and sent them in a file in that email. He sent it to everybody."

Rae's nose began to burn, as if all the blood had drained from her head and pooled in her left nostril. She felt a little woozy—enough so that she half stumbled, half walked over to the kitchen table. Her body did not feel like her own; it was empty, floating . . . floating . . . floating above her braids she'd piled atop her head, so they wouldn't get in the way as she poured, mixed, heated her pots; above the kitchen table, where Skye had written the most perfect list of "me," "he," and "we" on the lined worksheet, above the brownstone, Brooklyn, to the moon she'd taken to staring at most nights out on the fire escape, thinking about Diego, joy. What freedom felt like for a Black woman with a baby on her hip and a man who could not keep up.

"What do you mean he sent it to everybody?" she whispered. Then, softly, to Skye: "Baby, go put your homework in your bookbag. You did such a good job. Go play in the living room until dinner is ready, okay?"

"Mommy, your—"

"Skye, do like Mommy asked you, okay? Your bookbag is on the bench by the front door."

"But Mommy—"

"Skye! What did I say?!"

Skye bolted upright like a metal rod had been attached to her spine. She grabbed her worksheet and headed to the front door. Rae watched her disappear around the corner, then turned her attention back to the phone.

"Tell me everything you know," she said to Mal.

"Listen, I'm telling you now, he knows about your sidepiece and just like the little punk bitch he is, Roman sent every text message you ever sent Diego to anybody who means anything to you. All in one big, massive email."

"When?"

"I just checked my email so I'm just seeing it, but it looks like he sent it about an hour or so ago."

A second call beeped on Rae's line. "Hold on, Mal," Rae said, clicking over.

"Oh my God, Rae!" It was Treva. "Are you okay?"

"I know, I know already. Mal is on the other line," Rae said. She took off her apron and untucked her T-shirt from her sweatpants, looking for a bit of cool in the middle of the emotional heat wave that was making her clammy, dizzy.

"Listen to me, he's on a rampage," Treva said.

Rae's chest did a dance.

"Jermaine called to check on him and he's not right, Rae. I need you to get out of that house."

"I'm not leaving my damn house!" Rae snapped. "Why would I do that?"

"Because he told Jermaine he wanted to, and I quote, 'punch her in her fucking face.'"

Rae swallowed hard, blinked away tears. She heard Skye's feet pattering behind her and sucked it all in—the water in her eyes, the snot in her nose. The scream rumbling around in her chest, trying to make its way up from her esophagus, past her larynx, into the bile creeping toward her tongue. She was determined not to let her baby see her lose her shit.

"Does Jermaine know where he is right now?" Rae asked.

"No," Treva said. "I need you to get out of that house, Rae. You're not safe."

"I'm not leaving my damn house," Rae snapped. "What I look like running from the place where I pay every last one of the bills? Why would I take my baby from her home? Why do I have to leave? I didn't see him pack any bags when he brought that bitch to our house!"

"Baby, Rae, listen to me. This isn't about leaving your home. It's about being safe. I'm afraid for you."

"No, no. I'm not leaving. I'm staying in my damn house. Can you come get the baby?"

"I'm on my way."

Rae clicked back over to Mal. "That was Treva. She's on her way to get the baby."

"How about I come over and sit with you for a while," Mal said.

"No, no—it's okay. I'm okay. I'm just going to wait for him to get back is all. It's going to be fine. I'm fine."

Rae did not believe this—not even for a second. But she intended to stand her ground.

Rae called her mother, but she did not answer her phone or Rae's desperate messages, and so Rae bathed in the light of the moon on the fire escape and cried herself to sleep on the couch. She dreamed of New Jersey and a girl, young, a teenager—someone she did not know but she knew all the same. They were in a creek—one that looked a lot like the waterway that ran behind Rae's childhood house in New Jersey, the one LoLo laid down in, looking for rest. Rae couldn't count how many nightmares she'd had of her mother, down there in the dirty, rocky stream, writhing and fighting off her father, Ms. Daley, begging them to let her be free. Sometimes, the dreams would end with Rae standing over her mother, looking at her lifeless face staring off into space, the sun bouncing light and rainbows in the water covering her eyes. Other times, there would be no sun, no ribbons of color. Just gray skies and dusk—fireflies flickering like a siren of a hundred tiny flashlights, making LoLo's face, hair, eyes glimmer in their sparks. There was beauty and there was death, and there was Rae standing there over her mother's body, heartbroken and confused. Terrified. But she hadn't had that nightmare in quite some time.

This evening, she welcomed this particular dream. She needed this girl, and the girl, she obliged—stood up out that water and offered her hand. "Come on, don't be scared," she said, beckoning Rae to slide down the bank and join her. Rae, reluctant, had taken off her shoes and socks and carefully rolled up her jeans. "It's all right," the girl said. "I ain't gone let you fall. I never let you fall," she said, her hand extended, her smile wide.

"Yes, ma'am," Rae said to this girl, so much younger than her, but who moved, talked, commanded with an old soul that radiated all about her. Rae grabbed the girl's hand and dropped herself into the water. To her surprise, it was warm, almost inviting. But the soles of her feet, they weren't ready for the shock of the rocks on the creek's bed; they were bumpy and rough, some of them sharp, some of them scorching. The girl moved quickly over the rocks, her feet seemingly unfazed by the gravelly terrain. Rae watched her intensely as she shuffled from one foot to the other, trying to find a smooth rock on which to balance, on which to find some small measure of relief.

"There's freedom in the water," the girl said as she watched Rae's feet. "But you can't stay still. You must keep moving. Don't stand there, daughter. Dance. Move your feet forward and dance."

"It hurts, Mommy," Rae said. She broke down, tears blurring her ability to look for the smooth rocks on which to step.

"Stop crying and show yourself grace, and then you'll see the smooth ones. They're down there. You just gotta look for them with clear eyes."

Rae let go of the girl's hand so she could use both her fists to rub the tears out of her eyes—so she could see the smooth rocks. Sure enough, there they were, not in any particular order or path, but visible. Reachable.

Rae bounced onto one and then another, smooth, like a waltz, gliding forward with the water's current. She extended her hand back to grab the girl's hand into her own but felt nothing but air. She balanced and turned slowly, only to find that the girl had laid back down in the water, her eyes glistening, staring at a sun wrapped in a rainbow.

Sharp, rapid knocking jerked Rae out of her dream. She gasped, the shock of the sound making her bolt upright. Her eyes darted every which way, searching for Skye, afraid she'd fallen or gotten into something that brought danger or harm, and then, slowly it all came back to her—why she was on the couch, how she'd quickly packed up the baby and let her negotiate leaving in her Cinderella dress in exchange for making a speedy, tearless exit with her Auntie Treva, how she'd sat there all night, deep into the earliest hours of the morning, steeling herself for her husband's wrath.

More hard knocking.

Roman, she calculated, wouldn't be knocking; he had a key and would have simply brought the storm straight to her. Still, she thought, what was stopping him from sending someone else to do his bidding? He'd already made his bitch move to paint her chest with a scarlet letter; he could easily have been somewhere plotting more destruction. Hell hath no fury like a man who's been cheated on. Rae steeled herself.

"Rae, baby, you in there? Open the door!" More hard knocking, then pounding.

It was LoLo. Rae hustled herself off the couch and practically sprinted to the door. She flung it open to find her mother standing there, fist mid-air, ready for another pounding, an overnight bag slung over her shoulder.

Rae practically leaped into her arms.

"Whoa, whoa, whoa—you all right? Let me take a look at you," LoLo said, prying her daughter off her torso to give her a once-over, like she was a little girl who'd fallen off a swing. Satisfied Rae was physically intact, LoLo pulled her daughter to her and looked around the foyer of the brownstone. "Where is he?"

Rae sighed and fought the tears, to no avail. "I don't know. He left yesterday afternoon and didn't come back."

"You okay?" LoLo asked, letting her darting eyes settle on her daughter's face.

"No, Mommy," she said. "I'm not."

"Okay, okay," LoLo said, pulling her crying daughter to her chest. "Come on. Your mother's here."

"How did you know to come? How did you get here? Why . . ." Rae's questions tumbled from her lips as she held tight to her mother.

"That fool had the nerve to call my telephone talmbout, 'She cheated on me,' and 'I have the proof,' and 'She's a no-good so-and-so,'" LoLo said. "I told him, 'Nigga you must be out yo' mind if you think I'm going to let you talk crazy about my daughter. I don't care what she did, that's my daughter you talking about.' Told him just like that. Sure did."

"Did he send you the email, too?"

"I didn't open that mess," LoLo said, pushing back from her daughter and leading her to the couch. "He sounded like he was unraveling on the phone. I warned him that if he even thought to look at you sideways, he better remember I keeps Tommy's guns and I know how to use all of them. I suspect he picked up what I was putting down, but I figured I should hurry up and get up here just in case."

"Thank you, Mommy."

"Mmmhmm. Where's my grandbaby?"

"She's with Treva," Rae said, rubbing her eyes. She let her chest fill with air pulled deep from her gut. The tears washed anew. "I dreamed about somebody just now, a young girl."

LoLo pulled Rae close to her; she lay her daughter's head in the crook of her neck and clasped her hand to hers. "What happened in the dream?" she asked.

Rae hesitated. And then: "She was in the creek behind the house," she said slowly. "I used to have nightmares about that water, but this time, I was in there with this girl and I wasn't scared." LoLo shifted uncomfortably beneath her daughter's frame. Rae had told Tommy a few times about her recurring nightmare—her recollection of what had been—but he would never allow much more of a conversation beyond the simplest details, and usually, Rae didn't push. She was barely in her double digits when her mother laid down in that creek, so she didn't necessarily understand, back then, what was. As a mother, wife, grown woman, she wasn't sure she did now, either. But she felt compelled to tell her mother about this dream all the same. "She told me to walk across the rocks, but she laid down . . ." Rae whimpered, sniffled. "She laid down in the water."

"Shhh," LoLo said, rubbing Rae's shoulder, holding her tighter.

"Why did you lay down in the water, Mommy?"

"I don't . . . want to talk . . . ," LoLo stuttered.

"I want to know, Mommy. Please," she begged. "We had a good life, didn't we? The house was so nice. That great big ol' yard. We ate at the Ponderosa, you remember that? I liked those fries. The thick ones. And the hamburgers. They were so big and juicy—big as my face, it seemed like. That was fancy—you and Daddy eating steak. Why were you so sad, Mommy? Why were you in that water?"

LoLo rocked Rae like she was a little baby—back, forth. An ambulance whirred down the street past the house, its siren stabbing the Sunday awake. Just outside the living room window, in the Norway maple that stretched all the way up to the fourth floor, its branches spread wide for spring's welcome, a mama robin bounced around the nest she had meticulously built from dead twigs and leaves, bark and shed feathers, anxious, neck swiveling, as she chewed up a fat worm that had drowned in a mixture of rainwater and motor oil at the base of the tree. She regurgitated that worm's remains into each of her babies' mouths as they stretched their necks to the sky, alternately opening wide their beaks and shrilly calling out to their mama. She heard them. She fed them. She trusted that their daddy, bouncing around in a branch nearby, singing his lullabies not to soothe but to warn, had her back. They would dance this dance, those little swallows, over and over again, until their hatchlings had enough food in their bellies and enough strength in their feet and wings and enough time behind them to become fledglings. To hop-fly to a lower branch, a shrub, until they were strong enough to spread their wings and soar, to fight for their own survival, maybe build a nest of their own and fill it with babies that needed them, too.

LoLo held her breath until the ambulance siren escaped around the corner and the little birds tucked their bobbing beaks back down into the nest. When she breathed again, her air was shaky. "You know, he thought he was making a good life for us, your daddy. All he wanted was for us to be a family. He never had that growing up. Neither of us did. When we started going together, they were telling everybody having two-point-five kids and a picket fence was where it was at. And there he was, holding down double his portion. I suppose your daddy thought he was doing something, holding down two families, keeping secrets. Like we weren't going to feel that.

"I felt it, though. I did. He was always gone. Always, always off somewhere else . . . ," LoLo added before trailing off. "And then all of a sudden, we were packing up all our things and headed to Jersey." Rae felt her mother's heart beat against her head. It jumped, double-tapping on her ear. "That was around the time that lady hit you."

Rae sat up and slowly turned to her mother—looked her straight in the face. "I . . . I don't understand. What do you mean she hit me? What lady?"

"At the daycare, when you were a baby. Right before we left. Betina was a teacher there and she hit you over something, I don't remember why. I do remember going down to the daycare center ready to beat her ass for touching you. To this day, I still can't figure out why she didn't just tell me right then and there . . ."

"Tell you what?" Rae said. "I don't understand . . ."

"All she had to do was swing her belly in my face and say it."

"Say what, Mommy? What are you saying?"

"Betina is Tasheera's mother, Rae. TJ told me her name and I did the math, you know, and I figured out that she was a teacher at your daycare. The same one I threatened when she hit you. She was pregnant. It was a miracle that woman didn't tell me who she was right then and there. Your daddy probably figured, 'She not about to ruin my family.' So . . . so he moved us to New Jersey. That's when he took us, me, away from everyone I knew and everything I loved, so he wouldn't get caught. He switched up my whole life. My entire existence."

LoLo turned her head to hide her tears, but her stomach heaved as she tried to catch her sobs. Rae wrapped her arms around her mother's body—squeezed her tight. But she said nothing—she wanted to learn.

"All my life, people been taking away my choices. Every person who was supposed to protect me caged me up and chained my hands, you understand? My daddy, my brother, those monsters at the orphanage. My cousin. His wife. They all chained me like some animal," LoLo said. She grew quiet.

Then: "Tommy promised to protect me. And what he do? He cheated and had two babies on me and I was the one caged up like some animal in a cave all the way in New Jersey. Might as well have been Siberia. He took away my choice. Going up under that water . . . it was my way to take control. It was my way to get free."

Rae squeezed her mother harder still. "I'm sorry, Mommy. I'm so sorry."

LoLo tucked her hands beneath Rae's torso and pulled her up so she could look at her, eye to eye. "You don't need to apologize to me, daughter. You need to save that for your husband."

Rae reeled back and wriggled out of her mother's grip. "Apologize? You want me to apologize? For what?"

"You cheated on that man, Rae."

Rae jumped to her feet so quickly she tripped over the cocktail table, shaking it hard enough to knock over the picture frame holding a photo of her and Roman, taken when they were happy and new and making their way toward forever. "I had my reasons, Mommy! It'll be a cold day in hell—"

"You don't have to cuss at your mama, and you don't have to yell. I'm right here," LoLo said, quietly, trying to lower the temperature in the room. "What you did ain't right, Rae. Cheating on your mate is the worst kind of pain you could throw on somebody you claim you love. I know that down to my core."

Rae kept pacing, but she lowered her tone. "I did what I did for me. It wasn't about him. Let me ask you this: Why do men think we like hobbling around the house, chasing after kids and cooking and cleaning and scrubbing dirty drawers and stuff anyway? Like that's the life! We give up everything we are, everything we could be, to buy into this fantasy men created. I took my power back. And I won't be apologizing for it, to anybody."

"That's what we signed up for," LoLo reasoned. "That was the exchange."

"But did you want to be a slave to it? Did you know what you were giving up to have this family? All this time growing up, I thought that was the point, because that's what you did for Daddy, for my hero. You always acted like he was your hero, but really, heroes help people. They don't put them in shackles, they help them get free. Being in those shackles almost drove you mad, Mommy. Don't you see? It's why I'm mad. I'm mad, Mommy. I'm mad! I'm mad! I'm mad!" Rae squealed, until her throat throbbed and her face burned hot. She sat back down on the couch and took her mother's hands into her own. Took a beat.

"I know you're mad, but you're not comparing Tommy to that no-count husband of yours," LoLo said. "I know Tommy wasn't perfect, but he was a good man. A damn good man."

"Maybe the girl in my dream was trying to tell me that Daddy and Roman are different sides of the same coin," Rae said calmly. "Maybe she was telling me that I need to walk on water, instead of laying down and drowning in it."

Roman came back home on the Wednesday, first thing, just after LoLo had finished wiping the morning oats off her granddaughter's lips and shining her teeth with that strawberry toothpaste she liked so much more than the minty kind she claimed made her tongue burn. Roman rushed through the front door and slammed it, fixed on putting on a show. Rae stood at the kitchen counter, tucking Skye's turkey sandwich, apple slices, baggie of pretzels, and bottled water into her lunch box like some kind of puzzle, intent on continuing with the morning routine she'd carefully crafted to minimize disruption of Skye's school routine, despite that every bone, every cell in her body was ice. Frozen with fear. In the quiet moments when she was on the subway headed to work, or standing over the stove preparing dinner, or screaming into her pillow at 1 A.M., when her entire world was finding its rest, Rae calculated what she would say when, finally, she saw Roman—when, finally, he would reappear and claim his victimhood. Most of his things—clothes, shoes, toothbrush and such— were still at the house after all, and, besides, his welcome surely would be worn wherever he was laying his head. He wasn't at a hotel, that much Rae knew. He didn't have any money. He wasn't using any of their credit cards or bank debit cards for a hotel. And his ego, fragile, would need to be fed. It already had announced itself to their whole world via emails and phone calls and bar meet-ups with his boys. In a matter of days, their relationship was now a spectacle, a glass house with cloudy streaks coaxed by the light. Roman was a ram running at its walls, full speed. Rae knew it would be just a matter of time before he shattered the glass, before the shards would rain down on both their heads. *He will come soon,* she'd reasoned. *Be ready,* she'd warned. For anger. For accusations. Threats. Maybe violence.

Rae's breath, chest grew heavier with each step she heard heading toward the kitchen. Instinctively, her eyes searched for a weapon, something with which to defend herself. The thought broke her heart. This is what it had come to.

"Which one was it?" Roman yelled. With theater intense enough for a Broadway play, he slammed onto the kitchen table, one after the other, three pieces of lingerie, including the berry corset Rae had worn the night she seduced Diego. "The red one? This black one right here? This white one you wore on our honeymoon?"

The corset was nothing at all like the other lingerie, members of a small stash of pretty and sensible lingerie Rae had crumbled in the back of her panty drawer, beneath a stale lavender and vanilla sachet she collected years ago from some bin at Macy's, likely one near whatever bin her mother and her church lady friends found the silk chemises and satin and lace baby doll gowns they gifted her at her bridal shower. A flash of memory had Rae holding them up for the gift givers and attendees to ogle and woo, nervous giggles colored around lines of awkward encouragement: "That's so you can tend to your man," they'd said, and "LoLo gone get her grandbabies for sure with that one right there!" they'd said, too. Rae wore the lingerie on the honeymoon and, in the beginning of her marriage, on weekends after a date night or when she and Roman stayed in and got tipsy off beer or vodka and orange juice. None of it ever stayed on long; Roman was about getting down to business. Getting to the finish. Before long, Rae was pulling out those modest gowns only for special occasions—birthdays, anniversaries, a Christmas Eve or two. Before long, she wasn't pulling them out at all. It didn't matter to Roman. His indifference didn't matter to Rae. A lot of things didn't matter to either of them anymore. Hadn't for the longest time.

"Which one of these is the freak gear that nigga told you in your texts to wear only for him from now on?" Roman demanded.

"What are you talkin—"

"Answer me, dammit!" he said, slamming his fist on the kitchen table.

LoLo rushed into the kitchen, startling Roman. "Your daughter is in the other room. Or does that not matter to you?" LoLo sneered. "Keep your voice down." Then, to Rae: "Baby, you all right? Come with me."

"I . . . I just want to talk, Mrs. Lawrence," Roman said, quieter, holding his hands up in surrender. His whole body slumped in surrender.

"That's not what that sounded like," LoLo said.

"It's okay, Mommy," Rae said. "Can you take Skye to school? I don't want her to be here while we talk. Just . . . just take her out of here." She held out Skye's lunch; LoLo mean-mugged Roman and, finally, took the lunch box into her hand.

"Let me tell you something. One hair on her head. One," LoLo said, holding up her pointer finger. "They'll be pulling buckshot out your ass through New Year, hear?"

Hands still in the air, Roman nodded.

"I'll be right back, baby, don't you worry."

Rae nodded. Nothing between her and Roman moved until long after LoLo pulled the front door closed.

"You want some coffee?" she asked finally.

"What I want is to know how you could do this to me."

"How could I do what, Roman?" Rae asked. Her entire face scrunched with incredulity.

"You fucked another nigga!"

"You did, too. And?"

"That's what this is about? Payback?" Roman asked. "You still mad because you think I cheated on you? You busting up our family over some shit that didn't even happen?"

"You really gonna stand here and act like cheating is the reason our family doesn't work anymore? Is that what you tell yourself when you're paying our bills with my money?"

"Oh, so now it's your money, huh. 'Don't worry, Roman, we gonna build together. I can take care of us while you go after your dreams, Roman. We in this together, Roman.' Isn't that what you told me when we agreed you'd work while I write?"

"Oh, it was a mutual decision with our family's well-being at the top of mind? That's what quitting a good job while your wife was pregnant was designed to do? Without telling me? What else was I supposed to say?"

"What the hell are you even talking about right now?" Roman demanded. "You never said you had a problem with me going after my dream!"

"I shouldn't have had to!"

Rae covered her face with both her hands and rubbed. "Listen, just . . . sit down," she said. Rae pushed her lingerie to the side of the table and stared at it a bit before positioning her chair so that she could sit knee-to-knee with her husband. He hesitated, then followed her lead.

"Where were you?"

"Now you care?"

"I care that you left this house with my cell phone and just left your child here like she was some kind of collateral damage in your tantrum."

"Tantrum? I think I was more than entitled to my anger over my wife trying to ruin our family."

"But telling the whole world our personal business and leaving for five days without sending word on whether you were dead or alive, that was rational?"

"I wanted you to see what it would be like to be a single mom out here," he said. "You damn sure needed to see how important I am to this family."

Rae chuckled. "You know, I'm not sure what's more nuts: you thinking that telling everyone I cheated would make you look good, or that I wouldn't be able to take care of my daughter without you being here. You have no idea what you've done or what you have, do you?"

"I have a wife who cheated on me."

"No, you have a wife who is so stressed out her body is breaking down on her."

"That's on me? Your stress, that's my fault?"

Rae fell quiet as she searched for just the precise words to make Roman understand, but, like some complicated, high-stakes chess match, she met every thought, phrase that came to mind with the counterargument Roman would use to refute her. Then that pain—dull, at first, and then quickly, not—gripped her calf. She let it sear—let the pain, all of it, coax her tears. As she sat, weeping, finally, it came to her: it was Roman who was the knot in her calf, excruciating and hot and unbearable.

"You definitely didn't help make my stress any better, Roman," Rae said quietly.

"What, because I wouldn't clean the bathroom to your liking, Rae? That's it? The living room too dusty for you? You wanted me to mop and fix you dinner? Like a little bitch?"

"I wanted you to protect me, Roman!"

"Protect you? Protect . . . what are you even talking about, Rae?"

"I'm talking about having a husband who holds up his end of the bargain," Rae said. "All you've done is take, take, take, take. You've given nothing in return. I let everyone else tell me what our arrangement should be, and now I'm not so sure if that's even what I want from this marriage anyway."

"Bargain? Arrangement? I don't even know . . . the fuck you saying, Rae?" Roman said, sitting back in his chair.

"This. This arrangement between a husband and a wife," she said, slapping her chest and then his back and forth. "I thought this is what I wanted. But I never really knew what I wanted, Roman. I never even really gave it a serious thought."

"Oh wait, so you got some new dick and now you're so turned out you confused about why we're together? Ain't this some shit?" Roman said, punctuating his words with a fake laugh.

"Oh, it's funny? This is funny to you, Roman?" Rae asked.

"What's funny is you cheat on me and now you sitting here talking like I'm the one to blame," he said. "You haven't even apologized for that shit." He forced another fake laugh.

The sound of his chuckle was an alarm, blaring. It led Rae to her epiphany. "You know what's funny? You're the joke, Roman," Rae said, her voice practically a whisper. "You just keep missing the punch line. This is over."

"Nah, you wanted to talk. Let's talk, Rae."

"I don't mean the conversation. I mean us. We're through."

Roman stood up abruptly from his chair; Rae stiffened from the motion—braced herself for impact. But Roman did not strike; he wandered in circles, rubbing his scalp, shaking his head. "Rae," Roman asked quietly. "Did you ever love me?"

They were talking in circles, and he could not hear her over his anger and defensiveness and ego—over his aggressive need to frame the narrative. For eight years, she was human scaffolding, doing this rickety, dangerous, exhausting work all around his frame while he stretched toward the sky, this inanimate object trying to be glorious, but busy casting shadows on all that surrounded it. On her. She couldn't do it anymore. Finally, Rae had come to an understanding with herself that she wasn't obligated to. This was how Roman lost Rae for good. This was how Rae found herself. This was when she learned how to walk on the water.

Epilogue

They had been with her, the four of them, the entire time—organizing, directing, clearing paths. One would send little white feathers to make their presence known—would leave them on a pillow or in the middle of the darkest parts of the pattern on a carpet. One time when Rae was feeling a way about her baby waking up Christmas morning with Roman and his family and she was looking to drown her emotions at the bottom of a vodka soda, she opened the freezer and there was a white feather right there, sitting next to a pint of butter pecan Häagen-Dazs. Made her think of her daddy. Something sweet. The others, the women, they sent ladybugs. Orange ones. Sometimes just one, sometimes an entire swarm. A bunch of ladybugs show up, they call them a lovely, and that's what they were for Rae, something lovely, like when she was worrying herself about bills and she got to cleaning like she did when her nerves were giving her the business and all of a sudden "Ribbon in the Sky" was streaming on her speakers and there they were, dozens of orange ladybugs crawling on the window screens, the building's walls, the fire escape where she watched the moon. Fifty-two in all, by her count. All that stress rushed right out her shoulders. Every time, gone. She'd see the feather or the ladybugs and forget about her burdens and focus, instead, on what the seer said: "All your life, they've never let trouble find its way to you. You fall and they're a cloud up under your bottom. Your feet, they'll never touch the ground. The feathers and the ladybugs are a promise. You are protected." And Rae believed it. Believed it with every ounce of her being.

Scared her, though. Sometimes. Same seer said the one who sent feathers, the man, liked to sit in the big brown leather chairs near the window, the right one in particular. "He says he likes the way the light from the window hits it, and it's the best angle to watch the Mets games when you remember to turn them on." The seer didn't know Rae from Adam and most certainly had never seen the interior of Rae's home and so when she described the scene, how Rae watched those games to remember her daddy, to feel close to him, Rae burst into tears. Same for when Rae smelled the flowers—gardenia, occasionally jasmine or lavender. The seer said it was the two older women, both with a predilection for flowers, who would fill the room with the sweet scent to make their presence known. "Your father, your great grandmother. Your grandmother, they're always with you," the seer said. "You are protected." The youngest spirit, seer said, she was Rae's mother—liked to flit around her daughter in a swirl of light, going on and on about how much she loved her little baby. How she didn't want to leave her. Never would again. "Her love for you is immense, intense," seer said. "Don't be afraid. You are protected." Rae followed instruction—tentatively, at first, then ritualistically, like tithing, laying prayers at the altar, praying over her food. She set out flowers and libation, bourbon, coffee. Cake, sometimes cookies. Something sweet. She imagined that it was the four of them that made the flame in the candle flicker, the light dancing all up on the new walls she'd painted all on her own, in her new apartment she paid for all on her own, packed with new furniture she picked out all on her own. Sometimes she slept with the lights on, listening for the creaks. Sometimes, she fixed it so Skye thought it was her idea to sleep in her mother's bed. Soon enough, Rae wasn't afraid anymore. She wasn't afraid. She was doing her best. She was free.

Acknowledgments

I was twelve when I discovered my adoption certificate while snooping in my parents' private papers. I was shocked by the discovery, but also too scared to say anything to my family or ask them questions because, well, I had no business peeking into that metal box, for one, and two, saying, "I'm adopted" out loud would have made my place in the Millner family an alternate reality I wasn't ready to dissect or accept. Keeping my adoption secret made sense for my parents, so I made it make sense for me, too. For the longest time, that was beyond enough.

This changed, though, when I got pregnant with my own babies and questions about my health history became a thing: "Anyone in your family have diabetes or cancer?" "Do healthy pregnancies run in your family?" "What's in your blood?" My doctors wanted details. I couldn't give them. Suddenly, the information I thought wasn't important actually was. *What's in your blood?* As my babies kicked and stretched and found their home in my belly, on my breasts, that question morphed into *Who is in your blood?*

It's an answer I may never truly have. The night we buried my mother, my father gave me a small piece of my story, the only piece he knows: someone had left me, a baby, on the stoop of an orphanage, and four days later he and my mom went looking for a little girl and found me in a corner crib in the basement, arms outstretched, ready to go. That is the beginning and end of my "birth" story.

Over the years, I've used my imagination to fill in that story with color and light and grace: maybe my birth mother was young and scared and couldn't fathom raising a baby on her own. Maybe she was forced to leave me on that stoop by a family that refused to support her and her child. Maybe she was in an abusive relationship and feared her baby would get swooped into the violence. There are so many ways that it could have ended badly for me, a little defenseless baby. But instead, this woman, this angel, gave me life, and then gave me life again by giving me away. It was an incredible sacrifice. And a miracle that I ended up in my parents' arms.

It was my mediation on miracles, adoption, motherhood, Blackness, Black womanhood, choices, and blood that led me to *One Blood*. I wrote this story because I have many questions and zero answers about my past—because I am curious about it, but also scared of what I will find. Of whom I will hurt. I wrote this story because my birth mother and many more like her deserve context—deserve some color in the stark black-and-white judgment we reserve for women who give their babies away. I wrote this story for my mother and the Black women of her generation, who were led to believe that their very survival was wholly dependent on their being mothers and wives, and that this should be the sole source of their ambition—even as American racism conspired to stop Black women like my mother from stepping into and succeeding at those very roles.

Telling this story in this way allows me to air out what has gone unspoken all my life, with the intent of honoring the stories—indeed, the lives and plights—of the Black women in my own life who represent, in no small measure, the lives of so many Black women who've not enjoyed nearly enough time in the sun. That my mothers—and Black mothers like them—fought through this gauntlet of heartache, loss, subterfuge, patriarchy, and pain and came out on the other side of it is a miracle. A miracle that warrants exploration.

Know that this story, while containing some small measure of family lore, was born of my imagination and nursed in my dreams, literally. I am sure, deep down in my gut, that both my mothers delivered their heart songs into my subconsciousness—spoke clearly to me when I was sleeping and when I was awake, bent over both my computer and notepad. In the still, all I had to do was listen. Pay attention. And let them have their way. I am grateful for the gift of sight and their willingness to let me see them, hear them, feel their presence, and know their love. They are the thread that made it so that I could sew/sow these words. I thank you. I love you.

My daddy, James Millner, and my mommy, Bettye Millner, found me, housed me, fed me, clothed me, taught me, disciplined me, advocated for me, encouraged me, filled me, cheered for me, prayed for me. Loved me. The two of you are the blueprint for my humanness—how I came to be. I am forever grateful to you for your guiding hands and, with arms open wide, your insistence that I can fly. I thank you. I love you.

My daughters, Mari and Lila, are the source of my joy—the two who taught my heart to sing. It is a fool's bet to wager that the rearing of children is unidirectional; my girls—gorgeous, intelligent, funny, confident, practical, and passionate—most certainly raised up the adult me, mended my broken parts, and built me up to be stronger, better. Fearless. How lucky I am that the two of you chose me! Every single thing I do, whether grand or itty-bitty or somewhere in between, I do for you; the two of you are the very beat of my heart. My very breath. I thank you. I love you.

My editor, Monique Patterson, is a brilliant, sharp, thoughtful tactician who respects both story and storyteller. Where there is weakness, she lends the muscle, where there is fear, she instills confidence, where the terrain is sharp, she knows just the way to make it smooth—traversable. I am most grateful that she made me think, talked me through, laid hands, coaxed, pushed, and loved me through the writing. Monique, you believed in me and this story—even and especially on the days when I didn't quite believe it for myself. You changed my life when you said, "yes." I am forever grateful. I thank you. I love you.

My agent, Victoria Sanders, is the light in my dark corners. Not a day goes by that she is not encouraging me, extending her hand to help me, listening to my cockamamie ideas, and literally putting them all into motion. Victoria never doubts me—never doubts what I can do. You must understand what it means to a writer to have someone who believes in your abilities—tells you that your words, that you, are magic. This is not a paean to a stroker of ego; this is a love letter to the woman who cares about my career, but, even more, me, from the woman who extends that care in kind. Victoria, you and Diane are such a force in my life—beyond the page, beyond the deals, beyond the strategy, beyond our twenty-year working relationship turned friendship. You and Di are my sisters. I thank you. I love you.

Benee Knauer is the book doula who showed me how to breathe life into Grace, LoLo, and Rae, running me through writing drills that got me limber and loose enough to release what I'd been holding back; Karen Good Marable, my favorite writer, poured into me lessons about the art of painting with words, pressed podcasts and books and articles about good writing into my phone like a church mom does mints into a child's hands on early Sunday morning, and reminded me over and over and over again, "this is sacred"; Ida Harris told me I could do this thing and checked in on my heart when the words, the story, the dreams, the truth of it all, came weighing down, and she consistently told me that these words matter, *keep going*, reminding me that, like WuTang, *One Blood* is for the chir'ren. I love each of you. I thank you.

My family; Troy, Uncle Berkley, Barbara, Raymond, Chere, Vincent, Treva, Will, Amber, Pam, Melanie, Kenny, Belinda, Mel, and TeeTee: with you all, I feel safe. Protected. Happy. Loved. Being in your presence is like pulling the high jokers, the two of diamonds, all the aces, a couple kings, and, like, one club. That's a winning hand. Together, we run board. I thank you. I love you.

Angela Burt-Murray's limitless talent, clear-eyed focus, biting humor, and big heart are the wings that give me flight; Marion Rossi-Kunney, who is about as nutty as a can of Planters, makes me laugh every single day while inspiring me with her insistence that we remain faithful, even when it's inconvenient and difficult, and that we honor God, our bodies, and our whole selves because we deserve that much. I thank you. I love you both to pieces.

My tribe—Adriene Craft, Jenny Gee, Joyce Davis, Selassie Dugbarty, Tina Fynn, Mike Fynn, Semaj Johnson, Akilah Richards, Kris Richards, Mitzi Miller, Sili Recio, Cliff "Hollywood" Boyce, Siddiq Bello, Erskine Isaac, Kamau Bobb, James Harris, Stacey Patton, Michael Arceneaux, Bernadette Baker-Baughman, Miles Ezeilo, Cole Ezeilo, Esete Guta, and Mazi Chiles: each of you are the fabric in the grand quilt of community that keeps me covered and lifted, whether I'm writing or editing or mothering or actively seeking joy, sunshine, and peace—when I'm just being me. I thank each of you. I love you.

Tarana Burke, Demetria L. Lucas, Kirsten West Savali, Karen Waldrond, Aliya King Neil, Luvvie Ajayi Jones, Erika Nicole Kendall, Patrice Grell Yursik, Tayari Jones, Britni Danielle, Shay Stewart-Bouley, Marie

Leggette, Heather Barmore, Samantha Irby, Kelly Hurst, and Bassey Ikpi: in my darkest days, when I was walking through the fire, you heard my cries, shined a light, and helped me find my way. I'll never, ever forget that. Ever. O.G.'s for life. I thank each of you. I love you.

Macmillan is the publishing house that said "yes" to *One Blood*, and the company's dream team has worked tirelessly to make its birth a triumph. Mal Frazier, Anthony Parisi, Eileen Lawrence, Jennifer McClelland-Smith, Kathleen Carter, Khadija Lokhandwala, Linda Quinton, Saraciea Fennell, Sarah Reidy, Mara Delgado Sanchez, Katie Bassel, Tracey Guest, Brant Janeway, Erica Martirano, Lisa Senz, Kejana Ayala, Tom Thompson, Alexandra Hoopes, Michael Storrings, Suzie Doore, Margot Gray, Lisa Kramer, Marion Hertrich, Bettina Schrewe, Aurora Peccarisi, Sabrina Annoni, Ilaria Marzi, Marie Misandeau and each of my foreign publishers that believed in and embraced *One Blood* from its very inception, and so many others who used their powers in service of this book's success, as well as fine artist Tawny Chatmon, who graciously created the cover art based on a piece in her gorgeous *Deeply Embedded* series: I thank each of you. I am grateful.

I miss my Teddy, my faithful, sweet goldendoodle, who sat at my feet for almost sixteen years, through the writing of nineteen books, including most of the two years during which I wrote *One Blood*. He brought me unconditional love and peace in the middle of double chaos—the Covid pandemic and the racial reckoning following George Floyd's murder. With Teddy by my side, I always felt safe. I miss him. And now, our boisterous, energetic, adorable, petite goldendoodle, Franklin, steps in to continue on my writing journey. Welcome home, Frankie. I thank you. I love you.

Just bees and things and flowers,

—Denene